D1606436

House of Lies

By
S.R.Claridge

Global Publishing Group

Global Publishing Group

Printed in the United States of America

First trade edition: October 2012

10 9 8 7 6 5 4 3 2 1

ISBN 978-0-9898467-5-2

This book is dedicated to anyone who has fought to rescue a loved one from the grips of a cult.

~

A heartfelt thank you to my core group of editors (Cash, Jerrye, Gary, Beth and Matt) for their tireless hours of reading, editing and supporting my work. Thank you to the additional editors specific to this project (Holly, Shelly, Melanie) for their invaluable input.

Thank you to my family for their love and support, and to God for every blessing.

I am grateful to my readers and hope you will continue to enjoy my work.

~

A complete list of books by S.R.Claridge is located at the back of this book.

For previews, reviews, interviews and information about the author, visit SusanClaridge.com or find her on Facebook.

CHAPTER 1

Tess grabbed her cell phone and dashed into the bathroom of her tiny, one bedroom apartment, locking the door behind her. With trembling fingers, she sent a text: COME HERE! HURRY! Within moments she heard them burst into her apartment, hollering her name. Diving into the tub, she pulled the white shower curtain closed and prayed. She knew it was only a matter of time before they would kick through the door and take her.

Her body shook uncontrollably as she curled into a ball in the tub, her blonde, shoulder-length hair sticking against her clammy skin. "Open it up or we knock it down!" The men pounded on the door and yelled.

"Go away," Tess cried. "Leave me alone!"

Shrieking at the sound of the door being kicked open; Tess pulled her knees tighter to her chest and closed her eyes. She heard the sound of the shower curtain being ripped to one side and felt their hands gripping her arms and lifting her in one fluid motion. "Please," she sobbed. "Please don't do this."

"Shut up," one of the men barked. "Sagan wants to see you."

Tess hung like a limp blanket in their arms as she was taken from her apartment to the main building on the P3 campus, where she was handcuffed to a chair, in complete darkness, and told to wait on the Lord to speak to her. Voices in hushed tones and whispers filled the room and Tess clamped her eyes shut and kicked her feet. "Go away!" She cried.

"We must drain the evil from your body," one voice seethed and Tess felt something or someone slither passed her.

"We must cleanse you of your sin," another voice whispered and she felt a slight breeze on the other side as someone moved near.

"Please," Tess begged, "please let me go."

"We are here to change the nature and expression of Christianity on Earth and God has chosen you, Tess, to be a forerunner in this change. As it has been prophesized, Maxwell Sagan is to lead and you are to follow and expand the culture to the ends of the Earth."

Tess shook her head. "These are lies," her voice quivered.

"The only lies are the ones that you have allowed Satan to place into your mind, causing you to doubt," the voice whispered. "You must fight off the demons, Tess."

"We will kill your disbelief and restore you to your rightful place in Joel's Army," a voice whispered. She could sense that they were circling her, at least two of them, maybe three. "You are a manifested daughter of God, chosen to play a part in ushering in the return of Christ." She could hear their footsteps shuffling against the floor as they moved around her in the dark. "Don't you want Christ to return, Tess?"

"Yes," Tess cried.

"Don't you want to rid society of homosexuality?" The voices whispered.

"Yes," Tess uttered.

"And rid society of abortion?" They taunted.

"Yes," Tess sniveled.

"Then we must not be complacent. We must purge the church of all complacency and overcome all corruption. We must not be as trite as the humanitarians who stand for nothing and fall for everything. They are the Harlot Babylon, ignorantly paving the way for the Anti-Christ. They are utterly deceived. You don't want to pave the way for the Anti-Christ, do you Tess?"

Tess broke into sobs. "No," she cried.

"You are called to be on the cutting edge, to be a leader, promoting God's agenda, and ridding the Earth of all sin. As Joel said, we are to blow the trumpet, gather the people, fast and pray and turn our hearts completely to the Lord."

"Turn your heart to the Lord, Tess," one voice whispered and repeated it over and over.

"Blow the trumpet and gather the people," another voice whispered repeatedly.

"Turn your heart..."

"Blow the trumpet..."

"Gather the people..."

The words were spoken chant-like and Tess began to kick her feet and scream as she felt the first cut to her left shoulder. Warm blood ran down her arm and dripped to the floor. Next, she felt the piercing tip of a knife against her right shoulder and the sting as it sliced through her skin. She tried to cry out but weakness and disorientation consumed her and she slipped further into darkness.

CHAPTER 2

"What we do here isn't for everyone." His voice came from behind and Skylar Wilson didn't need to turn around to know who was speaking. She knew that cunning evil tone and it sent icy chills up and down her spine. It was Maxwell Sagan, the creator and leader of the P3 movement, the one idolized by hundreds of thousands of predominantly young people who came seeking validation only to be sucked into his distorted truths. Her older sister, Tess, was unfortunately one of those adoring followers who had dedicated her whole life to the movement, leaving behind a trail of wounded friendships, a broken marriage and a family that missed her. Maxwell was the man responsible for irrefutable damage to her sister's life and, as far as Skylar was concerned, he might as well have been the Anti-Christ. That's how deeply she despised him.

P3 stood for "Purposeful Powerful Prayer." It appeared to be a harmless 24/7 international prayer movement on the surface, but it was a dangerous secret society beneath. Skylar didn't know the extent of Maxwell's plan, but she knew that the underlying P3 agenda was more narcissistic than spiritual. Maxwell simply used spirituality as a guise to satisfy his needs, cleverly masking his real agenda beneath a blanket of pseudo-evangelical Christianity. For those not blinded by his charisma, the extensive trail of false prophets shed light on his ultimate goal. Power. What kind of power? Skylar couldn't be certain. She had spent countless hours over the past three years studying the P3 movement, hoping somehow to free her sister from its grip; but every attempt had failed and driven a wedge further between them. Several months ago, Skylar gave up the fight and she hadn't heard from Tess since; until today, when out of the blue, she received a text message from her sister. It read: COME HERE! HURRY! The moment Skylar read the text, tentacles of fear crept up the back of her neck and she knew something was terribly wrong.

Tucking her dark brown, shoulder length hair behind one ear, Skylar slowly turned to face Maxwell. She was both amazed and disgusted that he had the audacity to open his arms as if to embrace her. "The last time I saw you," he grinned, "you were just a little girl. How long has it been?"

Not long enough, Skylar thought, crossing her arms tightly against her chest to let him know she had no intention of hugging him. "Eighteen years," she answered flatly.

He placed one hand on each of her shoulders and grinned. "Eighteen years," he blanched with fake enthusiasm. "Time flies…" his voice trailed off and he smiled wickedly. "What a beautiful woman you've become; so much like your sister." Skylar wiggled from his grasp. She and Tess did look alike, despite the fact that Tess was four years older and had bleached blond hair. "It's those eyes," Sagan grinned. "Those beautiful, deep, Wilson blue eyes."

Skylar wasn't moved by his compliment. "I'm here to see my sister. Where is she?"

His sardonic grin grew wider, and she could see his beady eyes flash with an eerie awareness from behind his round-framed glasses. "You used to like me," he pouted.

"I was young and naïve."

"And now you're all grown up," he said, circling around her, as if he were studying her inside and out.

"I've grown enough to see through cult-leaders, false prophets and all-round assholes," she blurted. "Now, where's my sister?"

Raising both hands into the air, he shrugged his shoulders. "Like I said, what we do here isn't for everyone."

Skylar didn't know much about religion or the Bible, but she knew enough to know that what P3 was doing was wrong. "Funny, because I thought this was a Christ-based ministry, and isn't Christ for everyone?" She sarcastically rebutted and the smile disappeared from Maxwell's face.

He shook his head and made a clicking sound with his tongue. "Offense is normal for those who judge what they do not understand, but you have unwarranted offense toward me. You should be careful."

"How typical," Skylar blurted, "you're still up to your same old tricks of threatening people who disagree with you. One of these days this house of smoke and mirrors is going to blow up in your face."

He raised his eyebrows. "Now who's making threats?"

"That's not a threat, Maxwell, it's a promise." Skylar flipped her hair behind her shoulder. "In fact, it's not only a promise, it's a prophecy," she said, glaring sarcastically at him and using her fingers to make quotation marks around the word prophecy. "It might even be the first prophecy spoken in this building that actually comes true." Maxwell scowled and Skylar raised an eyebrow and grinned. "What's the matter? Truth hurts?"

"You should be careful," he snarled.

Skylar hadn't planned on having a confrontation with Maxwell, or calling him out on the fact that every prophetic word he or one of his cohorts predicted had all been proven false. But she couldn't deny that standing up to him felt good. His authority either intimidated or impressed most people, but not her. She found his short, stocky stature, defined jaw line, thinning auburn hair and fake-tanned skin distasteful. It wasn't that he was an unattractive man per se, but that the aura of evil and arrogance emanating from him left her physically nauseous and spiritually repulsed.

"Where is my sister?" Skylar demanded. The sadistic sneer returned to Maxwell's face.

"I haven't seen Tess," he stated, "but if I do, I'll tell her that you're here." He sauntered down the hall, raising his hands in the air and singing a praise song aloud; then inserted a key into one of the many white doors that lined the hall and disappeared inside.

Skylar knew he was lying about not having seen Tess, and it infuriated her; but there was nothing she could do but wait and hope that Tess would find her.

The P3 campus was large and consisted of many buildings, all of which were attached by long hallways. Conceivably, she could walk the compound all day and never find Tess, so she needed to choose one spot, in open view and stay there. To the left of the front doors of the main building was the entrance to what was called the Prayer Room. Straight ahead was a long, windowless hallway lined with white doors; all of which were closed. To the right was a shorter hallway that led to a coffee shop and a bookstore. Skylar chose the coffee shop and sent a text message to Tess, telling her to meet her either in the bookstore or the coffee shop as soon as possible. Purchasing a black coffee in a to-go cup, Skylar sipped it as she perused the bookstore, trying not to show outward disgust at the underlying theme behind the majority of the books offered. It was a mixture of mysticism and geopolitics; but mostly it was the writings and teachings of Maxwell Sagan. *Christ-based ministry, my ass,* she thought to herself. *This is a Maxwell Sagan-based ministry.*

"Excuse me," Skylar said, approaching a sandy haired, young woman behind the counter, whose sunken eyes and sullen demeanor made her look as if she hadn't eaten or slept in weeks. "Do you sell any Biblical study guides?" The woman stared blankly, as if she were either studying Skylar or completely zoning out. Skylar wasn't sure which. "You know," Skylar clarified, "like something that doesn't go into prophetic nonsense or contemplative meditation but just sort of walks you through the Bible?"

After a moment the woman uttered a soft "no," then gestured toward a shelf behind Skylar. "But we have a really good book called The Fire Within by Father Thomas Dubay," she paused to slowly inhale a breath as if it were labor-some, then added, "It's about Teresa of Avila and..."

"And contemplative prayer," Skylar cut her off. "And astral projection. I know." She rolled her eyes. "I've noticed you carry several books on those topics." Skylar's tone was more sarcastic than she had intended and she saw the woman's eyes nervously dart upward, to the left and then quickly back down to Skylar. Following her gaze, Skylar saw the security camera mounted in the far corner, facing the counter. *Constant surveillance of members.* She remarked in her head. *Typical cult activity.*

The woman rocked woozily and grabbed the counter to balance herself. "Are you okay?" Skylar asked, as the young woman became visibly nervous, fidgeting with her fingers. Panic shown in her light brown eyes, and she repeatedly glanced up at the camera. "Can I help you with something?" Skylar asked, sensing that she wanted to say something but was too afraid.

Her hands began trembling and her eyes grew even glassier as she slid backwards against the wall, slumping to the floor behind the counter. Skylar rushed to her side. "Are you all right?" She blurted. "Should I call 9-1-1?"

Tears streamed down the young woman's face. "No," she shook her head. "Please call my mom. I want to go home." She broke into sobs. "I want to go home."

Skylar pulled her cell phone from her jacket pocket and started to hand it to the young woman, but she pushed it away. "I can't!" She blurted. "I'm not allowed."

"What's the number?" Skylar asked, with her fingers perched and ready on the keypad.

"816-8..." was all that she said before two men entered the bookstore, one stopping in the doorway and the other rapidly approaching the counter. It was obvious that they were not there to buy a book. Skylar quickly slid her phone back into her pocket.

"My name is Ema Wright," the young woman said in what Skylar could only describe as a barely audible tone of desperation. Ema gripped Skylar's arm tightly, digging her fingernails into her skin. "Ema Wright," she mouthed again, her eyes pleading for help with such intensity that Skylar once again felt the icy chill of fear grip her.

Standing up as the man approached the counter, Skylar looked him squarely in the face and lied. "She fainted but she's conscious now. She said she didn't want me to call 9-1-1."

"I'll take it from here," the man gritted, sliding behind the counter and nudging Skylar out of the way.

"What's wrong with her?" Skylar asked.

"Probably the flu," he said, while lifting Ema from the floor. "It's been going around."

He carried Ema toward the door and set her down next to the other man, who looped his arm in hers, not as someone wanting to be helpful, but as someone escorting a captive.

"Ema?" Skylar called after her and Ema turned to look over her shoulder. "I'm going to be here for a while, waiting for my sister. If you feel better, maybe we could meet for a cup of coffee?"

Ema tried to smile but her lip quivered and tears ran down her pale cheeks. "That would be nice," she said softly.

"I'll wait for you in the coffee shop."

Ema gave a slight nod. Then, as the men inched her toward the exit, she stopped, looked one last time at Skylar and asked, "Who is your sister?"

"Tess Wilson," Skylar answered. Ema gasped.

CHAPTER 3

It had been three hours since Skylar's arrival at P3 and there was still no sign of Tess. She had called and text her cell numerous times with no response. Equally as disturbing was the fact that Ema never showed up at the coffee shop to meet her. Skylar didn't believe Ema had the flu. Most people with the flu aren't panic-stricken. In fact, Skylar surmised that Ema had purposely sunk behind the counter to prevent the surveillance camera from recording her asking for help. Whatever her reason, one thing was certain, Ema was afraid and wanted to go home. Skylar made a mental note to search for Ema's mother when she got back to her apartment. Since surveillance was everywhere on the P3 campus, she didn't want to risk further endangering Ema by seeking her out, although she had an unsettling angst that Ema was already in deep trouble. Skylar was also uncomfortable with Ema's reaction to hearing Tess's name. It was as if the name Tess Wilson had struck fear into the very core of Ema's being. Skylar wanted to know why.

Having polished off four cups of coffee, and in need of a bathroom, she headed down the hallway in front of the main doors to find one. The building was eerily vacant. She hadn't noticed it when she arrived, probably because Maxwell had immediately distracted her; but now she noticed how strangely empty it was.

Tess had been a part of P3 for ten years and Skylar had only been there a couple of times. She had visited once because her sister had invited her, and again, a few years later to research for herself the so-called prophetic movement and false teachings therein. Both times the building had been wall-to-wall people, so it seemed strange now to see it virtually vacant. The more she thought about it, the more she realized how odd it was for Maxwell to be at the door precisely when she arrived; as if he were expecting her. The mere thought caused goose bumps on Skylar's arms and she shuddered to shake off the fear.

Meandering down the long, white hallway, Skylar pulled on the doorknob of every door she passed; but they were all locked. She walked back up the hall toward the front doors, silently remarking how there was obviously no prophetic vision for interior décor because the windowless, white halls and white doors offered the warmth of an asylum. She passed two young men near the front doors and asked them for the whereabouts of a bathroom. Both looked pale and fragile. "That way," one mumbled while they continued walking.

"Thanks," Skylar answered but they didn't acknowledge her.

Nearing the Prayer Room, Skylar could hear voices coming from within so she crept closer. She could hear a worship team leading the congregation in what sounded more like a repetitive chant than an actual song. Quietly, Skylar pulled the door open just enough to peek her head in and watch. Now, she knew why the halls were empty, as people were packed liked sardines into the Prayer Room.

"Worthy is the Lamb. Worthy is the Lamb. Worthy is the Lamb," they sang over and over and over until seamlessly flowing into another chant-like phrase with only a slight variation in the melody. "Who was and is and is to come. Who was and is and is to come. Who was and is and is to come," they repeated for the next several minutes while Skylar scanned the room, looking for any sign of Tess or Ema. As she watched, she witnessed what could only be described as a sort of hypnosis fall over the congregation. Rows of people began to chant, to sway and to rock methodically. Several individuals twitched their bodies as if they were suffering from uncontrollable muscular spasms.

When the music stopped, a man rose from his chair on the left side of the stage and began to speak. Skylar recognized this man from the research she had done. She also knew of him from her many conversations with Tess. His name was Saul Latham and he was a senior leader in the international P3 movement. Tess claimed that both Saul and Maxwell were her brothers, her family; telling Skylar that her heart was knitted with theirs. This made Skylar want to vomit. Because Tess spoke so highly of Saul, Skylar had felt compelled to research him and his teachings, and had listened to him preach many times online; but she had never seen him in person. Now, out of curiosity, she slipped inside and slid into a seat in the back row.

"Welcome fellow Yahweh Separatists," Saul began, as he rocked back and forth on his heels. "As you know, we are living in a Jezebel generation." His voice raised and Skylar could see what could only be described as a flash of hatred in his eyes. He rubbed one hand over the top of his bald head and then down over his auburn and speckled gray moustache. "God is punishing this Jezebel generation for its homosexuality and pro-abortion ways." There were mumblings of agreement all around her. "Hurricane Katrina was God's punishment for homosexuality and the tornado in Joplin, Missouri was His reproof for abortion." Skylar couldn't believe her ears. She had heard him say these things online, but a part of her had hoped that the video had been tainted or the comments taken out of context. Now, watching him in person, his words and presence were far more powerful than she had ever imagined. "We must put an end to the hypocrisy in the church and in America and in the world." Even more unbelievable than his words was the fact that when she looked around the room, she appeared to be the only person offended by his remarks. "Better for a man to be dead than to be

homosexual," Saul hollered from the stage and the
congregation applauded. "Better for a woman to die
than to abort her baby," he screamed and the crowd
went wild.

If a pregnant woman dies the baby dies too.
Skylar rolled her eyes. *Asshole.*

"God is raising up His army in these last
days, to purge the church and defeat evil in society."
Cheers echoed across the room. "We can no longer
be passive about sin. We must overcome all barriers
of corruption in our government, in our education
system and in our culture!" He rocked violently back
and forth as he spoke, and it looked as if the rocking
was involuntary; almost like an unwanted tick.

You ARE the corruption. Skylar retorted in her
mind with a silent snort.

"We are to build the Kingdom of Heaven on
Earth and prepare the way for Christ's return. With
our prayers, oh holy children, we will move heaven
and usher in the return of our King!" Everyone,
except Skylar, was now jumping and cheering and
chanting, "Build a wall! Build a wall! Build a wall!"
After several minutes of this, Saul lifted his arms and
the crowd grew quiet again. He went on to explain
that he was not merely a teacher or a preacher, but
that he was a Prophet of God, and God was going to
send upon him the spirit of Elijah.

It took all of her strength not to snort aloud at
his ridiculous proclamations. *What a whack job!*
Skylar was pretty sure that of all the people on the
planet, Saul would be one of the very last entrusted
with the spirit of Elijah. Besides, she was pretty sure
that what he said wasn't even Biblical. The Bible
didn't instruct human beings to build the Kingdom of
Heaven on Earth, it said that Jesus would return and
HE would build a kingdom on Earth. Saul was
twisting Scripture and, even though she wasn't a
Bible scholar, it pissed Skylar off.

"The Lord told me it is my personal
commission to turn America back to Him," he

shouted in a raspy voice. Everyone leapt up again
and cheered. "The Lord told me that I was to be the
spiritual Charles Lindbergh and lead His children
through the proverbial arch of prophetic wisdom. I
saw it in a vision and it looked like the St. Louis Arch,
and I was leading God's people through it; and we
were taking flight."

*Oh, brother! Yet another self-appointed
prophet of God. The only arch you're leading anyone
through is the gateway to hell.* Forcing herself not to
roll her eyes or exhale too loudly, she rose from her
seat and sneaked out the door. Once in the hallway,
she wiggled her shoulders and shuddered as the
heebie-jeebies rushed over her. *How can so many
people believe these lies?* She wondered.

Continuing her search for a bathroom, Skylar
walked down another long hallway which jetted off to
the left. This hall, too, was painted white with no
pictures and no windows. All of the doors were
locked except the last door on the left, which opened
when she twisted the handle. Skylar hesitantly
pushed on the door and stepped inside. It was pitch
black, so she left the door slightly ajar while running
her hands along the wall to find the light switch.
When she finally found the switch and flipped it on,
she threw her hands over her mouth to muffle a
scream. The walls were painted dark red and a
blood-stained drain was located in the middle of the
concrete floor. A black leather office chair, with a
pair of handcuffs dangling from each of the arm rests,
sat in the center of the room; and a pool of fresh
blood covered the floor beneath the chair, and left a
tell-tale trail as it inched its way into the drain.
Skylar's heart beat violently as she took her cell
phone from her pocket and snapped a picture of the
chair and the floor beneath it; and then quickly
turned off the light and dashed back down the
hallway.

Torn between the urge to leave and the
nagging obligation to find Tess, Skylar went back to

the coffee shop and sat at a small round table near the front windows, in plain view. The need to use the restroom had been stifled by the fear of being alone in the hallways. What if a security camera had seen her taking a picture of the chair and the blood? Her heart was racing and she tried to take deep, slow breaths and calm down. Every part of her wanted to leave, but not without Tess; not when Tess had asked for her to come. For years she had been praying for Tess's eyes to be opened, and waiting for her to reach out. There was no way she would let fear get the best of her now.

Ordering another cup of coffee, Skylar stared out the window. *God, help me find Tess,* she prayed silently as she took a sip. When she had calmed down, she pulled out her phone, emailed herself the picture of the bloody chair, and then deleted it from her cell. She wondered if she should take the picture to the police, but dismissed the idea after logically convincing herself that she didn't have any real evidence of a crime being committed. *After all,* she thought, *it could have been fake blood, used for a skit or something.* Her mind tried to rationalize away the fear, but her gut told her something was very wrong.

She grabbed a magazine, called POP, which stood for the Power of Prayer, from the rack by the doorway; immediately noting that the entire rack was stocked with in-house published items. There were no People or The Week or Time magazines, and no USA Today or even the local KC Star newspaper. It was all internal P3 propaganda and Skylar couldn't help but give a mental eye roll. *Control information and you control everything and everyone,* she silently grimaced. *That's Cult 101.*

The POP magazine had articles highlighting the benefits of contemplative prayer, ironically denying any likeness to transcendental meditation. One story spoke of the spiritual experiences of Maxwell Sagan; and his so-called visits to Heaven and encounters with demons. *All made up fabrications,* she sighed. There was an article on Saul Latham, painting him as a good husband, a loving father and an evangelical Christian leader with a heart for the nations. Skylar rolled her eyes. The truth was Saul may very well have been a good husband and a loving father, but he was also a bigot. He may have had a heart for the nations, but only for those in the nations who were heterosexual and without sin. He was someone who prophesied falsely and twisted Scripture, using lies to influence the minds of a youthful generation. Skylar didn't like him almost as much as she despised Maxwell.

The most disturbing information in the magazine was the list of politicians and even Presidential candidates who were linking themselves to P3 by way of the National Ecclesiastical Transformation, or N.E.T. for short. Probably they were trying to increase campaign support, rally conservative voters to win elections, and were unaware of the core philosophies and dangerous roots of the N.E.T. Either that or they didn't care. Skylar wasn't sure which made a person more dangerous; ignorance or apathy. But she knew one thing, she wouldn't be voting for anyone connected to P3.

Closing the magazine, Skylar stared out the window, wondering how it was that her sister and all of these people could be deceived by the double-talk, blatant lies and manipulations of this movement. Then she thought back to when she had been sitting in the Prayer Room, watching and listening to Saul speak, and she cringed. Without a doubt there was an underlying power in his words; an authority that summoned people and commanded their attention. It was an authority that demanded high respect in the name of the God; but it wasn't God. Beneath it all, the foundation was false.

Sipping the last of her coffee, Skylar was about to get up and throw her cup into the trash can, when a blonde waitress, one she hadn't seen before, approached her. "Are you finished?" She asked.

"Yes, thank you."

The waitress picked up Skylar's cup. "Let me get that for you," she said. Then she held the empty cup against her white apron and purposefully angled it so that the outside bottom of the cup faced Skylar. "Can I get you anything else?" She asked, subtly lowering her eyes to the cup and then back to meet Skylar's.

Skylar followed the waitress's eyes down to the cup; her breath catching in her throat as she read what was written in black marker across the bottom. "Danger. Get out now!"

CHAPTER 4

Skylar's hands trembled as she gripped the steering wheel of her silver Nissan Altima, weaving down the side streets to find her way back to highway 435. She had taken the cup from the coffee shop, and hoped that it, coupled with the photograph of the bloody chair would be enough to take to the police. *God, please keep Tess safe,* she silently prayed as she drove; feeling a twinge of guilt for having left without her sister. Tears of worry pooled in her eyes.

Pulling onto the highway, her thoughts drifted to Tess and how the P3 nightmare began. Even as a teenager Tess had always had a deep love for God and when Maxwell met her and saw her passion, he used it to manipulate her. It had been painful to watch and just thinking about it again made Skylar sick to her stomach. Maxwell had convinced Tess that she was chosen to be a part of God's army. It was a teaching called the Manifest Sons of God, and it sucked Tess completely in; brainwashing her and thousands of others into thinking that God's chosen ones could not be deceived by anyone. How clever it was of Maxwell to teach his followers that a Christian was unable to be deceived. That statement alone helped validate his false teachings. Skylar thought back to one of the many heated conversations she had with Tess.

"This movement isn't Biblical," Skylar told Tess.

"It is," Tess rebutted, spouting prophesies that spoke of God's agenda.

"These prophecies are not in the Bible," Skylar protested. "You're not seeing clearly."

23

"I'm seeing all that God wants me to see as one of His chosen," Tess answered calmly. "These prophesies aren't in the Bible because they come from new prophets."

"We're ALL chosen by God for special, individual purposes in life," Skylar argued; but Tess shook her head.

"Not everyone is chosen to be a forerunner in ushering in the second coming of Christ," Tess explained. "Not everyone is to be in Joel's Army."

Skylar gripped the steering wheel tighter, as the replaying of the conversation in her mind brought back the same old frustration. "Joel's Army," she blurted aloud as she drove. *If that isn't the biggest load of crap I've ever heard, I don't know what is.*

The purpose of Joel's Army was to take by force any ground that was not Christian. Maxwell taught his followers that anyone born after 1973 could become a member of Joel's Army, wherein they were called by God to purge the church of sin and defeat evil in society. Of course, the definition of 'evil' was anything Maxwell wanted it to be, and according to Saul, homosexuality and abortion fell into that category. They called it 'cleansing the earth,' but it was really just masked bigotry. Skylar's stomach knotted. Maxwell Sagan, with the help of his so-called prophets, took the philosophies of Joel's Army, the Manifest Sons of God and the Latter Rain movement, meshed them together and formed his own unique theology of Dominionism. He had hand-selected each philosophy to fit his plan, tweaked the ones that didn't fit and came up with the P3 movement; proclaiming it to be the new order of Christianity sent down by God. A new order led, ironically enough, by Maxwell. It was narcissistic deception at its best and it made Skylar queasy.

The worst part was that Skylar had watched helplessly as an unnatural air of superiority overtook her sister. She knew it stemmed from the fact that Maxwell used prophetic ministry to justify the authenticity of his words, thereby creating an air of elitism in all P3 members; but Skylar was powerless to stop it. Even though Maxwell twisted Scripture to fit whatever his prophets were saying, his so-called prophets of God were still wrong. Skylar pointed this out to Tess, but Tess refused to accept it; proclaiming that the dreams and visions from God were true, but had merely been misspoken and misinterpreted by human error. Skylar thought back to one of their last conversations.

"God doesn't make mistakes," Skylar told Tess. "Can't you see that if a prophecy is inaccurate then it didn't come from God?"

"God doesn't make mistakes," Tess agreed, "but people do."

Skylar yanked on her own hair to indicate the conversation was driving her crazy. "Think logically," she begged. "Over thousands of years God chose fewer than fifty people to be Prophets, and those Prophets were never wrong. Maxwell Sagan has proclaimed more than that in the past several years and they've never been right, not once. They've ALL been proven false."

Skylar pleaded with Tess but her logic fell on deaf ears, as Tess coldly stated that they would have to agree to disagree. After that, Tess left her husband and moved to the P3 compound on a full-time basis. That was three years ago.

It was bad enough that her sister had been sucked into the P3 movement, but Maxwell's agenda extended far beyond Tess. His reach spread to hundreds of thousands of young people around the globe, offering them identity as chosen members in God's elite army. He brought hope to the hopeless through prophetic dreams, which Skylar knew were merely schemes to further his agenda, stroke his already inflated ego and increase his personal wealth. What made P3 so dangerous is that it shrouded itself in an evangelical Christian veil, when in actuality its teachings were based in heresy and mysticism, relying upon well-known cult tactics to isolate and control its followers. It short, P3 was a scam and Skylar knew it.

Though Officer Burnes confirmed that there were previous complaints about the goings on at the P3 campus, there was legally nothing that could be done about it. This made Skylar feel hopeless. "It's all speculation," he told her.

"Can't you investigate based on speculation?" Skylar questioned.

"Listen lady," Officer Burnes exhaled, rocking his chair back onto two legs. "P3 pays their taxes, they keep to themselves and they've brought jobs into an otherwise run-down, small community." He slammed his chair back down onto all four legs and leaned forward placing his forearms on top of the desk. "Even if I wanted to, I got no grounds to go in and investigate."

Skylar deflated, swallowing hard to keep the lump of emotion from rising any further into her throat. "But my sister's in there," she mumbled and looked up with pleading eyes.

"What's your sister's name again?" He pulled a manila file folder, marked P3, from his bottom drawer.

"Tess Wilson," Skylar answered, sitting up a little straighter and watching as he flipped through pages in the folder.

"Tess Wilson. Tess Wilson," he repeated aloud as he searched. "Wait a sec," he blurted. "Tess Wilson. I know that name." He pulled open the bottom desk drawer again and fumbled around, mumbling to himself about an article he'd read. Skylar tried to peek over the side of the desk to see what he was doing. "Here we go," he said, placing a POP magazine atop the desk."

"You subscribe to POP?"

"Nah, my wife picked it up. She likes to head over to P3 now and again for that all night prayer thing they got going on. I think she's nuts." He flipped through the magazine and stopped half-way through. "Yep, this is it," he announced, turning the magazine to face Skylar. There was a four by six sized picture of Tess and the headline read: Leading the Way

Skylar gasped and snatched the magazine from the desk to get a closer look.

"See, there," Officer Burnes said, "your sister's not a prisoner; in fact, from what this article says, she's one of the up and coming leaders. It says here she and this Saul fella are going to lead the way in St. Louis." Officer Burnes read from the magazine, "Saul Latham says he knew God was telling him to open a new P3 prayer house in St. Louis when God told him he was to be the spiritual Charles Lindbergh."

Skylar's stomach felt suddenly hollow. "That's not possible," she mouthed almost inaudibly.

"Sometimes we don't know folks as well as we think," he said, as if that was supposed to make her feel better.

She shook her head. "I know my sister and something isn't right." Tears filled Skylar's eyes. "Why would she send a text asking me to come quickly if she didn't need my help?"

He shrugged.

"And what about Ema?" Skylar looked intently into Officer Burnes' light brown, caramel colored eyes.

"You mean the girl that didn't come back to the coffee shop?" He rocked back onto two legs of his chair again, and Skylar was certain that the chair would collapse beneath the weight of his triple chin and enormous belly.

"She probably went back to her apartment and took a nap." He shrugged. "You said she didn't look well. Maybe she really did have the flu."

"Maybe," Skylar sighed.

"I'll tell you what," he said, sliding his business card across the desk. "Email me the picture you took of the bloody chair and I'll see what I can

27

do." He slammed his chair back onto four legs. "It's probably nothing though. I mean, it was probably just a prop or a practical joke to scare somebody."

"It worked," Skylar groaned, giving a half-witted grin and standing up. "Can I keep this magazine?"

"It's all yours."

Skylar thanked him and left. She wasn't hopeful, but at the very least, what had happened had now been documented. As she walked across the parking lot toward her car she noticed something sticking out from beneath the windshield wiper on the driver's side. It was a white piece of wide-lined notebook paper, folded neatly into four even squares. She unfolded the paper and read the cursive penmanship: Contact Stephen Braznovich

Skylar scanned the parking lot to see if the note deliverer was still there; but she saw no one. Once inside her car she sent a text message to Tess one more time, telling her that she loved her and would return to P3 tomorrow to find her. "Meet me in the coffee shop at 10:00am if you can." She wrote. Then she pulled out of the lot and headed for home.

~

Officer Burnes slid the P3 folder back into his bottom drawer and grabbed the receiver to the old, black, land-line phone that sat on his desk next to the picture of his wife, two sons and their German Shepherd dog. He dialed and waited until he heard a voice on the other end.

"It's done," he said.

"Any unexpected problems?" The man asked.

"Nope," Officer Burnes clucked. "I gave her the magazine just like you asked."

"Well done," the man answered. "The Lord has spoken that you have been a good and faithful servant."

The line went dead.

CHAPTER 5

Skylar tossed and turned in bed. She was riddled with guilt over having left without finding Tess, and tormented by the article that implied Tess was a leader in the P3 movement. Being a follower was one thing, but a leader; that was almost more than Skylar could bear. Her thoughts drifted between Tess, Ema and wondering who had left the note on her car telling her to contact Stephen Braznovich. It was 2:30am when she finally gave up on sleep, grabbed a notebook from her nightstand drawer and began jotting down everything that had happened that afternoon. Then she made a list of the next steps she planned to take. First: Contact Tess's ex-husband, Greg. Last she heard, he was still living somewhere in St.Louis. *Maybe Tess sent him text message for help too?* Though Skylar knew that was probably a long shot, as Greg had been furiously devastated when Tess left him; still, it was worth a try. Second: Find out who Stephen Braznovich was and why she was anonymously advised to contact him. Third: Find Ema Wright's mother and tell her that her daughter wanted to come home. Fourth: Go back to P3 and look for Tess. *This time I'll actually walk the campus,* she told herself. Fifth: Find the waitress from the coffee shop and ask her what type of danger she was referring to and why she had risked her own safety to warn her.

When the sun came up, Skylar was already showered and dressed. She had researched Stephen Braznovich on the computer and discovered that he was a Private Investigator in Kansas. She called and left a voicemail at 5:30am, stating her name and that it was imperative for them to meet as soon as possible. To her surprise, Braznovich returned her call within fifteen minutes and scheduled a meeting for 7:30am. "I have a full schedule today," he told her. "But I can squeeze you in first thing this morning."

She agreed to meet him at a hole-in-the-wall bar called the Backrow Tavern in Overland Park. She had driven by the bar many times, but had never gone in because it wasn't the sort of place a lady frequented unless she was covered in tattoos and drove a Harley. *At 7:30 in the morning, how dangerous can the place be?* Pulling into the parking lot, Skylar saw the line of motorcycles already parked out front. Unsure of what to expect, she pulled a Smith & Wesson .22 pistol from her glove compartment, checked the clip and slipped it into her purse. *A girl can never be too careful,* she told herself, repeating the words her father had said years ago, when he gave her the gun. She'd used it only at the shooting range to get certified, and she was hoping she wouldn't need it today.

Stepping out of her car and cinching her black, mid-length trench coat tighter around her waist, Skylar took a deep breath; and then she opened the door and stepped inside the tavern. The place was truly a hole-in-the-wall, small, dark and smoky. There were a handful of patrons sitting at the bar and Skylar guessed by their leather clothing and overall appearance that they belonged to the bikes out front. Everyone turned and stared as she entered and she felt her face flush with embarrassment. She was the obvious oddball in the group. Slowly approaching the bar, she opened her mouth to speak but before she could ask, the bartender flipped his head to the right and said, "He's back there."

Skylar paused. *How does he know who I'm looking for?* She wondered.

"Oh, and lady," the bartender grunted, "take this to him, would ya? My waitress ain't in yet." He handed her a cup of coffee and pointed to the back of the bar.

Skylar took the steaming coffee and tentatively walked to the right of the bar and down an aisle between booths. She noticed a man sitting in the last booth on the left, facing the door. When he looked up and met her eyes, he rose to his feet in gentlemanly fashion.

"You must be Skylar Wilson," he said, extending his right hand.

"Stephen Braznovich?"

"The one and only," he smiled and Skylar felt a flutter of nerves grip her stomach. He was better looking than she imagined, way better looking. In fact, he was almost breathtaking. Skylar blinked slowly, gawking at him, unable to find words.

"Is that for me?" He asked, motioning toward the coffee cup that was clutched tightly between her now clammy hands.

"Oh, yes, the bartender asked me to bring it to you." Her voice grew shaky and she nervously cleared her throat.

"Would you like to sit down Ms. Wilson?" He asked, with a certain amusement behind his eyes.

He's laughing at how nervous I am! Skylar slid into the booth across from him. "You're not at all what I expected," she said softly, tucking a piece of hair behind her ear.

"I hope that's a good thing," Stephen grinned with that dynamite smile; a sexy, boyish grin that made her go weak in the knees.

"I mean," she cleared her throat again and knotted her fingers together, "coming to a place like this, I wasn't sure what to expect."

"Fair enough," he smiled, folding his hands on the table. "Before we get down to business, can I get you something to eat or drink?"

Skylar's awkwardness grew. She hadn't eaten breakfast, but she felt too nervous to eat in front of him. Besides, she didn't want to order something if he wasn't ordering anything. Her face flushed as she hemmed and hawed, "I, um, well, I'm …"

"They make the best western omelet. Do you like eggs?" He interrupted, rescuing her from her mental clamoring.

"Yes," Skylar smiled sheepishly.

"Good. I'll be right back." Braznovich slid out of the booth and vanished up the aisle, while Skylar exhaled and gave herself a mental head slap. As she slid out of the booth and removed her trench coat, the knots in her stomach gave way to fluttering butterflies and she wasn't sure why she suddenly felt like a bumbling teenager. Was it the overwhelming nature of the whole situation, the trepidation she felt walking into such a seedy tavern, or the fact that Braznovich was remarkably good looking? The answer was obvious. It was Braznovich. It was as if his eyes alone, those dark, sparkly eyes, unraveled every tangible thought and stroked her in places that hadn't been stroked in a long time.   She took a deep breath and exhaled. *Keep it together, Skylar,* she scolded herself and slid back into the booth, folding her coat and setting it beneath her purse.

He returned carrying a cup of coffee for Skylar and a small carafe. "I drink a lot of coffee," he said, setting the carafe down and sliding in across from her. "It goes with the P.I. job description," he joked and Skylar noted how his smile shone through his eyes. There was something warm and likeable about him. Despite the fact that he looked muscular beneath his dark sport coat, and that his dark brown, tussled hair and tanned, olive skin made him a candidate for the cover of GQ, there was a depth and genuineness about him that fostered immediate trust.

"Do you always hang out in these types of taverns?" Skylar asked.

"Aw, this place is great," Braznovich leaned back in the booth. "It's a diamond in the ruff."

Skylar glanced around. "Well, you've got the rough part right," she teased and he chuckled aloud.

"Just wait until you try the omelet and you'll change your mind." He winked and Skylar felt her temperature rise. Taking a sip of coffee, she almost choked on it when he asked, "Is that a Smith & Wesson .22 sticking out of your purse?"

Skylar's eyes widened and she instinctively covered her purse with her elbow, pushing the gun further down. "I-I wasn't sure about coming here alone," she stuttered. "I didn't even know this place was open so early and I didn't know if you were normal or ..." her voice tapered off.

"I have always strived not to be normal, Ms. Wilson," he leaned in on his elbows and spoke in a whisper. "Normal equates to boring and boring is no fun." Deliberately leaning back in the booth, he grinned and Skylar's mouth went dry. *He looks fun. I like fun.*

"I'm judging from your wide-eyed reaction that you're not licensed to carry concealed," Braznovich leaned forward again and spoke in a half-hushed tone; his eyes smiling.

She smirked at him. "No, I'm not licensed, but if you saw it then it wasn't really concealed, now was it, Mr. Braznovich?" She raised her eyebrows, proud of her comeback.

"Touché' Ms. Wilson," he grinned.

"I may not be licensed, but I am certified and I'm a pretty damn good shot."

He raised his palms up, stick up style and leaned back. "Well, I can vouch for the pretty part," he said and she felt her face flush. *Did he just call me pretty? Does Mr. Drop-Dead-Gorgeous really think I'm pretty?* Her stomach wrenched into knots of excitement. "So, tell me Annie Oakley, what brings you to inquire about my services?"

Skylar rolled her eyes, and then took out her cell phone and showed Braznovich the text message from Tess. Next, she pulled out the picture of the chair with the blood stained floor and the cup with "Danger, Get Out Now" written on the bottom. She also gave Braznovich the POP magazine article about Tess. Then she explained what had happened with Ema in the bookstore and how she had found the note on her car at the police station, instructing her to contact him. She summed it up with a cliff-notes version of her deteriorating relationship with Tess due to the influence of the P3 movement. The moment Skylar mentioned P3, she saw the sparkle leave Braznovich's eyes and a look of disgust fill his face.

"So you want me to locate your sister?" He asked.

"Yes and no," Skylar answered. "I know Tess is at the P3 compound, but I need help finding her and getting her out."

Braznovich tightened his jaw and shook his head. "I don't do rescue missions, Ms. Wilson. If your sister is there, she's there voluntarily and you can't get her out."

"What if she's being held against her will?" Skylar argued.

"That's speculation. There's nothing here that tells me she is being forced to stay." He raised an eyebrow. "If anything, it appears she is one of the leaders."

"But what if she's not? What IF they won't let her leave?"

The bartender sauntered over to the table and set down two plates filled with the biggest western omelets Skylar had ever seen. Then he pulled a bottle of Tabasco from his pocket and handed it to Braznovich. "You know what I like," Braznovich grinned. "Thanks man." The bartender gave a nod and shuffled back up the aisle.

Skylar watched in amazement as he shook the Tabasco on his omelet until there wasn't a trace of egg to be seen. "Listen, Ms. Wilson, my fee is high and your job is filled with man-hours you can't afford."

Indignation rose in her gut and Skylar narrowed her brow. "How do you know what I can afford?"   "What I'm saying is that it isn't worth your money or my time." He shoveled in a fork full of omelet and washed it down with coffee. "You can't fight these people, and you can't rescue someone who doesn't want to be saved." He stared at her for a moment, the sparkle gone from his eyes. "These people are like drug addicts, and you can't force an addict to go clean. THEY have to want it."

"P3. It's the equivalent of spiritual heroin," Skylar uttered quietly. Sadly, it was true. Maxwell had designed P3 to become addictive; a drug only his methods of mantra-based music and centering meditation could provide. People thought they were touching God, but if that were the case then they would have the same experiences without the music and the meditation. If God were speaking to them inside P3, then He had the power to speak to them outside of P3. The problem was once people like Tess became addicted; they lost the ability to see that God wasn't speaking to them at all. It was all Maxwell and his demonic manipulations.

Skylar lowered her eyes to the table and poked at her omelet with her fork. Suddenly, she was no longer hungry. Her stomach knotted again and a lump of emotion began rising in her throat. "I'll pay you whatever it takes," she said softly. "I don't make a lot of money, but I can put some money down and then pay you monthly until it's paid off." She didn't like begging, but she didn't feel like she had another choice. "Please, just look into it," her voice cracked. "That's all I'm asking."

Skylar was visibly startled when a big, burly man with a cigarette in his hand, seemingly appeared out of nowhere and slid into the booth next to Braznovich, forcing him to move over. He was dressed in a pair of faded Levi's, black army boots and a white t-shirt covered by a blue and black flannel shirt that hung open. He looked to be about six foot four and had a short, military style haircut and dark brown bushy eyebrows. His stature lookcd powerful and even dangerous, but his chocolate brown eyes had the feel of a harmless teddy bear.

"Hey Braz," he growled with a smoker's voice. "What's shakin'?" He picked up Braznovich's cup of coffee and took a drink.

"Get your own," Braznovich snapped, shoving the printed picture, cup and POP magazine into a pile and blocking it beneath his forearm.

The man grinned. "Friends share," he said and exhaled a smoke ring above his head. "Speaking of friends, aren't you gonna introduce me to yours?" He asked, gesturing with his head toward Skylar.

Braznovich rolled his eyes. "Ms. Wilson this is Ernie James. Ernie James, Ms. Wilson."

Ernie gave Skylar a nod, picked up Braznovich's fork and shoveled a big bite of omelet into his mouth. "So what are you two kids discussing?"

Skylar opened her mouth to speak but Braznovich beat her to it. "Nothing," he said emphatically. "We're just having a nice breakfast. Or we were."

"Ooh, ouch," Ernie grimaced. "What's got you all testy this early?"

"Nothing." Braznovich grabbed the fork from Ernie's grasp and slammed it onto the table. "Max!" He yelled and a few seconds later the bartender appeared in the aisle. "Will you get Mr. Moocher here an omelet and some coffee?"

Max laughed out loud. "Hey, Ernie. I didn't see you come in."

"Slipped in the back," Ernie replied without taking his eyes off of Skylar. His scrutinizing stare made her feel uneasy, as if he were looking right through her. Inhaling his cigarette for what seemed like an unusually long period of time; Ernie held the smoke in his lungs and then exhaled it through his nose. He squint his eyes at Skylar and murmured, "I see."

You see what? Skylar wondered.

"No, you don't see anything," Braznovich interjected. "There's nothing to see."

Ernie grinned, inhaled and blew another ring above his head. "I see that Ms. Wilson carries a concealed Smith & Wesson .22," he said, reaching his arm across Braznovich and squishing his cigarette butt into the ashtray.

"How did you see that?" Skylar gasped and put her hand on top of her purse. She had pushed the gun to the bottom of her purse after Braznovich noticed it.

"I saw into your purse when I approached the table. I'm tall enough to have what you'd call a bird's eye view, and you're not very good at hiding it." Ernie grinned and lit another cigarette.

"Do you have to chain smoke first thing in the morning?" Braznovich barked, waving the smoke out of his face.

"I don't have to, but it helps me think." He turned his attention back to Skylar. "Now, let me guess. You're not a cop because that's not the standard piece issued around these parts. You're not FBI or CIA because you didn't see me coming and you don't have that jaded look about you." He leaned back and studied her. "There's something very familiar about you, though. I can't put my finger on it."

"Are you done?" Braznovich piped in.

"Not yet," Ernie answered him without taking his eyes off of Skylar. "When I walked up, you were asking Braz to take a look at something for you. Any chance I can take a look see too?"

"No!" Braznovich blurted and then gave Skylar a glare that told her not to share anything with Ernie.

"I guess not," Skylar winced.

Max brought Ernie's omelet and coffee, set it down on the table and headed back toward the bar. "Max," Ernie called after him. "What's got Braz all tense?"

Max turned and shrugged. "Dunno man. Haven't seen him like this since the time he took on that crazy cult on the Missouri side. That was bad shit, man. Bad shit." Max shook his head and meandered back to the bar.

Skylar's mouth fell open and she stared at Braznovich. "You took on P3?" All of a sudden revelation struck her. "So that's why I was told to contact you."

Ernie snapped his fingers. "Hot diggity damn, I knew you looked familiar," he pointed at Skylar. "You look like that Wilson girl. What's her name? The leader chick that ..." Ernie stopped abruptly. "Oh," a light of recognition flashed in his eyes.

"What?" Skylar stared from Ernie to Braznovich and back to Ernie. "The leader chick that what?" Neither one of them answered. "Would one of you tell me what's going on?" They both sat silent. "If it's about my sister I deserve to know."

Ernie elbowed Braznovich. "It's her sister, man, you should tell her."

"Yes, Mr. Braznovich, you should tell me," Skylar narrowed her eyes.

Braznovich ran his fingers through his hair and leaned back in the booth, popping his lips together and exhaling deeply. It was obvious that this was not a topic he wanted to discuss. "My nephew, Jonathan, is a member of P3, an intern there," he sighed and Skylar empathized with the anguish that washed across his face. "He cut his mother, my sister, completely out of his life; claiming he had sought higher wisdom and that this, quote 'higher wisdom' had told him to sever ties with all family members outside of P3. P3 members were to be his new family." Braznovich shook his head. "It was killing my sister and she came to me for help. She and I drove there, just to talk to him; but when we arrived, they refused to let us see him."

"How could they stop you?" Skylar blurted. "They can't legally stop you from seeing your own nephew?"

"Legally, no," Braznovich said. "But when we refused to leave, a woman came to speak with us and told us that Jonathan had received a prophecy stating that he would die if he were to speak to his mother or anyone in his family."

"What!" Skylar exclaimed louder than she intended, and then slumped down and lowered her voice. "That's bullshit. You don't really believe that do you?"

Braznovich shook his head.

"Your sister doesn't believe that, does she?" Skylar asked.

Braznovich didn't answer, but his eyes, burning with anger and sadness, spoke volumes. "My sister was afraid that something bad would happen to Jonathan if we stayed, so we left."

"Don't you know that what they claim to be 'prophetic words from God' are all crap?" Skylar was now leaning on the table with both elbows.

"What I know is that the people running P3 are very good at manipulating others by twisting truth and masking their threats," Braznovich explained calmly.

"So you gave up because of what one woman said to you?" Skylar cocked her head to the side and scrunched up her nose, as if to imply she thought his retreat was weak. "You had to have known that she was lying." Braznovich picked up his fork and swallowed down another bite of omelet. "That's why I want to get my sister out of there, to protect her from Maxwell Sagan and Saul Latham and all of the other liars at P3." The words were no sooner out of her mouth when Braznovich shot Ernie a glance and Ernie reciprocated with a nod. She watched as Braznovich set his fork down and exhaled slowly. "What?" Skylar asked, searching his face. "What aren't you telling me?"

"The woman who told us Jonathan would die if he didn't sever ties with his family..."

"...was a liar," Skylar sarcastically interjected.

"...was Tess," Braznovich gritted and Skylar gasped.

"My Tess?" She sat back in disbelief as he nodded his head up and down. She suddenly felt nauseated. *Tess was no liar. How could she have said something so terrible, unless, she believed it to be true? Was she THAT brainwashed?*

"My Tess threatened you?" Skylar uttered softly, her hope in saving her sister quickly fading.

"Not in so many words," Braznovich clarified. "But the leaders of P3 are very careful about choosing their words. She basically told us that Jonathan would die if we came around again."

"So, she was threatening his life?" The thought of it was almost more than Skylar could handle. What had happened to the Tess she knew? It was difficult to fathom Tess being a mere player in the P3 corruption, but a leader and a liar? Skylar couldn't wrap her head around the idea. "That's exactly what Maxwell and his so-called prophets did to a bunch of churches when they first moved into the area," Skylar spoke in monotone, as if she were recalling the events in her head. Braznovich lowered his eyes to the table and squirmed uncomfortably in the booth.

"I haven't heard this," Ernie said, taking sudden interest.

Skylar cleared her throat. It had been a while since she talked about or even thought about how the P3 movement gained its powerful footing in Kansas City. "This goes way back. When Tess first became involved with P3, I began researching it and learned that the foundation of the organization is built upon a mountain of lies."

"Like what lies?" Ernie asked.

"I would need to dig out my research notes to be able to tell you everything, but what I remember off the top my head is that when Maxwell Sagan first came to Kansas City, he threatened many of the pre-existing churches," Skylar explained.

"Threatened, how?" Ernie questioned.

"He used prophecy to force the churches to close or coerce them into joining his congregation. There's even testimony by several pastors stating that Maxwell himself predicted their deaths if they took any type of stand against his teachings."

"So what happened?" Ernie blew out a smoke ring above his head and then leaned forward. "Did these pastors complain or take legal action?"

"There were forty-five pastors in the city that stood up against Maxwell. The one leading the opposition put together a 200 plus page document and delivered it to the Apostolic Presbyters of the Network of Christian Ministries; but I'm not sure what became of it after that." Skylar deflated. "They obviously gave up the fight just like everyone else." She said, staring deliberately at Braznovich. She knew by his piercing glare that her message had been received.

"Maybe this Maxwell Sagan guy paid them off?" Ernie suggested.

"Maybe," Skylar shrugged. "He certainly had the means and motive to do it."

"Do not be carried away by varied and strange teachings. Hebrews 13:9" Braznovich uttered quietly, as if deep in thought, and Ernie exhaled smoke right over the top of his head.

"Impressive, man," Ernie grinned.

"My grandpa was a preacher and he used to warn me about the coming days of false prophets and deceitful teachings," Braznovich explained. "He used to say, 'take everything you hear back to the Scripture and ask God for yourself."

"That's good advice," Skylar said.

"I hope you can understand why I can't help you. I promised my sister that I would stay away from P3 so that Jonathan would remain safe,"

41

Braznovich said apologetically, but Skylar still felt a twinge of anger.

"So that's it? They win Jonathan and Tess and Ema and God only knows how many other innocent young people because we're all too afraid to fight against them?" She shook her head. "Don't you see that Maxwell uses totally fabricated prophesies to promote his movement?"

"I see it, but what do you expect me to do about it?" Braznovich seethed, anger flashing in his eyes. "I'm as sickened by it as you are."

"I don't think you are, Mr. Braznovich," Skylar retorted. "If you were you'd be doing something about it."

His jaw tightened and Skylar recognized a rage behind his alluring brown eyes; but there was also something else there. Sadness? Grief? Sorrow? He lowered his gaze before she could put her finger on it.

"My hands are tied," he gritted.

"Well, I don't care if they prophesy that I will die or that my sister will dic. Their prophecies have all been wrong."

"Wait a tick," Ernie huffed. "What do you mean ALL of their prophecies have been wrong?"

Skylar rolled her eyes. "I mean, all of the so-called P3 Prophets have been proven false."

"How is P3 still in business?" Ernie squinted at Skylar. "If they're always wrong, what makes people stay and new people come?"

Skylar shrugged. "That's the million dollar question. Even Maxwell admits that they've been wrong, and do you know what he excuse he gives?" It was a rhetorical question, with Skylar not pausing long enough for either of them to answer. "He says that their prophecies have been wrong because they we're going through a phase of restoration and because every prophecy is conditional."

"Conditional?" Ernie snorted. "What does that mean?"

Skylar answered his question with a shrug and an eye roll and then continued talking. "My favorite excuse was when he said that New Testament prophets were different from Old Testament prophets because Old Testament prophets were perfect, but New Testament prophets could make mistakes.'" Skylar slammed her hands down on the table, making Ernie jump with surprise. "What a bunch of bullshit!" She hollered. "They're outright liars and I don't care what it takes, I'm not backing down!" Her voice had grown louder than she intended, as years of frustration and anger surged through her veins. "I'm not giving up!" Breathless from her rant, she slammed her elbows atop the table and buried her face in her hands, embarrassed that she was on the verge of tears in front of two complete strangers. *Don't cry! Don't cry! Pull yourself together.*

An awkward silence filled the air between them and then Braznovich reached across the table, pulled Skylar's left hand from her face, and held it in both of his. Giving it a tender squeeze, he spoke softly, "I understand where you're coming from, I do; but you have to realize there is nothing you can do to save Tess."

That was a reality she wasn't willing or ready to face. Despite the fact that his hand touching hers sent warm ripples of excitement up her back and made her flush, she pulled it away; using a napkin to wipe away a tear that had escaped and trickled down her cheek.

"Ms. Wilson…" his voice was soothing and compassionate, but Skylar cut him off before he could continue.

"Did Jonathan ever reach out to you for help?" She asked.

Braznovich shook his head and inhaled deeply. "No."

Swallowing hard, Skylar set her jaw. "Well, Tess reached out to me and I'm not leaving her."

CHAPTER 6

Skylar felt deflated as she drove back to her apartment, made a fresh pot of coffee and plunked down onto the couch to wait for the coffee to finish brewing. She was disheartened by the fact that Braznovich had experience with P3 and was refusing to help her. She understood his reasons, but seeing him succumb to the fear tactics commonly used by P3 leadership to keep the Yahweh Separatists in and the rest of the remnant out, infuriated her. *They're not forcing me out!* She couldn't help but replay what he told her about Tess over and over in her mind. It was one thing to think Tess was led astray by Maxwell Sagan, but entirely another thing to believe she was deliberately deceiving others. It stung her heart.

Skylar closed her eyes, finally starting to relax when a knock on the door startled her. Leaping up, she looked through the peep hole, but saw no one. Skylar lived on the third floor of a small apartment building just across the Missouri Stateline. She was a freelance photographer, trying to get her business up and running, and couldn't yet afford to rent on the Kansas side. The neighborhood wasn't a place in which she'd walk alone after dark, but she had good neighbors and it was safe enough during the daylight hours. Peering through the peep hole again, just to make sure no one was there, she jerked the door open and a piece of wide-lined notebook paper, which had been wedged into the crack of the door jam, fell at her feet. Skylar picked it up, immediately noticing the same cursive penmanship used in the note that had been left on her car. However, this note contained only one word: DIVINITY

"Hello?" Skylar called out, rushing to the edge of the stairway that jetted off to right of her door and peering downward to see if she could catch a glimpse of someone leaving.

She jumped and shrieked when her next door neighbor's door thrust open and Mrs. Neiler appeared in the doorway, holding a broom. "What's all the racket?" Mrs. Neiler hollered with such ferocity that her voice bounced off of the walls and echoed down the stairwell. Mrs. Neiler was in her eighties and had recently gotten a new hearing aid. She was having trouble adjusting it so sometimes it was turned up too high and sometimes it was turned down too low. Skylar could always tell which by the volume of Mrs. Neiler's voice. When the aid was up, Mrs. Neiler talked softly and when the aid was down, she yelled to be able to hear herself.

"Nothing," Skylar hollered back. "Sorry to have disturbed you."

Mrs. Neiler grabbed her ears. "Bless my soul, child, you don't have to yell," she winced. "What are you trying to do, give an old woman a heart attack?" She shook her head in reprimanding fashion and returned to her apartment, mumbling something about the youth having no respect for their elders.

Skylar stepped back into her apartment, closed the door and locked the deadbolt. She was uncomfortable with the fact that the anonymous note deliverer not only knew what kind of car she drove, but also knew where she lived. She stared at the paper, trying to assign relevancy to the word 'DIVINITY.' When she couldn't, she went to her closet and dug out the thick black binder that held all of her P3 research notes. She was just about to dive in when another startling knock sent her airborne. Grabbing the .22 from her purse, Skylar rushed toward the door in hopes of catching whoever it was that was leaving her these mysterious clues; but this time, as she peered through the hole, Ernie James smiled and waved from the other side of the door.

"What are you doing here? How did you find me?" Skylar hollered through the door.

"That's two different questions," Ernie said. "Which one do you want me to answer first?"

Skylar opened the door just a crack, blocked it with her right leg and allowed her gaze to pass beyond Ernie. "Is Braznovich with you?"

"No, just me," Ernie shrugged and Skylar felt a wave of disappointment wash over her. "Now, before you shoot me, let me be up front and say I followed you home." Ernie glanced down at the .22 held tightly in Skylar's grip.

"So you're a stalker?" Skylar smirked and Ernie bellowed out a smoker's laugh.

"Some might say that. I'm a cop, sort of, so I only stalk when it's absolutely necessary."

Skylar narrowed her brows. "How are you a cop 'sort of'? You're either a cop or not a cop, right?"

"It's a long story." He drew a badge from his front pocket and held it up for Skylar to inspect. It looked real enough, at least from the little she knew of police badges. "I'm retired, but I still help out. Can I come in?" Ernie asked.

Skylar hesitated, staring blankly. Should she trust him? After all, despite his teddy bear-esque quality, he was nonetheless a complete stranger.

"You're trying to decide if you can trust me," Ernie mumbled, as if the reason for her delay in opening the door had just now registered in his brain. "Let me help you. You're approximately five feet, six inches tall and weigh around one hundred and twenty five pounds, right?"

"Uh-huh," Skylar answered, wondering what that had to do with anything.

"You've used your right knee to block the door against a six foot, four inch man, weighing a good two hundred and thirty pounds." Skylar glanced down at her knee, suddenly aware of how flimsy a blockade it was. "If I wanted to harm you, don't you think I would have barged in already?"

There was some logic there, though it could be a trap. Skylar stood frozen, her heart racing in her chest.

Ernie pulled his gun from the back of his jeans and held it up, handle-first toward Skylar. "Here," he grinned, "if I wanted to hurt you would I be handing you my only weapon, leaving you armed and me with nothing but my overwhelming charm?"

Skylar rolled her eyes and stepped back, allowing Ernie to enter. "Don't make me regret this," she uttered and he chuckled. Ernie made a beeline for the black faux leather couch, plopped down, crossing his hands behind his head and placing his feet atop the pale wood coffee table.

"Nice digs," he mumbled.

Skylar closed and bolted the door and then joined him by the couch. "So, are you here to arrest me for carrying concealed?"

Ernie chuckled, lowered his feet and sat up straight. "Nope. And since I could see it, it wasn't really concealed."

"That's what I said to Braznovich," she laughed.

"I'm here to help you find your sister." He pulled out a cigarette, packed it against the back of his left hand and lit up. "You don't mind if I smoke do you?" He asked, as the cigarette dangled from the side of his mouth.

"I guess not," Skylar said, hurrying to open the sliding door that led to a small balcony.

"Good, 'cuz I can't think without a smoke."

"I've noticed," Skylar mused. "What made you change your mind about helping me?"

"I didn't change my mind. I was always gonna help you. It's Braz that has the issue with it." Ernie took a drag and exhaled slowly. "Don't misunderstand him. He wants to help but loyalty to his sister forces him to stay away."

"I know," Skylar sighed. "But I keep thinking about the person who left the anonymous note on my car. They must have had reason to believe he could help me."

"Maybe they knew he took on P3 before?" Ernie said, raising himself off of the couch and walking toward the kitchen.

"But then we'd have to assume that they also knew he quit," Skylar pointed out.

"Maybe." Ernie shrugged, held the cigarette in his lips and then smacked his hands together. "You said you had some research notes?"

"Yes," Skylar pointed to the black binder that was sitting on the kitchen table and told him about the 'DIVINITY' note she received just moments before he arrived.

"Let's start by finding out what this DIVINITY means," he said and then blew a smoke ring over his head. "You take the binder and I'll jump on your laptop and cross-reference Maxwell Sagan and the word Divinity." Skylar agreed, slid her gun back into her purse, sat down at the table and opened the binder; while Ernie carried her laptop from the counter to the kitchen table and sat next to her. Skylar began to peruse her old research notes when Ernie blurted, "Well, I'll be damned."

"What?" Skylar glanced at the screen.

"The first fifteen listings match Maxwell Sagan with something being called the Divinity Design," Ernie said.

Skylar leaned in closer. "That's GOT to be what the note is referring to," she said excitedly.

Ernie clicked on one of the links. "Lookey here."

Skylar stood behind him and leaned over Ernie's shoulder as they both read the article describing the Divinity Design. The article said that the prophecy was received by Maxwell from an unknown prophet, which was then confirmed by another prophet and by a supernatural encounter Maxwell had involving both an angel and a demon. "This prophecy became the building block of the P3 movement and is still its foundational premise today," Ernie read.

Skylar shook her head in disgust. "It's not even from the Bible."

"If these guys are new prophets then what they said wouldn't be in the Bible," Ernie suggested.

"Don't go there," Skylar held up her palm in a talk-to-the-hand manner. "That opens up another can of worms."

"What worms?"

"Worms that ask how do we know if a prophet is real or if a prophet is false," Skylar explained. "Tess and I have gone round and round on this."

"Well, how DO we know?" Ernie got up, opened the sliding door wider and flicked his cigarette butt off the deck.

"There's a verse in the Bible that says to beware of false prophets and tells us that you will know them by their fruits..."

"Fruits?" Ernie interrupted.

Skylar retrieved her Bible from the oak bookshelf located against the wall across opposite the couch. She sat down next to Ernie and flipped through the pages, stopping in the book of Matthew. "It's here in Matthew 7:15-20. It says 'watch out for false prophets. They come to you in sheep's clothing, but inwardly they are ferocious wolves.'" She stopped reading and looked at Ernie, who was lighting up another cigarette. "That describes Maxwell all right," she uttered and then continued reading. "By their fruit you will recognize them.'"

"What does that mean?" Ernie rasped.

Skylar continued to read. "It says 'every good tree bears good fruit, but a bad tree bears bad fruit. A good tree cannot bear bad fruit, and a bad tree cannot bear good fruit. Thus, by their fruit you will recognize them.'"

Ernie leaned his head back and listened until she was finished reading; and then he blew smoke straight into the air. "So good people do good things and bad people do bad things. Am I missing anything?"

"It goes deeper than that because a good person can still make a mistake and do a bad thing," Skylar said. "I think it is referring to an on-going lifestyle. It takes a long time for a tree to grow and bear fruit and the whole tree has to be bad for it to consistently produce bad fruit."

"So we need to look at Maxwell Sagan's fruit?" Ernie laughed out loud. "I never thought I'd say THAT about another man."

Skylar smiled and grimaced at the same time. The thought was disgusting. "The problem with P3 is that on the surface, it looks like this big beautiful tree of fresh, shiny apples; but the poison is hidden inside."

"Like Snow White," Ernie said with his cigarette dangling to one side of his mouth.

Skylar smiled. "I didn't take you for a fairy tale guy."

"I'm deep, man. Really deep." He chuckled and blew smoke out of his nose.

Skylar waved her hand in the air to dissipate the smoke. "You look like a bull when you do that," she laughed.

"That's what Braz says." Ernie took a long drag and exhaled smoke through his nose again, and then directed his attention back to the computer screen. "Listen to this," he said and read aloud. "The Divinity Design was allegedly first received in 1984 but Maxwell Sagan refused to make it public until 2002; though it has been speculated that portions have still been withheld."

"That doesn't surprise me," Skylar said.

"It gets better," Ernie quipped, and read on. "Another version of the Divinity Design was released in 2006, which was not identical to the 2002 release; and yet another release came in 2009 with still more changes."

"If this prophecy were really from God, how could they make changes to it?" Skylar asked.

"Good question," Ernie said. "I'm no straight as an arrow guy, but I sure as hell don't have the kahunas to alter something that was given to me by God." He blew out a giant smoke ring above his head.

"Maxwell knows it's not from God, so he has no problem re-writing it to fit his ever-changing agenda." Skylar rolled her eyes. "He makes me sick."

"Listen to this," Ernie pointed to the computer screen as he read. "One might suggest that Maxwell Sagan's Divinity Design has been a self-fulfilling work of fiction."

"That's what I just said," Skylar blurted.

"I know," Ernie raised his eyebrows. "You're one smart cookie."

"Not smart enough, because I still can't connect the dots." Skylar plunked her head down on the table. "Like, who is leaving me these notes and why? Why did Tess send me a text? What does the Divinity Design have to do with finding my sister?"

"You're making a lot of assumptions," Ernie said.

She lifted her head and squint her eyes at him. "What do you mean?"

"You're assuming that you were given the word DIVINITY in order to help you find Tess, but that's speculation. And you're assuming that Tess was the one who text you for help, but that's speculation too. All you really know is that you received a text message from Tess's phone. You don't know for sure who sent the message."

Skylar was speechless. It never occurred to her that Tess might not have been the one sending the text. She narrowed her eyebrows and licked her lips, trying to play it all out in her mind.

"Is that your thinking face?" Ernie teased, mimicking her expression and chuckling aloud.

"At least I don't look like a bull shooting smoke out of my nose when I think," Skylar retorted.

Ernie's cell phone buzzed and interrupted their banter. "Braz, man, we were just talking about you." Several "uh-huhs," "no-shits," and "I'll be damns" later, he was off the phone and ushering Skylar toward the door.

"Where are we going?" Skylar persisted.

"I'll tell you in the car," he slapped his hands together excitedly. "Braz is on the job."

Really?! Excitement swelled inside and Skylar couldn't hide her ear-to-ear grin.

CHAPTER 7

Ernie drove with Skylar in the passenger seat of his black Ford pick-up, which was souped up with big tires and dark tinted windows. There was something about sitting so far above other drivers that made a person feel a certain sense of power. On the way to Menorah Medical Center in Overland Park, Ernie told Skylar what Braznovich had said on the phone; which was that a young woman had been found alongside highway 71 at 4:00am that morning, less than a couple of miles from the P3 complex. She was unconscious and without identification when they brought her in. They pulled into the hospital parking lot and, killing the engine, Ernie turned to face Skylar. She knew her concern was evident on her face.

"Does Braznovich think the young woman is Tess?" Skylar asked, fear laced in her voice. She took a deep breath and tried to calm her nerves. *Please don't let it be Tess. Please don't let it be Tess.*

"He didn't say that." Ernie gave her shoulder a pat that told her not to think that way.

"If they found her on the Missouri side, why did they bring her all the way to Menorah?" Skylar asked, as Menorah was on the Kansas side and there were clearly other hospitals closer to where she had been found.

Ernie shrugged. "Dunno. This is where the man who found her brought her. We'll have to ask him why." He opened the driver's door and flicked his cigarette butt onto the pavement as he stepped out.

Skylar climbed out of the passenger side and they met in front of the truck. "If he doesn't think it is Tess, than why does Braznovich want me here?"

"You can ask him that yourself." Ernie pointed to Braznovich, who was walking out of the front entrance of the hospital to meet them. Skylar took a deep breath and felt her face flush a little when she saw him. He was wearing black suit pants and a black, crisp t-shirt that lay tight around his well-built chest and muscular arms. There was no denying his air of confident power. He was sophisticated yet had certain athleticism, and he was hot; the kind of hot that made Skylar feel fidgety and nervous. He was the kind of hot that made her temperature rise just being in his presence; the kind of hot that would make girls swoon. Skylar's mouth grew dry and she nervously licked her lips, telling herself not to look too eager and excited to see him. *You're mad at him for not taking your case, remember?* Her subconscious remarked; but Skylar couldn't keep from smiling. Despite her anger she was indeed happy to see him again.

As he approached, Skylar could see the scowl on Braznovich's face. *Oh no, it isn't Tess is it?!* Without acknowledging her, he locked eyes with Ernie. "I need you to pull the cop card and get us in to talk to the victim. She's in ICU."

"Right on," Ernie said and headed toward the entrance.

Braznovich then turned to Skylar. "I'm not officially taking your case. This doesn't mean anything, but I have a feeling this woman can help you."

"Is it Tess?" Skylar blurted, her worst fear manifesting before him.

His face softened and he tenderly placed his hand on the outside of her shoulder and squeezed. "No, it's not Tess." Skylar breathed a sigh of relief that felt as if it traveled from her head all the way down to her toes, and her muscles began to unclench.

"Do we know for sure the victim is from P3?" Skylar asked.

"I know she is," Braznovich answered matter-of-factly. "Both of her arms were bandaged between the elbow and shoulder when she was found." Skylar narrowed her brows and shook her head to indicate she didn't understand the relevance. Taking Skylar by the arm, he led her away from the main doors. "If I'm right, her arms have been sliced by a very thin, sharp object; sharp enough to make the tiniest slither through the skin without causing severe tissue damage, or leaving a jagged scar."

Skylar instinctively rubbed her hands over her own shoulders and grimaced. "I don't understand."

"It's a form of corporal mortification, only this is different because I don't believe these wounds were self-inflicted." Skylar knew her ignorance was evident. "We don't have time for me to go into detail right now. I'll explain it all later. Besides, it's just a hunch."

"So you're saying someone at P3 cut her arms?" Skylar raised her eyebrows, the thought sickening her.

"I'm saying I think Maxwell Sagan has taken a very old Catholic ritual and mutilated it to fit his purpose." Braznovich ran his hand through his tussled hair. "Mortification has taken on many forms throughout history and even though some groups have abused it, for the most part, it is pure in its use and intent," he explained.

"What's the intent?"

"It was originally used by Catholic priests and nuns to elevate and purify a person in body and soul. Corporal Mortification can involve simple things of self-denial such as fasting, dressing in sackcloth or hair shirts that cause discomfort, sleeping without a pillow, taking vows of silence, all the way up to wearing a chain cilise with sharp points or whipping oneself with a knotted rope…" He stopped talking when Skylar shuddered. "The point is that the process of mortification was never meant to be something inflicted by another person, and it was rarely supposed to be bloody."

"What makes you think P3 is doing this?"

"I've had a hunch for a while now," he sighed. "I noticed a few things when I was at the campus with my sister last year."

Skylar could tell there was more to the story than what Braznovich was telling. She wanted to ask questions, but now wasn't the time.

"Anyway," he continued, "we know Maxwell Sagan has an affinity for Saint Teresa of Avila, right?" Skylar nodded, impressed that Braznovich seemed to have done his homework. "Teresa of Avila was obsessed with the practice of disciplines, including self-infliction of pain for the purification of the soul; such that she ordered her Carmelite nuns to apply disciplines to themselves daily."

Skylar studied Braznovich's eyes. "And you think he's not only into Teresa of Avila's mystic prayer rituals, but adopting her mortification practices as well?"

"Not adopting," Braznovich emphasized. "Dangerously twisting."

"Well, that wouldn't surprise me," Skylar uttered sarcastically. "He certainly twists everything else."

Ernie poked his head out of the front doors and motioned them inside. "I'll have to escort you," he said. "Braz, you're a special detective working on a high profile security case, of which you think our Jane Doe might be a part."

"Got it," Braznovich nodded.

"Skylar, you are a possible relative we've brought in to help identify the victim," Ernie explained.

Skylar didn't like hospitals and she particularly didn't like the ICU. Illness and death were things she feared and being around people that were fighting for their lives stretched her way beyond her comfort zone.

"Do you know who found her?" Skylar whispered to Braznovich as they followed Ernie into the ICU. She couldn't help but catch a whiff of his scent when she leaned toward him. He smelled like cool aftershave and warm musky cologne, an intoxicating distraction from their gloomy surroundings.

"I have his name and address but I haven't spoken with him yet. I plan on paying him a visit later this afternoon," Braznovich answered, leaning down to whisper in Skylar's ear, his close proximity sending chills through her.

Ernie entered the room first, and then Braznovich stopped in the doorway, ushering Skylar inside ahead of him. He placed his hand in the small of her back and guided her through the doorway and toward the bed. Skylar's senses were heightened by the awareness of his touch, and butterflies danced wildly in her stomach. *Oh, what this man does to me!*

The nurse informed Ernie that they only had fifteen minutes. "Good luck getting anything out of her," the nurse quipped. "She just stares, refusing to answer any questions; like she doesn't want to be helped." Exhaling an exasperated sigh, the nurse waddled out of the door, closing it behind her.

"She's a ray of frickin' sunshine, ain't she," Ernie muttered after she left.

When Skylar looked at the woman in the bed, her breath caught in her throat. She had an IV in her left arm, an oxygen tube in her nose and heart monitors stuck to her chest. Dried blood was caked in between her fingers and her skin looked ghostly gray. Skylar instinctively took a hold of Braznovich's arm and squeezed. "That's Ema," she whispered to him, her voice fading with emotion. "That's Ema Wright from the bookstore."

Ema must have heard her name because as soon as Skylar uttered it, she turned her head slightly in Skylar's direction. Nearing her bedside, Skylar took Ema's fingertips in hers, noting how icy cold they were. "Ema," she sniffed and pursed her lips to try to control the mixture of sadness and anger she felt. "Can you hear me?"

Ema's head nodded slightly.

"Who did this to you?" Skylar asked, but it became quickly clear that Ema was too weak to speak.

"Stick to yes and no questions," Ernie instructed.

Skylar fought to keep her composure as she swallowed hard and rephrased her question. "We're here to help you. Did someone at P3 do this to you?"

Ema nodded.

"Did they cut your arms? Is that why your arms are bandaged?"

Ema nodded again and started to cry.

Tears filled Skylar's eyes. "Do you know the name of the person who did this to you?"

Ema shook her head to indicate no.

"Were you blindfolded when it happened?"

Ema shook her head no.

"Were you in a dark room?"

Ema nodded.

All at once Skylar's mind flashed back to the picture of the room with the red walls, the black chair, the handcuffs and the blood all over the floor. Her pulse quickened and she felt queasy. "Ema," Skylar breathed in deeply, "were you handcuffed to a chair when they cut you?"

Tears flowed down Ema's face as tiny sobs of agony escaped her throat.

Skylar leaned closer and stroked her sandy brown hair. "It's going to be okay now," she told her. "You're safe now and everything will be okay."

Ema shook her head no and cried.

"No one will hurt you here," Skylar tried to reassure her, but Ema adamantly shook her head, trying to form words.

"M...M..." Ema's voice faded and Skylar could see the determination in her eyes to speak. "M..."

"Money?" Skylar blurted. "Magic?"

Ema shook her head and slowly licked her lips. "N.E..." her voice faded away again.

"Any?" Skylar shrugged at Ernie and Braznovich. "Any what?"

Ema shook her head and winced as if she were in pain.

"I'm sorry," Skylar told her. "Try again."

"N.E.T.," Ema sucked in a breath as if it were painful to breathe.

"N.E.T.," Skylar repeated. "National Ecclesiastical Transformation?" She blurted and Ema nodded her head. "What does the Divinity Design have to do with the National Ecclesiastical Transformation?"

Ema stared at Skylar as if she wanted to be able to telepathically communicate, and Skylar wished she could. "P...Pr...Pr..." Ema exhaled and tried once again to suck in a deep breath. Her eyes started to droop closed and Skylar could tell she was forcing them to open back up.

"Prayer?" Skylar guessed, but Ema didn't respond. "Um, prophet?" She guessed again, but Ema lay motionless. Skylar looked at Ernie and Braznovich. "I don't know the right questions to ask," she wailed.

"D..." Ema's voice grew faint. "D...d...d..."

"I don't know what D means?" Skylar said. "Dominus?" Skylar blurted.

"Who's Dominus?" Ernie asked.

"Dominus is the angel or rather, demon that Maxwell Sagan has spoken with on several occasions," Braznovich explained, and Skylar was shocked by his knowledge of P3 history. She made a mental note to ask him about it later.

All of a sudden Ema's body started violently convulsing and the heart monitor went from the methodic beep, beep, beep, to one long, ongoing beeping sound. Skylar squeezed Ema's fingers and called her name, but she was pushed aside by the nurse and several others who had immediately responded to the alarm.

"Code Blue!" A male nurse hollered as the alarm sounded.

"Clear," another nurse said, and then hit Ema's chest with the paddles. They all stared at the monitor.

"Clear," the nurse said again, and issued another hit to her chest.

Skylar couldn't breathe, as she watched everything happening as if it were in slow motion. She wasn't even aware of Ernie grabbing her arms and pulling her from the room, because her eyes were fixated on Ema's sunken face.

In the waiting room, Ernie jotted down the conversation between Skylar and Ema, Braznovich paced back and forth with his cell phone, utilizing every resource to locate Ema Wright's mother; while Skylar stared blankly at the floor, tears trickling down her chin and dropping to the carpet. She prayed for Ema, prayed that they would find Ema's mother and prayed for understanding. *Help me put the pieces together, God, please,* Skylar said in the quiet of her mind.

The doctor didn't have to say anything when he stepped into the waiting room. Skylar knew just by looking into his eyes that Ema was gone. "We'd like to conduct an autopsy and determine the exact cause of death," the doctor said.

"We'd like that too," Ernie piped in.

"Don't you need the family's approval to do an autopsy?" Skylar sniveled.

"Not if the individual dies of suspicious causes and has been unattended by a physician for a minimum of twenty-four hours," the doctor explained. "We're estimating this woman to be in her early twenties, which is an unusual age for cardiac arrest. I'm not saying it can't ever happen," he raised his eyebrows. "I'm just saying that it gives us cause to look into why it happened."

Ernie stayed to talk with the doctor while Skylar and Braznovich walked outside. Skylar felt dazed. She didn't even know Ema, and yet she felt this surreal connection to her. "I'll take you home," Braznovich said and looped his arm around her back.

Arriving at her apartment building, Braznovich walked Skylar to her door. "Are you going to be okay?" He asked, as she inserted her key and pushed the door open.

"Yeah," Skylar nodded. "I just keep thinking this is partly my fault. Maybe this happened because I talked with her in the bookstore." Tears started to well up in her eyes. "If I hadn't gone there, maybe she wouldn't have been punished." Suddenly Skylar was overcome with emotion and broke into sobs. Holding her against his chest, Braznovich maneuvered them inside and closed the door.

He led them to the couch, enfolded her in his arms, and gently stroked her hair as she wept against him. "Go ahead and let it out," he said softly. "Get it all out."

When she finished crying, she awkwardly separated herself from his embrace and apologized. "I don't normally break down like that," she said.

"I don't expect you normally have days like this," he rebutted, which made her smile.

"That is true," she agreed and an awkward moment of silence filled the space between them. Braznovich rose from the couch and Skylar followed suit. "Thank you for bringing me home and for taking me to see Ema."

Braznovich looked down at the floor momentarily and pursed his lips together. "You can stop thanking me," he said, lifting his gaze from the floor to her eyes. "We're officially in this together now, Ms. Wilson."

"You mean you're on the case?"

"Against my better judgment, yes, I'm on the case." He grinned and excitement swept over her.

They stood at the door for a brief moment of awkward silence. "Oh!" Skylar blurted, "I need to pay you." She reached toward her purse, which was sitting on the countertop to the right of the front door. "How does this work? Do I make a down payment to retain your services and pay you the rest as we go?" She retrieved her checkbook and a pen from her purse and then turned to see Braznovich smirking at her. "What?" Her eyes widened. *He's laughing at me again!* Her subconscious pouted, with a crossed-arm stomp of the foot.

"Let's not worry about the down payment, Ms. Wilson," he said smoothly. "Consider my services officially retained."

Skylar suddenly felt embarrassed and shame flushed her cheeks. She didn't want his charity. Dropping her head, she shifted her weight from side to side. "Look, I appreciate what you're doing, but I agreed to hire you and I intend to pay you." She glanced up. "I obviously don't have a lot, but if you'll let me make monthly payments..."

He reached over and tucked a piece of her hair behind her ear and then lifting her chin so their eyes met, he spoke, "Ms. Wilson, we will discuss payment options once I get a more in-depth look at your case." His touch sent warm shivers from her head to her toes. "Got it?" His tone was authoritative and his eyes sparkled with a piercing power that made her want to succumb to his every wish.

She nodded and he released her chin. Excitement and hope instantly filled her. Pure, unadulterated hope; hope in finding Tess and rescuing her from this cult once and for all. Hope of having a real relationship with her sister again, whom she missed so deeply it broke her heart. With the help of Braznovich and Ernie it might actually be possible. Without forethought, she threw her arms around his neck and shrieked, "I'm so excited I could kiss you!" No sooner had the words left her mouth, when a rush of humiliation filled her and her cheeks turned red. Did she really just say that out loud? Did she really just throw herself into this man's arms? *Omigosh!* She was mortified and immediately releasing her grip, she backed away, scrunched her eyes shut and shook her head. "I'm so sorry," she winced. "I – I don't know why I ..."

She felt his fingers against her lips and when she opened her eyes she saw that a big grin had spread across his face and illumed his eyes. "Ms. Wilson, I have a very strict policy never to mix business and pleasure," he explained. Skylar deflated. *Here comes the reprimand. This is so embarrassing!*

"Of course," she shifted her weight nervously. "I didn't mean to imply..."

He put his fingers to her lips again to silence her. "Once we get this whole thing figured out, I'm going to hold you to that kiss." He gave her a wink and was gone before Skylar could catch her breath, but the smile stayed glued on her face for the rest of the afternoon.

CHAPTER 8

When Tess awoke, she was lying in her bed in her apartment, with bandages wrapped around her arms and both Maxwell Sagan and Saul Latham were standing over her, praying. When they saw that she had awakened, Maxwell sat on the side of her bed and took her right hand in his.

Tess felt strangely disoriented. "What happened?" She asked, struggling to sit up.

"The Lord has shown me that you are chosen and often the chosen are the most attacked. I, myself, have been attacked by demons eight or ten times over the past several years. It's not your fault, Tess. The enemy will cast shadows of doubt, but you must fight them off with the authority given to you by the Lord."

Tess tried to force a memory but her mind was completely blank. "I was attacked?" She asked. "The last thing I remember was taking communion with you in the Prayer Room and then I came back here, I think."

Maxwell nodded. "Yes, we should have escorted you back to your apartment. That was our error. You were weak and vulnerable."

"Some of the interns heard screaming and we came up and found you were under great attack," Saul added.

"We helped rebuke two very strong demons that were confining you," Maxwell explained and Saul nodded in agreement.

Tess's eyes widened and she crossed her arms over her chest and ran her fingers over the bandages. "You mean the cutting demons?" They each nodded slowly. "Why do they cut?" Tess asked.

"It is symbolic," Saul explained, "of the devil trying to clip your wings so you cannot fly."

"But you are destined to fly high," Maxwell grinned. "Now, do you remember what it was that caused you to doubt in the first place and brought on the demons that attacked you?"

Tess tried to think back. She remembered the feeling of panic, of being nauseated and dizzy, and she recalled hiding in the bathtub; but she couldn't remember what had happened to make her believe something was wrong. She shook her head. "I don't know," she said.

Maxwell studied her face, looking deeply into her eyes. "We know you shared your feelings of doubt with Ema Wright, but did you share them with anyone else?"

The mention of Ema's name brought back a memory and Tess sat up straighter. "It was Ema who came to me with information..." her voice faded.

"Information about what?" Saul asked.

Tess stared at the comforter on the bed, trying to remember. She had lost a lot of blood and still felt lightheaded and weak. "I can't remember," she uttered.

"Did you contact anyone else?" Maxwell asked and Tess shrugged.

"I don't think so," she said softly.

Maxwell rose from her bed. "The Lord has told us that you are to fast and pray for twenty-one days, without ceasing. Perhaps then your memory will be restored. It is crucial we know who has been negatively affected by Ema Wright's deceitfulness, so that we may intervene on their behalf before demons run rampant spreading seeds of doubt."

"I understand," Tess said.

"We have assigned helpers to encourage and strengthen you over the next few weeks," Maxwell said.

Tess didn't speak, but gave a slight nod of her head. She felt so weak she couldn't imagine fasting and praying for twenty-one days.

"The Lord will give you strength," Saul said, as if he knew her thoughts. Then they left, locking the door from the outside.

Tess lay back down and stared up at the ceiling. She tried to remember something about the attack, but her mind was completely blank. A gentle tapping on her door brought an abrupt end to her thoughts. "Come in," Tess murmured and two young women entered. They were intern leaders who had now been reassigned to watch over Tess.

The blonde was named Caroline and the red-head with the bright green eyes was named Hannah. "Can we get you anything?" Hannah asked.

"Yes, we're here to support and encourage you," Caroline spoke with a southern drawl. "So you just let us know what we can do to make you comfortable."

"I don't remember what happened," Tess stated groggily. "They said it was the cutting demons." Tess shook her head. "Can you get Ema Wright for me? I need to speak with her."

Caroline and Hannah shot each other a fearful glance. "I think she's gone," Hannah said in a half-whisper.

"Yeah," Caroline agreed. "No one has seen her since yesterday."

"She didn't show up at her group meeting last night and her roommate said she never came back from her shift at the bookstore," Hannah added.

"What do you mean gone?" Tess asked. "Like she sneaked off campus?"

Caroline and Hannah shrugged.

CHAPTER 9

The next morning Skylar got out of bed, packed up her camera with the mega zoom lens and headed to P3. Her plan was to walk the entire compound and ask everyone she passed if they had seen Tess. She pulled her hair back into a low pony tail, put on some lipstick, blush and eyeliner; threw on a pair of blue jeans, black boots and black cashmere, button-up sweater and was out the door.

When she arrived at P3 she saw two police cars angled in front of the building and a crowd gathered around the main entrance. Skylar parked, hurriedly jumped out of her car and headed toward the commotion. Both fear and the hope that Tess might somehow be involved leapt within her. After all, if Tess was involved at least Skylar would get to see her and see that she was okay. Working her way through the crowd, Skylar saw that two police officers were trying to subdue a woman who was screaming obscenities and thrashing her arms and legs.

"What's going on?" Skylar asked a young man in the crowd.

"Dunno," he shrugged. "Rumor has it she's possessed."

Skylar inched her way closer and saw that one of the officers was Officer Burnes, the man she had spoken with at the police station. He was no match for this woman, even though she was half his size. She kicked him and spit on him while he and his partner struggled to subdue her. Creeping within earshot, Skylar snapped several pictures with her camera.

"Don't make me Taser you ma'am," Officer Burnes warned. "Let's leave quietly and peacefully and there won't be any problems."

"He killed my baby!" She wailed with a tone of agony and rage only a mother could understand. "He killed my Ema!"

A lump formed in Skylar's throat. This was Ema's mother. Braznovich must have found her and told her what had happened. Skylar felt a rush of guilt and a deep ache of compassion.

"He'll kill you too," she screamed at the crowd of young people gathered around. "He'll kill all of you!" She pointed her fingers at particular individuals in the crowd. "He'll kill you and you and you and you and your mother's will wail in the street just like me!" She pounded her fists against her own chest. "Just like me," she cried out, swinging her fist around and punching Officer Burnes in the jaw. "Murderer!" She pointed to the building and screamed in a voice that was so loud it was raspy with pain. "I'll kill you, Maxwell Sagan!" She screamed. "I swear I will kill you!" She dropped to her knees bellowing out the deep, agonizing moans of a grieving mother.

"Grab her now!" Officer Burnes hollered and both cops lunged forward to lift Ema's mother off of the ground. She no longer fought, but hung limp in their arms, sobbing as they carried her through the crowd and placed her in the back of one of the police cars.

Skylar stood speechless amongst the crowd. Her heart ached so deeply for Ema's mom that for a moment she thought she couldn't breathe. She wanted to get back into her car and drive to the station to talk with Ema's mother; but she knew there were no words to comfort her. Nothing Skylar or anyone else could say would heal her broken heart. Skylar fought back emotion and reminded herself that she needed to stay focused on finding Tess. *Besides,* she told herself, *Ema's mom will probably be at the station for a while, being that she punched a cop and threatened to kill Maxwell.* She made a mental plan to drive by the station on her way home.

"Maxwell would like everyone to gather in the Prayer Room immediately for a meeting," sounded a young man's voice over the outside intercom system. "This meeting is mandatory for all interns, students, volunteers and employees." The crowd immediately made a beeline for the Prayer Room, and Skylar followed along, hoping she would find Tess inside and curious to see how Maxwell would explain away the outburst from Ema Wright's mother.

The Prayer Room was packed and Skylar slipped behind a group of interns standing near the back, hoping to remain unseen by Maxwell. She adjusted the strap on her camera and hung it around her neck so that it dangled down by her stomach. Making sure the flash was turned off; she casually aimed upward and snapped pictures, hoping to capture the member's faces. Her hope was that Braznovich would recognize Jonathan in one of the photos. As everyone waited for Maxwell to make his grand appearance, Skylar eavesdropped on conversations around her; finding herself amazed by how few were actually discussing Ema or her mother. It was almost as if, for some, what happened outside wasn't out of the ordinary.

Knowing this was a rare opportunity to blend with the culture and find out anything she could about Tess, Skylar meandered through the crowd, carefully staying near the back of the room, where she would be blocked by others who were standing. Every now and then, she nonchalantly asked someone, "I haven't seen Tess Wilson in a while. Have you?"

The first young man she addressed shrugged and turned his back to her. The second and third answered with a curt "no." But the fourth person, a young woman, paused before answering. Skylar sensed her uneasiness, and thought she was stalling and trying to think of what to say.

"I haven't seen her," she uttered, shifting her weight from her right foot to her left foot and back to her right again. "Not for a few days anyway," her voice trembled as she spoke and Skylar noted she was a bundle of nerves.

"Are you an intern here?" Skylar asked, watching as the young woman grew even more visibly uncomfortable.

"Yes," she answered quickly, "but I'm only in my first year, so I don't really know much about the place."

"Did you know Ema Wright?" Skylar asked, and the young woman instantly lowered her eyes to the floor.

"Yes. I mean, I knew her pretty well." Skylar thought she detected genuine sadness in her face as the woman said, "I'm guessing that was her mother outside. I can't believe she's dead."

"Me either," Skylar sighed. "You don't by chance know an intern named Jonathan, do you?"

"You mean Jonathan James, one of the intern leaders? We call him J.J. He's right over there," she pointed to the front of the room. "He's in the red shirt."

"Thanks." Skylar started to walk away, but turned back quickly. "I'm sorry, I forgot your name."

"Lexi," she answered with a forced grin.

"That's a pretty name," Skylar smiled and then slowly meandered far enough away that she could casually turn and snap a picture of Lexi. Making her way toward the front of room, Skylar noticed there were three men wearing red shirts, all standing in the same vicinity. She wasn't sure which one was Jonathan, so she held the camera in front of her chest, as if she were merely carrying it, aimed it slightly upward and snapped several pictures in their general direction. Since she couldn't see what she was shooting, she snapped extra shots; hoping to have at least one clear shot of all three men to show Braznovich. Skylar continued scanning the room, eager to catch a glimpse of Tess, but she was nowhere to be seen. In fact she was so preoccupied with the search for her sister that she didn't even see Maxwell enter and take the stage.

"My beloved," Maxwell began, "we have been informed that one of our very own has passed and it is indeed a misfortune and a tragedy." He removed a microphone from its stand and paced back and forth on the stage as he spoke. "We were aware that one of our students was enduring hardship and assigned fellow classmates to help support and encourage her; but it wasn't enough. Ema Wright took her own life late last night."

What! Skylar almost couldn't believe what Maxwell was doing, and yet there was nothing she would put passed him. Anger boiled inside her and she fought the urge to scream "Liar!" at the top of her lungs. She couldn't believe he was painting Ema's death as a suicide. *What a snake! What an asshole!* Skylar silently seethed.

"We will dedicate thirty minutes of Prayer Room time this evening for those of you who knew Ema and would like to gather together and remember her."

Wow, a whole thirty minutes! Skylar's subconscious sarcastically spewed. *You son of a bitch!*

Once Maxwell left the stage the crowd began to exit the room in the same clumps and groups in which they had entered. Skylar milled around in the back, nonchalantly snapping pictures as people walked by. She wasn't sure why, but she felt driven to capture as many faces on film as she could.

When the last group filed out and there was no sign of Tess, Skylar sauntered back to her car, feeling dumbfounded by the injustice of what had happened to Ema and frustrated by having gained no information about Tess. Skylar opened the driver's door, scooted into the seat and gripped the steering wheel. Her hands trembled from the rage boiling within. She wanted to kill Maxwell the way he had killed Ema. "Someday you'll get yours," she mumbled aloud, as if she were speaking to Maxwell. "And I'll be there to watch you go down and remind you that paybacks are a bitch." Her teeth clenched and her jaw tightened as Skylar tried to control the overwhelming anger she felt. With tears pricking her eyes, she leaned her forehead against the steering wheel, exhaled and let the emotion escape her in quiet sobs. When the emotion subsided, she pulled her camera from where it hung around her neck and leaned over to place it on the passenger seat. With the camera still tightly in her grip, Skylar's heart suddenly stopped. A piece of white paper was stuck to the outside of the passenger window. She blinked slowly focusing on the words that were written on the page; words that sent her world into slow motion. The message was written in big bold letters: BOMB! RUN! With her heart leaping into her throat, Skylar yanked on the door handle and kicked the driver's door fully open, jumping away from her car. The sound of the explosion overtook her senses while the force of the blast propelled her forward onto the pavement, her knees and hands taking the brunt of the fall. She felt the intense heat on her back, a piercing ringing in her ears, and a pain that made her head feel like it was splitting wide open. For a moment Skylar lay face down on the ground, trying to process what had happened. She rolled over just enough to see what little was left of her Nissan Altima.

A crowd gathered quickly and Skylar could hear sirens off in the distance. Someone must have called for an ambulance. She tried to lift herself from the ground, but her head felt like it weighed a ton and her vision was blurred. Lying on her back, looking at all the faces gathering closer, she tried to focus her eyes. "Tess?" She called out. "Get Tess Wilson," she hollered, and swallowed hard as a wave of nausea overwhelmed her. She could see people talking but she couldn't hear what they were saying. Suddenly, Lexi's face came into view as she leaned down over Skylar. "Lexi?" Skylar fought to stay conscious and focus.

"Don't speak," Lexi said, bending down and gently lifting Skylar by the shoulders into a sitting position.

"I can't hear you," Skylar spoke loudly, like Mrs. Neiler when her hearing aid was turned down too low. Lexi nodded, picked up Skylar's camera and placed it in her hands, wrapping Skylar's fingers tightly around it and aiming it at the car.

"Take pictures," Lexi said, over-enunciating the words so Skylar could read her lips.

Skylar didn't have the strength to lift the camera, but she angled it on her lap and snapped several photos, unsure if she was getting anything other than pavement. A barrage of sirens filled the parking lot and Skylar flopped backwards, fighting her brain's beckoning to lose consciousness. While the fire department extinguished the flames consuming her car, the police dispersed the crowd so that the paramedics could work on Skylar. She was placed in a neck brace, moved onto a gurney and lifted into the ambulance. As they placed an oxygen mask on her face, and checked her vitals, Skylar kept her eyes locked on Lexi and the man in the red shirt that took Lexi by the arm and pulled her from the crowd.

CHAPTER 10

"Don't tell me to calm down," Skylar barked at Braznovich. "Someone just tried to blow me up!" She swung her legs over the side of the examination table and tried to lower herself into a standing position, but the dizziness forced her to sit.

"You have a concussion," Braznovich explained.

"Ya think!" Skylar sarcastically blurted.

Braznovich took her hand and gave it a squeeze. "Ms. Wilson, the best thing you can do right now is calm down so your body can rest and heal."

Skylar rolled her eyes. Asking her to be calm now was like asking the Pope to renounce Catholicism. It just wasn't going to happen.

"Here's what we're going to do," Braznovich explained. "Ernie is already looking into finding out who placed the bomb in your car. When you're released I'll drive you back to your apartment and help you pack."

"Pack for what?"

"It's not safe for you to stay there. Obviously someone knows where you live and what car you drive..."

"...drove," Skylar interrupted.

Braznovich sighed. "The point is you need to go stay with family for a while." Skylar hung her head and stared at the floor. "You do have family around don't you?"

"Tess is my only family," she said softly, pressing her lips together and trying to hide the wave of emotion that wanted to sweep her away. "Our parents have passed and Tess is all I have left."

74

The doctor entered the room and explained that Skylar could either be admitted for a night or she could be released if she had someone to watch her closely for the next twenty-four hours. The last place in the world she wanted to be was in a hospital, but she didn't have a choice. "I guess I'll have to stay," Skylar sighed.

"Good," the doctor noted. "I'll arrange to have you moved upstairs."

"No, that won't be necessary. I'll babysit her," Braznovich said and Skylar looked at him with wide-eyed surprise. *What?!* "I have a spare room," he uttered poignantly. "You'll stay with me until everything is back to normal."

She was speechless. First, he didn't ask her to stay, he told her she was staying and she wasn't sure how to respond to his authoritative tone. She could tell he was used to being in control and now he was exercising that control over her. A part of her wanted to refuse, only to prove that he didn't have the power to tell her what to do; the other part of her wanted to stay with him, to have him all to herself, to spend time alone with him, to bask in that musky aftershave scent and gaze into those sparkly, brown eyes.

"Okay. The nurse will be in with the release forms. Once those are complete, you're free to go," the doctor gave a nod and left.

"You don't have to do this," Skylar said.

"Now, Ms. Wilson, what kind of a gentleman would I be if I didn't rescue a damsel in distress?" He teased. "But don't expect much from my apartment. I'm a die-hard bachelor." He gave a wink and that strange tingly sensation warmed her again.

Skylar didn't pack much; a couple of changes of clothes, toothbrush, basic toiletries, her laptop, and P3 research notes. She grabbed her purse from the kitchen counter and was ready to go.

"Your purse wasn't in the car with you?" Braznovich asked.

"Nope," Skylar said, "and I'm thankful for that. Canceling all of my credit cards, getting a new debit card and checks would have been a nightmare. "Ugh," she grunted. "I don't even want to think about it."

"Do you always drive without your license?" Braznovich raised his eyebrows.

"No. I had my driver's license, debit card and cell phone in my pocket, in case I needed them. I don't like to leave my purse in the car, especially in that part of town," she explained. "I worry that someone will rob me blind."

"Good thinking, Ms. Wilson," Braznovich grinned and opened the apartment door.

As Skylar stepped into the hallway, Mrs. Neiler thrust open her door and hollered, "I told you to keep the noise down."

Both Skylar and Braznovich jumped. "Mrs. Neiler," Skylar shouted. She could tell by the volume of Mrs. Neiler's voice that her hearing aid was turned way down. "You need to adjust your hearing aid."

Mrs. Neiler reached up and turned the dial. "I adjusted it down because you were so loud earlier," she said in normal voice.

"I wasn't home earlier," Skylar rebutted. "You must have heard noise from someone else's apartment."

"No, it was from your apartment and I banged on the door and told you to keep it down." Mrs. Neiler was emphatic about what had happened and Skylar threw Braznovich a worried glance.

"About what time was that?" Braznovich asked her.

"It was 11:45 exactly." Mrs. Neiler pointed her finger into the air as she spoke. "I remember because I was hurrying to make my lunch and tea before my show came on at noon. I like to sit and eat my lunch on a TV tray while I watch my show," she explained.

"What kind of noise did you hear?" Skylar questioned.

"I heard a man's voice and a woman. They were talking really loud. I thought it was you."

"Do you remember anything they said?" Braznovich asked.

Mrs. Neiler scrunched up her face. "Not word for word. They said something about hurrying back for a meeting, and after I banged on the door and told them to keep it down, they said 'sorry.'"

Skylar and Braznovich thanked Mrs. Neiler and went back into Skylar's apartment. Braznovich put his finger to his lips to indicate Skylar shouldn't speak. He then pulled her close, placed his mouth right next to her ear and whispered, "My guess is that whoever was here, planted bugs."

Skylar felt a warm tingly rush of attraction when he pulled her close. She breathed in his musky scent and felt her stomach twist into jittery knots. She thought about turning her head slightly and letting her lips accidentally brush against his, but no sooner had the fantasy begun to play in her mind, when it came to a screeching halt. He released her and began searching the apartment.

They found four recording devices. One in the bedroom phone, one in the kitchen phone, one located beneath her bookshelf and one attached to the top of a lamp shade. Skylar watched Braznovich disconnect the devices and place them in a sandwich bag which he retrieved from the drawer to the left of the sink. Skylar felt suddenly violated. How long had someone been listening to her and watching her?

"Can I talk now?" She whispered.

"Yes, I've dismantled the devices. No one can hear you now."

"Unless we've missed some bugs?" Skylar's voice rose slightly as fear gripped her.

"Let's talk outside," Braznovich nodded and motioned her toward the door. Once in the hall, Braznovich continued. "I'll have Ernie bring a team in to dust your apartment for prints. Maybe we'll get lucky and they were stupid enough not to wear gloves."

"How long do you think they were spying on me?"

Braznovich shook his head and concern lit his eyes. "There's no way to know, but we have to assume at least the last several days. Probably the bugs were planted after Tess sent you the text."

Skylar took a deep breath and exhaled slowly. *Tess. What kind of trouble is she in? God, please let her be okay. Please let her be okay.*

"Do you have a key to lock up, or were they incinerated with your car?"

"I have a spare," Skylar grimaced and pulled her spare key from her purse. Turning to face the door, she tried to place the key in the lock, but her hands shook and it took several attempts. Braznovich must have noticed her trembling because he placed one hand on the door and leaned in closely from behind. She could feel his breath against her neck as he spoke softly. "Take a deep breath, Ms. Wilson, and try to relax. We'll get to the bottom of this."

Skylar nodded. The proximity of his lips to her neck was certainly distracting.

"I don't want you to return to your apartment for any reason," he spoke sternly. "Do you understand?"

Her muscles clenched and a warm sensation of sensual longing ran from her neck all the way down. She didn't know why, but this man had the power to unravel her without even touching her. Just the scent of him and the feel of his breath on her neck as he spoke, rendered her defenseless. Skylar cleared her throat and fought to maintain her composure.

"Yes, I understand," she answered quietly, still facing the door.

"They'll know we've disconnected the bugs," he explained, his mouth a mere inches from her ear. "And they might come back. I'll have Ernie schedule surveillance on your apartment."

Skylar drew in a shaky breath, turned the key and the dead bolt clicked. *Finally.* Now that the door was locked there was no more reason to stand facing it. She needed to turn around. She held her breath as she slowly turned to face him. This was a mistake. She never should have made eye contact. His deep brown eyes were hypnotizing and she was consumed with a longing to feel his lips on hers. Fearing that her wanting was written all over her face, she searched his eyes for any reciprocation of desire.

"We don't want anything to happen to you, Ms. Wilson," he said softly, almost tenderly. *Kiss me!* Her subconscious begged, but Skylar nervously lowered her eyes. "We should go," he said, abruptly dropping his arm from the door and turning toward the steps. Disappointment washed over her. She wanted him to kiss her, but scolded herself for the desire. After all, they'd just met and she knew nothing about him, other than the fact that he had the uncanny ability to make her hormones rage.

Braznovich lived on the Kansas side, in a three bedroom, split-level condominium; though one bedroom had been made into an office. For a bachelor, the place was immaculate, which he attributed to his cleaning service that came in every Wednesday. Stepping inside the front door, Skylar was taken aback by the size and warmth of the condo. The kitchen jetted off to the immediate left, with a long marble counter that divided it from the large family room. The family room had a beautiful stone fireplace with built in book shelves on either side that took up the entire wall to the left. Straight ahead were two sliding doors that opened onto a large covered deck, extending the full length of the condo. The doors were divided by a four foot long wall that held a built in television, DVD player and Xbox gaming system. To the right of the front door were French doors that opened into his office and just passed it, a hallway that led to two bedrooms, each with their own bathroom. All at once Skylar was impressed by his place and embarrassed by hers. He obviously made a lot more money than she did.

Settling into the guest room, Skylar booted up her laptop and pulled out her camera, hoping it had survived the dive onto the pavement and the explosion. She wanted to download the pictures from that morning to see if anything had turned out. The download was taking unusually long and Skylar feared that her camera had suffered irrefutable damage. But, thankfully, after several minutes, pictures began to appear on the screen and Skylar was pleased with what she saw. The photos were at odd angles but they were clear and faces could be recognized. She cropped faces and edited photos until the screen resembled a yearbook page. Beneath Lexi's picture she typed her name and beneath the three men in red, she typed Jonathan or J.J. and a question mark. She would show them to Braznovich later and see if one of these men were his nephew.

Skylar paused at the picture of Ema's mother, and stared at the screen, feeling a twinge of heartache. Tomorrow, when her head was less foggy, and her body less achy, she would take the notes from Ema's last conversation and talk to Ema's mother. Maybe Mrs. Wright knew something that would help them; something that would prevent this from happening to anyone else.

When she had finished looking at all of the photographs, Skylar pushed her laptop to the side of the bed and drifted off to sleep.

By the time Braznovich came into the kitchen, Skylar had made coffee and was scrambling eggs on the stove. "Good morning, Ms. Wilson," he said, with a tone of pleasant surprise. "You slept well last night.

I checked on you several times and you were sound asleep."

Skylar blushed. *I hope I wasn't snoring or drooling.*

"I remembered you liked eggs," Skylar said, quickly changing the subject. She dished them onto a plate and set it down on the table next to the Tabasco sauce. She then poured him a cup of coffee.

"You're not the hired help. You don't have to wait on me," he said, dousing his eggs with tabasco.

"I'm just earning my keep, Mr. Braznovich," she grinned.

He shoveled in a fork full of eggs and washed it down with a gulp of coffee. "On second thought, Ms. Wilson, you should keep earning your keep. I didn't realize you were a chef." He gave her a wink and lifted another fork full to his mouth.

"I'm glad you like it." She smiled and felt a flush of warmth fill her cheeks.

"Ernie text me and he's on his way over," Braznovich announced.

"Uh-oh, we better open the windows and start airing out the place now," Skylar quipped and Braznovich laughed out loud.

With a second pot of coffee brewing, Ernie, Skylar and Braznovich gathered around the large coffee table in the family room and discussed what had happened. Ernie took the over-sized arm chair by the fireplace and Skylar and Braznovich each took one side of the couch. Lighting up a cigarette, Ernie started the conversation. "I tried to get information on the explosion, but the officer handling the case is tight-lipped and downright uncooperative."

"How so?" Braznovich asked, getting up and opening both sliding glass doors a little farther.

"He wouldn't let me snoop around, for one." Ernie inhaled his cigarette and held it in his lungs, then exhaled as he spoke. "He pulled the jurisdiction card."

"What's the jurisdiction card?" Skylar asked.

"Some cops can be territorial," Braznovich explained.

"Why?" Skylar asked. "You'd think they would want all the help they could get to solve a case."

"Some do," Ernie said. "But others have ego issues. They'd rather solve it alone and get all the glory. The FBI is particularly fussy about it." He shook his head. "Anyway, I wasn't able to get a look at the car, but I did happen to overhear two officers talking and they said it was a standard tilt fuse model bomb. Nothing fancy."

"So anybody could have made it," Braznovich sighed. "That's what I was afraid of." Braznovich retrieved the coffee pot from the kitchen and filled everyone's cups. "What about prints?"

Ernie shrugged. "The way the fire department flooded the car, I doubt there are any prints left to find."

"What about the note?" Skylar asked. "The one that said 'BOMB! RUN!'"

Ernie raised his hands and dropped them back down. "No mention of it. It probably burned."

"Well, we know Maxwell is behind the bomb," Skylar quipped. "Can't you arrest him on suspicion of something or even attempted murder?"

Ernie chuckled and Braznovich tried to hide his smirk. Skylar felt a flush of humiliation. *Why was that such a stupid question?* "Listen," Braznovich said, reaching over and squeezing her shoulder. "I know you hate Maxwell and I know this is personal, but we have to go about it the right way or we don't stand a chance."

"We might not stand a chance anyway," Ernie muttered.

Skylar gritted her teeth. "We HAVE to stop Maxwell. There HAS to be a way. We just need to find it." She felt such a deep burning anger toward

Maxwell that she knew she'd never feel relief until he was brought to justice.

"Why do I get the feeling your motive here is deeper than just saving your sister?" Braznovich raised an eyebrow and glared at Skylar, causing her to squirm uncomfortably beneath his gaze.

"Is there something you need to tell us?" Ernie added.

"Something you'd like to share with the class?" Braznovich raised both brows.

Skylar shrugged. "No, not really. My motive is saving my sister. It's just, well..." she stopped talking and took a deep breath. It was a long story and Skylar didn't feel like going into all the gory details. She stared down at her fingers, knotting them together. "Maxwell came into our lives, my family's lives, a long time ago. I knew him before P3 ever existed."

Ernie blew a smoke ring above his head. "The plot thickens," he said.

Skylar fought hard to hold at bay the tears pricking at the back of her eyes. "Maxwell seduced Tess way back then, and left my family broken." Both men sat quietly listening, their eyes locked on Skylar. "We never had demon encounters in our home until he came into our lives. Things were normal and we were happy until he came around." A single tear escaped and ran down her cheek and she quickly brushed it away with the back of her hand. "He manipulated my sister and even my parents for a while, though they finally saw through him. After he entered the scene, my family fell apart and my parents were under constant demonic attack, we had terrible nightmares, heard strange voices..." her voice trailed off again. "It got so bad my mom called in a Catholic Priest to bless our house with Holy Water." Skylar wiped another tear. "I know it sounds unbelievable, and you can think I'm crazy if you want; but I know what he did to us and what he's still doing to Tess and I won't sit back and allow him to get away with it any longer." Her jaw tensed and anger rose in her voice. "He's worse than a demon and I will find a way to exercise him from my sister's life."

Ernie rose from his chair, walked toward the sliding door and flicked his cigarette butt outside. Then he pulled out a pack of Marlboro Reds and lit up another. "Personal vendettas are a dangerous game," he muttered. "Like playing chicken with an eighteen wheeler."

"What does that mean?" Skylar asked.

"It means Maxwell is a helluva lot more powerful and resourceful than we are," Braznovich answered, while running his hand quickly through his hair. "If we take him head on, we're likely to wind up road kill."

Skylar pursed her lips together and rolled her eyes. "So, what? We just give up? You want to quit just like you did last time?" She glared at Braznovich and saw his jaw tightened and a spark of anger flash in his eyes.

"Ms. Wilson," Braznovich said through clenched teeth, "everything you just told us is what we call speculation, meaning there's no proof. We have no evidence to support the notion that Maxwell Sagan consorts with demons and no evidence to support that he had anything to do with your car exploding."

Skylar narrowed her eyes. "We may not have evidence, Mr. Braznovich, but I know he did it. I KNOW it!" She glared at him, indignation rising from her gut. "Who else would benefit from getting me out of the way?"

Braznovich shook his head slowly from side to side. "This is all speculation and it gets us nowhere. Besides, why would Maxwell detonate a bomb in his own parking lot? He's smart enough to know it would bring the police and the kind of media attention he doesn't want."

"That brings up a good point," Ernie interjected. "We don't know if the bomb was supposed to detonate when it did, or if it was set on a timer that malfunctioned..."

"That is a good point," Braznovich stated.

"Another thing," Ernie said, slumping back into the arm chair and letting a cigarette hang from the corner of his mouth, "maybe Maxwell has the local police and even local media in his back pocket, which means he can put whatever spin he wants on a bomb going off at P3."

"Another good point," Braznovich said. "For all we know, it may give him exactly the attention he wants."

"Play himself up as the victim," Ernie added.

Skylar deflated. Someone tried to blow her up and it seemed there was nothing they could do about it. What if they tried again? Someone obviously wanted her out of the way, but who? And Why?

"Well, the good news is whoever set the bomb knows you survived it, so if they really want you dead they'll try again," Ernie rasped.

"That's what you call GOOD news?" Skylar gawked at him, her mouth falling wide open. This made Ernie laugh out loud.

"It's good news because we'll hopefully catch them this time," Braznovich explained.

"Hopefully?" Skylar blurted. "The word hopefully doesn't offer much security."

"Don't worry," Ernie chuckled. "There's a chance they were just trying to scare you away, and there won't be another attempt."

Skylar exhaled, slumping forward and using both hands to massage her neck and shoulders. She wasn't sure whether her aches were from the explosion or from fear-driven tension. "Allow me," Braznovich said as he scooted closer, moved her hands out of the way and began to massage her shoulders. "Why, Ms. Wilson, you're a knotted mess." His strong fingers dug into her muscles and Skylar winced beneath his touch. He worked his way up her neck, rubbing and pinching and kneading her muscles, and then back down over each shoulder until she finally started to relax. Actually, she did more than just relax; she melted into a soupy pool of desire.

"Can you send in a team this afternoon to get prints from Skylar's apartment?" Braznovich asked Ernie, as he continued stroking Skylar's back.

"Yep," Ernie grunted. "But I gotta tell you, I'm not real hopeful we're gonna find anything."

"I know," Braznovich sighed. "Whoever planted the bugs probably wore gloves."

Skylar pulled up the pictures that she had taken at P3 and showed the three men in red shirts to Braznovich. He immediately identified Jonathan, and Skylar saw a gleam of affection in his eye. He was obviously relieved to see that Jonathan was alive and well. "Is his last name James?" Skylar asked and Braznovich confirmed that it was. "He's an intern leader now. They call him J.J. for short."

"Great," Braznovich sarcastically spewed. "He's a leader. He's as good as gone forever now."

"Don't say that," Skylar moaned. He had obviously forgotten that Tess was a leader in the movement as well.

"I'm sorry," he stammered quickly. "I didn't mean that."

"I know." She gave an empathetic smile. She was struggling with the same feeling about Tess, wondering if a leader could be rescued. Or were the leaders so deeply indoctrinated that there was no hope? Skylar had to believe there was something in Tess that wanted out. Why else would she have sent a text for help? *IF the text really came from Tess,* her subconscious reminded.

Skylar showed Ernie and Braznovich the picture of Lexi and told them about their conversation in the Prayer Room and how Lexi was the only one who spoke to her after the explosion. All of a sudden

the memory of Lexi handing her the camera and
telling her to take pictures came rushing back to her.
"Oh my gosh!" Skylar gasped and began clicking
through the file of uploaded photos.

"What?" Ernie and Braznovich said in
unison.

As she searched the photos, she explained
how Lexi had retrieved her camera from the
pavement, had placed it in her lap, and pointed it at
the burning car, telling her to take pictures.

"Did you?" Ernie asked excitedly; smoke
pouring out of his nose.

"I think I did. I mean, I tried to." Skylar
pushed her arrow down key until she got to the very
bottom. "Here," she blurted. "Here it is!"

Ernie jumped up, circled behind the couch
and leaned over Skylar and Braznovich's shoulders to
see the screen. "Can you make it bigger?" He asked.

Skylar pulled the picture into her editing
software and cropped the edges, making the driver's
door section appear larger. "Well, lookey here," he
rasped, clenching his cigarette between his lips.
"There's your explosive device, right down there." He
pointed to a small silver square just beneath the
driver's door. "I'm going to need you to email me this
picture," he said to Skylar.

"I would like a printed copy as well,"
Braznovich added.

As soon as she finished emailing the picture
to both Ernie and Braznovich, she continued with the
story. "While I was in the ambulance I saw a man in
a red shirt, not Jonathan, escort Lexi away," Skylar
told them. "It was this man." She pointed to one of
the pictures. "I'm worried Lexi might be in trouble,
like Ema was, just for talking to me."

"Did people see her talking to you?"
Braznovich asked.

"There was a whole crowd gathered around,
so they must have. Besides, they have surveillance
cameras everywhere."

All of a sudden Ernie, who had returned to the comfort of the arm chair, leapt to his feet, clapped his hands together and blurted, "Hot diggity damn," with his cigarette hanging half out of his mouth. "That's it!" He said excitedly.

"What's it?" Skylar asked, as Ernie pulled the cigarette from his lips and kissed her on top the head. "Surveillance."

An a-ha expression came over Braznovich's face. "We'll subpoena their surveillance videos and be able to see exactly who planted the bomb in your car."

Skylar bit her lip. Something was nagging at her. "That won't work," she exhaled, and they both stared at her. "First of all, who issues a subpoena? And how do we know we can trust that person?" She looked from Braznovich to Ernie and back to Braznovich again. "Think about it, there are thousands of people in this city who are members of P3. Earlier you suggested that it's possible that Maxwell even has the police in his back pocket. If anyone tips them off, they'll destroy the video and we'll get nothing."

"You have a better idea?" Ernie sat back down and blew a smoke ring over his head.

Skylar shrugged. "What if we could tap into their surveillance system remotely without anyone knowing?"

"You mean hack in?" Braznovich asked and Skylar nodded.

"We could download whatever data we wanted without them being any the wiser." Silence filled the room as they all mulled over the idea.

"It's illegal," Braznovich said. "Anything we found would be inadmissible as evidence."

"It's only illegal if we get caught," Ernie scoffed. "And we wouldn't use it in court. We'd use it to blackmail people into giving us evidence that we could use in court."

"You're a scary man," Braznovich grimaced.

Ernie winked and grinned. "That's why you like me."

"I'm glad you're on my side, if that's what you mean," Braznovich mumbled.

Braznovich ran his fingers through his hair. "I know some computer geeks, but I don't think any of them are talented enough to pull this off. P3 probably has safeguards set up at every turn."

Ernie blew smoke out his nose. "Don't look at me. I'm technologically imbalanced."

"You mean technologically challenged," Braznovich corrected.

"That too," Ernie huffed. "I can Google something and check my email and that's it."

Skylar bit her lip. "I know someone, but I don't know if he'll do it. His name is Greg and he used to be married to Tess."

"You trust him?" Ernie asked. "I mean, you trust that he's not one of them?"

"He hates P3 even more than I do," Skylar nodded. "It destroyed his marriage. Trust me; he's not one of them."

While Ernie called Menorah Medical Center to see if Ema Wright's autopsy results were in, and Braznovich contacted Ema Wright's mother to schedule a time for all of them to meet, Skylar stepped into the spare bedroom and dialed Greg. She wasn't sure if he would take her call much less be willing to help. The last time they had spoken, he told her that he hated her family and wanted nothing to do with them. She couldn't blame him. He was speaking out of the brokenness Tess had caused when she left him, claiming he wasn't spiritual enough and was hindering her walk with God. That was just one tiny example of the elitist attitude P3 created in its members.

Skylar was surprised when he answered after the second ring. "Skylar Wilson, to what do I owe the pleasure?" Greg said with a hint of sarcasm.

"Thank you for taking my call," she said and took a deep breath. "I need help and you're the only person I know that might be capable of helping." She hadn't planned on blurting it out so bluntly, but she was glad that she had because it seemed to peak his interest long enough for her to fill him in on all that had transpired. When she finished explaining, Greg was quiet, so quiet that Skylar groaned, "Are you still there?"

"I'm here," he said, sounding shocked and not shocked at the same time. "I was afraid one day something like this would happen." Skylar heard Greg take a deep breath and exhale. "Honestly Skylar, when I saw your number on caller ID, I thought you were calling to tell me Tess drank the Kool-Aid and I had a funeral to attend."

"That's not funny."

"I know it's not. Believe me, every time I turn on the damn news I half-way expect to see another Jonestown incident with a news anchor that says international prayer house movement goes deadly, story at eleven."

"So, will you help me?" Skylar asked.

"Let me think about it. I'll call you back in a couple of hours."

Skylar hung up feeling hopeful. Greg could have ignored her call, but he didn't and he could have said no right away, but he didn't. He was thinking about it and right now, thinking was a good sign.

If they could prove Maxwell was behind the car bombing and prove he was connected to Ema Wright's death, maybe, just maybe, Tess's eyes would be opened and she, and thousands of others, would be freed. *Please help us find a way,* she silently prayed.

CHAPTER 11

Her apartment rendered no suspicious prints and neither did the bugging equipment. There was one positive thing though; Braznovich thought they could use the serial number on the bugging equipment to track where it had been ordered and to whom it had been shipped. "It's not like a person can walk into Wal-Mart and walk out with a bugging system," he explained. "This equipment was most likely ordered from a security company and if that's the case, we'll be able to find out who ordered it."

They all piled into Ernie's truck and headed to Ema Wright's mother's house, located on the Missouri side, about fifteen minutes from the P3 campus. Ernie drove, Skylar sat in the middle and Braznovich in the passenger seat. Each time her knee brushed against Braznovich's leg, she felt butterflies flutter in her stomach; so she tried to tense her knees together to keep from bumping him. He must have noticed her tension, because he reached over, pulled her right knee toward his, until it was touching and said, "Relax." *Easy for him to say.*

Ema's mother lived in an older neighborhood, where all of the homes were ranch style and made of brick, with big shutters and screened storm doors. The houses were separated further than typical suburban neighborhoods, giving the area a rural feel. What Skylar loved most about older neighborhoods were the big trees and this neighborhood had a lot of them. Ema's mother's house, and all of the homes on that side of the street, backed up to a wooded area. Skylar imagined Ema had probably played in the woods as a child, finding treasures and picking flowers, same as she did growing up; and a wave of sadness swept over her.

As soon as they pulled into the driveway Ema's mother appeared in the doorway, as if she were excitedly awaiting their arrival. "Come in, come in, come in," she said, holding the screen door open and motioning them in with her arm. Once they were all inside, she closed the door and locked it tight. "Come to the kitchen," she said and hurried passed them, down the hall to the back of the house. Skylar peaked around as they followed her passed a hallway on the right, and a living room on the left, which Skylar surmised connected to the dining area and kitchen.

The kitchen was small and painted white with blue flowered wallpaper and tan linoleum. The cabinets were light oak and matched the round kitchen table and chairs. A curtained window was above the sink, next to the backdoor and to the right was the dining room which, as Skylar predicted, connected to the living room through an arched walkway. Mrs. Wright pulled the curtains closed on the kitchen window and flipped on the overhead light. "Sit down," she said, motioning them toward the table, where she offered coffee and raspberry Danish. Braznovich and Skylar declined, but Ernie took both the coffee and the Danish and it appeared to make Mrs. Wright happy to feed him.

"I have something to show you," she said, letting her eyes dart around the table to make contact with each of them.

Mrs. Wright was thin and wiry. She had long dark hair with gray strands running through it, which she had pulled into a tight bun. She wasn't wearing any make-up or jewelry and her skin looked shiny and clean. She was dressed in brown loafers, tan pants and a floral-printed, pink blouse, covered with a white apron. Skylar guessed her to be in her mid-fifties. Pulling a pair of reading glasses from her apron pocket, Mrs. Wright grabbed a notebook from the long thin drawer located beneath the oven. She joined them at the table and took a deep breath, sliding the glasses onto her nose.

"I got this in the mail this morning," she told them, holding up the notebook and handing the envelope to Braznovich. The envelope was hand-written, in cursive and addressed to Carolyn Wright. "That's me," she said, tapping the name on the address line with her fingers. The return address was also Carolyn Wright's address.

"What is it?" Braznovich asked.

Skylar could see Mrs. Wright fight back emotion and it made her force back the urge to cry as well. "It's a journal," she said. "It's my Ema's journal." She clutched the notebook to her chest and hugged it.

"Do you know who sent it to you?" Braznovich asked.

"No," she shook her head. "There was no note inside."

"How do you know for certain its Ema's journal?" Ernie asked, shoveling in a bite of Danish.

"I know my Ema's handwriting," Mrs. Wright answered defensively. "And she wrote about stuff only she would know."

Skylar sat speechless. Just seeing Mrs. Wright's boney fingers clutch the notebook, knowing it was all that was left of her precious little girl, was almost more than Skylar could bear. Tears welled up in Mrs. Wright's eyes and Skylar's did the same.

"It tells the goings on at that place," Mrs. Wright gritted. "It tells what they did to my Ema," she said, her face a mixture of sadness and rage.

"May we read it?" Braznovich asked, and Mrs. Wright clutched the notebook tighter. "Mrs. Wright," Braznovich spoke softly, "there might be something inside Ema's journal that will help us save other people from suffering the same fate as your daughter."

Tears dripped from her eyes. "I want it back," she said. "You make copies and you bring it right back to me. You hear?"

Ernie was immediately up, out of his chair and out the door to make copies, while Braznovich and Skylar stayed behind to talk with Mrs. Wright. They talked about Ema's last conversation in the hospital and about Skylar's brief conversation with her in the P3 bookstore. "She missed you, and she wanted to come home," Skylar said. "She asked me to call you and I was dialing your number when those men showed up and took her away." Mrs. Wright broke into sobs and Skylar hugged her. "I'm so sorry," Skylar cried. "I'm so sorry."

Mrs. Wright regained her composure and stared down at the table, drawing on the edge of it with her finger. "My Ema's death won't be in vain. I promise you that." She nodded her head up and down. "I promise you that."

"That's why we're here," Braznovich interjected. "To make sure justice is served."

"Oh, there will be justice," Mrs. Wright said in a tone that told Skylar she just might hold true to her threat of killing Maxwell.

Braznovich reached over and tenderly placed his hand on top Mrs. Wright's fingers. "Mrs. Wright," he began in a soothing tone. "Maxwell Sagan is a powerful man..."

"He's the Anti-Christ," she interrupted him.

"He's powerful," Braznovich nodded. "The last thing we want to do is make him more powerful." He shifted in his chair, turning his whole body to face her. "We don't want there to be any reason for people to sympathize with him, or view him as someone being victimized. Do you understand?"

She nodded.

"We want to rid him of his power by dismantling his organization from the foundation up, so that people can see for themselves the lies he has spread." Skylar could see the compassion in

Braznovich's eyes as he studied Mrs. Wright's face. "Do you read the Bible, ma'am?" He asked and she nodded. "There's a verse my grandpa used to quote and it says, 'then you will know the truth and the truth will set you free.'" He paused and scrunched up his face like he was trying to think of something. "I think it's in John eight, verse thirty-two. Anyway, the point is that the only way we can free these young people from the manipulation of the P3 movement is to provide the truth and trust that the truth will indeed set them free."

Mrs. Wright nodded again, but Skylar could tell by her tightened jaw and pursed lips that her anger was more powerful than his words. "One way or another Maxwell will pay for what he's done. Everyone at P3 will pay." Anger flashed in her dark brown eyes and Braznovich and Skylar exchanged glances. Mrs. Wright shook her head. "You can't mock God and get away with it, you know," she reached across the table, retrieved a napkin and wiped the tears from her cheeks. Her lip quivered. "You can't twist God's Word and abuse folks with it and get away with it," she said, anger rising in her voice. "Folks around here aren't gonna tolerate it no more."

When Ernie returned, he gave the original notebook back to Mrs. Wright and then they said goodbye. Skylar promised to check in on Mrs. Wright in a couple of days; and Braznovich made her swear that she would refrain from any revengeful plans against Maxwell. "Give me time," he told her, "and I promise you I will shed light on the truth and avenge your daughter's death."

Mrs. Wright outwardly promised, but Skylar was certain by the gleam in her eye that she had her proverbial fingers crossed.

Climbing into Ernie's truck Braznovich mumbled, "We better solve this quick."

"Yeah, why?" Ernie asked.

"Because she's going to try to kill Maxwell," Skylar answered before Braznovich could.

"That frail little woman? What makes you think that?" Ernie snorted.

"Hell hath no fury as a woman scorn..." Braznovich said, his voice tapering off as he stared out the window.

CHAPTER 12

Arriving back at Braznovich's condo, they gathered around the coffee table while Ernie read from the Coroner's Report. It brought unexpected hope. A chemical substance called Rohypnol, known on the street as "roofies" and in the media as the "date rape" drug, was found in Ema Wright's body. In most people, the only negative effects from Rohypnol were black outs and memory loss; but in Ema Wright, the drug, coupled with her severe dehydration and previous blood loss, induced cardiac arrest. Ema's frail, starved body just gave out.

Skylar grimaced as Ernie read the report aloud.

"Was there any sign of sexual abuse?" Braznovich asked and Skylar instinctively put her hands over her mouth. The thought of Maxwell and sex in the same context was enough to make her nauseated.

"Nope," Ernie huffed. "Says here there was no sign of sexual abuse and no sign of alcohol in her system."

"I'm sure they aren't allowed to drink alcohol on the campus," Skylar remarked.

"If there was alcohol in her system then we'd have to look at the possibility that she sneaked off campus, met someone for drinks and that, that person slipped her a roofie," Ernie explained. "But with no alcohol, we can assume for now that the drug was given to her at P3."

"It's still speculation," Braznovich interjected, leaning back on the couch and staring up at the ceiling. "If there was no alcohol and no sexual abuse, what would be the purpose of administering Rohypnol?"

Ernie blew a smoke ring above his head. "Seems to me one advantage would be to create a blank slate in someone's mind; one you could fill in with any details you wanted."

"Like Men in Black," Skylar blurted.

"Men in Black?" Braznovich repeated. "The movie?"

Skylar nodded. "Uh-huh. Remember the little flashy thingy they would use to erase people's memory after an alien encounter?"

"And then they'd give them a new memory," Ernie added with an inflection of sudden awareness.

"Right," Skylar said. "Remember? Will Smith got irritated with Tommy Lee Jones for not giving people better memories."

"So you think Rohypnol is the P3's version of the flashy thingy," Braznovich smirked, as if the idea was ludicrous. *He's laughing at me again!* Skylar rolled her eyes.

"Depending on the person, Rohypnol can cause black outs lasting anywhere from 4 to 24 hours," Ernie interjected. "A lot can happen in that amount of time."

"What good is having someone passed out for 24 hours?" Skylar threw her hands in the air.

"I said black out, not passed out," Ernie emphasized. "Rohypnol causes memory loss, but conceivably a person can still walk, talk and function. They become uninhibited and they won't remember anything."

"So, they administer this drug and then tell people that they experienced something that didn't really happen," Skylar shook her head. Was Maxwell really capable of something as horrific as drugging people to manipulate their minds? *Of course he is!* Her subconscious screamed, and the mere thought of it made her angry.

"Or, get information out of them," Ernie said. "Information they won't remember sharing."

Braznovich snapped his fingers and sat up straighter. "Information that can later be used to give the appearance of an accurate prophetic word."

"That kind of mental manipulation could certainly build a strong foundation of belief," Ernie uttered.

"Belief in something false," Skylar blurted.

"Not to them," Braznovich added and shook his head in what looked like sheer disgust.

Skylar sat motionless. She knew Maxwell was a snake, but she never thought he would stoop low enough as to drug people in order to manipulate their minds. "So this proves there is foul play, right?" Skylar asked excitedly. "You can arrest him now, right?"

Braznovich shook his head and Ernie blurted, "Wrong."

What?! Skylar exclaimed. "Why not?"

"Because we can't prove who gave Ema the drug. For all we know, she could have taken it herself," Ernie explained, exhaling smoke through his nose.

"WE know she probably didn't," Braznovich said, "but in the eyes of the law, this is all speculation."

Skylar grunted and flipped backwards on the couch.

Ema's notebook was well over one hundred pages long, written on the back and front of each page. She noted in the front of the book that this was her secret journal, stating it was separate from the mandatory journal writing that was turned into the group leader each week. She also stated that it was difficult to write in the dark. "Sometimes, when the moon is exceedingly bright and it hits my window just perfectly, I can see the lines on the paper, as I hide beneath my comforter and write," Ema had written in one of her first entries.

Ernie divided the journal into three sections and they each took one, beginning their quest to understand what really happens behind P3's closed doors.

After an hour of silent reading, Braznovich rubbed his eyes and got up to make another pot of coffee while Ernie stepped out onto the patio and lit up a smoke. Skylar stood up, arched her back and stretched her arms above her head. She closed her eyes and slowly rolled her neck back and to the left and then front and to the right, trying to alleviate the tension in her muscles. She didn't realize Braznovich had come up behind her until she felt his hands on her shoulders.

"You're very tight, Ms. Wilson," he said quietly, squeezing and kneading her shoulders.

Skylar's breath caught in her chest. His touch made her flush with excitement, anticipation and wanting. "How does this feel?" He asked, massaging over her shoulders and up the back of her neck.

"It feels wonderful," Skylar sighed, dropping her head forward as he pressed his thumbs up the back of her neck, stroking away her tension.

"Am I next?" Ernie teased, walking in from the patio with a cigarette pursed between his lips. "I've got a pinched nerve right back here," he pointed to his back. "How abouts I strip down and you give me full body rub?"

Skylar giggled at the visual, while Braznovich released her shoulders. "I have a strict no stripping policy," he teased Ernie, "and it especially applies to you."

Ernie chuckled aloud, took his seat back in the arm chair and continued reading his section of Ema's journal. Skylar stood speechless. What did he mean by 'it especially applies' to Ernie? Was he implying that it wasn't okay for Ernie to strip but it would be okay if she were to strip? Or was she reading more into it? Was his massage an act of flirtation or was that just wishful thinking?

"Let's get back to work," Braznovich said, lowering himself onto the couch and returning his attention to Ema's writing.

The information in Ema's journal was both interesting and haunting. So far they hadn't found anything that could be useful in taking Maxwell down, but Skylar wasn't ready to give up. She felt such a connection to Ema that she felt she owed it to her and to Mrs. Wright to keep reading.

Returning to the couch, Skylar picked up her section of the journal and noticed that the next page was filled with unusual doodling. There were musical notes floating up the page and a cobblestone path that wound all the way around the margins, connecting at the bottom to make a complete circle. Poking through the cracks in the stones were vine-like creatures, almost resembling snakes, but they had hands and fingers and they were holding what looked to be little pieces of bread and small glasses of wine; like you would see in church when taking communion. In the center of the circular cobblestone path was a person. Although the person was wearing no clothing, the anatomy didn't allow for gender speculation. It was simply the outline of a naked human body. The person's eyes were closed but from them flowed a stream of tears that grew bigger as they fell down the page. Long pointed objects stabbed into each arm of the body and blood ran down the page. Skylar shuttered and set the notebook on the coffee table.

"What's the matter?" Ernie asked, obviously noticing she had stopped reading. Upon hearing Ernie's question, Braznovich glanced up from his pages.

Skylar pointed to the page filled with doodlings. "It confirms your corporal mortification theory," she said.

"Let me take a look see," Ernie mumbled and moved onto the couch, forcing Skylar to scoot over closer to where Braznovich sat. They all leaned in to analyze the page.

"The arms are definitely being cut," Ernie remarked and then leaned back and blew a large smoke ring above his head.

"But it doesn't tell us if she's cutting herself or if someone else is cutting her," Braznovich noted.

"What's the difference?" Skylar winced. "It's demented either way."

"The difference is corporal mortification isn't illegal. Mortifying someone else, even if it is for the sake of purifying their soul, is considered assault," Braznovich explained, his face a mere inches from Skylar's. Their eyes met once while he spoke, but only briefly, and Skylar nervously returned her gaze to the page.

Braznovich and Ernie both leaned against the back of the couch and continued reading their sections, while Skylar left her section setting on the coffee table and leaned forward, elbows on her knees to study it. After several moments, Ernie broke the silence. "Listen to this," he said, pulling the cigarette from his mouth and reading from one of the pages. "I've heard rumors that there are spies here, living among us. Our groups have become tighter and we are required to meet nightly instead of weekly. Our journals are to be turned in twice a week now and we are no longer allowed cell phone access, even on our day off. We cannot leave the campus for any reason and the Sacrament is now required to be taken once a week instead of once a month. Surveillance cameras have been doubled and even the bathrooms have cameras, angled away from the toilets, but still able to show who enters and how long they stay. I haven't seen cameras in our apartment, but I am certain we are being watched, which is why I write only at night, beneath my blanket, in the dark."

By the time Ernie finished reading, Skylar could feel her anger boiling all the way down to her toes. "They are prisoners in there," Skylar uttered.

"Not all of them," Braznovich said. "Ema was definitely a prisoner, but most of the members are there because they want to be there."

"They THINK they want to be there because they're brainwashed," Skylar protested.

"That's speculation," Braznovich said and Skylar grunted.

"The fact that they are being manipulated is not speculation!" She abruptly turned sideways, her right knee banging into Braznovich's left knee, forcing him to wince and lean forward. Ernie witnessed the collision and chuckled aloud.

Braznovich exhaled and rubbed his hand over his knee. "If something can't be proven then it is speculation."

Skylar glared at him, momentarily ignoring her attraction for him. *I hate when he talks down to me.*

"You two are missing the point," Ernie interjected, clearing his throat. "Ema wrote, and I quote, 'there are spies among us.'" He raised his eyebrows and grinned. "Spies are on our side."

Skylar felt her spirit lift and she whirled around to face Ernie, crashing her left knee into his right knee. "Ouch!" Ernie snorted.

"Not so funny now, is it?" Braznovich grinned.

"Sorry," Skylar murmured. "Does Ema name anyone? How can we find them? How many do you think there are?"

"Slow down there Ms. I've-Got-A-.22-And-Ready-To-Use-It," Braznovich chuckled. "This is all speculation."

Skylar slapped her hands against her knees. "Is everything speculation to you?" This made Ernie laugh out loud and sent him into a smoker's coughing fit, wherein he had to excuse himself to the

patio to regain composure.   Skylar glared at
Braznovich. "That's all you ever say." She waved her
arms in the air and mimicked him, "that's
speculation." She tapped her index finger against her
chin and made an overly dramatic thinking face.
"That's speculation." She leapt to her feet and pointed
into the air.   "Wait a minute, nope, I think that's
speculation!"

"Are you done?" Braznovich calmly asked and
then reached up, looped his fingers in the waistband
of her jeans and pulled her backwards onto the
couch. He gave her a sideways smirk, shook his head
and went back to reading. "Just so you know, Ms.
Wilson," he spoke while keeping his eyes on the page,
"I don't look like that when I talk."

"But you do say everything is speculation,"
Skylar argued. "Don't you believe in anything?"

Braznovich leaned forward, set the pages
down on top of the coffee table and exhaled what
Skylar thought to be a sigh of exasperation. He
turned sideways, bending his left knee so it sat up on
the couch and crossed his right knee over his left
foot. Draping his left arm over the back of the couch,
he left his fingers rest just inches from her shoulder.
"I pretty much believe everything, at least to some
degree," he began, sincerity shining in his eyes. "If I
allow myself to get wrapped up in what I believe to be
true, or what I want to be true then my judgment gets
clouded, and I don't see all the angles. I have to keep
my view untainted in order to see all of the options."
His eyes were so tender and warm that Skylar forgot
how annoyed she was and felt herself melting into
them. "See, you're looking at everything through the
lens of how to save your sister. I'm looking at
everything through the lens of how I can find the
truth. Do you see the difference?"

"Yes, but I want to find the truth too because
the truth will free Tess and Jonathan and hundreds
more," Skylar said.

"Maybe," he sighed and let his fingers fall against her shoulder, giving it a light squeeze. "And maybe the truth will be that none of them want to be freed."

Skylar pushed his fingers from her shoulder. "I don't believe that. I won't believe that. Ema wanted to be rescued and we were too late." She abruptly stood up and walked toward the hallway. "I'm not going to be too late for Tess or anyone else."

"Where are you going?" Braznovich called after her.

"To the bathroom," she hollered back. "Of course, unless you actually see me pee, it's all speculation."

Entering from the patio, Ernie caught the tail end of their conversation and, sitting down in the arm chair, he chuckled aloud. "She's a feisty one."

Braznovich nodded. "Yep."

"You like 'em feisty, though," Ernie smirked.

"That's speculation," Braznovich raised his eyebrows and grinned.

CHAPTER 13

It was 3:04am when the phone rang, startling Skylar awake. They had read late into the night, finishing Ema's journal. Braznovich answered the phone and Skylar could barely hear him talking through the bedroom wall. The next thing she knew, he knocked on her door and told her to get up and get dressed.

"What is it?" She asked.

"It's Mrs. Wright," Braznovich said in a tone that told Skylar the news wasn't good.

"Did she try to kill Maxwell?" Skylar didn't mean to sound hopeful, but she couldn't deny the fact that she wouldn't have deemed it entirely bad news if Mrs. Wright had killed him.

He shook his head. "No, she's been murdered."

Skylar gasped and felt a deep ache pierce her heart. She couldn't believe this was happening. Who would have killed that poor woman and why?

Braznovich walked down the hall to wake Ernie, who was snoring on the couch, while Skylar hurriedly pulled on a pair of jeans and a black sweater.

The drive to Mrs. Wright's house felt surreal, as she listened to Ernie and Braznovich bounce around ideas of who might have killed her, why someone would want her dead and how they might have gone about it. It was all speculation, and none of them had seen this coming. Skylar sat quietly between them. When they arrived at the house, there were two police cars on the street and an ambulance backed into the driveway. Skylar surmised it was probably parked that way so it was easier to load Mrs. Wright's body without the neighbors seeing. Ernie pulled up behind the cop cars in front of the house and killed the ignition. Per their instructions, Skylar stayed in the truck while Ernie flashed his badge and escorted Braznovich inside. She had no desire to see the body. She didn't even like seeing bodies in caskets at funeral homes. It gave her the creeps.

The front door was marked with yellow crime scene tape and the ambulance lights cast an eerie red glow on the white brick house. Skylar scrunched down in the truck and leaned her neck against the back of the seat, crossing her arms over her chest. Her thoughts drifted to Tess and she silently prayed, again asking God to keep Tess safe.

Several minutes had passed when she saw Officer Burnes come out of the front door and walk to the cop car parked directly in front of her. He took a cell phone from his inside jacket pocket and dialed. Skylar scrunched down further and reached toward the driver door, pressing the automatic window button and rolling the window down just enough for her to eavesdrop on his call. Thankfully Ernie had left the keys in the ignition so she was able to roll down the window. Officer Burnes shuffled his feet on the pavement, obviously waiting for whomever he dialed to answer.

"I thought you weren't going to pick up," he exhaled, sounding relieved to have made contact.

Skylar could only guess what the person on the other end of the call was saying, based solely on Officer Burnes' responses; but it was obvious they were discussing Mrs. Wright.

"Yeah, it's done," Officer Burnes said. "Suicide, just like you said." He paused and then uttered, "Yeah," I got the notebook. I'll deliver it in the morning."

Suicide! Something didn't feel right. Earlier today Mrs. Wright didn't seem like a woman on the verge of suicide. Skylar's pulse quickened as a terrible thought crept into her mind. Could Officer Burnes be working for P3? Who else would know about Ema's notebook? Who else would want it? Maxwell had already tried to pass Ema's death off as a suicide and it seemed to Skylar that he was now trying to do the same thing with her mother.

She stayed hidden until he disconnected his call and walked back inside the house. Then Skylar sneaked out of the truck and toward the police car. She didn't know what she was looking for, but something, anything to tell her whether he was a member of P3. She quietly opened the door and slid into the driver's seat, searching the middle console and running her fingers under the seats and between the cracks. She opened the glove compartment, but found nothing except the usual maintenance papers, small snow scraper, tire gage and a pair of gloves. Pulling open the ashtray, she was shocked to find a bugging device buried in a bunch of loose change. It looked similar to the one found in her apartment. Skylar crammed the device into the front pocket of her blue jeans, then found the lever for the trunk and popped it. Getting out of the car, she opened the trunk to take a quick peak and found the handwritten envelope Mrs. Wright had received from the anonymous person who mailed her Ema's journal, but the journal wasn't there. *Why would he separate the envelope from the journal?* Skylar wondered. Then she slipped the envelope under her black sweater and quietly closed the trunk.

Quickly climbing back into Ernie's truck, Skylar scrunched down; breathing a sigh of relief when she saw Ernie and Braznovich finally come out of the front door and head toward the truck.

"I don't like that Officer Burnes," Ernie said, climbing into the truck and starting the ignition.

"Me either," Skylar quipped and they both stared at her.

"He's just territorial," Braznovich shrugged.

"He's hiding something," Skylar and Ernie said almost in unison and then gawked at each other.

"That was weird," Braznovich commented.

As they drove, Skylar filled them in on Officer Burnes' telephone call and the items she had found in his car. Ernie chuckled and gave her a high-five, "You went on a mini-covert op while we were inside."

Braznovich frowned. "That was dangerous," he said flatly. "What if you would have gotten caught?"

"I didn't think of that at the time," Skylar shrugged, reaching in her pocket and pulling out the bugging device. "Here." She handed it to Braznovich and then retrieved the envelope from beneath her sweater and handed that to him as well.

"You have anything else hidden in your shirt that you want to show me?" He smirked.

"Maybe later," she grinned and then felt that all-too-familiar flush.

Braznovich raised one eyebrow and gave her a look that told her he was not only surprised by her bold comeback, but impressed as well.

"Well, I do," said Ernie, digging his hand into his right jean pocket as he drove, and retrieving a small, white note card with a picture of cooking utensils in the upper left hand corner. It looked as if it belonged in a recipe box. Written on the card was a name, time and place: Alexia Graham   3:00pm   KNP Lower

"Where'd you get that?" Braznovich asked.

"From Mrs. Wright's apron pocket," Ernie answered, while he dug into his flannel shirt pocket, retrieving a pack of Marlboro Reds.

"I didn't see it," Braznovich shook his head; as if it bothered him that Ernie found a clue he had overlooked. "I usually catch that stuff."

"You were trying to make nice with Officer Burnes when I found it," Ernie explained.

"Did Officer Burnes tell you it was a suicide?" Skylar asked.

"He tried to," Braznovich answered.

"This was no suicide," Ernie scoffed, lighting his cigarette and exhaling out the window.

"How do you know for sure?" Skylar asked.

"For one, she was baking a pie. Who stops in the middle of baking a pie and kills themself?" Ernie snorted.

"And two," Braznovich added. "Something was off with the way the body fell. We've seen plenty of suicide victims and that was a poor attempt at making it look like a suicide."

"Did you tell Officer Burnes that you didn't believe it was a suicide?" Skylar questioned.

"Oh yeah," Ernie rolled his eyes. "Mr. Speculation over here made sure he knew."

"So he knows we're onto him?" Skylar asked.

"Maybe," Ernie said. "That's what we're going to find out." He drove up the next street and parked between two houses, positioned perfectly so out the passenger window they had a clear view of Mrs. Wright's front door. Ernie killed the ignition and the lights. "I think Officer Burnes is uncooperative for a reason, and if he thinks Braz doesn't believe the suicide story, he's going to have to do something to render the evidence inconclusive."

"How?" Skylar stated.

"I have a hunch," Ernie mumbled again, while exhaling a ring of smoke over his head.

"Uh-oh," Braznovich uttered. "He's about to Wow us."

"Wow us?" Skylar repeated.

"Yep," Braznovich nodded. "Ernie has a specialty, and it's hunches. Incredibly accurate hunches." With that, Braznovich pulled a .45 from the back of his black jeans, checked the clip and then put the gun back.

"Good thinking," Ernie said and reached across Skylar into the glove box, retrieving a gun.

"You have your .22 with you?" Braznovich asked Skylar.

"Yes, it's in my purse in the backseat." She turned around, leaned over the seat and began digging through her purse.

"What's taking so long?" Ernie barked. "You don't hide it all that well."

"It must have fallen out when I threw my purse in the back," she mumbled and climbed over the seat and into the back cab area. She searched the seat and the floorboards. "Did you guys take my gun?"

"Why would we take your gun?" Braznovich uttered.

"Well, it's not here," Skylar started to feel panicked. "It's not in my purse."

"When was the last time you remember seeing it?" Ernie asked.

"In my apartment, the morning you came to see me," Skylar answered Ernie. "Once I let you in, I put it back in my purse and never took it out again."

"Are you sure?" Braznovich questioned.

"I'm positive."

"Did you put it in your car and it got blown up?" Ernie suggested, peering at her through the rearview mirror.

"No, I didn't take my purse with me. Remember," she said to Braznovich, "it was on the counter when we went to my apartment to pack my things." All of a sudden a light went off in her head and Skylar gasped.

The notion must have hit Braznovich at the same time because he uttered, "oh, no."

"What?" Ernie asked.

"Whoever planted the bugs in your apartment must have taken the gun from your purse," Braznovich winced.

"How would they even know I owned a gun?"

Braznovich and Ernie exchanged glances and then Ernie reached over the seat, grabbed Skylar's purse from her lap and began digging through it.

"Hey!" Skylar objected.

111

Braznovich placed his fingers on her lips to indicate she should be quiet. Seconds later, Ernie retrieved a small bugging device from the bottom of her purse and tossed it out the window.

"Ah, shit," Ernie barked. "Frame job?" He said to Braznovich, who exhaled and shook his head.

"What do you mean by 'frame job'?" Skylar blurted.

"They stole your gun for a reason," Braznovich moaned.

"For what reason? Like they're going to frame me for a murder?" Skylar gasped.

"Don't panic," Braznovich said. "This is all speculation."

"Yeah, but what isn't speculation is the fact that whoever planted the bug has been listening to us this whole time," Ernie said. "So they know we're onto Office Burnes..."

"And they know we're here," Braznovich interrupted.

"Yep." Ernie popped his lips together. "And they know we're here," he repeated.

Skylar didn't say a word. She could tell by the tension in the air that this was not good.

"Climb back up front," Ernie said to Skylar, "and don't worry about the gun. It's on our radar and we know what to look for."

Somehow his words didn't make Skylar feel any better. Besides, that was the gun her dad had given her. It had sentimental value more than anything else. Skylar climbed back over the seat clipping her ankle on the back of Braznovich's head and falling forward, her face in Ernie's lap and her butt sticking up in Braznovich's face.

Ernie rasped a smoker's chuckle. "I haven't had a woman in my truck in this position in a long time."

Skylar pushed back, removing her head from Ernie's lap, but inadvertently thrusting her butt backwards, closer to Braznovich's face. Braznovich placed his hands lightly against her bottom to keep her from pushing further back into him. Skylar gasped at the feel of his hands on her butt. *Omigosh! His hands are on my ass!* Her cheeks flushed with embarrassment. Skylar pushed up and tried to flip over, but her foot was wedged between the seat and Braznovich's shoulder. He tenderly took her ankle and pushed it free, flipping her onto her back, her head dangling by Ernie's leg and her legs up around Braznovich's head.

Ernie burst out laughing, filling the truck with a puff of smoke. "This just keeps getting better," he said.

Braznovich waved his hand in the air to dissipate the smoke and barked at Ernie to roll down the windows. Skylar grunted and tried to sit up without kicking Braznovich in the head.

"Ms. Wilson," he teased, "I had no idea you were so limber."

Skylar's flustered cheeks burned. "I'm sorry," she moaned, finally clamoring into a sitting position.

"Don't be," Braznovich smiled, his eyes sparkling. "It was a nice view." He gave her a wink and her stomach clenched into knots of excitement.

Finally regaining his composure, Ernie shook his head, "That was a hoot," he said and Skylar playfully smacked his knee.

"You ARE entertaining, Ms. Wilson," Braznovich added with a grin.

While they sat in the dark waiting and watching, Skylar studied the note card Ernie retrieved from Mrs. Wright's apron. "Do you think this means three o'clock today?" She asked.

"That could have been in there for months," Braznovich said. "We have no way of knowing."

"Any idea what KNP Lower means?" Skylar questioned.

"It's obviously an acronym for a location," Braznovich answered.

"Thanks, Sherlock," Ernie laughed. "We'd have never figured that out."

Officer Burnes left the house and drove up the street, leaving one police car still parked in front of the house. A moment later, the ambulance pulled out of the driveway and followed Burnes up the street.

"You know what really bothers me," Skylar whispered, rhetorically because she didn't wait for an answer. "If Officer Burnes is one of them, then I'm the reason that Ema and her mother are dead. I was the one that told Officer Burnes about Ema asking me to call her mother. They might never have known otherwise." This realization stung Skylar's heart.

"Ema was already being watched," Braznovich said. "It was just a matter of time before she tried to escape." He put his hand on her knee and gave it a light squeeze. "It's not your fault."

They sat several more minutes in silence.

"Are you going to share your hunch with us?" Skylar asked, turning her head toward Ernie. "Or are we just going to sit here all night?"

"Just a few more minutes," Ernie said, glancing down at his watch. "Any minute now Burnes is going to return to the house and try to destroy the evidence."

"What evidence?" Skylar asked.

"The body," Ernie and Braznovich answered almost in unison.

Skylar gawked at them. "The ambulance just left," she said, with a "duh" tone.

"They didn't take the body," Braznovich answered, keeping his eyes on the house.

"How do you know?"

"Burnes left a cop there to guard the body. So either that cop is working with Burnes or…" Braznovich began and Ernie cut him off.

"Or he's a dead man standing."

"Office Burnes is going to kill the other cop?" Skylar gasped.

No one answered. They were all distracted by the police car returning to Mrs. Wright's house. They watched as Officer Burnes got out of the car and disappeared inside the house. Skylar was speechless with surprise. "How did you know he would come back?"

"The guilty always return to the scene of the crime," Ernie said and flicked his cigarette butt out of the window. Then he looked at Braznovich. "Braz, he's gonna torch it and I need one thing from that house."

"Torch it? Like set the house on fire?" Skylar gasped, but they ignored her.

"I'll distract him," Braznovich said and then turned his attention to Skylar. "You stay here," he ordered and before she could argue they both jumped out of the truck and ran between the houses, across the street and toward Mrs. Wright's home. Braznovich went in through the front door and Ernie disappeared behind the house.

Skylar sat quietly in the dark, trying not to think about the fact that someone had been listening to their conversation and knew exactly where to find them.   What if they were watching right now and saw Ernie and Braznovich leave her alone? She instinctively leaned to both sides and made sure the doors were locked. Skylar couldn't stop thinking about who might have bugged her apartment and her purse? She knew it was someone working for Sagan, but who? *Was it Officer Burnes?* The question lingered in her mind only briefly before she concluded that he wasn't the one. *If he was listening then he would know we were here and he wouldn't risk coming back to tamper with Mrs. Wright's body; especially when Braznovich had already expressed disbelief in his suicide theory.* It didn't make sense. Why would Sagan go to all the trouble to bug her apartment unless he was worried that she had been given some sort of information that could be used against him? *Maybe he thinks that Tess has told me something and he's desperate to know what it is.*

Skylar leaned her head against the back of the seat, trying to force herself to relax, when a sudden explosion made every muscle in her body tense. She grabbed the dash, her heart racing when she noticed the explosion came from Mrs. Wright's home. Quickly sliding over to the passenger side door, Skylar crawled out, careful to stay low while running between the houses; anticipating that the neighbors would soon be filling the street to see what had happened. Flames shot high through the front of Mrs. Wright's home and Skylar feared Braznovich and Ernie were trapped inside, or even worse, dead. She approached the front door but the fire in the front of the house was too powerful for her to enter, so she ran to the back. For a brief moment she debated on whether to go inside, as every survival instinct tells a person not to run into a burning building. However, she couldn't ignore the fact that Ernie and Braznovich might need help and she rushed toward the back steps.

Sirens sounded in the distance and Skylar saw that two of the neighbors had already retrieved hoses and were spraying Mrs. Wright's house with water. She reached for the doorknob just as Officer Burnes came barreling out of it, smashing into Skylar and knocking her backwards, off of the concrete step and into the grass. Tripping over her legs, Skylar latched onto his ankle before he could manage to get to his feet and run. She screamed out for help, as Office Burnes violently thrust his leg up and down, kicking her in the chin and neck. It was only a matter of seconds, though it seemed much longer, and then Skylar felt the cold steel barrel of a gun against her forehead. She released her grip and put her hands up in a position of surrender. Before she could raise her eyes to look at him, Officer Burnes kicked her in the chest, knocking her backwards and then disappeared into the wooded area behind Mrs.

Wright's house. Breathless, from the wind being knocked out of her, Skylar struggled to her feet and headed back toward the house, just as Ernie and Braznovich rushed out, dragging Mrs. Wright's body. Ernie had a small box tucked under his left arm. He handed the box to Skylar and then they rushed back inside, returning with the body of the other officer, which they dropped next to Mrs. Wright.

Skylar put her hands to her face and fought the urge to gag, as the majority of the back of Mrs. Wright's head had been blown off and a large part of the officer's face was missing. Braznovich took off his jacket and threw it over the top half of their bodies.

Ernie looked at Skylar. "Where'd Officer Burnes go?"

Skylar pointed toward the woods. "He put a gun to my head," she panted. Ernie took off in a dead sprint into the woods while Braznovich took Skylar by the arm and hurried her back to the truck. Once they were in the truck, Braznovich started the ignition and turned to face Skylar, anger flashing in his eyes. "I thought I told you to stay here!" He scolded. "You could have gotten yourself killed!"

"I'm sorry. "I saw the explosion and I thought you and Ernie might be…" her voice cracked. "I thought you might need help."

"In the future, Ms. Wilson, don't think, just obey what I tell you," he seethed and Skylar slumped down, feeling like a child who had just been reprimanded by her favorite teacher.

By the time they drove out of the neighborhood, rescue vehicles were parked in front of Mrs. Wright's house and firemen had begun to battle the blaze.

Braznovich pulled out of the subdivision and took a left, down a road winding through the woods. "Keep your eyes peeled for any sign of Ernie or Officer Burnes," he instructed Skylar. There were no streetlights and the woods were dark so it was difficult to see anything.

"I thought the ambulance took Mrs. Wright's body earlier?" Skylar blurted out of the blue.

"We were supposed to think that," Braznovich said. "But when I cast doubt on the suicide angle, Officer Burnes had to find another way to destroy the evidence. He must have ordered the EMT's to leave the body."

"Why would they do that?" Skylar questioned.

"Either they're working with Officer Burnes, or he told them a special investigation was going to be conducted and the body was not yet to be moved," Braznovich surmised.

"Is that normal procedure?"

"It can be. Every case is different. Chances are he told the EMT's to come back in a couple hours or that he'd give them a call when the investigation was finished so they could pick up the body."

Braznovich's phone buzzed and he hit the speaker button. "Where are you?" He blurted.

"I'm in the woods, about fifty yards to your left. I can see your lights," Ernie answered.

"Any sign of Burnes?" Braznovich asked.

"Yeah," Ernie mumbled. "I'm looking at him right now and he's got a bullet in his brain."

"You shot him?" Skylar gasped.

"No, someone beat me to it," Ernie exhaled. "Stay put, I'm coming to you."

Braznovich disconnected the call and slammed his fists against the steering wheel. "Damnit!" He blurted. "We were so close."

Skylar looked down at the small box Ernie had given her. It was a recipe box and inside were note cards that matched the one Ernie had retrieved from Mrs. Wright's apron pocket. Skylar ran her fingers through the tabs, pulling out random cards and glancing at the recipes. She couldn't help but wonder why Ernie took it from Mrs. Wright's house. It seemed an odd thing to steal.

When Ernie thrust open the passenger door and climbed into the truck, he was out of breath. "I gotta quit smoking," he panted, which made Braznovich laugh out loud.

"Ya think?" Skylar teased.

They drove in silence for a few moments, while Ernie caught his breath and Braznovich found their way back to the freeway. Despite his earlier comment, Ernie cracked the window and lit up a smoke. "We got problems," he huffed.

"Thanks, Sherlock," Braznovich quipped.

"Whoever killed Officer Burnes had to have seen the three of us," he said, which made Skylar's stomach knot with nerves. "Now, either they were sent to kill Officer Burnes or they were sent to take all of us out."

"If they were sent to take all of us out, there are three possibilities," Braznovich began. "Either they didn't see us at all…"

"…which is unlikely," Ernie interrupted.

"Or they saw us and are secretly on our side," Braznovich said and Ernie shrugged. "Or they didn't think they could kill all three of us there and plan to kill us later." Skylar felt her eyes widen at the third option.

"I vote for option two," Skylar said.

"Unlikely," Ernie mumbled and exhaled smoke through his nose. "Chances are they killed Burnes so he wouldn't talk to us."

"Or they killed him because he talked to me," Skylar mumbled quietly. "They've killed everyone who has talked to me." Emotion caught in her throat.

"Well, they haven't killed us," Ernie said. "And they'll be sorry if they try."

They rode back to Braznovich's condo in silence.

CHAPTER 14

It was almost 6:00am by the time they reached the condo and a fresh pot of coffee was brewing. Though Braznovich urged her to go back to bed, Skylar knew she wouldn't be able to sleep. Too much had happened and too many thoughts were bouncing around in her head. Sleep would have to wait. She showered and threw on a pair of jeans that didn't smell smoky and weren't caked with mud from being dragged across the ground by Officer Burnes, and a clean black V-neck sweater she had borrowed from Braznovich. It was way too big and the arms hung down to her knees if she didn't roll them up, but it smelled of him and it made her feel somehow better. Then she joined Ernie and Braznovich in the family room.

"Did you ever talk to the guy who found Ema on the side of the road and took her to the hospital?" Skylar asked.

"Briefly," Braznovich answered. "He wasn't much for phone etiquette and hung up on me mid-sentence."

"Why?" She asked.

Braznovich shrugged. "The most interesting tidbit of information was when I asked why he drove Ema all the way to Menorah Medical Center instead of taking her to the nearest hospital. He told me it was because the hospitals on the Missouri side were crooked."

"Crooked?" Ernie raised an eyebrow. "What does that mean?"

"He said that the last two kids he had picked up on the side of the road and took to the nearest hospital were returned to P3 right away," Braznovich explained. "He had some choice words to say about 'them P3 folk'," he used his fingers to make quotation marks and spoke with a twang to mimic the man. "Anyway, I asked if he would be able to identify the other kids he picked up, and he yelled 'I don't trust you' into the phone and hung up." Braznovich held up his hands, "I didn't bother calling back."

"Maybe I could call him?" Skylar posed.

"You need to stay out of this before you get hurt," Braznovich scowled.

Skylar's defenses sprung alive. Who was he to tell her what to do? After all, he wouldn't even be working on this case if she hadn't brought it to his attention. *Maybe that's it,* she thought. *Maybe he wishes I had never come to him with this.* "I just thought maybe he would be more comfortable talking to a regular person as opposed to a private investigator or a cop," she explained, but Braznovich's expression didn't change.

"The answer is no," he said flatly.

Skylar's cell phone buzzed, and was a welcome interruption from the conversation. She took the call, excusing herself to the kitchen. When she got off the phone, she excitedly returned to the family room and plunked down on the couch. "That was Greg," she said, a smile flooding her face. "He's already half way here from St. Louis and will call back after he has checked into his hotel and sets up his equipment."

"So, he's in?" Braznovich sounded surprised.

"He's in," Skylar shrieked excitedly. "He said he already has the schematics to the P3 campus buildings and with the type of security they're using, he doesn't foresee any problems getting around it."

Skylar felt hopeful once again. If they use the surveillance cameras to prove Maxwell planted the bomb in her car, they'd have grounds to arrest him; and with him out of the way, it would surely be easier to convince people to open their eyes and see the truth. That was the hope anyway. Also, Skylar hoped Greg would be able to tap into the surveillance feed and locate Tess. She knew if she could just see Tess and know she was all right, she would feel better.

Braznovich filled coffee, handing a cup to each of them and then joined Skylar on the couch. Placing her cup on the coffee table, she lifted the recipe box from the table and opened the lid, once again, running her fingers along the alphabetical tabs inside. There were probably two hundred note cards, all with little utensils in the upper left hand corner. She flipped through the cards, randomly selecting one and reading the recipe. Apple Dumplings. Bread pudding. Chocolate Cake. She set the box down and looked at Ernie. "Why did you take her recipe box?"

Ernie shrugged his shoulders. "I had a hunch."

Skylar picked up the note card that was found in Mrs. Wright's apron pocket and held it next to the Apple Dumplings card from the box. The note cards were identical. They were both written in black ink. The one difference was that "Apple Dumplings," and all the recipe names, were written on the title line of the card; whereas on the card found in her pocket, "Alexia Graham 3:00pm KNP Lower" was written under the ingredient section.

Skylar retrieved her laptop from the spare bedroom and returned to the couch in the family room. She searched by the words KNP Lower in Kansas City, Missouri and found the name of a park. Kernodle Park surrounded a lake and had an upper and lower section. Her heart leapt with excitement. She shared the information with Braznovich and Ernie and told them she was going to go there at 3:00 and see if Alexia Graham showed up.

Braznovich shook his head. "No."

"What do you mean 'no'?" Skylar asked.

"I mean it isn't safe." His jaw tightened. "They've bugged your apartment, blown up your car and murdered everyone you've come in contact with these last couple of days. For whatever reason, Ms. Wilson, you are a threat to someone and for your own safety and the safety of those around you, you need to lay low." Braznovich's voice was stern and the sparkle that was normally in his eyes had been replaced by a stern glare.

"What am I supposed to do, Mr. Braznovich?" She over-enunciated his name with sarcasm. "Sit here and twiddle my thumbs when God knows what could be happening to Tess right now?"

Braznovich sauntered to the kitchen, shaking his head. "The card probably indicates an old appointment anyway," he mumbled.

"Then why was it in her apron pocket?" Skylar retorted.

"She could have forgotten to take it out," he said.

"Or she could have purposefully put it in there as a reminder of the meeting," Skylar argued.

Walking back into the family room with a fresh cup of coffee, he rolled his eyes at Skylar. "The semantics are irrelevant. You're not going and that's final."

Indignation flared inside and Skylar could feel her cheeks redden with anger. She clenched her teeth and leapt to her feet, ready to give him a solid, verbal lashing, when Ernie interrupted.

"I'll go with her," he said. "It can't hurt to take a look see. We'll stay at a distance, not interact with this Alexia Graham person, if she even shows up. If she does, we'll snap some pictures with that fancy camera of yours." Skylar smiled at Ernie, who gave her a quick wink and Braznovich threw up his hands and stormed from the room.

"I'm taking a shower," Braznovich huffed, disappearing down the hall.

"What's wrong with him?" Skylar grimaced.

"He gets uptight when people he cares about are in danger."

"Is he that worried about Jonathan?" Skylar asked. "I mean, he didn't seem that worried before, and we have no reason to think Jonathan in any real danger right now, do we?" *And at least we have a recent picture of Jonathan to confirm he's alive and well. I don't even know where Tess is.*

Ernie lit up a cigarette and walked to the sliding door. "I was talking about you," he said, opening the door and stepping outside.

His words shocked Skylar. *He cares about me?* Other than a fleeting fantasy here and there, the thought had never really crossed her mind. She obviously found him attractive, warm and likeable, but was the attraction more than one-sided? Maybe he massaged her shoulders because he cared about her? Skylar sank back onto the couch and stared blankly at the floor. *I thought I was a nuisance to him, someone that occasionally amused him, but for the most part was a pain in his ass.* If he liked her at all, she thought it was because her attraction to him was so evident that it stroked his ego and that she was probably nothing more than a fun flirtation. It never dawned on her that he might genuinely care for her.

With Ernie still on the patio, Skylar slid off of the couch and tiptoed down the hall toward Braznovich's bedroom. She suddenly felt guilty for upsetting him and thought maybe they could talk, sort of clear the air. Standing outside his bedroom door for several seconds, Skylar tried to muster the courage to knock; uncertain of how she would start the conversation. Just as she raised her hand to tap, the door flew open and startled her. She gasped, and he instinctively grabbed her by the shoulders and slammed her backwards against the wall. Realizing it was her, he quickly released his grip. "Ms. Wilson, my apologies," he said, breathlessly. "I think I'm wound a little tight with everything that's transpired."

"We're all wound a little tight," Skylar sighed.

"Did I hurt you?" He asked, placing his hand on the small of her back and leading her into his bedroom.

Skylar shook her head. She wasn't hurt, just nervous. Very nervous. Stepping into his room, the scent of musky aftershave overtook her and she inhaled deeply. Braznovich turned to face her and for the first time she noticed that he was freshly showered, wearing nothing more than a white towel wrapped around his waist. His dark hair was damp and tussled, like it had recently been towel dried, and his eyes were sparkling. Skylar felt her breath quicken and butterflies flutter in her stomach as she tensed beneath his gaze. She wanted to speak but the sound caught in her throat, so she licked her lips and swallowed. Their eyes locked and seemed to engage in a conversation of their own. She was certain hers spoke of every fantasized notion she'd had since the morning they met; and his, for the first time, flashed with desire. *He IS attracted to me!* Her subconscious shrieked with delight. Keeping his eyes on hers, he reached behind her and shut the door, slowly pushing the lock until it clicked. Then, taking one step closer, he placed his hands on her waist and gently pushed her backwards until she was leaning against the door. Her heart beat wildly as the anticipation of his kiss began to fill her mind.

"I don't mix business and pleasure," he whispered in her ear with his lips so close to her neck that she could feel his breath escaping.

"Oh?" She uttered almost incoherently.

His lips brushed lightly against her ear lobe and then softly against her neck. "So, I'm going to have to quit your case," he said, bringing his lips so close to hers that the longing was almost more than she could bear.

"Okay," she whispered, granting him the permission he needed to pull her into a deep kiss. His muscular arms wrapped around her, one on the small of her back urging her hips forward against him; and the other on the back of her neck, looping his fingers in her hair and tugging gently so that her head tilted slightly upward, into the perfect position to receive the fullness of his kiss. Every inhibition was swept away as their tongues danced wildly. After several moments, he whirled her around, lifted her unto the bed and lay down beside her.

"Ms. Wilson," he whispered. "This is moving too quickly."

"It is," Skylar agreed. "This was...um... unexpected."

"Would you like to stop?"

No! Her heart cringed. Did he want to stop? Did he think she was easy? "Do you want to stop?" She asked hesitantly.

"No," he answered without hesitation. "But I don't want to hurry either." His eyes flashed with lustful desire. "I have a personal policy never to gulp fine wine."

Is he comparing me to fine wine?

Without another word, he sat up, pulled Skylar to a sitting position and lifted the black sweater over her head. "My sweater looks good on you," he said, "but I think I like it better crumpled on my floor." He tossed the sweater off of the bed and then reached over and unfastened the front hook on her bra, releasing her breasts for his viewing. Gazing down at her and cupping his hands beneath each breast, he moaned, "You are exquisite."

Skylar wasn't accustomed to being naked in front of men, especially in broad daylight. She was, generally speaking, an only-have-sex-with-the-lights-off kind of girl, so she felt embarrassed to have her breasts so plainly exposed and pulled her knees up to cover herself.

Braznovich shook his head in scolding fashion, tugged at her ankles, pulling her legs straight, and revealing her breasts once more. "I want to look at you," he said. He then unfastened her jeans, moved to the bottom of the bed and pulled them off, leaving her wearing only her panties. Her stomach quivered with nerves as he ran his eyes the full length of her body and then returned to meet her gaze. "Ms. Wilson..." he began but she cut him off.

"Call me Skylar," she sighed and his smile grew.

"Skylar," he whispered, running his hands up the inside of her calves, to the inside of her thighs and gently over her panties. "I've been thinking about this since the moment we met," he murmured. *He has?!* "I'd like you to lay back and relax while I kiss all over your body." It wasn't a question, it was a statement. He wasn't requesting permission, he was giving instructions. Was this really happening? Was she dreaming or was one of the hottest men she'd ever seen about to pleasure her? This was so different than anything she'd ever experienced. Skylar hadn't had many lovers, but she'd had a few and past experience taught her that first encounters were typically rushed and unfulfilling; at least for the woman. It was usually two people awkwardly fumbling around in the dark; gulping the fine wine. Skylar panted with desire as she tentatively obeyed Braznovich's command, leaning backward and laying her head on the pillow.

"Now, close your eyes and relax your muscles," he instructed. This was hard to do. Every muscle was tense with anticipation.

"Brazno..." she began, but he quickly hushed her, moving up her body with his tongue.

"Shhhhh," he whispered. "Just enjoy." He took turns placing each nipple in his mouth, rolling his tongue in quick circles around it and sucking hard until it stood erect. He blew softly on each breast and she let out a quiet moan of pleasure. "You like?" He asked.

"Yes," she sighed.

Working his tongue over her rib cage, around her belly button and down to the top of her panties, he planted tender kisses everywhere, simultaneously massaging her breasts with his skillful fingers. Skylar was on the verge of ecstasy. "Let's see what else you like," he murmured and slid her panties down. Skylar felt her face flush as her most private area was exposed. "You're beautiful," he said, his fingers drawing tiny circles where her panties used to be.

Skylar looked down at him and saw unbridled desire aflame in his eyes. He was burning to have her and she wanted to be taken. Sitting up, she reached for his shoulders, to pull him on top.

"No," he whispered.

"No?" Skylar puzzled.

"Not yet," he uttered. "I'm going to pleasure you first. Now, lay back."

How could she argue with that? Hot and giving? He was every woman's dream. This was unprecedented. She did as she was told, while Braznovich pulled her legs further apart. His tongue worked magic and his touch was everything she had fantasized and more. Finally, trembling with passion, Skylar arched into him, gripping the sheets and moaning with pleasure.

"How was that?" He asked.

"Incredible," she answered breathlessly.

"Good," he said and moved up the length of her body, pulling off his towel in one fluid motion and letting his erection press firmly against her. "I'd like to make-love to you now," he said, his nose brushing hers; and before she could speak he drove inside her. She winced from his sheer girth, but it felt good. She lifted her legs and wrapped them around his waist as he thrust forcefully into her, their bodies dancing to a rhythm only known to lovers. He paused, groaning deeply as he surrendered to climatic tension and sweet release.

Rolling to her side, he planted a tiny kiss on her neck and then wrapped his arms around her and pulled her against his chest. "I think we needed to get that out of the way," he said.

"When I came in here to sort of clear the air, this wasn't what I had in mind." Skylar drew tiny circles on his chest with her finger.

"Disappointed?"

Skylar giggled. "No, I'm pleased you don't gulp your wine," she teased.

Leaving Skylar sleeping in his bed, Braznovich got dressed and sauntered into the family room.

"You two get rid of the tension?" Ernie grinned.

"Yep," Braznovich nodded.

"You need a cigarette?" Ernie teased and a smile spread across Braznovich's face. Ernie pursed his lips together and shook his head. "You're one lucky son-of-a-bitch."

CHAPTER 15

At 2:50 Ernie and Skylar crept through the trees that surrounded the lower section of the lake in Kernodle Park. There were two benches about fifty yards from one another sitting near the edge of the lake. Ernie and Skylar positioned themselves in the clump of trees between the two, so they could see if anyone came to either spot.

"Remember," Ernie said, "we're here to see who shows up, but we're not making contact because it could endanger that person, not to mention us."

"Got it," Skylar nodded. "I'm just going to get pictures and we can determine who it is later." Skylar adjusted the lens on her camera and looked through, making sure everything was set.

At exactly 3:00pm a woman, wearing a dark gray hoodie, gray sweatpants and running shoes approached the bench to their left. Skylar looked through the lens, zooming in and snapping pictures. "It's Lexi," she whispered to Ernie. "It's the girl that talked with me after the car bomb."

"You don't seem surprised," Ernie noted.

"I had a feeling about her to begin with," Skylar explained. "Then, when I saw the name Alexia on the recipe card, I thought it possible that people called her Lexi for short."

"You're not a bad little PI, you know it." Ernie patted her shoulder.

Skylar lowered the camera. "Now that we know it's her, do you think I can go talk to her?"

Ernie shook his head. "No. If she's the spy from Ema's journal, we need to assume she is under constant surveillance and stay away. That's the only way to protect her identity."

Skylar knew Ernie was right, but she wanted so badly to talk to Lexi. She snapped a few more photographs and noted that Lexi looked like she was stalling for time. She glanced around, as if she were looking for someone. She pretended to stretch her legs on the bench and looked at her watch several times. Skylar could tell from her body language that the more time that passed, the more anxious Lexi grew. When she placed her right hand in the pocket of her hoodie, Skylar grabbed the camera and zoomed in.

"What's she doing?" Ernie asked.

"She's pulling something from her pocket." Skylar zoomed in further, watching as Lexi took a small item from her pocket and quickly wedged it underneath the rungs in the wooden bench. She then pretended to stretch her legs for a few more seconds and ran off in the same direction from which she'd come. "She stuck something in the bench," Skylar told Ernie.

Once Lexi was out of sight, Ernie instructed Skylar to stay put and made a dash for the bench.

Back in Ernie's truck, he pulled out the item and handed it to Skylar. "It's a memory stick," Skylar said aloud, and she couldn't wait to return to Braznovich's condo and see what was on it.

Skylar, Ernie and Braznovich huddled around Skylar's laptop to see what was on the memory stick. There were twelve different folders. She clicked on the one labeled "Divinity Design." It contained the actual document received by Maxwell Sagan in 1984, as well as the released versions from 2002, 2006 and 2009. Skylar immediately emailed the file to Braznovich, who starting printing copies for each of them to read.

The next folder was labeled "N.E.T.," in which two files were saved. Clicking on the first one labeled "Video One," Skylar read the notation aloud. "Here is a video of a private meeting, led by Maxwell Sagan, Saul Latham, Mort Radburn (the founder of NET) and two of the upcoming presidential candidates: Senator, Randy Patterson and Congresswoman, Micah Belmont."

Skylar clicked on the video feed and they watched intently. It was obviously being recorded without the knowledge of those in the room. The recording device was placed somewhere above and angled downward. Maxwell welcomed everyone and they all sat in a circle of folding chairs. "As you know," Maxwell began, "it is our commission to lay the foundation of the new global church, as we have been doing all these years." He rose from his chair and paced around the circle. "There is no more crucial hour than now to govern and dominate the world politically and spiritually. God has a global agenda and He has been restoring his prophets and apostles, His army, to take back that power. It is our job to exert as much influence in every area of society to increase the values of the Kingdom of God."

"To rid our nation of homosexuality and abortion," Saul interjected.

Maxwell returned to his seat and addressed the candidates directly. "With your commitment to govern and dominate our systems and promote the new order of a one world church, we will support you with all of our resources."

Mort Radburn added with an arrogant smirk, "And our resources are great."

Maxwell grinned. "We have strength not only in our country but in Africa, Latin America and Asia. We are millions strong and growing by the hour."

"What happens to those who do not agree with you?" Senator Patterson asked.

"All obstacles are removed by the hand of God," Maxwell stated flatly without batting an eye.

"We've arranged rallies for you in several states over the next six months. Texas and then Detroit and then here, in Kansas City, and then

Denver," Saul said. "We will be joining you on the campaign to ensure that you have the votes from everyone in all of our organizations."

"It is our plan that you, Randy, will take the helm and you, Micah, will be at his side," Mort explained.

"Let not your ego be bruised, Micah," Maxwell added. "The Lord has made the man to be the head of His household and the woman to be his helper." Maxwell clapped his hands together. "Now, before you leave, let us commune together and pray."

The door opened and a man Skylar recognized as the man in the red shirt who had escorted Lexi from the car bombing, stepped inside carrying a silver tray of Sacrament. Maxwell gave each person a tiny piece of bread and a small cup of wine, and then extended his arms outward and prayed, "May Joel's Army be ushered forth and blessed by the leadership of Senator Patterson, the next President of the United States and his soon-to-be Vice President, Micah Belmont." The video feed ended.

Skylar shuddered. The whole thing gave her the heebie-jeebies. She then clicked the next file beneath the N.E.T. heading, labeled "Video Two."

The video displayed the same room wherein both candidates still sat, but their body language had changed. Micah complained of feeling nauseated and dizzy and several minutes later she jumped up and dry-heaved into a small rectangular trash can that sat in the far corner. Patterson sat motionless, looking as if he were stoned.

"What do you think of all this," Micah asked Patterson, slumping back down in her chair and not bothering to sit up straight or cross her legs.

"I think if we hitch our wagon to these fellows, we're going to win the election," he slurred.

"Who will win? Me or You?" Micah asked, leaning closer to him.

"God will win," Patterson said. "Remember, the man leads and the woman follows. I will be President and you will be my Vice President."

Skylar paused the video. "What's wrong with them?" She posed aloud. "They look drunk or stoned or something."

Ernie and Braznovich exchanged glances and blurted almost in unison, "Rohypnol."

"The Rohypnol is in the Sacrament," Ernie said and moved to the arm chair to light up a cigarette.

"You mean he's poisoning the symbolic blood of Christ?" Skylar was so appalled and angry that tears stung the back of her eyes. "How dare he!" She seethed.

"I'm not even religious and that pisses me off," Ernie said, exhaling smoke forcefully out of his nose.

"I wish Mrs. Wright would have killed Maxwell," Skylar raged.

"That wouldn't do any good," Braznovich sighed. "This thing is much bigger than just one man."

"I still wish he was dead," Skylar crossed her arms and scowled.

"Let's watch," Braznovich said, placing his hand on Skylar's knee. She hit play and Ernie returned to the couch so he could see the screen.

A man entered and handed each candidate a thick stack of papers. "Maxwell asked that you complete these before you leave this afternoon," he said.

"Where's Mort?" Senator Patterson blurted. "How come he doesn't have to fill out a questionnaire?"

"I believe Mr. Radburn has already left," the young man answered and then left the room.

Skylar paused the video. "Wait a minute; if they're on Rohypnol will they be able to complete the questionnaire?"

"Yep," Ernie blurted, "but they probably won't remember doing it."

Skylar hit play and the video resumed. They watched as Senator Patterson flipped through the pages, seemingly annoyed by the length of the questionnaire, while Micah began filling in answers. "Oh, look at question three," she said gleefully and read it aloud. "What is your fondest childhood memory?" A smile filled her face. "Mine would have to be when I was nine years old and my dad bought us a miniature pony. I wanted a horse but my dad said they ate too much and pooped too much so we got a pony instead." She giggled aloud. "We named her Zuzu and I loved her. I used to feed her sugar cubes every afternoon after school."

Patterson scanned the questions. "Here's an interesting one," he said. "What is a secret you've never told anyone?"

Micah giggled and blushed like a schoolgirl, covering her face with her hands. "I kissed my eighth grade science teacher," she said. "A tongue kiss and everything."

Patterson chuckled. "You naughty little girl," he scolded and for a brief second Skylar thought she witnessed an attraction between them.

"What's YOUR deepest darkest secret?" Micah asked him.

He looked to be deep in thought and sank lower in his seat as if he felt remorseful. "When I was a door-to-door salesman I had sex with several of my customers."

"You Don Juan, you," Micah teased and brushed her hand lightly against his shoulder.

"I feel bad," he said. "I wasn't married yet but I was dating my wife at the time and I didn't treat my future bride or any of those ladies with much respect."

"It's okay," Micah said. "We all did naughty things in our younger years." She placed her hand on his leg.

135

Skylar paused the video again. "I don't understand the relevance here," she said.

"I've got a hunch," Ernie said as he rose from the couch and walked toward the sliding door. "I suspect that this information will come out later either to threaten the candidates into doing whatever Maxwell wants..."

Braznovich cut him off, "or to prophetically deliver a word from God."

"A word that contains information only God could know because neither one of them will remember this conversation or the fact that they filled out a questionnaire," Ernie added.

Holy crap! Maxwell's plan was brilliant, brilliantly evil, but brilliant nonetheless. Only a man without a conscience could drug people using the symbolic blood of Christ and then extract information from them that they wouldn't remember sharing, and use it against them as a weapon of corruption and control.

"So what do we do?" Skylar looked from Braznovich to Ernie and back to Braznovich. "Can we take this video to the police or to the media?"

Braznovich leaned back on the couch and folded his hands behind his head. "We have no proof of Rohypnol being administered."

"It's all speculation," Skylar mumbled and rolled her eyes. *So, how do we prove that Maxwell is manipulating people?* Skylar thought, but her thoughts were interrupted by the low, long growl that came from her stomach. It was so loud even Ernie, standing across the room, whirled around and gawked at her.

"I think we should eat," Braznovich said, raising his eyebrows and glancing at her stomach.

Skylar felt her face flush with embarrassment. "I'm obviously not one of those women who starves herself to look good," she sighed.

"You wouldn't last a day at P3," Ernie joked.

Braznovich pulled Skylar off of the couch and they went into the kitchen to whip up dinner, while Ernie sat at Skylar's laptop reading from the files on the memory stick. "Listen to this," he hollered. "Remember how Maxwell said they had millions of people in Africa, Latin America and Asia?"

"Uh-huh," Skylar answered.

"And remember how Patterson asked what happened to people who opposed him?" Ernie said.

"Yes," Braznovich answered.

"Well," Ernie exhaled a smoke ring above his head. "I think I found out what Maxwell meant when he said God would remove them." Ernie leaned in closer to the computer screen and read aloud. "P3 purchased land in Zimbabwe under the guise of doing missions work. They named the land the Eden Plantation and they preached the need for lengthy prayer sessions to overcome the evil of complacency found in the current church movements."

"Sounds familiar," Skylar sarcastically quipped.

"It gets worse," Ernie said, continuing to read. "P3 began to control all incoming and outgoing mail and all phone calls at the Eden Plantation were censored. The on-site pastor opposed these confinements and when P3 refused to lift their surveillance, he and his family escaped the movement."

"Escaped being the operative word in that sentence," Braznovich snorted.

Ernie read on. "A year later, when members of the Eden Plantation again took opposition against the ideals of the growing P3 movement, the entire farm of almost one hundred people, with the exception of one small child, was hacked to death by what the Zimbabwe government labeled a team of mysterious bandits."

"Hacked to death?" Skylar repeated.

"Yep," Ernie huffed. "It seems that's Maxwell's definition of God getting rid of his opposition."

Skylar slammed a pot onto the stove. "Why didn't anyone do anything about it? If they knew P3 was behind it…"

Braznovich cut her off. "P3 was the land owner. There's probably zero evidence to support the notion that Maxwell had the entire farm wiped out because they opposed him."

Ernie pulled his cigarette from his mouth. "Let's all say it together."

And they all blurted. "It's speculation."

CHAPTER 16

Greg called Skylar and they scheduled to meet him at his hotel room at 8:00pm. It was already 6:30pm by the time they had finished eating and cleaned up the kitchen. Ernie announced that he was running home to shower and change clothes and would meet them in the lobby at the Holiday Inn on highway 71 at 8:00pm sharp.

Skylar went to the guest room to get cleaned up as well. Just reading about Maxwell's dirty politics made her feel grimy. The shower in the guest bathroom was small and square shaped with a glass door. Skylar tossed a towel over the top of the glass, then opened the door and stepped in. The warm water felt good against her skin and she closed her eyes and tried to relax. She just started to lather up when she heard the bathroom door creak open and the lights turned off. "Braznovich?" She called out.

"It's me," he said, pulling the glass shower door open and stepping inside. "I came to see if you needed any help?"

"I learned to bathe myself when I was little, but I suppose it never hurts to have an extra pair of hands," Skylar blushed.

"Oh yes, more hands are always better," he smiled.

He had left the bathroom door slightly ajar so the light from the bedroom gave just enough visibility for her to see the wanting in his gaze. She scooted over to share the warm water and he pulled her close, kissing her neck and working his way toward her lips; his hands on an exploration of passion. It was the best shower Skylar had had in a long time.

Blowing her hair dry, she couldn't escape the surreal feeling that came with making love to Braznovich, much less the fact that it had happened twice in one day. She hadn't been to bed with a man in a long time, longer than she wanted to admit; and she didn't realize how much she had missed a man's touch. It felt good, better than good, mind blowing incredible, actually. She wondered if they would sleep together in his room tonight or if she would stay in the spare bedroom? She wondered if he had genuine feelings for her or if they just sort of fell together out of lust and convenience? *When I move back to my apartment, will he still want to see me?* Skylar shook off the questions for now. There were more important things to focus on, like meeting Greg, rescuing Tess and proving Maxwell was evil.

"Don't you two look all chipper," Ernie remarked as they walked into the lobby of the Holiday Inn Express.

Skylar blushed and Braznovich grinned. "I feel chipper," he said.

"Lucky son-of-a-gun," Ernie mumbled under his breath.

They took the elevator to the third floor, and knocked on the door to room 344. Greg forcefully whipped open the door after the first knock, with a look of panic on his face. "I didn't know if you'd make it," he blurted.

"I told you we were coming," Skylar answered, a little confused by his reaction.

"Yeah, but, after I saw the news I thought maybe they had picked you up," Greg was almost breathless as he ushered them inside.

"What are you talking about?" Skylar asked.

Greg clicked the television to a local news station and Skylar's heart stalled. There, on the screen, was her picture and a notation that read WANTED. They quietly listened as the reporter read from the prompt. "Twenty-nine year old Skylar

140

Wilson is wanted for questioning in the murder of Kansas City Police Officer David Burnes. Burnes was shot and killed early this morning while responding to a 9-1-1 call in a residential neighborhood. Skylar Wilson is also wanted for questioning in the murder of Kansas City resident, fifty-six year old, Cecila Wright."

Greg muted the television and stared at Skylar. "You know I have to ask, did you do it?"

Skylar's mouth fell open. "No!"

"Mrs. Wright might have been shot with Skylar's .22, but Officer Burnes wasn't," Ernie said.

"How do you know?" Greg asked.

"'Cuz I saw him up close and personal and the hole in his head wasn't made by a .22. I'm guessing it was a .45."

"So, Skylar's being framed?" Greg's voice elevated with disbelief and fear.

Braznovich shot Ernie a glance and Ernie nodded, "I'm on it." He grabbed his cell phone and stepped into the hallway.

Skylar's heart was pounding from the adrenaline surge of unadulterated fear. "It was my gun," she said more to herself than to Braznovich or Greg.

"It was your gun?" Greg repeated.

Skylar stood motionless, staring at her picture on the television while Braznovich introduced himself and filled Greg in on what had transpired. "If what you're telling me is true," Greg said, "then you were with Skylar at the time of the murder. You're her alibi."

"In a non-P3-corrupted precinct that would be true," Braznovich answered. "The problem is we don't know how many other officers are on the P3 payroll or what kind of tainted case they're building."

Skylar's mind was a whirlwind of terrible thoughts. She could only imagine how Maxwell would twist this and use it against her with Tess. Would Tess actually believe Skylar was capable of killing someone? What about all of her customers and friends? Would anyone believe she was innocent? The truth was no one really knew her well enough to believe in her innocence. She could imagine her neighbors being interviewed on the news and remarking how, like all of the other whackos in the world who suddenly went postal; she was quiet and kept to herself. Skylar stood in a daze, tears streaming down both cheeks. She didn't notice Ernie had returned or that Greg was frantically packing up his equipment.

She turned her head slightly as Braznovich touched her left arm. "I know you're in shock, but I need you to look at me." He took her face in his hands and stared into her eyes. "We have to get out of here now. Right now, Skylar."

Skylar nodded, thankful he was with her.

Braznovich, Skylar and Ernie took the stairs to the first floor and left through the rear entrance of the hotel, while Greg went out through the front doors and loaded everything into his car. Once outside, Ernie ran to get his truck and picked them up in back of the building.

"Give me your cell phone," Braznovich said to Skylar and she dug into her purse and handed it to him. He removed the SYM card, disconnected the battery and threw the phone into a dumpster in the corner of the lot.

"Why did you do that?" Skylar gasped.

"The police are looking for you now." Braznovich took her arm and helped her slide into the front seat of Ernie's truck. "They're checking your phone records, they're scouring your apartment and your photography studio, they're talking to your friends, customers and neighbors, and they're locking onto your cell phone via satellite," Braznovich explained all in one breath. He then gave Ernie a nod. "You know where to take her."

"I'll meet up with you soon," he said to Skylar, leaning in and kissing her lightly on the lips. "Don't worry, we'll get this fixed." Skylar felt as if she might hyperventilate as Braznovich closed the door and Ernie peeled out of the parking lot.

"Where are we going?" She asked, her mouth completely dry and her stomach queasy.

"Braz knows a place you won't be found," Ernie answered.

"What am I going to do?" She looked at Ernie, emotion welling up inside.

"You're going to stay hidden," he said.

"Can we report my gun stolen?"

"Already did." His expression was grim. "I got a hunch that won't be taken into account." He lit a cigarette and cracked his window about two inches. "Crawl in the back and stay down," he instructed her. Skylar crawled over the seat into the back cab area of the truck and curled into a little ball on the seat. She couldn't stop the tears as she closed her eyes, wanting to pray but not even sure what to say.

Please help me, she whispered in her heart.

CHAPTER 17

It felt as if they drove forever and Skylar dozed off in the back cab of Ernie's truck. She dreamt of her parents and of Tess and the old house where she grew up. She missed it and she missed all of them even more. None of this would be happening if Maxwell Sagan had never entered their lives. She thought back to how everything changed the moment they met Maxwell and started attending the church in the county where Maxwell preached. She remembered how Maxwell sucked Tess in even back then, and how Tess became obsessed with everything spiritual; leaving her friends and family by the wayside. Tears streamed down her cheeks.

Ernie's phone jolted her from her thoughts and Skylar lay there listening, surmising from his responses that it was Braznovich on the other end of the call. When he disconnected, Skylar leaned up on one elbow and asked, "Can you tell me where we're going?"

"A small farm in Stillwell," Ernie answered. "It's not much farther." The air from Ernie's slightly opened window made Skylar shiver and she tucked her arms inside her sweater and curled them against her chest to stay warm.

Arriving at the farm, Ernie told her it was safe to sit up and Skylar watched as they drove down a long gravel road through the woods and toward a clearing. At the end of the road was a log cabin and a barn. It looked like something from Little House on the Prairie days, only this cabin had electricity and plumbing.

"What is this place?" Skylar asked as Ernie pulled the car to the side of the cabin and put it in park.

"It belonged to Braz's grandpa. It's a real special place and Braz doesn't bring anyone here," Ernie winked. "I guess he thinks you're real special." He opened the door and stepped outside while Skylar crawled over the seat and slid out of the driver's door.

They walked toward the cabin, Skylar noticing for the first time that Ernie shuffled his feet when he walked. It wasn't noticeable on pavement or grass or indoors, but on the gravel it made a funny dragging sound. They ascended the three long wooden steps that led to the front porch, complete with a wooden bench swing. Skylar peered through the window next to the door. "Can we get in?" She asked Ernie.

"Yep," he said, jingling his keys in front of her face.

"I thought you said he doesn't let anyone come here?"

"Braz thinks I'm real special too." He winked, unlocked the door and held it open for Skylar to step inside. She was immediately taken aback by the size of the cabin. It was deceptively small from the outside and enormous from the inside. The front door opened into one giant room with log support beams strewn throughout. A staircase to the immediate left led to a loft that circled the entire cabin, with doors jetting off. Just beyond the staircase was a bathroom and then an open kitchen, with a long marble countertop dividing it from the dining room table, which sat in a nook with three giant bay windows overlooking a pond. Directly across from the front door was a glass sliding door that opened onto a porch that was covered by the deck above it. To the immediate right of the front door were built in book shelves filled with books, a dark green leather arm chair and a cream colored, fuzzy rug. Further to the right was a stone fireplace adorned with a center-mounted deer head and flanked by two elk heads, one above and to the right and one below and to the left. In the middle of the room was a large rectangular rug that must have been twenty by twenty in size. It was dark brown with swirling patterns that looked like green and orange leaves. Matching curtains hung on each window. In the center of the rug sat a brown leather couch, two matching leather chairs and a green corduroy recliner that looked like it had been there for centuries.

"The bedrooms are upstairs," Ernie said, breezing by her and heading for the fridge. "Hot diggity dog, it's still here," he yelped, grabbing a bottle of 1843 Bourbon from the refrigerator and holding it up to show Skylar. "This is exactly what I need right now."

"Make it a double," Skylar sighed and joined him at the counter. Ernie poured them each a glass and Skylar remarked how her dad used to drink the same Bourbon when she was growing up.

"No kidding?" Ernie said. "Very few people around these parts have heard of it."

"I know," she remarked. "That's because it's a St. Louis Bourbon and they don't sell it west of Columbia, Missouri."

Ernie took a long drink and then made an "ah" sound. "I wonder why that is?"

Skylar shrugged. "I dunno. But I used to buy several bottles whenever I'd go back to St. Louis. I guess I forgot how much I liked it."

"St. Louis or the 1843?" Ernie asked.

Skylar felt emotion welling up and she fought to keep it at bay. "Both," she answered quietly. "After my parents died and Tess moved to the P3 compound, there was no real reason for me to make the trip anymore."

"Do you still have friends there?" Ernie topped off their glasses.

The thought of her friends brought a smile. "I do actually," she said. "They're the kind you can go months without talking to and then pick right back up as if only an hour has gone by."

"Those are the best kind," Ernie winked and raised his glass in toasting fashion. "To good friends."

They clinked their glasses and drank. "I need me a smoke," he announced, shuffling to the slider and cracking it open.

Ernie told her Braznovich was picking up supplies and that he and Greg would be joining them shortly. She tried to relax, but it wasn't easy. Her stomach tightened into jittery knots and her head throbbed. At Ernie's urging, Skylar took some Ibuprofen and curled up in the corduroy recliner, closing her eyes. Emotionally exhausted from worry, sleep beckoned her and she didn't fight it.

Clanging dishes in the kitchen jolted her awake and Skylar sat up, immediately noticing that she had been covered by a snuggly brown blanket and there was a fire blazing in the fireplace.

"Well, lookey who decided to join us," Ernie announced when he saw her sit up.

"How long was I asleep?" Skylar asked feeling sleepily disoriented.

"Couple of hours," he said. "Braz and Greg are getting things set up in the library."

Skylar scooted off the chair and peered over at the book shelves which sat to the right of the front door. She assumed that was the library section of the room, but Braznovich and Greg weren't there. "The library?" She questioned and Ernie grinned.

"You fell asleep before I could give you the full tour." He raised his eyebrows into his forehead and walked toward the left side of the fireplace.

Skylar watched as Ernie reached his fingers around the side of one of the fireplace stones, and released a lever that opened a narrow door in the stone. The door opened inward and Ernie stepped inside. "Follow me," he said and disappeared down a stone staircase that curved around below the

fireplace and opened into a large room. Skylar
followed him, completely in awe.

The walls were stone and there were no
windows. Lights hung overhead and cast a dim,
yellowish glow around the room. A large white fuzzy
rug filled the center of the room and two brown suede
couches faced one another with an oval coffee table in
between. Floor to ceiling shelves lined the far wall
and the entire wall to the right, holding hundreds of
books, some that looked to be very old. Two leather
studded armed chairs sat in the far corner with an
end table and a lamp between them.

"Behold the library," Ernie grinned and held
his arms out, gesturing over-dramatically, in Vannah
White fashion.

"It's beautiful," Skylar awed.

"There's more," Ernie said and opened a dark
wooden door to the left of the steps. When the door
opened Skylar could hear the voices of Braznovich
and Greg. She hurriedly followed Ernie inside.

"Look who's awake," Braznovich smiled upon
seeing her.

The room was filled with electronic
equipment. A forty inch screen was inset in the wall
straight ahead, with several smaller screens
surrounding it. A wooden desk ran the length of the
far wall and the wall to the left of the door. There
were drawers on the ends and a stainless steel
trashcan in the left corner. Several laptops sat atop
the desk with wires running to the inset screens and
to several electronic devices, a printer/copier/fax
unit, a paper shredder and several others Skylar
couldn't identify. To the right of the door was a large
wooden armoire and Skylar surmised it probably held
computer supplies, like ink, paper, etc.

Greg was scurrying about the room, attaching
wires and clicking away at numerous keyboards,
booting up everything he needed to hack into the P3
security system.

"Can you hack in from here?" Skylar asked Greg.

"I can hack in from anywhere," he answered without looking up from what he was doing.

Braznovich took Skylar by the hand and led her back toward the stone staircase. "Let me show you to your room. I have something for you."

As they climbed the stone steps to the main level, Skylar snickered softly. "You're like Batman," she teased, "with your own private, underground lair."

He entwined his fingers with hers. "You have no idea. Wait until you see my bat mobile."

They ascended the staircase that led from the main level to the loft and walked passed two bedrooms and one bathroom, then into a master suite. "This is your room," Skylar said, feeling a little awkward about the prospect of sharing a room with him.

"You're right, it is my room." He squeezed her fingers gently. "Greg will use one spare room and Ernie the other." Wrapping his arms around her waist, he pulled her close and gazed down into her eyes. "After what happened this afternoon and this evening, I suppose I am guilty of assuming you would be comfortable sharing my room." He kissed her lightly on the lips and then she squirmed from his grip, and walked toward the glass doors that opened onto a deck made out of logs, overlooking the pond and the woods.

Opening the doors, Skylar stepped onto the deck and drew in a deep breath. The air was crisp and cool and smelled of pine trees.

Braznovich followed her outside, wrapped his arms around her waist from behind and rest his chin on the top of her head. "What's wrong?" He asked softly.

"Everything," she exhaled.

"I'll tell you what, why don't you stay in here and I'll bunk with Ernie."

Skylar whirled around to face him. "No!"

He raised his eyebrows in surprise.

"That's not what I meant. Being with you doesn't feel wrong it's everything else that's wrong." She shook her head. She wasn't explaining herself very well. "I would like to stay with you, unless you'd rather share a bed with Ernie." She shyly glanced up at him, feeling her face flush.

"Well, Ernie snuggles great, though he does hog the covers and snores like a grizzly..." Braznovich teased, holding up his hands in scale fashion and acting like he was weighing out which option would be better, sleeping with Ernie or sleeping with Skylar. Skylar laughed out loud and playfully smacked his arm.

"If you can't decide between me and Ernie, I think we have bigger problems," she laughed, meandering back inside.

"By the way, I hope you don't mind but I took the liberty of picking up some clothes for you." He closed and locked the glass doors.

"You went to my apartment?"

"No, your apartment will be crawling with cops," he said. "I stopped into Steinmart and grabbed a few things to tide you over."

He pointed to the bags that sat atop the king size bed and Skylar made a beeline toward them. She pulled out two cashmere sweaters, one light blue and the other smoky gray, a pair of Lucky Brand blue jeans, silk black pajamas, a toothbrush, toothpaste, shampoo, a hair brush, some basic make-up and several pairs of satin panties.

"I guessed on size," he sheepishly grinned.

Skylar felt overwhelmed by his kindness and by the amount of money he had spent on her; not to mention embarrassed by the fact that he had bought her panties. No man had ever bought her a pair of panties. "I can't believe you did this," she whispered. "I'll pay you back."

He took the panties from her hands and dropped them back into the clothing bag, and then wrapped his arms around her waist and pulled her close. "If you try to pay me for the clothes, I'll take them back and then you'll have nothing to wear but your beautiful birthday suit." He kissed her lips and then suddenly pulled back. "On second thought, maybe I WILL take the clothes back." He smiled and his eyes sparkled with affection and warmth, everything Skylar needed at that very moment to know she wasn't alone.

CHAPTER 18

When Greg's equipment was set up and he had successfully hacked into the P3 security system, he began scanning archived footage of the main parking lot on the day Skylar's car blew up. "Found anything yet?" Ernie asked, returning from a smoke break.

"Near as I can tell, two people approached Skylar's car while she was inside; but I can't get a clear visual of either one of them."

"Why not?" Ernie asked.

Greg backed the footage up several frames and paused it. "The first person to approach the car is wearing a red hoodie and with the camera angle and the shadow from the hood I can't get a clear view of his face," Greg explained.

"Or her face," Braznovich interjected.

Greg shrugged his shoulders. "Could be a woman, but the tennis shoes are men's shoes and he's wearing men's boxers."

"How can you see the boxers through his jeans?" Skylar asked, squinting at the screen.

"Right here," Greg pointed. "When he bends down by the driver's door you can see the top of a pair of boxers." He paused the frame and they all stared at it.

"Sure looks like a guy," Braznovich admitted, "but we don't know for a fact."

"We don't want to be guilty of gender speculation," Skylar teased and Braznovich flashed her an expression that said 'very funny.'

Ernie chuckled and then moved in closer toward the screen. "The bomb has a magnetic coating with a pre-set timing device," he said so confidently that it drew Braznovich's attention.

"How do you know?" Braznovich asked.

"He's only at the car for about five seconds; just long enough to stick the bomb under the driver's side of the vehicle," Ernie explained. "He didn't wire or set anything."

Braznovich leaned in toward the monitor screen. "Greg, can you zoom in closer and see if he has anything in his pockets?"

"His pockets?" Skylar asked.

"I don't think the bomb had a pre-set timer because how would anyone have known precisely when you would be getting into your car to leave?" Braznovich ran his fingers quickly through his hair. "Besides, you said you sat there for at least a minute before noticing the note, right?" Skylar nodded. "And as soon as you saw the note you leapt from the car, which is when the bomb exploded."

"Right," Skylar said.

Braznovich squinted at the screen. "I think the bomb has a detonator switch."

"That's a more delicate design," Ernie added. "Do you think they have the equipment and know-how for something like that?"

Braznovich never took his eyes off the screen as he spoke. "I think their resources are limitless."

Greg maneuvered the video and zoomed in on the man's jean pockets, his hands, and his jacket pockets. There was no indication that he had a detonator in his possession. After printing two pictures of him, Greg moved several frames forward on the surveillance feed to where the second person approached Skylar's car. It was obvious by her walk that this person was a woman, even though her body was covered by a long black trench coat with a hood and her face was covered with large, round framed black glasses and a black turtle neck, stretched over her chin. The only part of her face that was visible was her lips. She pulled a piece of paper from her coat pocket and tried to open the passenger door. The door was locked and after tugging on it two times, she wedged the note into the window and hurried away.

"Can you follow her?" Ernie blurted to Greg.

"I have to pull up multiple feeds, but I should be able to track where she went, if that's what you're asking," Greg replied.

"I want to know if she got into a car and drove off or went into a building on the P3 campus," Ernie said, and then blurted. "I gotta have a smoke. I can't think without a smoke."

Hours later and after numerous complaints from Ernie about not being able to smoke in the downstairs library, and not being able to think clearly without a smoke, they all moved upstairs to the main floor. They moved Greg's computer upstairs and he reconfigured the printer for a wireless connection. Then Greg hooked his computer to the larger television that hung above the fireplace so anything he pulled up on surveillance could be easily viewed by everyone in the room. He printed off several pictures of the woman at the car and then asked Skylar to retrieve the pictures from the printer downstairs.

On her way back through the library, she noticed a manila envelope stuck between two books on the shelf closest to the staircase. It stood out because the books were almost all hardback and dark in color, and the envelope was lighter. Curiosity drove her to pull it out and read what was written in cursive handwriting on the outside of the envelope. It read: Goodwin's Personal Report. Skylar's mind raced to assign meaning to the twinge of familiarity she felt when seeing the name Goodwin. All of a sudden awareness filled her and she felt her mouth fall open. Goodwin was the name of the pastor who stood up against the P3 movement when they first arrived in town. He was one of the men Maxwell Sagan had physically threatened and he was the one who rallied the forty-five churches to stand against

P3. The Goodwin Doctrine was the 233 page document that was sent to the Apostolic Presbyters of the Network of Christian Ministries. It was the document that had never been refuted and the one she had described to Braznovich and Ernie the first time they met.

Skylar opened the envelope and pulled out a handwritten note that lay on top of a stack of papers. It was addressed to Braznovich's grandfather, Franklin Braznovich, and was written from Mrs. Goodwin.

"Dear Franklin," Skylar read silently. "It is in deepest mourning that I write this letter and out of the agony of my despair that I come to you for guidance. It has been one month since my Edward has passed and I know now that it was at the hand of that devil of a man, Maxwell Sagan." Skylar swallowed hard and read on. "As you know, Edward was threatened that if he took a stand against Maxwell he would surely die, but we sought the Lord together and felt certain it was the right thing to do. I still believe Edward obeyed the Lord's will in this. When Edward did not stop pursuing repentance from Sagan, Maxwell tried to destroy his reputation as a pastor and damage our marriage. I fear he succeeded in many ways." Skylar's hands began to tremble from anger as she continued to read. "My Edward was accused of adulterous affairs with two women. At first, I believed the accusations, but Edward was always an honest man and when he continued to protest his innocence to me, I dug deeper and have now found evidence that Maxwell paid these women to spread lies about my husband.   If only I could have told Edward I believed him before he died." Skylar's heart ached for Goodwin's widow. "Franklin, you are one of a few men my Edward trusted and so I hand the torch to you. I was told Edward died from a heart attack, but when I received the coroner's report, it stated the heart attack was induced by a chemical substance. I have never heard of such a substance and I am certain Edward had not either. My husband never used drugs and was not on any medication at the time of his death. I know in the center of my heart that he was murdered by Maxwell Sagan. Will you help me prove it and not let my Edward's death be in vain? Enclosed is written testimony from the two women paid off by Maxwell Sagan and a copy of the coroner's report." A single tear ran down Skylar's left cheek. "Lovingly, Helen Goodwin."

Skylar slid the letter back inside the envelope and wiped the tears from her face. She felt nauseated with anger and she wondered if Braznovich knew his grandfather was friends with Goodwin and that Goodwin had been allegedly murdered by Sagan. *Maybe he doesn't know,* Skylar thought to herself. *If he did know he surely would have disclosed the information at our first meeting when I spoke of the Goodwin Doctrine.* Then she remembered that she never mentioned Goodwin by name, so maybe Braznovich didn't put two and two together. Then again, he never said he didn't know what she was talking about that first morning. It was Ernie who asked all the questions, not Braznovich. She stared at the envelope, debating whether or not she should carry it upstairs and ask Braznovich if he had seen it. *If he had seen it, surely he would have investigated it further.*

"Did you get lost?" Braznovich hollered down the steps and startled Skylar.

"I'm coming," she yelled upward and quickly slid the envelope back between the books on the shelf. She decided that she needed to get a good look at the alleged proof in the envelope before she confessed to snooping around. She wondered if Braznovich's grandfather took action against P3 after receiving this letter from Goodwin's wife. And if so, what was the result? *Surely he conducted some form of investigation or follow-up*, she thought; *and if he did, he must have left notes behind.* She determined that after everyone was asleep she would sneak back down to the library and snoop around; then she would ask Braznovich about all of her findings.

Greg had scanned all of the surveillance archives from the parking lot and was now working on the hundreds of cameras inside the various buildings. Skylar could tell by the intensity in his glare that he was searching hard for any sign of Tess. Though he had previously proclaimed to hate her, Skylar knew that that was just the hurt talking and that deep down he still loved Tess. She could see it behind his eyes. If he didn't still love her, why else would he be here?

Ernie brought Greg a cup of coffee, and Greg placed his laptop on the coffee table and took the cup with a genuine look of gratitude. "You need to take a break," Ernie said. "Your eyes are all glassy and red from staring at that computer too long."

Greg rubbed his eyes with one hand and held the coffee steady with the other. "I know," he agreed. "There are just so many cameras I feel like I can't stop or it'll take forever to get through the archived files. San Quentin doesn't have this many cameras."

That statement alone summed up Skylar's thoughts on P3. It was worse than a prison.

"Seriously," Greg continued. "They don't just have security cameras to guard against break-ins or even break-outs; they have surveillance specifically designed to track movements within the building."

"What do you mean?" Ernie asked.

"The cameras are purposefully placed so that anyone entering or leaving a room can be seen, and their time of entry and exit is recorded. They literally cannot go anywhere without being watched." Greg rubbed his eyes. "I knew it was bad, but I didn't know it was this bad."

"Ema wrote about the cameras in her journal, remember?" Skylar added. "She said she didn't think they were in the bathroom stalls, but they were

157

definitely recording when a person entered and left the bathroom."

"A bunch of sickos," Ernie huffed.

"Is there a way you can link our laptops so that each of us can check a different surveillance feed at the same time?" Braznovich asked.

"That would speed things up," Greg nodded, "but I'm not sure if it's doable while maintaining our secure status."

"What does that mean?" Ernie asked.

"Hackers get in and get out quick, to avoid being caught," Greg explained. "I'm already lingering in their system longer than I should be."

Braznovich sat down in the armed chair across from Greg. An expression of concern lit his brow. "Let me ask you this. If they discover they've been hacked, will they be able to trace your location?"

"No, I made sure of that," Greg answered confidently and then blew on his coffee to cool it down. "Besides, I'll know the moment they discover there's been an intrusion."

Ernie's cell buzzed and he stepped outside onto the deck, lit up a cigarette and took the call. When he came back in, his face was reddened with anger and he spewed obscenities. Skylar stared wide-eyed. She had never seen Ernie so upset. Even in the throes of chaos he always had a whimsical joke or sarcastic quip to lighten the mood. Now, he was visibly agitated.

"What's up?" Braznovich asked, watching Ernie intently. Skylar guessed by the expression on Braznovich's face that he hadn't seen Ernie behave this way very often either.

"They just pulled a woman's body out of one of the lakes at Kernodle Park."

Skylar felt her heart stall. *Was it Tess?* She thought it but didn't ask it aloud. If she didn't verbalize it then maybe it wouldn't be true. She sank down onto the couch next to Greg.

"ID?" Braznovich asked and Ernie shook his head to indicate no. "Let's go," Braznovich said, grabbing his keys from the kitchen counter. As he followed Ernie out of the door, Braznovich turned to Skylar and Greg. "I don't know what time we'll be back. There's food in the kitchen. Don't leave the house for any reason." His face was stern and his eyes, determined. "If anyone comes here, go down into the library and stay there until we return. You'll be safe there."

"No one knows about your secret lair, Batman?" Skylar smiled.

"Do as you're told," he shook his finger at her and Skylar nodded. She knew it wasn't safe for her to be seen by anyone. It was sorely ironic to think that P3 had now made her a prisoner of sorts as well.

As soon as Braznovich and Ernie were gone, Skylar left Greg sitting on the family room couch scanning surveillance video, while she went back down to the library. She pulled the manila envelope from between the books and opened it, taking out the letter from Goodwin's widow, the two letters of testimony from the women paid off to accuse Edward Goodwin of engaging in sexual relations with them, and the Coroner's report. Skylar scanned the Coroner's report first and her eyes immediately stopped on one all-to-familiar word. Rohypnol. *I knew it!* She then read through the letters of testimony from the two women, feeling sickened by the reality of what transpired. Maxwell Sagan paid each woman five hundred dollars to lie and say they had sex with Edward Goodwin.

Setting the envelope and letters down on the edge of the staircase, Skylar stood back and scanned the book shelves. *If I was Franklin Braznovich and I received that letter from the widow of a trusted friend, I would have definitely dug deeper into it.* She tapped her index finger against her top lip and walked slowly in front of the book shelves. *So, where would he have stashed his notes?* Skylar ran her fingers across the books on the top shelf, stopping every so often to pull out a book and flip through its pages. She searched for folders or envelopes or loose pieces of paper that might have been tucked between the books, but she found nothing. She did the same with the lower shelves. Frustrated from coming up empty handed, Skylar sank down into a chair and sighed heavily. *What did you expect?* She berated herself. *After all, it's been like years since that letter was written. Even if Franklin had researched deeper, his notes were probably long gone.* She leaned her head against the back of the chair and closed her eyes, trying to distract herself from the terrible thought that wanted to permeate her mind. Was Tess the woman found in the lake?

"Whoo-hoo!" Greg hollered from the floor above her. "Skylar! Skylar! Come here, quick!"

Skylar leapt to her feet at the sound of Greg's yelp and dashed up the stone staircase. "What is it?" Her heart was racing.

"It's Tess!" He exclaimed with genuine excitement.

Skylar dove onto the couch, toward the computer screen and stared at a visual image of her sister, sitting on the side of a bed in what looked like a small one room apartment. "How old is this image?" Skylar blurted.

"It's live," Greg smiled.

She stared at Greg, and asked again. "When exactly was this taken?" Before she got too excited she needed to verify one last time that Tess was truly alive.

Greg grabbed Skylar's shoulders and grinned from ear to ear. "Skylar, it's a live feed. It's happening right now."

"So Tess is alive?" Skylar couldn't bring herself to look away from the screen as relief flood her heart and tears filled her eyes.

"Tess is alive," Greg confirmed and then exhaled and leaned back on the couch. Skylar could tell that he had been as worried as she was, fearing that they were going to find out Tess was the body pulled from the lake.

"You've been searching for Tess the whole time, haven't you?"

Greg made a squeamish face. "Not the whole time. I mean, I ran the archived parking lot surveillance from the day of your car bombing…"

Skylar cut him off. "But since then, you've been running live feed trying to find her, haven't you?"

"Guilty," he said.

"That's why you didn't want to hook up the other laptops and let each of us help scan through the archived feeds," Skylar said, snapping her fingers in an I-get-it-now fashion.

"I figured we could always go back and look at the archived data after we found out if Tess was still there and if she was all right," he explained.

"You still love her don't you?" Skylar leaned back on the couch.

"Guilty again," he sighed.

CHAPTER 19

After Skylar and Greg dined on frozen lasagna and butter bread, Greg went back to monitoring Tess's apartment and Skylar continued searching the library. Upon finding nothing, she grabbed a large hardback Bible from the top shelf and carried it and the manila envelope upstairs. She planned to lie in bed and read until Ernie and Braznovich returned. On her way upstairs she stopped on the main level and covered Greg, who had fallen asleep on the couch, with a brown comforter which she found hanging over the back of the armed chair. His computer screen still displayed the images of Tess in her apartment. She noticed Greg had made notations on a piece of paper as to when people entered Tess's apartment, a brief description of them, their perceived reason for entering and the time they came and left. Skylar was impressed with how detailed Greg was and even more impressed with how much he still loved Tess.

Once in the master suite, Skylar tossed the Bible and envelope on top of the bed and went into the bathroom to shower and change into her new satin pajamas. When she came out of the bathroom she noticed the corner of a small, white piece of paper sticking out of the front of the Bible. She hadn't seen it before and surmised it must have shifted into plain view when she tossed the Bible onto the bed. It had a verse written on it that read: *"Even from your own number men will arise and distort the truth in order to draw away disciples after them. Acts 20:29."* Chills darted up the back of her neck. If that didn't describe Maxwell Sagan she didn't know what did. Maxwell was the king of distorting truth.

She crawled into bed and opened the Bible to Acts 20:29, wanting to read the verses before and after it; but there she found another small, white piece of paper with another verse written on it. It read: *"For such men are false apostles, deceitful workmen, masquerading as apostles of Christ. And no wonder, for Satan himself masquerades as an angel of light. It is not surprising, then, if his servants masquerade as servants of righteousness. Their end will be what their actions deserve. 2 Corinthians 11:13-15."* Skylar sat for a moment and stared, wondering if it were possible that Maxwell could actually be the Anti-Christ. What would that mean for the world? What would it mean for Tess? She dismissed the thought, almost as quickly as it came and turned in the Bible to 2 Corinthians, chapter eleven. Verse eleven had been underlined in red ink and written in the margin next to the verse was the name Maxwell Sagan. Skylar closed the Bible and stared at the ceiling. She had a feeling that Braznovich's grandfather had extensively researched Sagan and the P3 movement. *If only I could find his notes,* she thought. *Maybe something in them would help us take P3 down.*

Skylar dozed off reading and woke up abruptly when she heard a tapping on the bedroom door. She shot up in bed and saw Greg standing in the doorway.

"Come downstairs quick," he blurted. "You've got to see this."

It was 3:30am and Braznovich and Ernie still hadn't returned. She followed Greg downstairs and sat down on the couch, facing his computer.

"I woke up and couldn't go back to sleep so I started to jump around to various surveillance cameras and see if anything was happening on the P3 campus," Greg explained. "I mean, being that they advertise prayer 24/7 I figured there would at least have to be a few people in the prayer room at all times, right?" Skylar shrugged and nodded in agreement. "I started watching these people in the prayer room and something's not right."

"What do you mean?" Skylar leaned in closer to the screen.

"Look at them. I mean, really look at them. It's like they're drugged or something and then, the longer they're in there they start twitching and jerking and some of them fall over and flop around on the floor." Greg shook his head. "If I believed in any of this I'd say they were possessed."

Skylar stared at the computer. Greg was right; it did look like they were possessed. She half way expected someone's head to spin around and for them to vomit pea soup.

Did Maxwell drug particular people before they entered the prayer room so to manipulate their minds and cause them to believe they were having a God encounter? Or were these people really meditating and calling forth demonic spirits that were then taking over their bodies? The thought made Skylar shudder.

Warming two cups of Earl Grey tea, Skylar rejoined Greg on the couch. He had hooked up another laptop, keeping one on the feed to Tess's apartment and using the other to scan the feed from various cameras. A third laptop was set up to tap into the Kansas City police department records to try and determine which officers had ties to P3 and which ones might be clean. Greg pulled up the police report on Skylar. "Do you want to know what evidence they have against you?" He asked.

"They shouldn't have any evidence against me," Skylar snorted. "I didn't kill anyone."

"It sure looks like you did." Greg shook his head and Skylar leaned closer to the screen. She couldn't believe what was in the report. It stated that the .22 used to kill Officer Burnes, another Officer named Martinez and Mrs. Wright was registered to her and had her fingerprints on it. This wasn't surprising since it was her gun that someone had stolen from her purse. The report also stated that her prints were found on the clothing of Officer Burnes and Mrs. Wright. Skylar rolled her eyes. Again, this wasn't hard to believe because she had been in Mrs. Wright's kitchen and hugged her the afternoon of her death; and she had tackled Officer Burnes to the ground that evening. It stood to reason that her DNA and prints were all over the crime scene. Adding fuel to the fire was the fact that several of Mrs. Wright's neighbors gave a description of Skylar, fleeing the scene; and one had even snapped a picture of her running toward the house. Skylar moaned and flopped backwards on the couch.

"I thought Ernie said the gun used to kill Burnes wasn't a .22," Greg commented.

"It wasn't," Skylar replied. "This report is a lie, but if we can't prove Maxwell or someone at P3 is behind this, I'm going to end up in prison for real."

"For life," Greg added and Skylar glared at him. "Sorry."

Greg went back to monitoring surveillance cameras and Skylar went downstairs to the library to continue snooping, but she didn't find anything else P3 related. A little after 4:30 in the morning she heard Braznovich and Ernie come in and she hurried upstairs to greet them. Ernie looked haggard and Braznovich, utterly exhausted.

"What are you doing awake?" Braznovich asked Skylar, but before she could answer Greg piped in and explained the strange activity in the prayer room.

"I thought they were possessed," he said.

"Maybe they are," Ernie barked, heading for the sliding door to light up a cigarette.

"He's testy," Braznovich rolled his eyes. "I wouldn't let him smoke in my car."

"From now on we take my truck," Ernie huffed.

Braznovich took off his black sport coat and draped it over the chair, and then proceeded to the kitchen where he poured himself an 1843, minus the ice, and drank it down in one gulp. Taking a deep breath he caught Skylar's questioning eyes.

"It was Lexi," he murmured. "She was shot in the head and dumped in the lake."

Skylar gasped, covering her mouth with both hands. She felt like she'd been kicked in the chest. "Because she talked to me," Skylar mouthed. "She died because she talked to me."

"It isn't your fault," Braznovich walked toward her, but Skylar backed away. "You didn't know this would happen."

Skylar felt like she might throw up as grief, anger and guilt consumed her. Everyone she came into contact with at P3 was dead. Sweet, scared Ema, Mrs. Wright, Officer Burnes and now Lexi.

"Oh, crap!" Greg blurted, clicking at his keyboard and sending his signal to the giant television. "Get a load of this."

They all stared up at the television while the newsroom anchor reported: "Police have pulled the body of twenty-two year old, Alexia Graham, from Kernodle Lake. Witnesses confirmed she was killed by twenty-nine year old, Skylar Wilson, who police believe to be on a killing spree. Wilson is wanted for questioning in three deaths, all in connection with P3 ministries, the 24/7 international prayer house movement in Kansas City, Missouri run by founder, Maxwell Sagan. Wilson allegedly set off a car bomb earlier this week in the P3 parking lot and is believed to be armed and dangerous." A picture of Skylar filled the screen and Braznovich instructed Greg to kill the feed, just as Skylar broke into sobs, sinking into the armed chair.

She pulled her knees up to her chest and wrapped her arms around them, burying her face. "They're going to put me in prison for the rest of my life," she sobbed.

"They'll have to find you first," Braznovich said.

"And then they'll have to come through me," Ernie added, blowing smoke through his nose. "And that ain't no easy task." Skylar looked up and met eyes with Ernie. He offered her a keep-your-chin-up smile and Skylar gave a slight nod. She knew Braznovich and Ernie would do everything they could to protect her; the problem was she feared they wouldn't be able to do enough.

"We all need some sleep," Braznovich said, pulling Skylar from the chair and leading her to the steps. "Let's grab a couple of hours and reconvene at 7:30."

Ernie flicked his cigarette butt out of the sliding door. "Things always look better after some shut-eye."

Braznovich led Skylar up the stairs and into the master suite, where he immediately noticed the Bible, manila envelope and letters strewn across the bed.

He left her standing in the center of the room and moved quickly to the bed, picking up the letters and skimming through them. "You've been snooping in my library," he whispered. "Why?" Compassion had left his eyes and was suddenly replaced with anger.

Skylar swallowed hard. "I didn't realize the library was off limits," she justified.

"It isn't off limits, but my grandfather's things are." He shook the papers at her. "Are you happy now?" He was visibly irritated, as he picked up his grandfather's Bible, shoved the papers inside and slammed it down atop the dresser. "My grandfather's papers are off limits," he seethed. "Do you understand me, Ms. Wilson? Off limits!"

So, it's back to Ms. Wilson instead of Skylar.
"I'm sorry," she stammered.

"His papers are no one's business!" His expression was rage filled. "This is none of your business, you got it?"

Ernie tapped twice and then walked in. "I heard yelling in here. Everything okay?"

Skylar didn't say a word. What could she say? She was left absolutely speechless by Braznovich's reaction.

"Everything's fine," Braznovich barked, storming into the bathroom, slamming the door and then turning on the shower.

She could feel Ernie's studying gaze. "A lover's quarrel or something I need to know?"

Tears dripped from Skylar's chin. "Probably something you should know, but he's going to have to be the one to tell you," she said softly. "Can we switch rooms tonight?" She knew she was asking a lot, as trading rooms would mean that he and Braznovich would have to sleep in the same bed. Realizing it was rude of her to ask two grown men to squish into one bed, albeit a king size, she shook her head. "Never mind, I'll just crash on the couch."

"No," Ernie blurted, holding up his hand to indicate Skylar should halt. "He'll just carry your sorry ass back upstairs and none of us will get any sleep. I'll switch rooms. Maybe I can calm him down and get him to talk."

"Thank you," Skylar uttered.

"Can you give me a hint as to what upset him?" Ernie asked.

"Something about his grandfather..." her voice cracked. "That's all I should say." She crept down the hall into Ernie's room and closed the door behind her. Once she was tucked beneath the sheets, she buried her face in the pillow and wept.

CHAPTER 20

Skylar waited until she heard Ernie and Braznovich descend the staircase to the main level and then she sneaked into the master suite, showered and dressed in her new panties, Lucky Brand jeans and blue cashmere sweater. She dried her hair, applied some eye liner, lipstick, blush and mascara and then stood back from the mirror and took in her reflection. Her eyes were puffy and red from crying and her cheeks were sunken in. She was beginning to look as malnourished as most of the people at P3.

By the time Skylar came downstairs, Greg, Ernie and Braznovich were already sipping coffee around the kitchen table. "We saved you some eggs," Greg said. "They're in the oven warming."

"Thanks," Skylar mumbled and retrieved the plate of eggs without making eye contact with Braznovich.

"Hurry and eat," Braznovich said, rising from his chair and rinsing his coffee cup. "Then meet me in the barn."

That's it?! No I'm sorry for being such a jerk last night? No explanation or acknowledgment whatsoever? Anger boiled in her gut.

Braznovich left the kitchen just as Skylar sat down with her eggs and coffee. A lump formed in her throat and drove away what little appetite she had, so she pushed her plate to the side, picked up her coffee cup, blew on the top of it and sipped it carefully. "Why does he want me to go to the barn?" Skylar asked Ernie.

Ernie shrugged. "But if he told you to go, you should go."

Skylar rolled her eyes. Who does he think he is, bossing her around after he treated her so poorly last night?

"I know what you're thinking," Ernie nudged her. "But if you don't go, you'll make it worse."

"Worse?" Skylar sarcastically repeated. "How could things be any worse?"

"You could be in jail," Greg interjected. "I'm just sayin'."

"I'm finishing my coffee and then I'm leaving," Skylar said flatly.

"And going where?" Ernie uttered. "There's a warrant out for your arrest. You're wanted for questioning in four murders. You take off from here and you're as good as dead. Let me paint a clear picture for you, these cops, the ones on the P3 payroll, they're going to shoot first and ask later. They don't care about justice, they care about the P3 agenda." Skylar squirmed beneath Ernie's piercing stare.

"Fine," Skylar sighed. "I'll go to the barn."

"That-a girl," Ernie grinned. "I knew you'd see the light."

"But I'm still pissed about how he treated me last night," Skylar blurted, shoving a fork full of eggs into her mouth and then storming across the family room and out the sliding door.

Greg shook his head side-to-side. "The Wilson girls are fiery," he said.

"I bet you miss that," Ernie grinned.

"I sure do."

Skylar walked across the deck, down three giant log steps, around the small pond and toward the barn. The large barn doors were closed so she made her way around the structure to the right until she found another door. Just as she was about to knock, Braznovich opened it and ushered her inside. His face was stern and his eyes, cold, making Skylar's defenses leap alive. She crossed her arms. After all,

what had she done to warrant his anger? *Nothing!*
Her subconscious screamed. *I've done nothing wrong!
All I did was search for information about P3. What's
so wrong with that?! HE was the one withholding
information.*

"I want to show you something," he said,
interrupting her thoughts. Like the house, the barn
was larger on the inside than it outwardly appeared,
and beautiful. It was made of the same logs as the
house, had a large, antler chandelier hanging from
the center of the ceiling, and a loft that held shelves
of books instead of bales of hay. The floor was made
of pale, polished wood, and Skylar noticed
immediately that the only thing this barn was lacking
were windows. A small sky light at the very top of the
ceiling was the only natural light source, but
surprisingly it illumed the entire room. Along the
wall to the right sat five horse stalls, but no horses. In
fact, the stalls were so clean Skylar wondered if a
horse had ever set foot inside. Along the wall to the
left sat four Harley Davidson motorcycles, and
directly ahead was a shiny, black Lamborghini that
looked like it belonged on a showroom floor. Skylar's
mouth fell open.

"This is the barn?" She mumbled.

"Yep."

"*Your* barn?" She asked, wondering mostly
about the Lamborghini and the Harleys.

"Is there a problem, Ms. Wilson?" He feigned
nonchalance.

Skylar ran her fingers softly over the seat of
one of the Harleys. "Do you ride?"

Braznovich smiled and Skylar noted that his
eyes lit up like a little kid. "I do," he said. "Or I used
to." He patted the seat. "I haven't had a lot of time
lately."

"Do you miss it?"

"I do," he sighed. "It's what you would call my
escape."

"And the Lamborghini?" She asked, walking next to it and gently touching the side of the car. He was obviously wealthier than she imagined. Way wealthier. "The P.I. business is more lucrative than I realized."

"My business does alright," he acknowledged, "but the Harleys, the Lamborghini and the cabin were gifted to me from my grandfather."

"I thought you said he was preacher?" Skylar was confused, as she knew most small town preachers didn't earn the kind of money needed to purchase expensive motorcycles and cars.

"He was. The money came from my grandmother's side." Braznovich's lips curved into a slight grin when he spoke of his grandmother. "My grandmother was very good friends with the Waltons."

Skylar could feel her eyeballs widen. "As in Sam Walton, founder of Wal-Mart?"

"The one and only. Sam's sister and my grandmother were very close, and needless to say, Sam Walton took good care of his friends and family."

"Wow," she mouthed almost inaudibly.

"Talk about good people," Braznovich's smile filled his entire face. "They don't make kinder, more genuine folks than people like the Waltons."

"I've heard that about them," Skylar said. "But to give your grandmother so much mon..."

Braznovich cut her off. "Let's just say that people who held Wal-Mart stock in the very beginning, benefited greatly." He gave Skylar a wink. "Besides, my grandfather also made some wise investments through the years. He sure liked his stocks," Braznovich ran his hand alongside the top of the Lamborghini.

"This is my bat mobile." He beamed and Skylar laughed.

"You really are Batman. Do you ever drive it?" She asked because it looked like it had never left the showroom.

"I've driven her only once," he sighed. "She's an investment."

"Don't cars de-value once you drive them off the lot?"

Braznovich smirked, and Skylar suddenly felt foolish. "Yes, most cars lose their value as soon as they leave the lot, but this baby is a mint condition 1964 Lamborghini 350GT. There were only one hundred and twenty of these models manufactured worldwide. It's worth more today than when I got it."

Taking Skylar's arm, he led her away from the car and into the last horse stall, opening the gate and closing it behind her. He bent down near the center of the floor and pushed a tiny button located in the crevice of two pieces of wood flooring. A panel of boards dropped slightly and slid sideways, beneath the floor, revealing what looked like a giant safe. It had a keypad on top and Braznovich stooped down and punched in a sequence of numbers. With a loud click, the door unlocked and slid sideways, revealing a metal ladder which descended approximately nine feet into complete darkness. Braznovich climbed onto the ladder. "Follow me," he ordered.

Trepidation filled her, but curiosity won, and Skylar turned around, lowered herself backwards into the hole and down the ladder. With only three rungs remaining, Braznovich reached up and grabbed her waist. "Let go. I've got you," he said, his voice direct and forceful.

"I'm capable of climbing down a ladder, Mr. Braznovich," she gritted, over-emphasizing the mister in his name. After all, last night he reverted back to calling her Ms. Wilson instead of Skylar, so she thought, out of sarcastic spite, she'd return the favor.

"Release your grip, Ms. Wilson, or I'll swat that sweet ass right here," his tone was unwavering and Skylar wasn't sure how to respond. Was this a real threat? Surely not, and she wasn't going to let him off the hook so easily. He was downright mean to her last night and the last thing she was going to do was plunge herself right back into his arms. She gripped the ladder rung tighter.

"I can climb down the ladder by myself," she said sharply. The words were barely out of her mouth when she felt the sting of his slap on her bottom. "Ow," she gasped. Before she could say anything more, he slapped her bottom again, this time a little harder.

"Release your grip and lean backwards," he said again.

"No!" Skylar retorted angrily. This had now become a battle of wills.

"It's going to hurt a lot more when I pull those jeans down," he warned.

He wouldn't! Would he?

With one hand already around her waist, he was able to quickly unfasten the button on her jeans. "Are you going to let go, or are these coming down?" He tugged on her jeans.

"Fine!" Skylar gritted her teeth and let go of the rung, falling backwards into his muscular arms.

"You are a stubborn woman," he winced.

"And you're bossy," she quipped.

He laughed out loud and then took several steps when Skylar noticed a sloshing sound. "Are you standing in water?"

"Yes, Ms. Wilson, I'm standing in a foot and a half of water, which is why I didn't want you to climb all the way down."

She suddenly felt flush with foolishness. *Why didn't he just tell me that? Here he was trying to help me and I thought he was being a jerk!* "I'm sorry," she said, wrapping her arms around his neck as he sloshed through the water.

"We'll deal with your stubborn disobedience later," he said firmly and trudged forward.

What did that mean? She decided to momentarily dismiss the thought. "Are we in a sewer pipe?"

"Similar piping, but this isn't sewage. It's rain water that's leaked in." He was breathing heavy. "I need to adjust you higher, over my shoulder, so I can use my hands to open the next door."

Before Skylar could question or comment, he lifted her higher and flipped her over his shoulder, so that her hands dangled by his backside. She winced as his shoulder dug into her hip bone. She heard him fumbling with what sounded like another combination lock, then a door slid open and he maneuvered them through, closing it quickly behind them.

Skylar noticed that the sloshing sound had stopped. "Is the water gone?"

"Yes, there's a draining system that keeps the water from entering this room."

"Can you put me down now?" She asked sassily.

Braznovich paused momentarily and then issued another swat to her bottom.

"Ow!" She yelped. "What was that for?"

"For not listening. For being sassy. For snooping around. Should I go on?" His tone was no longer angry, but carried a twinge of amusement. Sliding her off of his shoulder, he set her down in front of him. It was pitch black. "Don't move," he ordered. "I'm going to turn on the lights."

She heard his footsteps lead away and within several seconds the room illumed with a soft light. Skylar squinted as her eyes adjusted, taking in her new surroundings. Concrete walls, bunk beds, shelves of clothing and canned goods, a generator, flashlights, camping lanterns, first aid supplies and several guns, ranging from shot guns to hand guns. "What is this place?" She gasped. "Is it a bomb shelter?"

"Sort of," Braznovich said, raising his eyebrows. "It's more like a P3 shelter."

He walked to a two feet by two feet sized safe that sat on one of the shelves, worked the combination and opened the door. Inside was a stack of folders, notebooks and loose leaf papers. Braznovich stepped aside and motioned Skylar to come near. "These are my grandfather's notes on P3. This is what you were searching for in the library."

Skylar couldn't believe her eyes and she couldn't wait to dive into his notes. "You're grandfather built this shelter?"

Braznovich nodded. "He was convinced that Maxwell Sagan was the Anti-Christ and that P3 would usher in the end times, killing more Christians than Hitler killed Jews." His eyes were suddenly filled with an emotion Skylar couldn't define. It was something between sadness and grief. "My grandfather's obsession with P3 was very personal..."

"I know," Skylar said softly. "I read the letter from Goodwin's wife. Your grandfather and Goodwin must have been very close."

Braznovich exhaled. "Goodwin's death started everything, at least for my grandfather, but that wasn't what drove his obsession against the P3 movement." He walked over to the bunk beds and sat down on the bottom bunk, careful not to hit his head on the bed above. "After my grandfather received Helen Goodwin's letter, he took my grandmother with him to the P3 prayer room. He wanted to see for himself what went on there, and he immediately sensed that something was wrong. He used to say there was evil a foot at P3." Braznovich ran his hand quickly through his hair and looked as if he were replaying a memory in his mind. "He interviewed every pastor from the Goodwin Doctrine and hundreds of others who had left the movement. His opposition to P3 became widely known and Sagan threatened that God would punish him if he didn't stop."

"So, did he stop?" Skylar sat down next to Braznovich.

"No, he was stronger than me," he sighed. "He never gave up."

Skylar didn't know what to say. Was Braznovich admitting that he was wrong in quitting? Was he sorry he hadn't pursued saving Jonathan? "Why *did* you quit?" Skylar tentatively asked, afraid to anger him, but wanting to understand his reasons.

"Because these people are dangerous, Skylar," he blurted emphatically. "If you mess with them, you get hurt, and for what? If Sagan is the Anti-Christ, then he's going to do what he's predestined to do and no one can stop him. Not Goodwin. Not my grandfather. Not you and not me."

"And if he's not the Anti-Christ?" Skylar asked.

He placed his hand on her knee, his expression softening. "I quit because I didn't want anyone else I cared about to get hurt."

"Anyone else? Who got hurt?"

Braznovich cleared his throat. "Shortly after Sagan threatened my grandfather, their house caught on fire and my grandmother was killed."

"She was killed in the fire?" Skylar exclaimed and Braznovich nodded. *That's awful!*

"Fire fighters confirmed that the fire was a result of arson, but no one was ever convicted."

"Your grandfather got out alive?" She asked.

"He was away at the time, meeting with the Assembly of Presbyters, ironically meeting about the P3 corruption. He knew Sagan was behind the attack, but he could never prove it. It was all speculation."

Speculation. That had to be the most frustrating word in the English language. She placed her hand on Braznovich's knee and gave it a tender squeeze. "I'm so sorry," she said softly.

"I watched P3 create a rage in my grandfather that eventually destroyed him. His hatred of the movement fueled his desire to rescue everyone who had fallen under Sagan's deception. 'The Great Deceiver,' he used to call Sagan."

"Your grandfather was a wise man," Skylar said.

Braznovich shook his head. "No, a wise man would have realized that you can't free people who won't admit they're enslaved, and he would have walked away."

Skylar entwined her fingers with his and stroked the top of his thumb. "I think maybe your grandfather was trying to remove the blinders so that the people in P3 would be able to realize they were enslaved and want to be freed."

"But at what cost?" Braznovich released her hand and stood up. "Why put your loved ones at risk on the off chance that you may or may not help some stranger see the light?"

"Because Maxwell Sagan has destroyed hundreds of families and thousands of lives and he'll hurt countless more if no one stands against him," Skylar felt her defenses rising.

"Standing against a man like Sagan is asking for trouble." Braznovich looked at Skylar and tucked a stray piece of hair behind her ear. "It's not worth the risk."

"If even one person is freed from his deception, I'd say it is worth it."

"Not if ten die in the process," he argued. "And not if you're one of the ones that get hurt or worse..." His voice trailed off.

"I'll be fine." She feigned nonchalance, not wanting him to know how scared she really felt.

He took her face in both hands. "You can't control Maxwell Sagan. He's already attempted to blow you up and succeeded at killing four people and making the world believe you did it." His eyes were piercingly stern. "I don't want to see anything happen to you."

Skylar's heart leapt into a wild, rhythmic beat. *He cares about me, deep down, in a real way. He cares about me.* She couldn't stop the smile from stretching across her lips.

"It's not funny, Skylar, this man wants you dead."

Skylar lowered her eyes to the floor, letting his words sink in. Was he right? She knew Maxwell wanted her out of the way, but did he really want her dead?

"You're not untouchable," Braznovich continued, "and when you are careless about your own safety, you hurt the people that care about you." He pulled her chin up so that her eyes met his gaze. "People like me."

Braznovich leaned forward and placed his lips, ever so gently against hers, leaving a light, lingering kiss. She leaned into him, sending an obvious signal that she wanted more, but this wasn't the time.

"Let me ask you something. Do you believe he's the Anti-Christ?"

"No," Braznovich answered flatly. "Not a chance."

"Then you have to believe that he can be stopped," Skylar's voice sounded surprisingly optimistic even to her. "You have to believe that if we find enough evidence against him, he can be stopped, right?"

"Maxwell's resources are unlimited and his pockets are deep, deeper than you know. He has some of the world's most powerful men eating out of his hands, and P3 has grown into a worldwide brand." Braznovich shook his head. "Our odds at beating him aren't good."

Skylar leaned her head against his shoulder. "We have truth on our side, God's truth and you know what they say? The truth will set you free."

He wrapped his arm around her. "I hope so."

CHAPTER 21

By the time Skylar and Braznovich returned from the barn with all of his grandfather's research notes, Ernie had left to go to the grocery store and Greg was back on the couch, scanning surveillance feed. He had set up more computers, so the entire coffee table was covered in monitors and wires. Skylar sat down on the couch with the pile of research notes, opened a manila folder from the top of the pile, and took out a photograph of what she guessed was Braznovich's grandmother's burial ceremony. A younger Braznovich stood next to a man she presumed to be his grandfather, Franklin; and they were looking toward a casket, which sat next to a large, rectangular hole in the ground. The casket was covered in flowers, mainly white lilies and white daisies. A crowd of people, thirty or more, were gathered behind Braznovich and his grandfather and they were all dressed in black.

Greg exhaled an annoyed sigh, drawing Skylar's attention from the photograph.

"How is Tess?" She asked. "Is she still in the apartment?"

"Yep," Greg answered. "She's on monitor five." He pointed to the screen at the end of the table and Skylar noted, in typical, anal Greg fashion, he had numbered and labeled each monitor using yellow sticky pad notes. Monitor five read '5 Tess.'

"I like your little labels," Skylar teased and Greg flipped her off. "Ooh, somebody's testy," she laughed.

"I don't know why you're not testy," he snapped. "Have you forgotten what's going on?'

Skylar's smile faded quickly as reality smacked her in the face. "What are you so pissed about?"

"I don't know. Maybe it's the fact that your picture is plastered across all major networks and the police are interrogating anyone you've ever known, including my elderly parents," he barked.

"Oh no, I'm so sorry, Greg," Skylar said. "Are your parents okay?"

"No, they're being harassed by the police and my mom is in tears, thinking I'm in some kind of trouble too."

Skylar's eyes widened. "You didn't tell them where you are, did you?"

"Of course not, but I'm going to have to tell them something soon. I'm worried my mom's gonna have a heart attack." He exhaled an exasperated sigh and returned to clicking the keys on his keyboard.

"Has anything been going on with Tess?" She tried changing the subject.

"She sleeps a lot," he answered flatly. "In fact, she sleeps enough for all of us."

"She's probably weak from fasting again," Skylar rolled her eyes. Fasting was the source of many arguments through the years. It wasn't that Skylar didn't believe in fasting; after all, the Bible said to fast and pray. Skylar just didn't believe in leaders invoking mandatory fasts on their congregations through tactics of guilt and peer pressure. She believed fasting was a very personal act of obedience to God and that God would speak to a person's heart if they were to fast while seeking Him. Tess had gone on several forty day fasts led by Maxwell Sagan himself, and each time she and Skylar ended up arguing. Skylar would tell her it wasn't healthy and Tess would balk in defense of Maxwell's ultra-Godly plan. In the end Skylar's words always fell short.

"I gotta tell you, Skylar, I don't know why we're trying to rescue her," Greg belted. "She doesn't look like she even wants to be rescued."

Skylar stared at monitor five, watching Tess sleep. She looked so peaceful when she was sleeping. "She text me for help, that's why." With a lump rising in her throat, Skylar stared at the monitor and silently prayed for Tess. Suddenly, two women entered Tess's room and Skylar leapt up with excitement. "Who are these girls? Have you seen them before?" Her shriek drew Greg's attention to monitor five.

"Oh, that's Hannah and Caroline. I think they've been assigned to watch her."

"How do you know?

"Late last night, when I was scanning archived feed from Tess's apartment, I watched Maxwell and Saul enter her room, pray with her, take communion and right after that Hannah and Caroline showed up and haven't left her alone since."

"So you think they've been assigned to help her?"

"Yeah, if 'help her' is code for watch her like a hawk," he sarcastically quipped.

"Do we know anything about Hannah and Caroline?" Are they leaders? Did they know Lexi or Ema? Could they be spies? Skylar licked her lips. If she knew if one of them could be trusted, maybe she could somehow get them a message to take to Tess.

"They share an apartment, but they're rarely in it. Hannah's the redhead and Caroline's the blonde. If you hit control HC on monitor three, you'll be able to see the live feed of their apartment," Greg explained.

Skylar hit control HC and took a quick peek into their apartment. It looked very similar to Tess's only theirs had two beds instead of one. It was as uninviting as everything else she'd seen on the P3 campus. Stark, white, plain. *Maxwell obviously doesn't spend any of his millions on interior design.* She grunted and then felt Braznovich's hands on the back of her shoulders. He had sneaked behind her without her noticing. "You're supposed to be digging through my grandfather's notes," he scolded, "not conniving a way to reach Tess."

How did he know what I was thinking? "But if one of these girls, either Hannah or Caroline, can be trusted, maybe we could get word to Tess and..."

"No, Skylar," Braznovich interrupted. "You're not talking to anyone." He said it in a way that let her know there was no room for objection.

Skylar scowled and his grip on her shoulders tightened. Leaning down, he placed his lips next to her ear. "If I'm not mistaken your jeans are still unbuttoned," he whispered so only she could hear. Glancing down at her waist, she quickly realized he was right. She had forgotten to fasten them after he had threatened to paddle her in the barn. "Let it be a reminder of what can happen when you stubbornly refuse to follow instructions," he smirked and she flushed. Part of her thought he wouldn't dare and the other part was curious to find out if he actually would.

He and gave her shoulders a tender squeeze. "Remember, talking to anyone at P3 can put their life in danger." He planted a tender kiss on the top of her head. "I don't want to see anymore dead bodies being pulled from a lake."

Skylar inwardly cringed as Braznovich turned and walked toward the loft steps. She knew he didn't mean to hurt her, but his words pierced deep into her heart, reminding her that Ema, Mrs. Wright and even Officer Burnes might still be alive if she had stayed away. *Did I get Lexi killed too?* She pondered and felt a rush of guilt. It was probable that Skylar had been seen talking to Lexi in the Prayer Room and again after the car bomb; but had anyone seen her and Ernie witness Lexi planting the flash drive in the bench at Kernodle Lake? *Surely not,* she told herself, but her pulse quickened as fear once again crept into her thoughts. If Lexi had been seen planting the flash drive, and Ernie had been seen retrieving it; then someone knew they had the drive.

Skylar felt the color drain from her face. What if someone was one step ahead of them? What if they had been followed? Leaping from the couch, she raced upstairs and into the master suite where she found Braznovich outside on the balcony, talking on his cell phone. She stood in the doorway and watched him. He looked handsome and relaxed, leaning his elbows against the railing, completely unaware that she was drinking him in. He had changed out of his khaki's, probably because they had gotten all wet in the barn, and was now wearing a pair of faded Levi's and a black t-shirt. His biceps bulged from the confines of his shirt sleeves and Skylar was suddenly flushed with a desire that chased away the fear that had brought her upstairs in the first place. She swallowed hard and let her eyes traverse his body.

"I've got it under control," he spoke into the phone. "She isn't going anywhere."

Who isn't going anywhere? What does he have under control? Skylar's ears perked, trying to fine tune her eavesdropping skills.

"Trust me," he exhaled. "She doesn't suspect a thing. I've got her busy searching through grandfather's notes."

Curiosity was killing her and Skylar crept closer.

"I'll keep her distracted; you just get everything else set in motion. I want to be done with this as soon as possible. She's not exactly easy to get along with," he muttered. "Yeah, stubborn as hell is an understatement." Braznovich stood up straight and ran his fingers through his hair. "She drives me crazy."

He's talking about me, Skylar gasped. *He gave ME his grandfather's notes to read. He called ME stubborn when we were downstairs, just a few minutes ago.* Skylar's stomach hollowed and all of a sudden she felt as if she wanted to burst into tears. *Did he sleep with me just to keep me distracted?* Her mind reeled. *Distracted from what? What is he setting in motion?* Skylar's hands began to tremble and she suddenly fought to catch her breath. She quietly backed up and stepped inside.

Hearing Braznovich wrap up the call, she rushed into the bathroom, closed and locked the door.

Seconds later Braznovich knocked. "Skylar? Are you in there?"

Oh, now it's Skylar again. What happened to Ms. Wilson? Skylar closed the toilet seat and plunked down. She didn't know what to think, much less what to say. Was it possible that Braznovich was a P3 sympathizer? *NO!* And what about Ernie? Could either of them be trusted?

"Are you okay?" He asked, tapping on the door again.

"I'm...um...I'm not feeling well," Skylar uttered. "I'm sick to my stomach."

"Do you need help? Can I get you anything?" He called through the door.

"No," she answered flatly. "I'll be fine." She wanted him to go away, to leave her alone so she could sort through her thoughts. She wanted to talk to Greg. If there was anyone who could be trusted as a solid hater of P3, it was Greg; but how could she talk to him without Braznovich overhearing? "I'll meet you downstairs," she said quietly, hoping he would take the hint to leave.

"Okay," he conceded. "I'm going down to the library. Meet me down there when you feel up to it."

"Alright," Skylar said.

Waiting until she heard him walk away, Skylar opened the bathroom door, tiptoed across the bedroom and listened to make sure he went downstairs. When she heard him tell Greg that he was going down to the library, Skylar closed the bedroom door and locked it. Her heart was racing. It was amazing how one simple conversation could change everything. Only moments before, she had been lusting to be in his arms, and now her only thought was to escape and get as far away from Braznovich as possible. She stepped out onto the balcony and inhaled deeply, trying to force herself to calm down. *Should I sneak downstairs and talk to Greg?* She wondered. *Then maybe he and I can leave together?* Skylar's stomach trembled and her lip quivered as she fought back the urge to cry. Staring out at the barn, an idea popped into her head. There was a way she could sneak out, get to a payphone and call Greg on his cell to explain. That way, Greg could remain on the inside and keep tabs on what Ernie and Braznovich were up to.

Skylar hurried inside to where her purse and laptop sat on the floor next to the nightstand. She flipped open her laptop with the flash drive still connected, and copied all the files to her hard drive. Then she emailed those files to Greg with a note that read: KEEP THESE FOR EVIDENCE. While the files were uploading, Skylar dug through her purse, pulling out her driver's license, credit card and a ten dollar bill. It was the only cash she had. Remembering Braznovich's warning that the police were monitoring everything, she dropped the credit card back into her purse. It would be too tempting to use if she had it with her. Ten dollars wasn't much. She clicked SEND on the email and shoved the flash drive into the front pocket of her jeans. Then seeing Braznovich's wallet sitting on top the dresser, she grabbed it, flipped it open and removed the wad of cash. He had two hundred dollars, all in twenties. Skylar took one hundred dollars and placed it back in his wallet, and then shoved the other hundred dollars into her pocket with her ten dollar bill and her driver's license. *We'll consider this payment for services rendered,* her mind sarcastically justified, with a stab of pain that stung her heart. She liked him, maybe even came close to loving him. He was definitely someone she could have fallen in love with, but now she realized she meant nothing to him. It was all an act. A game. An assignment to keep her distracted. A twinge of heartache gripped her, but Skylar pushed the emotion down. There was no time to cry over what might have been.

Aware that Braznovich would eventually come to check on her, she rushed onto the patio, swung her leg over the railing at the far corner and shimmied down the corner post. She winced as a splinter dug into her left thumb. Once her feet hit the ground, she ran toward the barn and slipped inside the side door. Taking a second to catch her breath, she dug her fingernail into her thumb, just below the splinter, and pushed it upward and out. The pain stopped the moment the splinter was out and Skylar shoved her thumb into her mouth to get rid of the tiny droplet of blood.

Skylar paused as she beheld the breathtaking Lamborghini. Was she really about to steal his car? Her heart raced. She'd never stolen anything before. Opening the door, she reached inside, feeling for the ignition. No keys. She searched the entire car, under the floor mats, beneath the seats, in the glove box, everywhere, but there were no keys; not even a hide-a-key underneath. Panic gripped her. What was she going to do now? Suddenly, Skylar turned and faced the Harleys. It had been a long time since she had been on a bike and she had never ridden one this big. In fact, she had only driven a motorcycle a couple times in college, and it was a small Yamaha. If memory served, the last time she was on a bike, she crashed it into a parked car. *Are there any keys?* She searched the first bike and immediately found the key in the seat pack. Her hands trembled as she took it out and placed it in the ignition. A perfect fit. Skylar swallowed hard.

"Okay," she sighed aloud, "now I need a helmet." She remembered seeing a shelf of helmets in one of the horse stalls. She tried on the first two, but they were way too big. The third one was black and shiny and a better fit. She slipped it on and fastened it around her chin.

The large barn door worked on a remote, like a garage door, and Skylar found the button on the side of the wall next to the door. As the door slowly raised, Skylar lifted the kickstand and pushed the bike out of the barn. It was heavy and she had to put all of her weight into moving it. Once outside, she pushed the bike down the gravel drive until she could no longer see the house through the trees, and then straddled the Harley and turned the key. *Here we go!* The engine roared beneath her, and Skylar gasped at the sheer power. Taking a deep breath, she revved the engine, pushed forward off the ground, lifting her feet and thrusting the bike into forward motion. Panic gripped her as she felt the raw power of the beast between her legs; and she tightened her palms around the handlebars. Thundering down the rest of the gravel drive, Skylar turned right on the outer road and headed back toward the Missouri state line. She knew exactly where to go, and told herself that upon arriving, she would call Greg and tell him everything.

Tears stung her eyes as she roared down the two lane highway, thankful that few drivers were on the road. The longer she rode, the more comfortable she became with the bike and finally began to relax her white knuckled grip. As she passed a tiny gas station, Skylar wanted to stop for a drink of water and to use the restroom, but she feared Braznovich may have already discovered that she was gone and would be hot on her trail. It wouldn't take him long to notice that she had stolen one of his Harleys since she wasn't able to close the barn door behind her. Then, turning onto a dirt road, heading east, memories of the last time she had been on this road flood her mind. It was almost two years ago and she had driven away from his house in a hurry; riddled with guilt and ashamed of her actions. His name was Rod and he was her rebound guy, well, at least for one night. After being dumped by the man she swore was Mr. Right, Skylar drowned her heartache in bourbon at a local bar and woke up the next morning in Rod's bed. It was not one of her prouder moments. Now, she impressed herself by remembering the way to his house, even though she couldn't remember his last name.

Skylar pulled up in front of the two-story, old Victorian framed house, covered in chipped country blue paint with a white, wrap around porch that looked like it was ready to fall off. Killing the engine, she removed her helmet and took a deep breath. She never thought she'd see Rod again, much less be pulling up to his house on a stolen bike to ask for help. Suffice it to say, she had hit an all-time low. She climbed off the bike, set the helmet on top of the seat, and then flipped her head forward and back up again to free her hair from the helmet-head feeling. When she looked up, Rod was standing on the porch, staring at her. He was bare footed, wearing a pair of faded jeans, ripped at the knees and no shirt. He held a black mug in his hand and looked somehow different than she remembered, although her memory had been formed through a drunken haze. She recalled that he was tall and slender, but now he looked more filled out, tan and muscular and his chest and arms were covered with tattoos. His hair was dark and long and he wore it pulled back into a low pony tail.

Skylar took one step forward. "Rod?" She tentatively asked. "Do you...I mean, um... I'm sure you don't remember me..." she stuttered, suddenly overcome with nerves.

"Oh, I remember you, sweet thing." He took a swig from his mug. "I'm surprised you remember me the way you shot out of here that morning." His ice blue eyes pierced through her and his tone and expression were unreadable. Was he angry? Was he hurt?

Skylar swallowed and licked her lips. "That was a bad time in my life."

"Worse than right now?"   He asked with an expression revealing that he knew she was in some kind of trouble.

"No."

"Nice ride," Rod said, changing the subject and motioning toward the Harley.

"I stole it," Skylar blurted, unsure why she confessed. The words just popped out before she could stop them.

His lips curled into a slight grin. "Well, then, I guess we should hide it."

Skylar smiled and exhaled in relief. He was going to help her. At the very least, she could use the bathroom, get some water, call Greg and figure out what to do without worrying about the police or Braznovich.

Rod moved the Harley to a shed that sat behind the house and then escorted Skylar inside through the back door, which opened into the kitchen. The walls were painted light blue with a peeling floral wallpaper border around the top; and the floor was old white linoleum, worn and speckled by yellow and brown stains. A square, two-seater, silver metal table sat against the far wall, topped with newspapers and Busch beer cans, some of which were crushed.

"You want a beer?" Rod offered, opening the fridge and pulling out two cans.

"Why not," Skylar mumbled, and took the beer. "Thanks."

She followed him down the hallway which emptied into the family room. It was covered in dark blue shag carpet. A brown leather couch, patched with duct tape, sat behind a light wood coffee table and a big screen television stood against the far wall, next to a large window that overlooked the front porch. The television looked like the only modern addition to the home. Skylar scanned the room, her eyes instantly fixating on two guns that were lying on the coffee table.

Rod sat down on the couch and crossed his bare feet atop it. "Sit. Let's have a chat," he said, taking a long swig of his beer.

Skylar sat on the opposite end of the couch. There was so much to tell, but where should she begin? She took a sip of beer and tried to think of a way to sum everything up. "It's a long story," she began. "My sister is in danger..."

Twenty minutes later Skylar stopped talking and met his steely glare. She couldn't tell what he was thinking. Did he believe her? She knew how crazy it sounded. He probably thought she was off her rocker. Had coming here been a mistake? Would Rod turn her into the police? Without a word, he rose from the couch, disappeared down the hallway and returned a few seconds later carrying two beers. He handed one to Skylar and then plunked down on the couch with a heavy sigh.

"That's quite a story," he said.

Her eyes widened. "It's true," she said pointedly. "I swear."

He gave a nod. "I believe you. I mean, I believe your sister is in P3 and I believe you didn't kill anybody."

"But?"

Rod abruptly stood up. "But, I have something to show you."

She followed him back into the kitchen and through a door that led to the basement. The staircase was wooden and narrow, without a railing. Upon reaching the bottom, he pulled a string and one light bulb illumed the room in dim light. Tables were set up along the walls, each one covered with guns, ammunition and explosive devices. Taped to the walls above the tables were newspaper articles, pictures and documents all relating to P3. Skylar felt her eyeballs bulging from her head. She couldn't hide her surprise.

"What is all this?" She moved from table to table, scanning the articles, taking it all in. There were pictures of Ema and Mrs. Wright and Officer Burnes. Skylar gasped when she came face to face with a picture of herself and the word WANTED written in big, black, bold lettering across the bottom. "You already knew everything I told you," she uttered beneath her breath.

"Well, I didn't know you were clean," he remarked, picking up a 357 magnum, slamming the clip into place and holding it out for Skylar to take. "Try this on for size."

Skylar took the gun. It fit nicely in her hand. "Why?"

"You said your .22 was stolen. It's a loaner."

She breathed a sigh of relief. He believed her and he wasn't going to turn her in. "Thanks, Rod," she spoke softly. "This means more than you know. I don't have many people I can trust."

"Let me ask you something. Do you believe in all that prophecy crap?" Rod studied her.

"I believe God can and probably does give people prophetic words and visions, but I don't bclicve He's talking directly to anyone in the P3 organization. And I'd bet my life on the fact that Maxwell Sagan has NEVER heard directly from God."

A broad smile spread across his face, signaling that Skylar had answered to his liking. "Do you believe in fate?"

"I suppose so." Where was he going with this?

"You showing up on my doorstep is no coincidence. You are the confirmation I've been seeking."

"Confirmation?"

"Yep. Folks around these parts are done with this cult nonsense." He picked up a shot gun, peered through the scope, and pretended to take a shot. "It's taken over Kansas City, and we've got our own plans to take back our town. We're meeting tonight to finalize everything. They'll be excited to meet you."

"Why?"

"Sister to one of the up and coming leaders of the P3 movement…" He rubbed his hands greedily together. "Your reputation precedes you."

"What if your friends think I'm guilty of killing Mrs. Wright or Lexi or Officer Burnes?

"I'll set them straight. Besides, everyone knows you didn't kill Officer Burnes," Rod said matter-of-factly.

"How do they know that?"

"Because we killed him."

Skylar gasped. "Why?"

"I told you, we're taking our town back, one-by-one if we have to. Burnes killed Mrs. Wright, so we killed Burnes."

CHAPTER 22

It was 8:00 p.m. and Rod's house was buzzing. He had set up folding chairs in the basement and it was now filled wall-to-wall with people. Most of them were Kansas City residents, tired of putting up with the corruption; but some were mourning parents from other towns, suffering from the same heartache Skylar felt over Tess. They had lost their loved ones to Maxwell Sagan's lies.

Rod introduced Skylar and told her story to the group, which applauded her tenacious desire to free her sister and vowed to help. Skylar then told them about Greg and how he had hacked into the P3 security system and was running up-to-date survcillance. Rod stood behind Skylar and placed his hands on her shoulders, addressing the group. "You can see that Skylar coming to us at this *precise* time is no coincidence."

Why the emphasis on this precise time? Skylar didn't understand.

"This Friday, we take down P3 and take our city back!" Rod hollered and the group erupted into cheers, throwing their fists into the air.

"What's this Friday?" Skylar asked, with an uncertain fear prickling up the back of her neck. Something wasn't right about this. Skylar sank into a folding chair and listened to their plan unfold.

"We've infiltrated the construction company that has been contracted for the next phase of building on the P3 campus. They're currently working on an apartment building on the east side of the complex." Rod pointed to several men that stood in the back of the basement. "Frank's the foreman," he said, pointing to a tall, dark haired man, who returned his introduction with a nod. "Mitch is second in command." Rod pointed to another man who raised his hand and gave a slight wave. "Then there's Andrew, George, Craig and Jason." Each man gave a nod toward Skylar. "They're all part of the construction crew."

"How did they get on the crew?" Skylar questioned.

"We've been planning our revenge for a couple of years now. See, folks around these parts aren't happy with what's happening at P3. Ema and Lexi aren't the first kids to end up dead. We're tired of Sagan walking around like he's some goddamned untouchable." Several people hooted and yelped in agreement. "So, when we got wind that P3 was taking bids for the next phase of build out, we made sure our men were hired." Rod grinned. "Sagan might have more resources, but we've got our share of connections." He spoke with a certain sense of pride. "And we're gonna show him just how touchable he really is." Rod gave her a wink. "That's a prophecy you can bank on." Everyone applauded.

"So, what's your plan?" Skylar asked.

"Friday evening we bring Armageddon to P3." The room filled with cheers again.

Armageddon? What does that mean? Skylar felt her breath catch in her chest. "What are you going to do?"

"Bring the fire of hell to Sagan," Rod said and everyone burst into cheers again.

"You're going to burn down the campus?" Skylar tried not to let shock or concern seep into her voice.

"We're not going to burn it down. We're gonna blow the mother up." Cheers erupted inside the room, as people applauded and threw their fists into the air. Skylar swallowed hard. This was unbelievable.

"How?" She asked.

"We're gonna start at the back of the campus, and one-by-one, blow up the buildings." Rod's steely blue eyes gleamed with revenge. "One-by-one."

Skylar's stomach twisted into knots. "What about all the people?"

"What about them?" Rod said.

"Yeah," a small, older woman yelled. "They made their bed, let them burn in it."

"See, that's the beauty of the plan. Maxwell installed an eight foot, electric fence around the perimeter of the campus, so the only way in or out is through the main building. We start the explosions in the back, forcing all the people to run toward the front, and then ..." Rod's voice tapered off and he made an exploding sound with his lips and gestured with his hands. "We blow up the Prayer Room and Sagan's office, both located in the main building..."

Where everyone will be congregating, trying to get out.

Skylar's mouth felt suddenly dry. These people were as radical as those at P3, only to the opposite extreme. She understood hating Maxwell. She understood wanting revenge for everyone he had corrupted, threatened, deceived and even killed. But this was going too far. Killing innocent people wasn't any different than what Maxwell was doing to them. Skylar froze, her heart pounding loudly in her ears. She couldn't tell them that she thought this was a bad idea. They might view her as being a P3 sympathizer and do God knows what to her. Turn her into the police? Give her back to Braznovich? Or worse? Skylar licked her lips, trying to generate saliva.

"How many people do you estimate will die?" Skylar asked.

"Hundreds," Frank, the foreman, said.

"If we're lucky!" Another man blurted from the crowd.

"What about Sagan?" Skylar asked.

"We figure Sagan will try to save himself, so we got some special snipers that will be stationed in the front to take him out the minute he makes a run for it."

"Looks like you've thought of everything," Skylar mumbled.

"Like I said, sweet thing, we've been planning this for a couple of years."

Skylar had an overwhelming urge to flee, but she knew she had to play her cards right. She needed Rod to trust her, to think she was on his side so that she could find out the exact location of each explosive device, report the information to Greg and hope that he could somehow get people off of the campus before the first blast. If he couldn't, at the very least, maybe he could get an anonymous tip to the police, who could notify Sagan and have the campus evacuated. Admittedly, Skylar wouldn't mind seeing the P3 compound go up in smoke; but she didn't want innocent lives taken. There was a big difference between hating someone and killing them. There was a big difference between blowing up buildings and murdering people. Skylar excused herself from the meeting, explaining that she hadn't been feeling well and needed some fresh air. As she climbed the basement staircase, Skylar's skin was clammy and her hands were trembling. She stepped outside the back door and inhaled the night air.

Her brain was on overload. She couldn't believe that Rod and his group appeared to take pride in the fact that they killed Officer Burnes. All the more reason she needed to behave as if she was on board with Rod's plan. If they killed a cop, killing her would be no problem at all.

Once everyone had gone home, Rod joined Skylar on the back steps and lit up a joint. He inhaled long and hard, and then extended it toward Skylar, offering her a hit. She shook her head. "I'm not feeling well," she said, feigning illness.

"Are you worried about Tess?"

His question caught her off guard. Was he testing her loyalty? Was he trying to read whether she would sabotage their plan in some way to save her sister? If she answered incorrectly, would he lock her up in the basement or turn her over to the police? Skylar felt her temperature rise and her face flush with fear.

"Um..." she stuttered and tucked a stray piece of hair behind her left ear. "She's my sister."

Rod nodded and took another hit. Exhaling above his head, he wrapped his large hand around the back of Skylar's neck and pulled her toward him. "If you want to save her, I'll help you, but we gotta keep it on the down low."

Skylar's eyes widened. Was he serious or was this just a test? He smiled and planted a kiss right in the middle of her lips. "Come inside. I want to show you something else." He turned and she followed him back through the kitchen, down the hallway and up the staircase which led to a small landing with three doors; two opened into bedrooms and one into a bathroom. The bathroom was situated between the bedroom doors. "Come in my room," he said, striding through the doorway to the left.

Skylar paused at the door. She had a vague recollection of their night together. It wasn't something she wanted to repeat. "Rod, I have a boyfriend," she lied.

"Disappointing," he sighed, "but not the reason I've asked you up here."

Her curiosity peaked. If he wasn't going to seduce her, why else would he led her to his bedroom? He flipped on the overhead light and she took two steps into the room. It was a mess, just as she remembered; just what you'd expect of a typical bachelor. She couldn't help comparing Rod, the typical bachelor, with Braznovich, the atypical, neat and tidy, control freak. The thought of him brought a twinge of guilt for having stolen his money and his bike, but she pushed it away. He deserved it. He lied

to her, used her and slept with her to keep her distracted. What kind of a person does that?
Someone secretly working for Sagan!

Rod plunked down on the bed, took another hit from his joint and pointed at the dresser. Skylar followed his finger to a framed picture setting on top of the dresser. It was of a young man, maybe in his early twenties. He had dark hair and blue eyes, just like Rod, except his hair was cut short. "Is this you when you were younger?" Skylar asked, picking up the frame and analyzing it closer.

"Nah," he shook his head and Skylar saw a sense of sadness shroud his face. "That's Lenny, my little brother."

"I didn't realize you had a brother." Skylar thought it odd that he kept an eight by ten framed picture of his brother on his dresser, but she didn't comment. To each his own. "Where does Lenny live?"

"He doesn't." Skylar looked up quickly and met Rod's glare. The sadness on his face morphed into anger and then bordered on rage. "He hasn't lived for two years, eleven months and twenty-five days."

But who's counting?

"This Friday will be the three year anniversary of his death." Rod leaned forward, took the frame from Skylar's hand and pulled her down next to him. He stared intently at Lenny's picture. "He was gonna be a lawyer. He was so goddamned smart. Sharp as a tack. He was gonna make something of himself. He was."

Skylar nodded, studying Rod's face, trying to fit the pieces together. It seemed to be no coincidence that blowing up the P3 campus was planned for the three year anniversary of Lenny's death. Skylar drew in a deep breath. "How did he die?"

"He flew too close to the flame." Rod shook his head. "He knocked on the gates of hell and the devil devoured him."

"How?" She placed her hand on Rod's knee. "How did the devil devour him?" Skylar could see Rod struggling with emotion. His lips tensed and he swallowed hard. "You can tell me," she persuaded.

He cleared his throat. "He was in his last semester of Journalism School at Mizzou and then he planned to go to Law School. He had already been accepted and everything. Lenny was the first in our family to go to college. I was real proud of him. Then, he got wind of P3 and he went there to interview Sagan. He went there to do a story." Rod abruptly stood up, opened his top dresser drawer and pulled out a newspaper. "It was one helluva piece he wrote," he said with pride in his voice. "After the article was printed, he started getting anonymous death threats. Three days later he was found dead in his apartment."

"I'm so sorry," Skylar whispered.

"We were gonna order an autopsy, but his body was accidentally cremated." Rod drew his fingers up to make quotation marks around the word accidentally.

"What?" Anger rose in Skylar's gut. "How can they accidentally cremate someone?"

Rod shrugged. "They said the paperwork got mixed up, but the truth is Sagan controls everyone in this town. Everyone." He sat back down on the bed, his shoulders slumping. "He paid them off. I know it."

"Were you ever able to prove it?"

"No. The police said we didn't have a case and coincidentally, the funeral director who signed off on the cremation was killed in a car accident days after Lenny died."

Maxwell really does get rid of every obstacle. Skylar sat in quiet disbelief. How many people has Maxwell murdered? In any case, she now understood why Rod had become a gun-toting radical, hell bent on blowing P3 up. She couldn't condone it, but she could certainly understand how he got here. If it had been Tess instead of Lenny, Skylar would probably feel the same way.

Placing Lenny's picture back on top of the dresser, Rod turned to Skylar. "I'll show you where you can sleep." He started for the hallway, but Skylar reached out and slid her hand into his, stopping him in his tracks.

"Thank you for telling me about your brother," she said softly, gazing up at him. "I understand now."

He gave her hand a quick squeeze and pulled her to her feet. "Let's get some sleep. Tomorrow we'll lay out a strategy on how to get Tess out before we destroy the complex." A part of her wanted to object, to point out that Tess wasn't the only person in need of rescuing; but somehow she knew her argument would fall on deaf ears. Besides, putting herself at risk wasn't going to save Tess, or anyone for that matter. She needed to play along and hope Greg could find a way to minimize the danger for everyone.

Keeping her hand in his, he led her across the hall and into the spare bedroom. "It ain't much, but it's a roof over your head."

Skylar surveyed the room. Small twin bed, covered in a solid blue quilt and a pillow with a floral sham. Light blue cotton curtains covered the window and a light oak nightstand sat next to the bed. A small lamp with a white, stained lampshade sat atop the nightstand. "It's perfect. Thank you."

"There's an extra toothbrush and some toothpaste in the bathroom drawer. I'll get you a change of clothes tomorrow."

They said goodnight and Rod left Skylar to her own thoughts. She locked the bedroom door, pulled the 357 magnum from the back of her jeans and set it on the nightstand; and then crawled into bed, opting to sleep with the lamp on. Her thoughts drifted from Tess to Braznovich. She still found it hard to believe that Braznovich was a P3 sympathizer, though it certainly explained why he didn't want to take her case in the first place. She berated herself for falling for him so quickly, and especially for falling into his bed. Despite how generous a lover he was, she vowed never to let him touch her again.

As for Rod, she wished she had her computer so she could look up Lenny and see if Rod was telling the truth. She couldn't imagine why he would lie, but after everything that had happened, she was leery of trusting anyone. Rod's voice replayed in her mind. "Sagan controls everything. Everything." She knew he controlled the Kansas City police, or at least some of them, and he was certainly able to pay off funeral directors, coroners, and prostitutes. His evil tentacles stretched deeper and wider than even Skylar had imagined. As mental and emotional exhaustion got the best of her, Skylar let her eyelids close, saying a silent prayer for Tess and reminding herself that the first thing she needed to do in the morning was find a way to discreetly contact Greg.

CHAPTER 23

Rod was still snoring when Skylar slipped the 357 magnum into the back of her jeans, crept into the bathroom, brushed her teeth and splashed cold water on her face. Gazing at her image in the mirror, she noted how pale and tired she appeared. Dark circles lined her eyes and her cheekbones protruded more than usual. She felt hollow and realized she hadn't eaten since breakfast yesterday. After making her way downstairs into the kitchen, Skylar quietly opened the fridge, in search of something to eat. It was filled with beer. She opened several cupboards, finally finding a box of saltine crackers. *Beggars can't be choosers,* she sighed and opened the box. She then found a plastic cup and filled it with tap water.

It wasn't much but it would have to do for now. It was a breakfast fit for a prisoner and the irony struck her that they were all prisoners to the P3 movement. One way or another, Maxwell Sagan controlled them, using lies, threats, manipulation and even the death of their loved ones. They moved like marionettes on the strings of his sinister will. *Well, not anymore! I'm going to make sure the Sagan puppet master is tied up and choked by his own strings.*

Skylar rummaged through the kitchen drawers until she found a piece of scrap paper and a pen; and then jotted a note to Rod, explaining that she was borrowing his pick-up to run to the corner mart for eggs and bread. "I'll make us breakfast when I get back," she wrote and then took his keys from the countertop and sneaked out the back door.

Pulling into the gas station mini mart, Skylar suddenly remembered that her face had been plastered all over the television, as a wanted criminal. She found a pair of dark sunglasses in the glove box and a bass fishing, baseball cap in the backseat. After slipping the glasses on, she carefully tucked her hair beneath the hat and checked her reflection. Confident that her identity was well hidden, she stepped tentatively inside the mini mart. Skylar walked quickly to the refrigerator section, selecting a carton of eggs and a small carton of milk. She pulled a loaf of bread from the bakery shelf on the way to the register.

"Did you get gas?" The man behind the counter asked with little enthusiasm.

Skylar shook her head. "Just this."

She paid for the groceries with some of the money she had taken from Braznovich's wallet. Then she asked for twenty dollars in quarters. The man paused and then took the twenty dollar bill, opened his register and counted out five piles of four quarters each. "Knock yourself out," he mumbled, pushing the piles of quarters across the counter toward Skylar.

She quickly shoved them into her jean pockets and headed back to the truck, groceries in hand.

"Now, to find a payphone," she exhaled aloud, as she climbed behind the wheel and started the ignition. She decided not to use the payphone at the same mini mart because she didn't want to stay in any one place too long and arouse suspicion. A few miles down the road, she pulled into a 7-11, parked near the back of the building and headed straight to the payphone. Her first call was to 4-1-1, requesting the number to the campaign headquarters for Presidential candidate, Senator Randy Patterson. She found a pen in Rod's truck but no paper, so she jotted the number down on the inside of her left wrist. Then, taking a deep breath, she inserted a handful of quarters and dialed the number.

"Senator Patterson for President," a woman with a nasal tone answered. "How may I direct your call?"

Skylar hesitated. Her heart was racing and she wasn't sure how or where to begin. "I need to speak with Mr...um...Senator Patterson," she said, breathlessly. "It's urgent."

"What is this regarding?" The woman asked in monotone, as if she received urgent phone calls every day and whatever Skylar had to say was most certainly unimportant.

Skylar's mind whirled. How should she begin? What could she say that would make this woman put her call through? Her mouth went dry and she licked her lips and inhaled through her nose. "Tell him I have a video recording of he and Micah Belmont that I believe he will find very interesting."

"Hold please," the woman barked and then elevator music flooded Skylar's ear.

Please put the call through. Please put the call through. If she could prove that Maxwell was manipulating people in high powered positions, surely his empire would crumble. Skylar believed Patterson was the key to making this evidence public.

"To whom am I speaking?" Came a man's voice through the receiver.

"Senator Patterson?"

"No, this is Clayton Richmond, Senator Patterson's campaign manager. To whom am I speaking?" He sounded young, maybe early thirties, and his tone was no nonsense.

"Mr. Richmond, it is urgent that I speak with Senator Patterson directly," Skylar said, trying to sound calm.

Clayton chuckled, obviously amused by her request. "All of the Senator's calls go through me. I'm sure you can understand that he does not have the time to entertain crank callers. Neither do I, for that matter."

"I'm not a crank caller," Skylar objected and then let out a sigh. She could see how this looked from his perspective. "This is an urgent matter. A life and death matter. Can you at least relay a message to Mr. Patterson for me?" Clayton didn't answer. "If you relay my message and he doesn't want to speak to me, then I won't bother you again. Please?"

"All right, but I'll need to know your name."

"I'll give the Senator my name if he decides to speak with me," Skylar retorted, knowing it was too dangerous to trust anyone with her identity.

"Very well," he exhaled drolly. "What is your message?"

Skylar swallowed slowly and nibbled on her bottom lip. She needed to choose her words carefully. "Please tell Senator Patterson that I have a video recording of him and Micah Belmont at the P3 campus in Kansas City, Missouri, where he met with Maxwell Sagan and Saul Latham and the President of the N.E.T. Sagan drugged them with Rohypnol and they filled out a questionnaire…" her voice trailed off as Clayton burst into laughter.

"Miss, I assure you Senator Patterson has attended no such meeting, nor does he associate with any radical groups from the right or the left. You have quite an active imagination," he chuckled.

"In the conversation he said he had sex with many women when he was a door-to-door salesman," Skylar blurted.

"Oh, really?" His voice dripped disdain. "And I suppose you were one of those women and you now want to be compensated for the sinful act against you. Or have you birthed his love child, perhaps?"

"No!" Skylar rolled her eyes. He was obviously trying to understand her angle, and suddenly Skylar realized that she needed to have an angle or her call would never be put through. She tightened her lip and spoke forcefully into the phone. "Listen, either Senator Patterson speaks with me directly, or I take my video to the media."

Clayton's voice lowered and she could hear his smile fade. "Give me one moment."

Elevator music filled her ears again, suddenly interrupted by an automated voice that told her to deposit two dollars into the phone. Skylar quickly dug into her pocket and then released the quarters one-by-one into the payphone slot. "Thank you," said the automated voice.

Moments later Clayton returned to the line. "The Senator will meet with you in person. He does not discuss important matters over the phone. From where are you calling?"

Skylar's heart leapt. He was going to meet with her. But where? When? How could she be sure it wasn't a trap? She chewed on her lower lip. "Tell Patterson to fly into the Johnson County Executive Airport in Olathe. That's in Kansas. I'll meet him behind hangar three."

"Senator Patterson has a very tight schedule. He can't just drop everything and fly to meet with every Tom, Dick and Harry," Clayton argued.

"I'm not just any Tom, Dick and Harry. If he doesn't come immediately, this video goes public," Skylar retorted.

"It will take us several hours..." Clayton began but Skylar interrupted.

"I will meet you at 1:00pm. That gives you plenty of time. Only you and Senator Patterson." Skylar's voice didn't waiver as she made her demands. "If you aren't there by 1:00pm sharp, I go to the media with a video that will destroy his career forever." With trembling fingers, she hung up the phone. She hated playing the role of the psychotic blackmailer, but what choice did she have? Rod was going to blow up the P3 campus in five days unless she could figure out a way to dismantle it first. Proving Maxwell manipulated people with drugs and lies would be the first step in freeing everyone trapped under his spell. If Patterson were on her side, then maybe the District Attorney would order every P3 member tested for Rohypnol. Maybe they would find samples of Rohypnol-laced Sacramental wine. Maybe they would find the chair with the handcuffs and discover how many young people had fallen prey to Maxwell's twisted idea of forced mortification. Skylar's mind whirled with possibilities. Exposing Maxwell would be the happiest day of Skylar's life.

Her next phone call was to Greg and she knew she'd have to make it quick, as he would most likely be tracing the call. Greg was genuinely surprised to hear her voice. "Oh, thank God!" He blurted. "We've been worried and Braznovich is beside himself. Where are you?"

Before she could answer, Braznovich took the phone from Greg. "Where the hell are you?" He demanded.

"Put Greg on the phone now or I hang up and you won't hear from me again." Her voice was steady and she was pretty proud of herself for maintaining her composure. She heard him curse loudly and then Greg came back on the line.

"What's going on, Skylar? Why did you take off?" Greg sounded genuinely perplexed and even a little betrayed.

"I don't have much time, so listen. I'm safe, for now, but we've got to figure out a way to get everyone off the P3 campus before Friday evening." He started firing questions at her, and without giving away names and location, she filled in the blanks, including her plan to meet with Senator Patterson.

"I'm going to have to tell Braznovich and Ernie," he uttered.

"Damn right you are!" She heard Braznovich yell through the phone and she guessed he was probably standing right behind Greg, attempting to overhear every word. *Tell Mr.Control Freak to take a chill pill!* She rolled her eyes and bit her tongue. No sense adding fuel to the fire. He was obviously pissed.

"Are you safe?" She asked Greg.

"Yes. I don't know why you left," he spoke softly. "Everything here is fine."

"It's not fine. I overheard Braznovich on the phone. I heard him say he was purposefully distracting me with his grandfather's notes. I heard him say everything was going according to plan, and that I was stubborn and hard to deal with..." Anger rose in her throat. "He's working for P3!"

"I don't know what you heard, but I don't believe he's with them. He hates them, Skylar, almost as much as you and I do." Greg's voice was convincing and a part of her wanted to believe him, but it was too risky. "Just be careful."

"Ditto," he said.

"I'll call you after I meet with Patterson. In the meantime, I need you to anonymously email Micah Belmont the video coverage of her and Patterson at P3."

"Okay, but what good will that do?" Greg asked.

"I'm hoping she'll contact Patterson right away, even send it to him, and that will convince him to show up for our meeting."

"I'll do it right now," Greg assured her.

"Greg...." Her voice cracked with emotion. "Do you still have a lock on Tess? Is she okay?"

"She's sleeping. Don't worry; I'll keep an eye on her. How can I contact you?"

"You can't."

Skylar hung up the receiver and wiped away a stray tear that was inching its way down her cheek. She needed to hurry back to Rod's house, make him breakfast for him and fill him in on Patterson, Belmont and the Rohypnol.

CHAPTER 24

Braznovich slammed his fist into the back of the couch, his face red with anger.

"Take it easy, man," Ernie mumbled and exhaled a smoke ring toward the sliding door. "She's not goin' nowhere."

"I don't even know where she is, or if she's safe, or why she left." He threw his hands in the air.

"I can answer all those questions," Greg said, "but on one condition."

"What?" Braznovich hissed.

"You don't chase her down and bring her back, at least not right away. She has a plan that just might work."

Braznovich stared at Greg, the kind of stare that could preclude a stiff punch in the face. "This ought to be good," he sarcastically mumbled.

Ernie flicked his cigarette butt out the door and closed it. "It just might be," he said. "She's one sharp cookie."

"She bases everything on speculation. She doesn't care at all about the facts. This is a big game to her and she doesn't realize she can wind up dead." Braznovich ran his fingers through his hair, pulling at the roots and grunting frustration.

"I know what you're feeling," Greg said. "You're afraid you've lost her. She's out of your reach and out of control and there's no way you can stop the train or even get her off the tracks before she's run over." It was obvious that he was speaking from experience. "I've been there. Hell, who am I kidding, I'm still there." He motioned toward the surveillance feed of Tess sleeping. "The difference between me and you is that the woman you love is on your side, she just doesn't realize it."

Braznovich shifted his weight uncomfortably from his right foot to his left and back again. Love. That was a strong word and not one he was accustomed to using. "Let's be clear. Ms. Wilson is a client and it is my job to protect my clients. Period." Braznovich's jaw was set as he stormed across the room and out the front door, slamming it behind him.

Ernie put his hand on Greg's shoulder. "You walked into that one."

"He's got it bad, huh?" Greg grimaced.

"Let's just say Braz ain't used to women walking out on him. It's usually the other way around."

"So this is all about ego? He doesn't really care for her?" Greg asked.

Ernie shook his head. "He cares. That's why he feels so out of control. He'll come around, but first he has to come to terms with how much he cares. I've never seen him fall so hard so fast." Ernie sat down on the couch and stared at the computer screens. "Now, tell me our girl's plan and let's figure out a way to help her."

Greg took a deep breath. "Basically, she's trapped between two radical groups; one being P3, who we know is capable of murder and the other an extremist group of locals who are planning to blow up the complex this Friday."

Ernie raised his eyebrows into his forehead.

"There's more," Greg said. "She's meeting with Presidential candidate, Randy Patterson, at 1:00pm today to show him the video recording of him and VP candidate, Micah Belmont, recorded when they were at the P3 campus...." Ernie cut him off.

"I've seen the video. What is she hoping to accomplish with this meeting?"

Greg shrugged. "I think she's trying to discredit Sagan and publically expose his practice of administering Rohypnol to unsuspecting victims."

Ernie smacked his lips together. "I gotta hand it to her. She's using all of her resources."

"Her plan might work," Greg interjected. "If Patterson sees the video and orders a blood test or gets a search warrant issued and Rohypnol is found on the premises, P3 won't be a very popular place to visit." He cleared his throat. "I mean, think about that information going public and every parent bursting through the doors, demanding to see their child. If anything, it will upset Sagan's world for a while."

"A warrant will be issued through local jurisdiction first, and for all we know most of the local law enforcement are on the P3 payroll." Braznovich said, having sneaked in the sliding door without them noticing.

"So?" Greg asked.

"So, it means they will destroy any Rohypnol they find before a federal warrant can be served," Braznovich explained. "See, Skylar doesn't think these things through."

"But we do," Ernie grinned. "It's a helluva plan. It just needs some tweaking."

"What kind of tweaking?" Greg asked.

"If Patterson gets a search warrant issued, we make sure Rohypnol is found on the campus," Ernie said, while rising from the couch and removing another cigarette from the pack he kept in his front shirt pocket.

"You want to plant false evidence?" Braznovich raised an eyebrow.

"I like to think of it as fighting fire with fire," Ernie grinned.

CHAPTER 25

Skylar whipped up scrambled eggs and toast, rinsed out an old Mr. Coffee she found on the pantry floor, next to a canister of Folgers, and set a pot to brew. Before long the stale beer scent that had previously hung in the kitchen was replaced by the pleasant aroma of coffee beans and buttery toast. She threw away all the beer cans that sat atop the counter and the kitchen table, and then wiped down the counters with Windex and paper towels. It was the only cleaning solution she could find so it would have to do. Then she hand washed two plates, two glasses, two forks and two knives and set the table. She kept the toast and eggs warming in the oven until Rod stumbled downstairs and into the kitchen.

Peering through one eye slit open, he surveyed the kitchen. "Holy Moley, somethin' smells good," he rasped. "I just came down for a beer, but somethin' smells better."

Skylar giggled at him. His hair was messed up and he was barely awake. "I sure hope my breakfast tastes better than a beer," she teased. "Otherwise, I'm good for nothing."

He pulled open the oven and peeked inside. "You cooked?"

"I figured it was the least I could do; you're letting me stay here and all."

"Where'd you get the food?"

"I borrowed your truck and drove up to the mini mart." The minute the words left her mouth his expression changed.

"Are you crazy?" He let the oven door slam closed. "You can't go traipsing around this neck of

the woods.   The police will be all over you." He
rushed down the hall and peered through the family
room window. "Did anyone follow you?"

"No," Skylar uttered, surprised by Rod's
paranoid reaction. "I wore your glasses and hat and
no one knew who I was."

"You can't take my truck," he frowned at her.
"It's registered to this address and if anyone get
suspicious of you, the plates will lead them here."

"Oh. I didn't think about the plates." Skylar
had been more concerned about taking Braznovich's
bike, afraid it might help him locate her. Rod's
license plates never entered her mind.

Rod shuffled back down the hall and sat down
at the kitchen table. "You gotta think like a convict."
He said, tapping his fingers against his head. "You
gotta realize you're being hunted and you gotta be
careful."

Skylar fixed Rod a plate, a cup of coffee,
poured a glass of milk and carried it to the table.
"Forgive me," she smiled. "I'm not used to being a
convict."

Rod shoveled in a forkful of eggs and followed
it with a bite of toast. "You better start thinking like
one, if you want to stay alive."

Skylar nodded. She knew he was right, but
was struck by how low she had fallen. One day an
honest photographer, trying to make a living and the
next, a thief and a liar, blackmailing Presidential
candidates and running from the police; and all
because of Maxwell Sagan.

As she watched Rod devour his eggs, her
thoughts drifted to Braznovich and his tabasco
covered omelet. Butterflies danced in her stomach as
she recalled his smile, his laugh, his muscular arms,
his bossy demands, the way his lips felt against hers
and, most of all, his touch. How could she not have
fallen for him? He was the textbook definition of
every girl's dream.

"Penny for your thoughts?" Rod blurted, halting her reverie.

Skylar shook her head. "Nothing. Everything."

"You were thinking about him. I could see it in your eyes."

"Who?" Skylar puzzled.

"Your boyfriend. You must be really into him, 'cuz your face sort of lights up when you think about him."

Skylar grinned, despite the sense of sadness that weighed heavily upon her.

"He's a lucky guy," Rod said. "Real damn lucky guy."

After breakfast, Skylar cleared the dishes and they retreated to the basement to discuss plans for what had become known as Armageddon Friday. Rod opened a map of the P3 complex and showed Skylar exactly where and when the explosions would occur. Tess's apartment building sat close to the main entrance, which meant it would be one of the last buildings blown up. This was good news, if there were anything good about planning an attack like this one.

"Tess is here," Skylar pointed to the structure just to the left of the main building, which housed the Prayer Room and Sagan's office.

"I know," Rod uttered. "That's what that gold star means." Skylar looked more closely at the map, now focusing on several gold stars that appeared to be strategically placed throughout the complex. "Each gold star represents a leader in the P3 movement and a target we want to make sure we don't miss."

Skylar swallowed back her emotion. They were purposefully planning to kill her sister. It was difficult enough to hear, much less having to pretend that she condoned it. Tears pricked the back of her eyes as Rod studied her face. "I told you, I'll try to help you get Tess out before everything goes down."

Skylar nodded. *But what about all the other people? What about all the Lexi's and Ema's trapped inside? They don't deserve to die. None of them deserve to die, well, maybe Sagan does.* A twinge of guilt gripped her for thinking he should die, but Skylar quickly pushed it away. Maxwell Sagan purposely twisted God's Word for the purpose of manipulating and harming others. He wasn't innocently deceived. He was egotistically deliberate. Should someone pay with their life for that? Skylar didn't know, but she was struggling to find even an ounce of compassion for the likes of Sagan.

"The bombs are set to start at the rear and work their way forward. At precisely 7:53pm the first explosive will detonate."

"7:53pm?" Skylar repeated, thinking that seemed a randomly odd time to start.

"Lenny died precisely at 7:53pm, three years ago," Rod explained, and then corrected himself. "Well, we don't know the precise time of death, but at 7:53pm I got the phone call telling me he was dead." Skylar slowly nodded that she understood and Rod continued. "Each explosive will detonate in six minute intervals from that time forward, so the first one is at 7:53, then 7:59, 8:05, 8:11, 8:17, 8:23 and the finale begins at 8:29."

"So, Tess's building blows at 8:23?" Skylar reiterated.

"Yep. You'll have until that moment to get her out and until 8:29 to get out of the main entrance." Rod's eyes flashed with fury and it made Skylar shudder within her skin. She hated Maxwell Sagan more than anyone. She despised what he did to people, but, despite that hate, she couldn't reconcile the mass killing of hundreds, if not thousands of P3 members.

"How do I get in?" Skylar asked.

Rod rolled up the map. "We'll put you in with the construction crew; give you a vest, hard hat, the works. That'll get you past security and onto the campus, but from there you're on your own."

Skylar nodded. She understood. If she didn't make it out the main entrance with Tess by 8:29pm, she was as good as dead. "Wait a second," Skylar gasped. "How do you know the leaders, the ones marked with the gold stars, will die in the explosions?"

Rod grinned. "We've got back up personnel assigned to each gold star. If they happen to make it out of their respective buildings, we take them down." Rod made a shooting motion with his hand.

Skylar's eyes widened. "What happens when I get Tess out of her building? Will your back-up gun us down?"

"I'll be the back-up for Tess," he stated matter-of-factly.

"You've been personally assigned to kill my sister?" Skylar couldn't hide the indignation rising in her voice. "Were you just randomly selected to kill Tess or did you choose her?"

For a brief moment anger flashed in Rod's eyes and then he lowered his gaze to the floor and pursed his lips together, as if he were considering how to respond. His pause was answer enough. Rod had chosen Tess as his personal prey.

"Why?" Skylar uttered, the question sticking in her throat. "Why would you choose her?" She couldn't help but wonder if he had chosen Tess because she was Skylar's sister, and because Skylar had out after their one night stand and never returned his phone calls. Could his choice have been motivated by revenge?

"You should be thankful!" Rod spewed. "If I wasn't assigned to kill her, I wouldn't be in a position to help you save her." Rod pulled the string on the basement light bulb and left Skylar standing momentarily in the dark. "The Lord works in mysterious ways," he mumbled, ascending the staircase.

CHAPTER 26

After watching the video of Senator Patterson and Micah Belmont at P3, learning that Rohypnol was found in Ema's body and seeing a picture of the chair, blood and handcuffs, Rod agreed to escort Skylar to the meeting with Senator Patterson and Clayton Richmond. Although unwavering in his determination to go ahead with Armageddon Friday, he appeared excited about the prospect of making Sagan's indiscretions public. "The more dirty laundry we air, the more public support we'll have for destroying the place," he told Skylar. That wasn't exactly how she wanted things to play out, but there was no sense trying to change his mind. He was dead set on blowing the place up.

Pulling into the Johnson County Executive Airport, Rod took the outer road and followed it all the way around until they reached hangar three. He parked the truck around the far side of the building, where it would be hidden from oncoming traffic. Then they each stepped out and walked toward the rear entrance door.

"Why this hangar?" Rod asked.

"Because it's vacant," she explained. "It was damaged in a storm and shut down pending repairs." She pulled open the door and stepped inside. Rod followed. "I did a photo shoot here last month."

After giving the hangar a quick once over and making sure Skylar was alone, Rod returned to the truck, drove up the street and waited. Skylar asked Rod to leave because she was afraid that Patterson would not talk openly if he were there; and she was certain that Patterson would have security guards who would search Rod, if he were anywhere near the hangar. Because of what Rod had planned for Armageddon Friday, Skylar didn't want any kind of public association with him.

One o'clock came and went and Skylar began to nervously chew on her fingernail. At one thirty she peaked outside the hangar. Rod was due to come back for her at two o'clock, or whenever he saw Patterson's entourage leave. Unsettling thoughts filled her mind. What if Patterson's people had somehow discovered who she was and had called the police? What if they were on their way to arrest her right now? She paced back and forth and tried to calm her nerves with slow deep breaths. Logic told her that if Patterson had gone to the police, they would have arrived prior to one o'clock and been waiting for her.

At one forty-five the rear door opened and Skylar whirled around on her heels to see Braznovich standing with his hands on his hips. Instinctively she pulled the 357 magnum from the back of her jeans and pointed it at him, warning him not to come closer. His gait was sure and steady, as if he were unaffected by the gun. "I should flip you over my knee right now," he blurted, striding right up to her until the 357 touched his chest.

She was speechless. *The nerve! Who does he think he is!* Skylar felt suddenly torn between feeling happy to see him, angry at the fact that he betrayed her trust, and fearful that his presence would jeopardize her meeting with Patterson. "Get out of here," she said through clenched teeth.

He took the gun from her hand, checked the safety and handed it back to her. "I see you've upgraded from the .22," he said. "Let me guess, you're not licensed for this one at all."

She rolled her eyes and slid it back into the waistband of her jeans and pulled her shirt over it. He knew darn good and well she wasn't licensed. "I borrowed it from a friend."

"Is this the same friend that's going to blow up the P3 campus?" His tone was disapproving.

"That's speculation," she uttered sarcastically.

Braznovich took her by the wrist and pulled her toward the door. "We're leaving. Now."

"I'm not going anywhere with you." Skylar ripped her arm from his grasp.

"You're being ridiculous and you're in over your head. You don't know who you're dealing with."

Skylar narrowed her eyes and glared at him. "No, I didn't know who I was dealing with, but I do now."

He exhaled a loud, exasperated sigh. "You've got it all wrong, Skylar."

"Not anymore, I don't." She crossed her arms over her chest. "I'm not going anywhere with you."

Braznovich pulled his phone from his pocket, opened the internet browser window and showed Skylar the headline. "Vice Presidential Hopeful, Micah Belmont, Found Dead in Hotel Room"

Skylar's mouth fell open. "That's right," Braznovich said. "Found dead, less than an hour ago." He shoved his phone back into his pocket. "Coincidentally she died after receiving Greg's email with the video of her and Patterson at P3." His expression and tone told Skylar what she already intuitively knew to be true; it was no coincidence.

"How?" Skylar uttered.

"We don't know yet, but what we do know is that she received the email around 9:00am this morning and she called Maxwell Sagan from her hotel room at 9:17am."

Skylar's mouth went dry and tears formed in her eyes. She felt stunned. Had she gotten Micah Belton killed too? It was inconceivable, but she knew Sagan's resources extended far into the upper echelon of the political world. "What about Patterson?" She mumbled, fear filling her gut. "Is he dead too? Is that why he didn't show up?"

Braznovich shrugged. "I don't know, but if someone at P3 knows about your plan to meet with Patterson, then we need to get out of here, and sooner than later." He placed both hands on the outside of her shoulders. "Please, come with me."

Skylar wiggled from his arms. "No. I heard what you said about me." A lump formed in her throat and she swallowed hard to hold back the emotion. "You have an interesting way of keeping me 'distracted.'" She used her fingers to make quotation marks around the word 'distracted.'

"Skylar, I don't..." he began, but she interrupted him.

"Save your breath," she blurted. "I heard what you said."

"I don't know what you heard but..."

"But nothing. You used me, plain and simple."

Braznovich tightened his lip. "I have no idea what you're talking about, but you're really starting to piss me off."

"I'm pissing YOU off?" Skylar huffed. "You're unbelievable!" She pushed against his chest with both palms, forcing him to take a step backwards. "I heard you say I was difficult to get along with...and driving you crazy...and that you were using your grandfather's notes to keep me distracted...and that everything was going according to plan and being set in motion and..."

Braznovich cut her rant short by placing his fingertips against her lips. Tears emptied onto her cheeks and she pushed his hand away from her face. A certain softness filled his brown eyes and the sparkle she had missed suddenly returned. "Is that why you left?" He asked, as if a light bulb had just gone off in his brain.

Skylar tearfully nodded and lowered her eyes to the floor.

Lifting her chin, Braznovich smiled. "I was talking about my sister, not you."

Skylar's eyes opened wider.

"Skylar, when my sister heard of Ema's death and Mrs. Wright and Officer Burnes, and the car blowing up at P3, she was frantic with worry. She was ready to fly here and drag Jonathan home herself." He ran his fingers through his hair and shook his head. "She was irrational and I was worried that if she went to P3, she'd be the next body we found, so I assured her that I was working on getting Jonathan out and distracted her by sending her some of grandfather's study notes on P3. I figured if I could make her think that she was actually helping by looking for clues, she would stay put and stay safe." He let out a frustrated sigh. "I wasn't talking about you."

Skylar flushed with a sense of foolishness and embarrassment. She had jumped the gun, again.

"And just so we're clear…" he paused, his smile fading. "I don't use people and I don't use sex to distract women."

She didn't know what to say.

He pulled her closer, wrapping his arms around her and letting her head rest against his chest. "Don't leave again," he said in a way that let Skylar know that he was serious.

"I didn't want to drive you crazy," she whispered.

Stroking her hair he chuckled. "You do drive me crazy, but in a good way."

She lifted her head from his chest and gazed upward. "I'm sorry," she said.

Leaning down to place a tender kiss on her lips, he said, "Not as sorry as you're going to be." Then he playfully swatted her bottom. "Now, can we please get out of here?"

Skylar nodded and they exited through the rear door, her hand tightly secured in his. "Oh, I'll have to stop and let Rod know what's happening."

"Already took care of it," he answered confidently.

"What?" Skylar puzzled. How would he have known Rod and where to find him? She hadn't even given Greg this information. Was he tracking her the whole time? *No, if he knew that I was at Rod's house, he would have stormed the place and dragged me back last night.*

"We watched Rod drop you off, search the hangar and leave again. Ernie followed him while I came in here to meet with you," Braznovich explained, opening the passenger door and helping Skylar climb into the shiny, black Hummer.

"Whose car is this?" Skylar had never been in a Hummer and it was impressive to say the least. It had tan leather seats and tinted windows.

"Mine," he winked.

He must be loaded. "So, why did Ernie follow Rod?" She asked.

"Well, hopefully for you, Rod took Ernie to the location of my bike and it is currently being transported back to my barn." He climbed behind the wheel and gave Skylar a sideways glance. "You steal one of my motorcycles again and I will whip you good."

She flushed at his threat. Would he really? "I didn't steal it. I borrowed it. And I wasn't planning of taking one of your bikes. I was going to take the Lamborghini, but I couldn't find the keys."

Braznovich shook his head. "Good thing."

CHAPTER 27

The motorcycle was now safely back in the barn and upon returning to his grandfather's house, Braznovich made a beeline to check on it. Ernie stepped onto the back porch to light up a smoke, chuckling as Braznovich hurried passed him. "I told you," Ernie hollered after him, "there's not a scratch on it. Can't even tell it was driven."

"I'll be the judge of that," Braznovich grunted.

Skylar joined Ernie on the porch. "Is he always this anal and controlling?"

"Only about the things he loves." Ernie gave her a wink and then stepped closer and draped his big, burly arm around Skylar's shoulder. *The things he loves,* she repeated in her mind. Could it be that Braznovich loved her? Could that be the reason he was often so overbearing and controlling? They'd known each other such a short time that the notion seemed ludicrous; and yet, she couldn't deny that he had a certain hold on her heart. Ernie pulled her closer, interrupting her thoughts and blowing a smoke ring right above her head. "You pull another stunt like that, running off like that, and you're gonna answer to me," he scolded. "You got it?"

"Got it," Skylar smiled. She knew that it was his way of reprimanding her for leaving and also showing her that he cared. The fact was she cared too, more than she thought possible after such a short time. Ernie was like the big brother she never had and Braznovich, well, Braznovich was an enigma. He was a mystery, not like any man she'd ever met; a perplexing mixture of authority and humility, gentleness and power, humor and logic. Running off to Rod's house made her realize how wounded she

225

had been when she thought Braznovich was against her and how deeply she cared for him.

"We had a misunderstanding," Skylar said sheepishly.

Leaning down, Ernie whispered in her ear. "If there's one guy you can trust, it's Braz. You can take that to the bank."

As Braznovich approached, he scowled and waved his arms in the air to dissipate Ernie's smoke. "I can smell that all the way over here."

"Then hold your nose," Ernie quipped and purposefully exhaled in Braznovich's direction.

Braznovich gave him an annoyed glare and Skylar couldn't help but laugh. They appeared to have a love hate relationship, playfully harassing each other like siblings.

Greg was watching CNN when they walked inside, and quipped how he couldn't believe Belmont had been killed. Muting the television, Greg mumbled, "Unbelievable."

Skylar sank into the couch. "It's my fault," she said, almost inaudibly. "I contacted Patterson and now look what's happened." Skylar stared blankly, speaking in monotone amazement. "When Micah received the video, I thought she would call Patterson first thing. I never thought she would call Sagan."

"Your plan backfired, but that doesn't mean Sagan murdering Micah Belmont is your fault," Ernie said, as he flicked his cigarette butt outside and pulled the sliding door closed.

"That's speculation," Braznovich said. "We don't have proof that Sagan had Belmont killed."

Ernie rolled his eyes. "Right."

Skylar still couldn't believe it. How could Sagan be powerful enough to murder a Vice Presidential candidate of the United States? Who else did he control?

"You know what gets me," Greg said softly. "When you read interviews with Maxwell Sagan, he paints himself as just one of the common folk, coming from a poor family with six siblings; never finishing school because he couldn't afford it. He and his wife live in a tiny, unassuming home and he drives a real piece of crap car…" his voice trailed off and he shook his head. "If he's just a poor, little nobody, how does he have all these big wig connections?"

"It's all a front," Ernie said. "The humble poverty is a front."

"But, why?" Greg mumbled. "Why does he need to pretend to be common? Where does that get him?"

"The flashy preachers are the ones who get busted," Ernie answered.

"It's true," Braznovich said. "A pastor with wealth is a red flag for the IRS. It's the hot shot preachers with their mega-churches, mega-buildings, mega-houses, boats and cars that get busted on misuse of funds…"

"And their empires crumble," Ernie chimed in.

"Sagan's smarter than that," Braznovich added. "But just because he's smart enough to hide it, doesn't mean he hasn't amassed an empire for himself. He has an empire all right, it's just underground."

"Underground," Ernie repeated. "That's an ironic choice of words. It's like demonic dinero." Ernie chuckled, raising one eyebrow and rubbing his thumb back and forth across the tips of his fingers to indicate that he was talking about money.

"It IS demonic dinero," Greg agreed. "I can see that as a headline."

"What can I say, I'm a creative guy," Ernie teased.

"Maxwell won't flaunt his money because money isn't his ammo," Skylar said. "It never has been."

"But he makes a fortune, between what he charges the P3 interns, the kickbacks from his wife's

Real-estate business and..." Greg was interrupted by Ernie.

"What Real-estate business?" He asked, meandering toward the door.

"His wife owns her own Real-estate company and she sells homes to P3, which pays her a substantial realtor fee. Because the homes are then church property, Sagan pays no taxes on the transactions. It's all legal, technically, but when you research the number of homes she has sold to P3, his claiming their life to be 'common' becomes laughable. And that's not even taking into account rental properties and student housing fees," Greg spewed. "He's a joke."

"He doesn't care about cars or boats or million dollar homes," Skylar said. "He only wants power. A lot of right-wing reports claim that Sagan gives all of the proceeds from his books to charitable organizations but that's all a front too."

"Yeah, especially since he's the one who claims that humanitarianism and charitable acts facilitate a sinful attitude of compromise that pave the way for the Anti-Christ," Greg chided.

Ernie snapped his fingers. "Is Sagan the whack job that called Oprah Winfrey the Anti-Christ? I remember that story."

"No, he said Oprah was the Harlot Babylon," Skylar corrected. "The pre-cursor to the Anti-Christ."

Ernie chuckled aloud. "What a tool."

"Sagan doesn't care about helping people. He uses his money to feed his ego and amass more power," Skylar moaned. "That's his only goal."

"I don't get why people can't see through him," Greg said.

"Because he's charismatic," Ernie said and flashed jazz hands, which made everyone smile.

"He's demonic. He's actually consorting with demons and they blind people from seeing the truth," Skylar explained.

Greg shook his head. "I don't know if I believe in all that demon crap. I think of him more as a magician."

"What about women?" Ernie asked, sliding the door open and lighting up another cigarette. "How many pastors have been cast down for committing adultery?"

"Sadly, it's too many to count," Braznovich answered.

"Adultery's better than what some Catholic Priests have been accused of," Greg suggested and Skylar gave him a disgusted look and hurled a couch pillow at him.

"Gross," Skylar moaned. "Besides, women aren't Maxwell's ammo either."

"Tess was his ammo," Greg bitterly spewed.

"But not like that," Skylar said softly. "Tess met him when she was young and impressionable and Maxwell manipulated her, but..."

"But she let him," Greg interrupted.

"He was married when he met Tess." Skylar tucked a piece of hair behind her ear. "I think Tess adored him and he liked being adored. What's more, Tess's love for the Lord got all mixed up in her emotions for Sagan but instead of acknowledging that she was at an impressionable age and setting her straight, he began brainwashing her and used her to feed his ego. He used her adoration to build himself up, to feel powerful." Skylar could see Greg's jaw tensing and she knew this was an uncomfortable topic for him. It had to be. When Tess left Greg for P3, he must have felt like she had left him for Maxwell; and in a way, Skylar knew she had. Tess gave up her whole life for Maxwell. If Maxwell said jump, Tess leapt. That's how brainwashed she had become. Maxwell's prophetic nonsense had become Tess's gauge on reality. She was living proof that even the purest of hearts could be manipulated and drawn like a moth to a dark, demonized flame.

"So how do we take a man like this down?" Greg asked, throwing his hands in the air.

"Sounds like the town folks are going to do it for us," Braznovich exhaled.

"Seems sort of apropos," Ernie mumbled.

"Despite the irony, we need to get the interns and students out before they're blown to smithereens," Braznovich said.

"Agreed," Ernie said. "Rod's not changing his mind and since P3 has corrupted the local police department, we can't turn him into the cops. It would be a death sentence for him and all the folks."

"So suddenly we've become the judges, getting to decide who lives and who dies," Greg uttered. "If we turn Rod and the local folks in, they will surely be massacred, but if we don't, the P3 students will be blown up..." his voice trailed off.

"It's a helluva quandary," Ernie mumbled.

"Well, we can't turn Rod in," Skylar blurted. "He's a good guy."

"Good guys don't plan events called Armageddon Friday," Braznovich slighted and it made Ernie chuckle.

"Yep, that's usually a red flag," Ernie said, exhaling a giant smoke ring and watching as it dissipated over the patio.

Skylar stood up, clearing her throat with deliberate attitude. "Believe me, if you're comparing Rod to Maxwell, Rod is definitely the lesser of two evils."

"There's a fine line between good and evil," Braznovich said.

"And a finer line between acts of love and actions of hate," Ernie muttered as he took a long drag and then flicked his cigarette butt outside, immediately lighting up another.

"We're not turning Rod into the cops, so we're just going to have to find a way to evacuate the campus before any of the bombs go off," Skylar said pointedly. "Greg, do you have any ideas?"

Greg shook his head. "No, at least nothing yet. The only thing I've thought of is that I can set off the fire alarms and sprinkler systems ahead of time. That might get people moving out of the buildings, but I don't think there's a way to guarantee everyone's safety. There are going to be casualties."

Moving to the kitchen table, they spent the rest of the evening discussing Rod's plans for Armageddon Friday. Skylar drew a diagram of the buildings and then outlined where and when the bombs were set to blow and Greg scanned schematics of the buildings, studying whether or not he could dismantle their override system. "If I can set off the sprinklers and kill their override program, the water will flood the buildings, and at least combat the fires from the explosions," Greg explained.

"Good plan," Ernie commended and Greg grinned. Skylar could tell he was completely in his element.

"But we need to get everyone off the campus before 8:29pm," Skylar told them.

"Why 8:29pm?" Braznovich questioned.

"That's when the main building will blow and Rod called that explosion the 'finale' so I'm guessing it will be big."

"Big and deadly," Ernie added.

"Rod's plan is to start the bombs in the rear, causing everyone to funnel toward the main entrance..." Skylar began and Braznovich interrupted.

"Then he blows up the main building and takes out as many people as possible." Braznovich grimaced. "Nice friends you have," he said to Skylar.

"He's not my friend...I mean, he wasn't my friend..." Skylar was getting frustrated.

"He wasn't your friend but he is your friend now?" Braznovich raised his eyebrows. "What changed your mind, the fact that he's a mass murderer?" His sarcasm was so thick it was almost palatable.

"Rod hasn't killed anyone…"

"Yet!" Braznovich seethed and Skylar glared at him.

"Lighten up, you two," Ernie interjected. "We've all got some friends in low places." Ernie started singing, "I got friends in low places where the whiskey runs and the beer chases my blues away…" He stopped and looked around the table. "C'mon, join in, you know you want to."

"Whiskey sounds good," Skylar blurted, standing up abruptly and fetching the 1843 bottle from the fridge. She plunked into her chair, unscrewed the lid and took a swig straight from the bottle.

"You ever heard of a glass, Ms. Wilson?" Braznovich sneered.

"Nope," Skylar responded, accentuating the 'p' and taking another swig.

"I'll take some of that," Ernie said and took a swig from the bottle. He passed it to Braznovich. "C'mon, it'll take the edge off."

Braznovich retrieved a glass, filled it with ice and poured the 1843 over it. Raising his glass in toasting fashion, he said, "Here's to low places and our friends who lurk in them." And then he drank it down in one swallow.

Several swigs later, Skylar fixed a platter of red grapes, Havarti cheese and wheat thin crackers. She felt famished and realized that she hadn't eaten since breakfast, and the bourbon on an empty stomach was making her nauseated. The guys must have been hungry too because the cheese and crackers quickly disappeared.

"Tonight is Wednesday, which gives us less than forty eight hours before the first bomb," Greg recanted aloud. "That's not a lot of time to come up with a plan."

"How many men are in Rod's group?" Braznovich asked.

"I don't know, maybe thirty or so," Skylar answered, trying to remember how many people were in Rod's basement for the planning meeting.

"Do you think there's a way we could get on campus ahead of time and disarm the bombs?" Braznovich directed his question to Ernie, who shook his head.

"We don't know what kind of bombs their using, if they have a detonator that's already been armed or if they're using a remote. It's too risky and we'd most likely need a bomb specialist to ensure they were disarmed safely," Ernie explained.

"There's no way to talk Rod out of this?" Greg asked.

Skylar shook her head.

"No can do," Ernie answered. "He's hell bent on sticking to his plan and I think the whole town is behind him."

"The town IS behind him," Skylar agreed. "Mrs. Wright told us the same thing before she died. Remember? She said the folks around these parts weren't going to take it much longer."

Braznovich was visibly rattled. "How can they think this is the right way to handle the situation?" He ran his hand through his tussled hair and grunted. "How can they justify acting like terrorists? Who gives this Rod guy, or anyone for that matter, the right to play God?"

"Who gives Sagan the right?" Skylar argued. "He's the only one playing God."

"So now you think that it's okay to blow up a bunch of people just because you don't agree with their beliefs?" Braznovich narrowed his brows and scowled at her.

"I never said it was okay. I don't want anyone to die, but..."

"But what?" Braznovich's voice grew louder.

"But it's understandable!" Skylar hollered, leaping to her feet and slamming her palms on top the table.

"Not to me," Braznovich uttered. "It's not understandable to me."

Silence filled the air between them and Skylar presumed that no one knew what to say. Ernie moved to the sink, opened the window above it and lit up a cigarette, while Greg intently studied the drawings in front of him. This was a moral issue, a spiritual issue and an emotional issue all clumped into one big mess. Was it justified to seek revenge against someone who had destroyed your family or your marriage or killed your loved ones? Was it right to fight against the injustice, if fighting meant there would be more casualties? In an ideal world they could prove that Sagan was using narcotics to manipulate, brainwash and threaten people into following him. In an ideal world they could find concrete evidence that Sagan was behind the deaths of Goodwin, Ema, Mrs. Wright, Officer Burnes, Lexi, Rod's brother, Micah Belmont, all the innocent people in that African Village and probably more; but this wasn't an ideal world. This was the real world and they were out of time.

Skylar locked eyes with Braznovich from across the table. "Maxwell murdered Rod's little brother. On Friday at exactly 7:53pm his brother will have died three years ago."

"Was his brother a member of P3?" Greg asked.

"No. He was a journalism student who interviewed Maxwell and wrote a paper on what he believed to be true about P3 and Maxwell's so-called prophetic ministry. He started getting death threats and a couple of days later, he was found dead." Skylar slowly lowered herself into her chair and exhaled. "Maxwell has been behind the deaths of more people than we even realize and it has to stop. He must be stopped." She fought to keep her lip from quivering as she directed her gaze to Braznovich. "Rod isn't a terrorist or a mass murderer. He's just a regular guy with a broken heart and he doesn't want anyone else to feel the loss and the pain that Maxwell has inflicted on him."

Braznovich pursed his lips together and lowered his eyes to the table. Skylar couldn't tell what he was thinking. "Greg," Braznovich said, "find a way to evacuate those buildings. We want as few casualties as possible." He turned around to face Ernie. "We're going to need manpower; men we can trust."

"Roger Dodger," Ernie grinned and winked at Skylar.

"No killing," Braznovich addressed all of them. "We're going in to save lives, not take them." Skylar smiled at him and he blinked slowly and gave her a nod. "We'll need a direct route in and out..." Braznovich began but Skylar interrupted.

"Can I borrow one of your phones?" She asked. When Braznovich mentioned a direct route in and out, it made Skylar realize that she hadn't spoken with Rod since Ernie took the motorcycle from him; and she wanted to make sure he would still help her get Tess out.

"Who do you need to call?" Braznovich asked, with a look of skepticism. "Anyone you contact, you endanger."

"I need to call Rod and make sure everything is still on."

Braznovich shot Ernie a sideways glance and Ernie raised an eyebrow. "I told you, there was no talking him out of Armageddon Friday," Ernie said. "Everything's still on."

"No...um...I mean I need to know if OUR plans are still on."

"YOUR plans?" Braznovich looked at her from beneath narrowed brows and she couldn't tell if his expression was one of concern, anger or jealousy.

"Rod is going to get me onto the campus as one of the construction workers and then he'll help me get Tess out."

"Absolutely not," Braznovich stated sternly.

Skylar gawked at him. "I'm going in to get my sister," she said flatly.

"It's not negotiable."

"You got that right," she huffed. "I'm going in. Period."

"It's too dangerous."

Skylar crossed her arms atop the table. Who the hell did he think he was? He had no right to tell her what she could and couldn't do, and especially when it pertained to Tess. She was going in and that was that.

His jaw tensed and Skylar could only imagine what he was thinking. "We'll discuss this later," he said through clenched teeth.

"I'd like to be a fly on the wall for that conversation," Ernie joked.

It felt good to take a warm shower and slip into the silky pajamas Braznovich had bought for her. He was already in bed when Skylar came out of the bathroom. Lying on his back, with his hands tucked behind his head, he stared up at the ceiling. His chest was bare and the blanket sat just below his belly button, revealing his muscular six-pack. Even though she was angry at him, Skylar couldn't help but drink him in with her eyes.

Sliding in next to him, she lay on her back and stared up at the ceiling. "Are you still mad at me?" She asked.

"You exasperate me."

"Ditto."

He shifted onto his side to face her, and propped himself up with his right arm, extending his left and placing it on her stomach. "I don't want you to be a part of what happens on Friday," he said.

She turned to face him, lying on her left side and weaving the fingers of her right hand between his. "Don't make me borrow your Lamborghini to go save my sister," she whispered, teasingly.

He shook his head. "What am I going to do with you?"

"I have a few ideas," she grinned, dragging her teeth over his lower lip.

Braznovich rolled over, the sparkle returning to his eyes as he climbed on top of her. "Are you flirting with me, Ms. Wilson?" He leaned down and ran his tongue up the side of her neck, planting tender kisses along the way.

"Possibly," she moaned.

"Possibly?" He pulled back and looked into her eyes.

"I'd say that's speculation," she grinned and he let out a chuckle, drawing closer and closing his lips on hers in a tender kiss.

"I don't want you to leave here again. Do you understand?" His eyes grew serious and his stare felt as if it were piercing through her. Skylar tried to read what was behind them. Was it fear? Was he afraid something would happen to her? Did he care for her as much as she had begun to care for him? Did he love her? *No. Surely, not. We barely know each other.* Was he so anal and controlling that he felt the need to lay down rules for her to follow? If that were the case, Skylar was certain that their relationship wouldn't last. Obedience wasn't exactly Skylar's forte. In fact, some might argue that she struggled to uphold the simplest of regulations.

She scooted out from under him and pushed him onto his back so that she was leaning over him. "I know you're upset that I left, but if I hadn't gone, I would never have discovered Rod's plans for Friday. The Lord works in mysterious ways," she smiled.

He gave her a stern look. "As Ernie would say, it's ironic; but don't do it again."

"I have to go with Rod on Friday." She studied his face as she spoke. "I don't have a choice."

"You stay here and I'll go with Rod to get Tess."

"And I'll do what? Sit here and twiddle my thumbs, not sure if you've found her or if either of you has made it out alive?" Skylar pushed off of him and flopped onto her back. "I can't do that."

Silence filled the air between them. They were at an impasse.

"Skylar, if the police get wind of this plan they'll be there waiting for Rod and his group to show up. You are wanted for questioning in several murders and until we can prove your innocence, you can't risk being arrested."

"They won't get wind of the plan," Skylar sighed. *He's just being paranoid.*

"Maybe not, but even if they don't, once the first bomb explodes that place will be crawling with cops. Do you think they won't notice you trying to coax your sister from one of the buildings?"

"So what? They'll just think I'm one of the many students fleeing for my life." Skylar turned onto her side, facing Braznovich and propping herself on her elbow.

"Your face has been plastered all over the news and on every wall of every precinct in a five state area. Don't think for a moment that every cop doesn't have your face burned into his memory." Braznovich gritted his teeth and narrowed his eyes. "Do you want to wind up dead?"

Skylar rolled her eyes. *He's cute, but paranoid.*

"You, of all people, should know what we're up against. These people are worse than the mob. They're worse than terrorists. They just took out a Vice Presidential candidate of the United States. I don't think that has sunk into your head yet." He reached over and tucked a piece of her hair behind her ear. "Skylar, these aren't people you need to be antagonizing."

"I know. I know who Sagan is and I know what he's capable of." She fought back the emotion rising in her throat. "I know he's a killer…" her voice broke and she cleared her throat and licked her lips. "But he's caused my sister and my family and even me, to some degree, to become something we never wanted to become, to live something we never wanted to live, and if we don't fight him, who will?" She dropped her gaze from his eyes to the bed, not wanting him to see that she was holding back tears. "Sagan is a cult leader. He's a spiritual bully and the only way to stop a bully from bullying is to hit back."

Braznovich took her chin and raised her eyes to meet his, wiping a stray tear that trickled down her cheek. "Okay," he whispered. "Then we fight back. Together."

She leaned into him, her lips touching his and opening into a kiss that started tender and grew more passionate. Weaving his fingers through the back of her hair, he pulled her closer until their bodies were so closely intertwined; it was as if they were one.

CHAPTER 28

"I've got an idea," Greg said from the couch, clicking rapidly across his computer keyboard with one hand and shoving a piece of buttered toast in his mouth with the other.

"How early did you get up?" Skylar asked, groggily coming down the stairs and heading toward the kitchen to make a pot of coffee.

"I never went to sleep," he answered hurriedly and in a voice that was slightly more high-pitched than normal.

Skylar rubbed her eyes. "How much coffee have you had?"

"Three or four pots, give or take." He fidgeted on the couch, bouncing his knee up and down.

Skylar poured the remaining little bit of coffee into a cup and made a new pot and then joined Greg on the couch. "You're wired," she smirked, noticing that he couldn't sit still.

"I know. I feel kind of jittery."

"You're eyes are all bulgy and red. You need sleep." Skylar took a sip of her coffee and then set the cup on top of the coffee table, next to the computer monitor that displayed Tess's apartment. "Were you up all night watching Tess?"

"No. I told you, I have an idea and I stayed up compiling data."

"What sort of data? What's your idea?" Skylar's curiosity peaked. Had he come up with a way to evacuate the P3 campus?

"Don't get excited, I don't have an evacuation plan yet, but I'm working on it. I just wish we had more time."

"Me too," she sighed. Armageddon Friday was tomorrow and they still didn't have a fool-proof plan to protect the students and interns from Rod's bombs.

Braznovich came down the steps, showered and smelling of musky aftershave. No sooner had he said good morning when Ernie came bounding through the front door, with a cigarette pursed tightly between his lips and two paper grocery bags clutched in his arms. "It's about time you sleepy heads got up," he barked. "Don't you know tomorrow is Armageddon and we got work to do." He left a trail of smoke from the front door to the kitchen and Braznovich waved his arms in the air to dissipate it.

"Do you have to walk in with a lit cigarette?" Braznovich complained.

"I don't have to, but it would be wasteful to throw it out when it's only half smoked." Ernie grinned and Braznovich scowled. "Besides, you know I can't think unless I smoke."

Once everyone had gotten coffee and bagels with cream cheese, they settled into the family room to hear Greg's idea. Ernie took a seat in the armed chair, Skylar sat on the couch next to Greg and Braznovich paced in front of the fireplace with coffee in hand. Greg explained that he was compiling data that could be used to build a substantial case against Sagan. "After I saw the video of Patterson and Belmont at P3, I got to wondering how many other political candidates had fallen prey to Sagan's game," Greg said. "I mean, P3 has been around for years. Sagan has had a long time to work his way into the upper echelon of the political world."

"Go on," Braznovich said.

"I started digging through the archived surveillance feeds and, for the life of me, I couldn't find anything."

"Nothing?" Skylar was genuinely surprised.

"Nothing," Greg repeated. "So I replayed the Patterson/Belmont video and noticed that it didn't come from one of the security cameras. It came from an independent source."

"What does that mean?" Skylar asked.

"It means the camera was secretly planted in that room," Braznovich answered. "Which we had already assumed."

"It also means I have no way of hacking into the feed because I don't have any idea what system it's running on or from where it's being generated."

"I don't understand," Skylar uttered. "I was under the impression you had GOOD news."

"Let me finish." Greg took a sip of coffee, returned his cup to the coffee table and then rubbed his bloodshot eyes with both hands. "The room that Patterson and Belmont were in is so secret that Sagan doesn't even have his own security cameras in it."

"How do you know?" Ernie questioned.

"I told you, I spent all night digging through the archived surveillance feed of every camera on the campus. The Patterson/Belmont video was not recorded by P3 security cameras."

"Which means?" Ernie asked.

"There's a room without cameras," Greg uttered and then began digging through a pile of building schematics that were lying on the couch until he found the one that displayed the main building. He held it up. "See this little camera icon? These denote P3 security cameras. Now, here is Sagan's private office. It sits right behind the Prayer Room in the main building." Greg pointed to the rooms on the page and they all nodded indicating that they were following along. "The Prayer Room has four security cameras, plus one on the outside of each door so they can easily see who is coming and going," he explained. "Sagan's office has one on the outside of his door, but none on the inside. The room at the end of this hallway has one on the outside of the door to record who comes and goes, but none on the inside to show what happens behind closed doors.

All of the other rooms in this building have security cameras installed inside."

"Let me see that," Skylar mumbled and took the page from Greg. She studied it momentarily, turning it so it was as if she were standing in front of the main entrance. "That room down the long hallway is where I saw the chair with the handcuffs and blood on the floor."

"That explains why there are no cameras inside," Ernie said. He rose from the chair and headed to the sliding door to light up.

"Where are we going with this?" Braznovich asked.

"Like I said, all the other rooms in the main building have security cameras on the doors and inside the rooms themselves, except Sagan's office, the room with the bloodied, handcuffed-chair, and this one." Greg held up another schematic of the building. He had drawn a giant red circle around a room that appeared to be located directly behind Sagan's office.

"Wait a second," Braznovich leaned in closer and pointed. "Sagan's office is the last door on the left side of that hallway, so how can there be a room behind it. How do you access that room?"

A grin spread across Greg's face. "The only access is through Sagan's office."

"How do you know?" Skylar asked.

"I don't see any doorways or access points anywhere on these drawings," Braznovich uttered.

Greg clicked on his computer and brought up a slideshow which he had created during the night. The first slide was of Patterson, Belmont and NET head, Mort Radburn, entering Sagan's office. The second slide was of Mort Radburn leaving Sagan's office. The third slide was of Patterson and Belmont leaving Sagan's office."

"I see where you're going with this," Braznovich said. "You're assuming that Patterson, Belmont and Mort Radburn were only together for one meeting; the one for which we have video coverage, but that's speculation. For all we know, they could have met a hundred times."

Greg shook his head and directed their attention back to the slideshow. The next several slides were of Mort Radburn being escorted into the building, and of Patterson and Belmont exiting their limousine and being escorted inside.

"This still doesn't prove anything," Braznovich uttered.

"In the video Sagan tells Patterson and Belmont that they will run in this election for the offices of President and Vice President. Then this Saul Latham dude tells them that he has arranged rallies for them in Texas, Detroit, Kansas City and Denver. Those were the rallies from this year," Greg explained. "This video was made sometime within the last twelve months, probably within the last six months."

"Go on," Braznovich nodded.

"I told you," Greg sounded frustrated, "I scanned all of the surveillance feed from the past twelve months and this is the only occasion where Radburn, Patterson and Belmont arrived at the same time and entered Sagan's office at the same time."

"But they didn't leave at the same time," Ernie added.

"Right," Greg said. "Radburn left several hours before Patterson and Belmont, which we can see from the time stamp on the surveillance feed."

"They didn't leave together because Sagan asked Patterson and Belmont to stay so that he could slip them the Rohypnol and have them complete the questionnaires," Skylar said.

"Actually," Greg sputtered, "if the Rohypnol was in the communion wine, it was issued while everyone was still in the room."

"Meaning?" Braznovich asked.

"Meaning there's a possibility that Mort Radburn knows about the use of the Rohypnol and helped facilitate the meeting with Sagan for the express purpose of drugging Patterson and Belmont." Greg's fingers trembled slightly, probably from all the caffeine he had ingested throughout the night.

"That's all speculation," Braznovich uttered and Skylar rolled her eyes. "We can't waltz in and accuse the President of the National Ecclesiastical Transformation of being privy to or supporting the use of drugs." Braznovich ran his hand quickly through his still damp hair. "I know you've worked hard and if we had more time this might be something we could dig deeper into; but right now, it doesn't help us."

"I'm not finished yet," Greg beamed. "I know the difference between evidence and assumption. What all of this proves is that there is a secret room that can only be accessed through Sagan's office."

Ernie flicked his cigarette butt out the slider door and closed it. "I see what you're getting at," he interjected. "Lexi brought us one video, but there could be hundreds more."

"Exactly!" Greg blurted. "There could be enough incriminating evidence to lock him away for life."

Skylar liked the sound of that. Maxwell imprisoned, never able to manipulate, brainwash or use another innocent person. Talk about heaven on earth.

"What's more," Greg added, "is that it proves there is someone on the inside working against Sagan; someone who is close enough that he or she is allowed access to this private room."

"Someone in his upper echelon of leaders," Ernie added.

"Like Saul Latham or Miriam Edwin." Skylar posed, though she didn't believe for one minute either of them was working against Sagan.

"Who is Miriam Edwin?" Ernie asked.

"A worship leader, one of his top. Her music is all over the P3 world and from what I've read she's responsible for creating most of the mantra-hypnotic songs they use. You can watch her on God TV," Skylar explained.

"There's a God TV?" Ernie chuckled.

"Yep." Skylar took a sip of coffee. She'd watched God TV numerous times during her study of the P3 movement. Just the thought of it made the back of her neck prickle.

Ernie moved back to the sliding door and lit up another cigarette. "God TV... for all your P3 needs." He waved his hand in the air as if making the phrase into a billboard. He chuckled aloud and spoke in a broadcaster voice. "God TV...bringing demonic activity into your home daily."

"That'll do," Braznovich interrupted, steering the conversation back on track. "It would have to be someone who enters Sagan's office regularly."

"Yes," Greg agreed. "Someone who would have permission to enter his office and the secret room without Sagan being present."

"There can't be that many people with access to Sagan's office," Skylar said quietly. "What about the guy in the video who brings in the Sacrament?" Her eyes grew wider. "He's the same one who pulled Lexi away from the crowd after my car was bombed. Maybe he and Lexi were working together?"

Greg pulled up the video feed and paused it on the man's face. "Yes!" Skylar exclaimed. "That's him!"

"It's possible," Braznovich said. "He obviously has access to the room, at least when Sagan is present."

"Get me a clear print out of his face and I'll see if I can get an ID," Ernie said. "Maybe he's a local kid and somebody around town knows him."

"Anyway," Greg continued. "If we could get access to the video feed from the secret room, we'd be able to see who Sagan has met with, hear what was said and know how many of them may have been slipped Rohypnol. Then we could contact those people directly."

"Or we could turn over our findings to the District Attorney," Braznovich advised.

"No good," Ernie grumbled. "The minute the D.A. confronts Sagan with this sort of information, Sagan will find a way to keep him quiet."

"God removes all obstacles, remember?" Skylar said sarcastically.

"He does it in interesting ways though," Greg said.

"How so?" Skylar asked.

"Last night I read some interesting testimony on the internal workings of P3 from ex-students, interns and even ex-employees who worked closely with Sagan. The interesting part is that these are people of all ages, from different parts of the country, in no way related to one another; and yet they all tell a similar story." Greg pulled up a Word document of notes he had made from various testimonies. "For example," he continued, "this ex-student of the Sagan's School of Ministry states that when she began to question what she calls 'anti-scriptural' teachings, she was, and I quote, 'red flagged.' She was basically ostracized from her group, told her doubts were harmful to the other believers, and transferred to a P3 location in Canada, where they were better equipped to handle her so-called demons of doubt."

"Sagan is one sick bastard," Ernie mumbled.

"Anyway," Greg continued, "here's another testimony from an ex-employee who claims that Sagan watches the prayer room from a hidden peep hole in his office and selects which person or persons will have a so-called God encounter."

"HE selects the person?" Ernie scoffed. "You would think God would want to choose who was going to have a God encounter."

Skylar's temperature began rising as the anger in her gut increased. She placed her half eaten bagel on the coffee table and leaned back on the couch. Talking about Sagan and his lies made her lose her appetite.

Greg scanned through his notes. "Over and over people are saying the same things. Demons. Lies. False prophesies. And here's the scariest one of them all. A man says, 'Sagan is out of control and so are his followers. People will do anything he says, starve themselves and their children, even kill for him. I've seen it done. He demonizes the young and the weak and tells them they are encountering God, but God is nowhere present at P3.'"

"I don't think there's anything in the world that could make me starve myself," Ernie said.

"What about starving your baby to death?" Greg interjected with sarcasm.

"Somebody did that?" Ernie blurted.

"Yep, I read the story last night. A local couple went on one of Sagan's fasts and made the kid fast with them," Greg explained. "Kid died and Sagan denied ever influencing them to fast."

"What an asshole," Ernie mumbled.

Chills darted up the back of Skylar's neck as the realization of who and what they were up against sunk in. The silence was broken when Ernie spewed. "It's sickening."

"It's wrong," Skylar added.

"It's speculation," Braznovich said. "It's all hearsay unless we can find physical evidence."

As the morning slipped away, their quest began to feel more and more hopeless. So many people had already died. How many more would die tomorrow night if they couldn't find a way to shut the P3 machine down?

CHAPTER 29

Shortly after breakfast, Ernie left in search of someone who could identify the man with access to the secret room. Skylar washed the breakfast dishes, made all of the beds and straightened up the family room as much as she could with all the computers, wires and schematics lying about. She was going stir crazy, cooped up in the house. She wanted to do something to help bring them closer to nailing Sagan, but there was nothing she could do. Leaving the safety and seclusion of Braznovich's house was tainted with the risk of being recognized and arrested; and even if she could talk with people, it would only endanger them.

"C'mon," Braznovich said, taking her by the hand. "Let's go for a walk."

Skylar threw on a pair of blue jeans, her smoky gray Cashmere sweater and black Converse tennis shoes. "Where are we going?" She asked as he pulled open the sliding door and guided her onto the patio.

"I want to show you something."

He took her hand and led her past the pond, around the side of the barn and into the thick woods. The trees were beautiful with their leaves turning autumn colors and beginning to fall to the ground. Skylar loved the crunching sound of dry leaves beneath her feet and the smell of autumn. It reminded her of her childhood. She had grown up in a house surrounded by woods, with a long, gravel driveway. That place would always be home in her heart.

The air felt cool on her cheeks and nose, as she inhaled deeply, trying to coax her body to relax. Under normal circumstances, a walk through the woods would put her at ease, she would indulge the playful urge to get muddy in the creek or the dangerous impulse to balance on a broken log or even skip rocks across the pond; but today she was not at ease. Her mind was preoccupied with the possibilities of what might happen on Armageddon Friday.

Braznovich led her to a large oak tree that sprawled majestically up into the sky. He leaned down and stared near the base of the tree. "Here it is," he said. "Look."

Skylar bent down next to him and surveyed the tree. "I don't see anything."

"It's small, but it says SB + SW."

Skylar squinted and leaned in closer. Sure enough, the carving was just as he said. She stood up and studied his face.

"It wasn't prophetic," he grinned. "SW were the initials of the first girl I kissed. Sally Watts." Skylar smiled, watching his eyes sparkle as he recalled the memory. "I was twelve and she was older. I was so nervous I kissed her on her nose first and then finally found my way to her lips."

This was a side of Braznovich she'd never seen. A softer, less controlling side and Skylar was intrigued. "Where is Sally Watts now?"

"I don't know. I lost track of her sometime after my sophomore year. Her grandparents lived just through the woods, so we sort of grew up together. Every summer, when she came to visit her grandparents, we'd meet here."

"You never dated in high school or anything?"

"No, she didn't live around here so I only saw her in the summer and our romance was limited to the woods." He placed his hand against the tree and gazed at it, a certain tenderness filling his face.

"Do you miss her?"

He chuckled. "No, that was years ago. I miss the excitement of seeing her appear through the trees. I used to get so nervous, wondering every summer if she'd still like me."

"What happened to her?"

The smile left his eyes and he dropped his hand from the tree. "One summer she just didn't show up."

"I'm sorry," Skylar whispered.

"She was my first love and when I became a private investigator, she was the first person I looked into finding."

"Did you find her? Did you talk to her again?"

"No. I found out her grandfather had passed away during my sophomore year of high school and that her grandmother sold the house and moved to Illinois to live with Sally and her parents."

"That explains why she never came back," Skylar said and he nodded in agreement, but she got the feeling that the closure didn't completely remove the sting from his heart. There was sadness in his expression that told her there was more to this story. "Where is Sally now?"

Braznovich took Skylar's hand in his and they started walking deeper into woods. "She's in Illinois. She got married right out of high school and had two kids. Daughters."

They walked for a moment in silence. Skylar was wondering why he was telling her all of this and if there were more to the story; but she felt uncomfortable asking for details.

"I saw her a year ago," he offered. "She called my office and I met with her."

"Was she just tracking down an old friend or…" her voice trailed off as a thought entered her mind. *He's still seeing Sally, that's what he's trying to tell me. She's probably divorced and he's in love with her and trying to give me the backstory to break it to me gently.* "I see," Skylar said, giving his fingers a tender squeeze and then releasing his hand. "Thank

251

you for telling me." Skylar turned back toward the house. "We should probably get back in case Ernie returns with helpful information."

Braznovich grabbed her arm and spun her around to face him. "I don't know what's going on in that head of yours, but let me set one thing straight." He stared into her eyes. "I have feelings for you, Ms. Wilson. Feelings that are deeper than they should be considering the short time I've known you." Butterflies fluttered in her belly. She was completely unprepared for this level of honesty. "I'm not involved with Sally Watts or any other woman for that matter. I'd like to become more involved with you, provided we live through tomorrow evening." His lips curled at the edges into a slight smile and his eyes searched hers, as if he were seeking a consensual response.

"I thought you were trying to tell me that you and Sally reconnected and that you were..."

"No," he cut her off.

"When Sally vanished from my life, I was hurt, to say the least. I came to the woods every day and waited. It crushed me and it made me feel out of control, vulnerable. I vowed never to feel that way again and I never have, until the day you stole my bike and ran away from me." The sparkle left his eyes and Skylar saw a flash of anger appear and then disappear as quickly as it had come.

"I said I was sorry for that," Skylar said quietly.

"I know." He intertwined his fingers with hers and they started walking deeper into the woods again.

"Why did Sally come to see you last year?"

"Because one of her daughters had become involved in P3 and she wanted me to investigate the organization and tell her if I thought it was a cult."

"What did you tell her?" Skylar couldn't believe how far and wide P3 reached and how many people were negatively affected by Sagan's dark tentacles.

"I told her that by all definitions of a cult, P3 fit the bill and I encouraged her to get her daughter out." Braznovich sighed heavily.

"But she didn't, did she?" Skylar could tell by his expression that this story didn't have a happy ending.

"She tried, but it was too late."

"What do you mean? It's never too late. You can't just give up like that." Skylar stopped walking, slid her hand abruptly from his and put both hands on her hips. "Why do you do that? Why do you just quit?"

"I didn't quit..." he began but Skylar interrupted him.

"You quit on Jonathan and you quit on Sally's daughter. Why?" Skylar demanded.

Braznovich's jaw tightened and he pursed his lips together. "Sally's oldest daughter, AnnMarie, got involved in P3 during a summer camp. Sally thought it was a good influence in Annemarie's life and so she let her younger daughter go to a local house of prayer in Illinois. Everything seemed okay at first, but then AnnMarie started fasting and Sally got worried. She said AnnMarie had lost touch with reality, that she spent all of her time fasting and meditating and that she refused to come home, even on holidays. Sally came to me but by the time I looked into it, AnnMarie had collapsed. She told her mother about the demons cutting her arms and how Sagan saved her. She was dead before we could do anything."

Skylar grunted and drew her hands into fists. She was so angry, she wanted to hit something or scream.

"Sagan labeled her death a suicide, releasing a statement in Charisma Magazine that his flock can get over-zealous for the Lord but that he, in no way, encourages them to fast to the point of starvation."

"That's bullshit!" Skylar blurted. "We have testimony after testimony of students who have told us that they were not allowed off campus and that the only place on campus that sells food was shut down. They are passively aggressively FORCING these kids to fast!" Skylar's blood was boiling now, to the point that she felt breathless.

"Calm down," Braznovich said slowly and Skylar tried but she couldn't.

"What about the younger sister? Where is she?"

"Her name is Hannah. She's at P3, guarding Tess."

Skylar's knees buckled and she flopped to the ground, anger and stress overwhelming her. She couldn't handle her own rage and process the agony Sally Watts must be experiencing, having lost one child and have the other standing on the threshold of death. Tears poured from her eyes and dripped from her chin as she sat on the ground, sobbing and silently praying for God's intervention, for His help, for His mercy, for His cleansing and for His power to rid the earth of P3 forever.

Braznovich knelt in front of her in the leaves and pulled her close while she wept.

"We have to stop him," Skylar sobbed. "It isn't right what he's doing. He's hurting people. He's destroying lives and he's doing it in the name of God." It made her want to vomit. "We have to stop this," she cried.

Braznovich stroked her hair. "We will. We will."

CHAPTER 30

Upon returning to the house, they found Greg taking a much needed nap on the couch and Braznovich and Skylar crept quietly upstairs to the bedroom. Skylar's eyes were red and puffy from crying and the anger in her gut was ever present. More than anything now, she wanted to find the evidence that would put Sagan behind bars for life. But how? They were running out of time.

Braznovich led Skylar to the master suite and nudged her to sit down on the bed. He knelt in front of her and unlaced her tennis shoes, sliding them off. Weaving his fingers in hers, he pulled her to her feet, releasing her hands once she was standing and sliding the cashmere sweater over her head in one swift motion. He ran his hands up her back, unhooked her black, lacy bra and slid the straps down each arm, all the while keeping his eyes on hers. Unbuttoning his black collared shirt, she slid it slowly down his arms, letting her fingers linger momentarily on his biceps and anticipating the moment when his lips would meet hers. A warm rush of wanting filled her as he unfastened her blue jeans and pushed them to the floor. He ran his index finger along the top of her panties while she fumbled with his jeans, until she finally got them unfastened and lowered. Placing his right hand in the small of her back and gripping her neck, he forcefully pulled her into him, his tongue dancing wildly with hers in a kiss that left nothing to be desired. It was an outpouring of every emotion, a tension building between them and igniting a heat Skylar had never before felt. He lowered her onto the bed, his lips never leaving hers, as they rid each other of their remaining clothes; and then, completely naked in each other's arms, Braznovich slid slowly inside her. She moaned with pleasure, gripping his muscular arms as their bodies became one. In that moment, the fear, the rage, the world melted away and Skylar lost herself in the euphoria of his touch.

When Skylar awoke Braznovich was downstairs talking to Ernie and Greg. She wrapped herself in the quilt from the bed and sneaked to the edge of the stairs to eavesdrop.

"I don't want her going tomorrow night," Braznovich said. "It's too dangerous."

"I don't know how you're gonna stop her," Ernie retorted.

"I'll find a way."

"Good luck with that," Greg chided. "The Wilson girls are as stubborn as they come."

"I'm beginning to see that," Braznovich teased.

As he approached the staircase, Skylar made a dash back to the bedroom and jumped into bed, just as Braznovich entered the room. He closed and locked the door behind him. Skylar shut her eyes, trying to feign sleep as he drew near and sat down on the side of the bed. "I know you're awake," he said flatly. "And I know you were listening to our conversation."

Skylar slit open one eye. "That's speculation," she teased.

"I saw the edge of the quilt sticking out from the stairs. How do you explain that, Ms. Wilson?"

She shrugged. "Can you prove that you saw it?"

In one quick motion, he spun her over and slapped her bare ass. "That's for eavesdropping." Before she could process what was happening, he slapped the other cheek. "And that's for lying about it." Skylar flipped over and pulled the quilt up to her chin. Was she appalled? *No.* Should she be? That question would take longer to answer. Oddly enough she felt turned on, just like she did the other day in the barn when he pulled her over his shoulder and slapped her on the bottom. She'd never encountered a man this bold and assertive and something about it intrigued her. Suddenly she couldn't control her urge to giggle. She was overcome with laughter and pulling the quilt over her head, she hid her face from his scrutinizing glare.

"Are you laughing at me, Ms. Wilson?" He asked, but she was laughing too hard to be able to answer. "Well, we'll just see about that," he teased, with a seductive undertow in his voice; and standing up, Braznovich quickly removed his clothing and crawled beneath the quilt.

Skylar stopped laughing when his nakedness pressed against her and she could feel his desire. "Again?" She smiled.

"Again," he grinned, the sparkle returning to his gaze. "And again and again and again," he whispered, drawing closer until his lips closed on hers.

Skylar was surprised at how deeply she had fallen for him and how quickly. When this P3 thing was all over she would certainly need time to sit down and analyze her feelings, making sure the magnitude of her emotion for him wasn't simply masking the stress of their current situation. She wasn't one to profess love pre-maturely, if indeed it was love they shared. Only time would tell. For now, she was determined to focus only on the facts. Fact one, she was drawn to him with a physical lust unlike she'd ever felt. *And, wow! Was he good in bed!* Fact two, he made her laugh at a time in her life when laughter didn't come easy. It felt good. Fact three, she felt safe with him and he was a great protector. Fact four, even though they hadn't engaged in deep philosophical discussions, she could tell he had a good heart, an honest upbringing and that they shared many of the same values. Did all of that equate to love, Skylar didn't know; but she was certainly willing to stick around and find out.

   That evening they dined on spaghetti and meatballs, salad, bread and wine. Ernie made the meatballs from scratch, bragging that his mother was half Italian and her secret recipe was to die for. "I'm no chef," he said, wrapping a large, white towel around his waist as a makeshift apron and tucking it securely into the back of his jeans. "But I make a mean meatball." He was right, they were delicious.
   Skylar made the salad, which ended up being a compilation of every vegetable she could find in the refrigerator, tossed with Italian dressing and sprinkled with ground pepper. Braznovich disappeared to his Bat cave and reappeared carrying two bottles of Silver Oak Cabernet. Skylar gave him a cockeyed look, questioning where he had gotten the wine.
   "You haven't seen the wine cellar yet," he said with a wink and planted a tender kiss on her lips as he passed by. Skylar was puzzled because she didn't remember seeing an entrance to a wine cellar when she was downstairs.
   Finding placemats and cloth napkins in one of the kitchen drawers, Skylar went the extra mile to make the table look pretty. She folded the napkins into triangles and stood them up on each plate and then placed a jar candle she had found in the family room, in the center of the table. At her request, Greg set up one of the computers to play a mellow mix of music consisting of Sinatra, Colbie Calliat, Michael Buble and many other artists she liked. Once the plates were served, Ernie lit the candle, Braznovich dimmed the lights and they all took their seats around the table.

Greg picked up his fork and Skylar immediately cleared her throat. "I was thinking we could say a prayer," Skylar said quietly.

"That's a good idea," Braznovich agreed, taking her hand and extending his other hand to Ernie, while Skylar reached her other hand toward Greg.

Greg replaced his fork and took Skylar's hand, reaching simultaneously for Ernie's. Ernie scowled. "This ain't right. How come each of you gets to hold a pretty lady's hand and I'm stuck holding hands with you two."

"Luck of the draw, I guess," Braznovich grinned.

"Lucky bastard," Ernie mumbled under his breath.

Braznovich said grace and prayed for the protection of everyone at P3, closing with, "God, please protect each of us that goes in to rescue our loved ones. Amen."

Despite the fact that the dinner was delicious, the atmosphere romantic, and the company enjoyable, there was still a sense of sadness hanging in the room. It was the night before Armageddon Friday and they were out of time.

A few bites into their meal, Ernie took his knife and clanged it gently against his glass. "A toast," he said, raising his wine glass. "I'll go first and everyone join in." He took a deep breath and exhaled slowly. "To fighting for what's right."

They all touched glasses and took a sip.

Braznovich went next. "To shedding light on the truth."

They clinked their glasses again and took another sip of wine.

"To surviving tomorrow night," Skylar said, offering up her glass. They all sipped again.

"To finding solid proof," Greg added and they all sipped again.

Ernie chuckled a loud, raspy smoker's laugh. "To fighting for what's right. To shedding light on the truth. To surviving tomorrow night and to finding solid proof," he repeated. "We're poets and we don't even know it."

Braznovich's phone buzzed and he excused himself from the table, stepping outside the sliding door to answer it. A few moments later he poked his head in and asked Ernie to join him on the patio. Greg and Skylar cleared the dishes and Skylar tried to act nonchalant, as if not knowing what they were discussing wasn't driving her crazy.

"What do you think that's all about?" Greg asked, breaking the silence.

Skylar shrugged. "I don't know."

"Why can't they talk about it in front of us?" Greg said with a hint of frustration. "I mean, we're all in this shit hole together, right?"

Skylar didn't say anything, but she was thinking the same thing. What could be so private that they'd have to go outside to discuss it? Should she barge out there and demand to know? *No.* She didn't want to be perceived as the overbearing, nagging woman, but the longer they stayed outside the more she fought the urge to crash their conversation.

Once the dishes were cleared and the kitchen cleaned, Skylar joined Greg on the couch. "What's Tess up to?" She asked and he pointed to the monitor.

"Sleeping, as usual, or maybe she's meditating. It's hard to tell anymore," Greg scoffed. "I gotta tell you, Skylar, I don't think she wants out. I wouldn't be surprised if she refused to leave with you tomorrow."

"Then why did she text me?" Skylar rebutted. "I think she wants help. I think deep down she knows this is all wrong but she's in so deep she doesn't know how to get out. It's become her identity and I think she's afraid she'll be nobody without it."

"I hope you're right."

"I am right." Skylar exhaled. "This is all happening for a reason."

"You think so?" Greg's tone revealed his skepticism.

"I know so. If Tess hadn't text me when she did, I wouldn't have gone to P3 and if I hadn't gone to P3, I wouldn't have ended up at the police station. If I hadn't ended up at the police station, I wouldn't have received the anonymous note that led me to Braznovich; and if I hadn't met Braznovich, I wouldn't have had a reason to doubt him and run off to Rod's house. If I hadn't gone to Rod's house, I would never have known about Armageddon Friday, and if we hadn't found out about Armageddon Friday, Tess and all of the others would have been brutally attacked with no chance of making it out alive." She took a deep breath before continuing. "See, it's all been orchestrated from above. With God there are no surprises."

"I wish I had your faith," he sighed.

"Well, have faith," Ernie dramatically shouted, as he and Braznovich burst through the slider. They were both visibly excited.

"We have a plan," Braznovich said, rubbing his palms together.

"More wine?" Ernie called from the kitchen and everyone answered with a simultaneous yes.

Ernie refilled the glasses and handed one to each of them.

"So, what's this new plan?" Skylar asked.

Ernie took a seat in the armed chair. "Well, first, I found our mystery man with access to the secret room. He held up the picture Skylar had snapped when she was in the prayer room. His name is Johnny McCulley and he's twenty-six years old. His parents, a Mr. & Mrs. McCulley, live in mid-Missouri. They are quiet, law-abiding, God-fearing folks and are against P3. Mrs. McCulley calls it a cult and claims it has ruined their lives."

"I know the feeling," Greg murmured.

"So, what does this mean?" Skylar asked.

"We convinced Mr. & Mrs. McCulley to help us. They will arrive at the P3 campus tomorrow morning and ask to see Johnny privately," Ernie explained.

"What if he refuses to see them?" Skylar posed, knowing that was a distinct possibility.

"He won't," Braznovich answered. "We found out that Johnny had a younger sibling, a sister, who died of a rare form of cancer when she was a teenager. His mother claims that he never recovered from losing her, and because of his grief, sought comfort at P3."

"I'm still not following..." Skylar's voice trailed off.

"We've falsified medical documents to make it appear as if Mrs. McCulley has terminal cancer and has been given only a few months to live. The McCulley's aren't just going to P3 to inform Johnny that mom is dying, but to ask him to lay hands on her, or whatever they do to heal the sick," Ernie explained.

"They're going to pretend to have had a change of heart and ask Johnny to accept them into the P3 community," Braznovich detailed.

"That's frickin' brilliant!" Greg blurted.

Skylar's eyes widened. "Do you think he'll buy it?"

"I do," Braznovich said. "What's more, they're going to request that Johnny ask Sagan and all of the leaders to lay hands on her and pray."

"While they do that," Ernie chimed in, "we'll have another person sneak into Sagan's office, find the secret room and see if she can transmit a message to whoever is monitoring that camera."

"She?" Skylar questioned.

"Sally Watts," Braznovich answered. "She's on her way into town tonight."

"What if she gets caught?" Skylar gasped.

"We're counting on her not getting caught, but if she does, at least she has a justifiable reason to be in the building," Braznovich said. "She can always say she came to see Hannah."

"The Hannah who is guarding Tess," Skylar informed Greg.

Greg's face shown surprise. "How in the world did you find Hannah's mother?"

"It's a long story," Skylar quipped.

"So what message is this Sally lady supposed to transmit?" Greg asked.

"You tell us," Ernie said. "She'll sneak into the secret room and be able to speak directly to whoever is monitoring that room."

It was as if a light bulb went off in Greg's head and his face lit up. "This is brilliant!" A grin slowly filled his face. "She could tell them about the bombs and urge them to evacuate the campus. She could tell them that we need concrete evidence to prove the use of Rohypnol. She could tell them that we have the video that Lexi tried to deliver to her contact, and then ask this person to either contact us directly or send us the uplinks to everything they've ever recorded..." his voice trailed off and Skylar could see the wheels rapidly spinning in his brain. "They could have all the evidence we need to take Sagan down. Whoever this is could have enough evidence against the P3 leaders to shut down the operation worldwide."

"Or at least create enough doubt that people will begin doing their own research before getting involved," Ernie added.

Braznovich paced in front of the fireplace. "I wish we could convince Rod to stop his Armageddon plan. All it's going to do is further victimize these young people and martyr any of the fallen leaders."

"In his attempt to destroy it, he could make the movement stronger," Ernie rasped. The thought of this made Skylar's stomach twist into nauseating knots. "Unless we can shut down P3 first," Ernie added.

"That's why we need concrete evidence of what Sagan is doing," Braznovich reiterated.

"If Sally's message gets through we might have that evidence tomorrow." Greg sounded hopeful.

"The challenge is that we aren't going to know if Sally's message is received and if any action is taken until tomorrow," Braznovich ran his fingers through his hair. "It doesn't give us a lot of planning time."

"The alternative is to go to the police and tell them of Rod's Armageddon plan," Greg said.

"We've already covered this. The answer is no." Skylar tightened her lip and glared at Greg. "Until we know for sure that there are cops who are NOT on the P3 payroll, we can't trust any of them. If we turn Rod's people them into the police and the information gets back to Sagan, he might have them all killed." Skylar grimaced. "I don't want that blood on my hands."

"Agreed," Ernie interjected. "The deeper I'm digging into Kansas City, the more I'm convinced that Sagan pretty much owns everything and everyone."

"I was thinking," Skylar said quietly. "Can we have the McCulley's plant a bug on Sagan?" Skylar shifted on the couch, looping one leg up and draping the other leg over the top. "I mean, it won't help us in stopping Armageddon Friday, but it could help us gather the evidence we need going forward." All three of them stared at her, as if she had suddenly sprouted another head. "What?" She sheepishly asked.

Ernie jumped out of the armed chair, grabbed Skylar's face and planted a kiss on the top of her head. "You're one sharp cookie," he said, pulling open the slider and lighting up a cigarette. "One sharp cookie."

Braznovich looked to Ernie. "Do we have the equipment we would need to do something like this?"

"Yep. Greg and I can have it easily set up so that all the McCulleys have to do is to find a place to plant it," Ernie responded. "Do you think they have the wherewithal to pull it off?"

"I think it's worth asking them to try," Braznovich uttered.

"What if they get caught?" Skylar posed and no one answered. It was obvious that no one wanted to consider that possibility or ponder the outcome.

Greg piped in. "I'd like to wire them so I can hear everything that's going on. I'd also like to wire Sally so I can communicate with her while she's in Sagan's office and the secret room. I'd also like to put a camera on her so we can see what she sees."

"That's a great idea," Braznovich said.

"We could also have Sally plant a bug in Sagan's office," Skylar said.

"Yes," Greg agreed.

"I can pick Sally up in the morning when I get the McCulley's and bring them all here," Ernie offered.

"No," Braznovich responded. "You get the McCulley's. I'll get Sally."

A twinge of jealousy gripped Skylar. Why couldn't Ernie pick Sally up? Why was Braznovich adamant about doing it? *Stop acting like a teenager,* she scolded herself. *He doesn't still have feelings for Sally.*

"But we're not bringing anyone back here," Braznovich said. "Have the earpiece and the camera ready and I'll show her what to do."

Braznovich sat down beside Skylar and draped his arm around her shoulder. "Ernie's right," he said quietly, "you're one smart cookie and Mmmm, I do like cookies." He licked his lips and Skylar laughed, her momentary insecurity over Sally fading. Whatever she and Braznovich shared, it was uniquely wonderful and in the midst of all the chaos, he was a welcome distraction.

A certain excitement filled the room. They all felt it. There was hope again. They couldn't stop Rod's plans for Armageddon, but if they had someone on the inside to help evacuate the campus, maybe there wouldn't be as many casualties, or maybe none. If the evidence they needed happened to fall into their laps before Rod's plan was set into motion, they could take Sagan down and save lives at the same time. It could be a win-win situation and it all hinged on whether or not Sally could get into the secret room to transmit their message.

Ernie raised his wine glass. "To the McCulleys and Sally Watts." They all raised their glasses and drank. "May God help them succeed."

And they all said, "Amen."

CHAPTER 31

It was seven in the morning on Armageddon Friday when Ernie left to meet Mr. and Mrs. McCulley and Braznovich left to meet Sally. Skylar had barely slept. Her mind was a jumble of what ifs and prayers. She prayed for the safety of everyone on the P3 campus, prayed Sally's message would be received in time and that they would get the evidence they needed to shut Sagan down, prayed she would be able to get Tess out and prayed they wouldn't get caught.

Showering and then sliding on her blue jeans and a black, button down blouse, Skylar descended the steps to find Greg on the couch, typing away at his computer. "Good morning," Skylar groaned. "What are you working on?"

"Just making sure I can monitor the McCulleys and Sally when they go in," he answered, never looking up from his screen.

"Do you want coffee?" Skylar asked, shuffling to the kitchen and pouring herself a cup.

"Already got it."

Skylar peeled and ate a hard-boiled egg, minus the yoke and then joined Greg on the couch.

"Here we go!" Greg said, excitedly, showing Skylar the text he had just received from Ernie. It read: GO TIME, which meant the McCulleys were ready. Moments later, he received a text from Braznovich indicating that Sally was in position and ready. Jumping off the couch Greg set each monitor to display a different surveillance feed, and then he sent the parking lot camera feed to the large television above the fireplace. "We're live," he said anxiously. "We should see the McCulleys arrive first. As soon as they meet with Johnny and hopefully with Sagan, I'll text Sally that it's safe to proceed."

Skylar took a deep breath. What if Sagan doesn't agree to meet with them? What if Sally can't get into Sagan's office? She pushed the questions from her mind. There were too many ways this thing could go wrong and if she concentrated on all of the 'what ifs' she'd go crazy. Right now, she needed to be calm and force herself to focus on the positive.

"Here they are," Greg said excitedly, pointing at the television. They watched in silence as Mr. and Mrs. McCulley got out of their silver Cadillac and slowly made their way toward the main entrance. Mrs. McCulley had plump, rounded hips beneath her blue floral dress and Mr. McCulley was bone skinny with bright white hair and thick silver-rimmed glasses. As soon as the McCulley's walked through the main entrance, Greg switched the feed to the inside camera, where they watched a young woman greet them and usher them down the hallway, into a small, white room. Greg switched the feed so that they could view this room. It was stark white and had no pictures on the walls. The lighting was fluorescent and gray and blue plaid chairs lined the walls. There were no magazines, no coffee machine, nothing to offer any sense of comfort. The McCulley's were visibly nervous. Skylar could see tears in Mrs. McCulley's eyes as they sat down, and Mr. McCulley took her hand in his.

"They look scared shitless," Greg sighed.

"Wouldn't you be?" Skylar's question was rhetorical. They both knew the answer. It was an undeniable yes. She studied them on the screen. Mrs. McCulley's hands trembled as she pulled a handkerchief from her handbag and wiped a stray tear from her cheek. Mr. McCulley draped his arm around the back of his wife's chair and exhaled. It looked as if the weight of the world rested upon them. A wave of guilt rushed over Skylar. Was it right to send them in? Was it justified to put these people, who had already been through so much, through this type of stress? Was it right to endanger their lives on the off chance that they may or may not gain enough information to stop Maxwell? "I hope we're doing the right thing," Skylar uttered.

"We don't have a choice," Greg responded. "We can't just let innocent people get blown up."

"But they look so frail and frightened..." her voice faded.

"Looking that way will help make their story believable," Greg said. "I have a good feeling about this."

Moments later the door opened and the same young woman escorted them out of the holding room, down the hall and directly into Sagan's office. The office door opened and closed causing Greg and Skylar to lose visual contact. "I'm switching us to audio now," Greg said. "Hopefully we can pick up their voices on the bug that is in Mrs. McCulley's purse."

"The bug he's supposed to plant on Sagan?"

"No, that's in Mr. McCulley's jacket pocket. Ernie thought it was too risky to wire the McCulleys so he put a bug in her purse. That way, on the off chance that it's found, they have plausible deniability."

Skylar rolled her eyes. "Sagan won't buy that they didn't know it was there," she scoffed.

Greg shrugged. "It was the best we could do."

Greg and Skylar stopped talking when they heard Sagan's voice. "Mr. and Mrs. McCulley," Maxwell welcomed them, his voice oozing with fake sincerity. Skylar's stomach turned and she made a gagging gesture at Greg.   "Johnny will join us here momentarily," Sagan said, "but I wanted to meet with you first."

"Thank you for seeing us," Mr. McCulley said.

"Please be seated," Sagan uttered and Greg and Skylar heard the squeaking of what sounded like a leather office chair. "Johnny was surprised to receive your message this morning. I believe this is the first time you have visited, is it not?"

"Yes, sir," Mr. McCulley answered.

"If I may speak directly, I was under the impression that you and Johnny had agreed to disagree as to the nature of what we do here," Sagan snarled. "So, you can only imagine the level of curiosity associated with your being here today."

"If I may speak to that?" Mrs. McCulley spoke softly and Skylar guessed she was asking Mr. McCulley's permission to address Sagan directly, which he must have granted because she continued. "We are getting up in years and there comes a time when life's circumstances have a way of making disagreements seem trivial." Mrs. McCulley's voice trembled. "Johnny is all we have left and we don't want to be separated from him. We're not above admitting that we may have misjudged him and you."

Skylar thought she could almost hear Sagan's cunning grin spread arrogantly across his face.

"Mr. Sagan, we've come a long way and we'd like to see our son now," Mr. McCulley said.

"Of course," Sagan said.

Moments later, they heard the door open and Johnny enter. "Oh, my Johnny!" Mrs. McCulley wailed and Skylar could only imagine how Mrs. McCulley must have leapt to her feet and thrown her arms around him.

"Son!" Mr. McCulley gasped.

Skylar found it odd that Johnny hadn't spoken at all yet. Not a word. Was it because he had an emotional knot lodged in his throat? Or was he just emotionless and cold? Skylar wished she were a fly on the wall.

"Johnny, your mother and I would like to speak with you in private," Mr. McCulley said.

"Whatever you have to tell me can be said in front of Maxwell," Johnny mumbled, and Skylar had the distinct feeling that he had been instructed to say this.

There were scuffling noises and it sounded as if chairs were being moved around and everyone was being seated. "Here goes nothing," Greg said. "They better sell the story and figure out a way to get out of his office."

"They will," Skylar said and chewed, nervously on her fingernail. *They have to!*

"Johnny," Sagan began, "is there something you would like to say to your parents?"

"Yeah, I don't know why you're here, but I don't believe you've had a change of heart," Johnny said in an accusatory tone. He sounded downright mean and Skylar was shocked.

"What a jerk!" Greg blurted.

"He's brainwashed," Skylar said. "You have to remember that he's been brainwashed against them."

"Don't you dare speak to your mother that way," Mr. McCulley scorned.

"It's okay," Mrs. McCulley sniveled. "We haven't been fair." There was a brief moment of silence and then Mrs. McCulley began telling the story that Skylar knew she had probably spent all night rehearsing. It was her turn to give an Emmy winning performance and she did just that. She moaned and cried and even broke into sobs as she told her son and Sagan that she had been diagnosed with Stage Four Lymphoma and given only six to eight weeks to live. "There's nothing they can do," she cried.

Sagan managed an insincere, "I'm sorry." Johnny said nothing.

"Son," Mrs. McCulley continued, "when I go, you are all your father has left. I couldn't bear it if you were estranged. I couldn't bear it," she wept.

Mr. McCulley cleared his throat. "We've been doing a lot of praying and asking for answers and we started to think that maybe we were wrong about what you do here."

"Typical," Johnny uttered. "You need help so NOW you turn to God."

"If that were my kid," Greg seethed, "I'd smack the crap out of him right there in the office."

Me too!

"Johnny," Sagan scolded, "it is often in the hour of need that God's salvation comes. He never turns away from the longing heart."

"Will you pray for me?" Mrs. McCulley cried. "Will you lay your hands on me and ask God to heal me? I don't want to die like your sister did. I don't want to leave you," Mrs. McCulley sobbed.

"Boy, she really knows how to lay it on thick," Greg mumbled.

"Yes, mom, of course we'll pray for you. Of course we will," Johnny said and it was the first sign of sympathy Skylar heard in his voice.

"It's working," Skylar whispered excitedly to Greg.

"Mr. Sagan," Mr. McCulley began, his voice shaky with emotion. "We've heard a lot about this prayer room of yours. We looked on the computer and we saw a lot of people getting healed so we got to thinking that if you and Johnny and your leaders laid hands on my wife in the prayer room..." his voice faded and he cleared his throat. "Well, we believe God will heal her."

Silence filled the room and the anticipation of Sagan's response was almost more than Skylar could bear. She crossed her fingers on both hands and closed her eyes. What was taking him so long to answer?

Finally, Sagan uttered, "Certainly, and may the Lord honor your faith with His restoration." Skylar wanted to leap off the couch and dance around the room. "Johnny, take your parents to the Prayer Room and I will summon some of the other leaders to join us."

Greg and Skylar watched the hall camera feed as Johnny and the McCulleys exited Sagan's office and made their way to the Prayer Room. She tried to get a read on Johnny, but his face looked stoic and unaffected by the news he'd just received. What kind of person wouldn't be in tears upon hearing that his mother was dying? Skylar couldn't fathom it. Fifteen minutes passed before Sagan finally sauntered out of his office. Saul Latham met him half way down the hall, followed by three other leaders, and they all entered the Prayer Room together.

Greg grabbed his cell phone and text Braznovich. "All clear."

That very moment Greg switched the main entrance surveillance feed to the television screen and they watched as Sally Watts adjusted her purse strap on her shoulder and walked through the main entrance door. "Is that Sally?" Greg asked.

"I don't know," Skylar mumbled. "I've never seen her before."

"Oh." Greg sounded surprised. He picked up the small microphone that was connected to his laptop and spoke into it. "Sally, if you can hear me okay, stop inside the door and tap your right foot two times on the floor."

The woman on the screen stopped and tapped her right foot two times. "Yep, that's her," Greg uttered.

Skylar swallowed hard. Sally looked much younger than Skylar had imagined. She had long dark hair that hung below her shoulders in natural waves and big, chocolate brown eyes. She was thin and prettier than Skylar had hoped. "Good," Greg said to Sally, "now proceed straight down the hallway in front of you until you reach the last door on the left."

Sally followed his instructions, but upon gripping the knob to Sagan's office, panic lit her face and she glanced up at the surveillance camera.

"Holy crap! It's locked!" Greg seethed. "Son of a ...."

"Wait," Skylar interrupted. "She's got it."

Sally reached into her purse, pulled out what looked like a small pocket knife, but it had smaller tools attached to it. She worked at the lock until it finally clicked open and then she hurried inside.

"Well, I'll be damned," Greg uttered. "She's handy."

They lost visual as soon as Sally entered Sagan's office.

"Okay, now," Greg said to Skylar, "I'm switching to two-way audio." He clicked at his keyboard. "Sally, can you hear me."

"Yes," she whispered. "I'm in but I'm not seeing another room."

"It's there," Greg assured her. "It might be hidden behind a bookcase or a painting or another large object. Look around."

"There's a giant tapestry that looks like the Shroud of Christ," Sally whispered. "I'll check behind it." They listened as she maneuvered around the office. "Yes," she said. "I've found the door. It's behind the tapestry."

They heard the door open and Sally's footsteps as she entered the hidden room.

"Close the door behind you and see if you can locate the hidden camera. It's located somewhere above, maybe in a ceiling tile or a vent," Greg instructed.

Sally followed Greg's instructions, keeping them informed of her every move. "I can't find a camera," she whispered.

"Do you think it was removed?" Skylar asked. "Either by the person who planted it or because it was discovered?"

The thought was upsetting. It would blow their entire plan. "Keep looking," Greg said to Sally.

Greg and Skylar stared at each other, locking eyes and fearing the worst.

"I found something," Sally said quietly. "It looks like a tiny black ball, but I think it's a camera."

"All right, we'll move forward as if it is. Do you remember what to say?" Greg asked her.

"Yes," she whispered. They heard Sally take a deep breath and then she began. "My name is Sally Watts and my daughter was murdered by the people of P3. My other daughter is a brainwashed member of this cult and I want to get her out. I've been sent here to ask you for help, not just for my daughter, but for every child ensnared here."

"That wasn't what we rehearsed," Greg said to Skylar, but Skylar couldn't blame Sally for adlibbing. If this was her one shot to save Hannah, who could blame her for taking it?

Sally continued. "Tonight there will be an attack on the P3 campus, something being called Armageddon Friday. People will be killed unless you can evacuate the campus before 7:00pm. We have tried to stop this attack but we cannot. Please help us. We have the video you made and gave to Lexi to deliver. We know about the Rohypnol, but we need concrete evidence to take to the District Attorney. We know about countless murders but we can't go to the police because many officers work for Sagan. Whoever you are, please help us." Sally drank in another deep breath. "Here is the email address where you can send any video evidence you have: AgainstP3@hotmail.com   We've all risked our lives to reach you. Please help us protect these kids and shut down this cult once and for all."

"Good, Sally," Greg praised. "Now get the hell out of there."

Skylar breathed a sigh of relief as they saw Sally exit Sagan's office, rush down the hallway and out of the building. "Thank God," she murmured.

"Now, we wait," Greg said.

"And hope for the best," Skylar added.

CHAPTER 32

Waiting was the worst part. It was agonizing. Greg stared at his laptop and Skylar paced behind the couch, every so often peering over his shoulder and asking if he'd received an email yet. "I promise you'll be the first to know," Greg sarcastically spewed after Skylar had asked for the umpteenth time.

Ernie returned an hour later, announcing that the McCulley's were unable to plant a bug on Sagan. "Mr. McCulley felt it was too risky and would endanger him and his wife if they were caught," Ernie explained.

"That's understandable," Skylar sighed.

"But it sucks," Greg added. "I'd liked to have heard what he said in private."

"You and me both," Ernie uttered, making a beeline to the sliding door and lighting up a smoke. "Where's Braz?" He asked.

"He's not back yet," Skylar answered and saw a flash of concern on Ernie's face.

"What's wrong?" Skylar asked, her stomach suddenly hollowing.

"Nah, nothing," Ernie tried to appear nonchalant, but Skylar could see that something was on his mind. He blew smoke out of his nose and turned around to face the barn.

"Do you think something is wrong?" Skylar questioned. "Do you think something happened to him?"

"Nothing's happened," Greg interjected. "At least nothing happened on the P3 campus." Greg pulled up the parking lot surveillance feed. "Sally left the building here," he pointed. Skylar peered over his shoulder at the computer screen, watching Sally exit the building and get into her car. "Braznovich followed her off the lot. See?" Greg pointed to the screen and Skylar saw Braznovich's Hummer pull out and leave the lot behind Sally.

"He probably met up with her for a debriefing," Ernie suggested, but Skylar didn't feel better about it. In fact, she felt that ever-present twinge of jealousy and she hated that feeling. Skylar glanced at the clock. It was 11:45am. "What time did Sally leave the campus?" She asked Greg.

He pulled up the main entrance feed and looked at the timestamp. "10:20am," he said.

Skylar's mood fell. Braznovich had been alone with Sally for the past hour and twenty-five minutes. *That's an awfully long debriefing.*

At noon, Skylar made ham and cheese sandwiches and served them to Ernie and Greg with potato chips and iced tea. Braznovich still hadn't returned. She borrowed Ernie's phone and called Rod, ensuring their plans were still on and arranging to meet him at the mini-mart up the street from his house at 6:45pm. She hung up the phone and felt the pit in her stomach deepen. At 3:00 Braznovich was still M.I.A. and Greg hadn't received an email from the mystery contact at P3. It felt as if everything was caving in around them.

Skylar excused herself to the master bedroom and flopped across the bed. She was both worried about Braznovich and angry that he had disappeared, presumably with Sally for so long. He could have at least checked in with Ernie or Greg to let them know that he was okay. Skylar rolled to her side and tried to stifle the tears that began filling her eyes. The truth was she was scared. She was about to walk into a war zone tonight and she felt unprepared. She was involved in a romance with a man who was obviously accustomed to entertaining and wooing lots of women, and she felt out of her league. She was going to try to save her sister, whom she wasn't even sure wanted saving, and she felt afraid for both of their lives. There was no room for failure, but in the face of Armageddon Friday, Skylar was having difficulty defining success. Was there any scenario that would result in zero casualties? The answer was no, at least not without a miracle of God.

At 5:20pm Ernie knocked on the bedroom door and awakened Skylar. Poking his head in, he told her dinner was almost ready and that they had one hour before they needed to leave. "Is he home yet?" She sat up and groggily asked.

"No," Ernie said. "But he's okay. He text and said he had some things to take care of and would see us tonight."

Now that she knew he was safe, anger began to replace sadness. He was probably in some sleazy motel room screwing Sally's brains out. *Who am I kidding? He wouldn't take her to a seedy motel. They're probably in a Penthouse suite somewhere, drinking champagne and toasting to first love.* Skylar sat up, draped her legs over the side of the bed and slid on her tennis shoes. Now, she was pissed. She brushed her teeth, touched up her make-up and went downstairs to join Ernie and Greg for dinner. Ernie had grilled steaks and Greg had made a batch of macaroni and cheese. They had set the table with paper plates.

"It ain't fine dining," Ernie joked, "but it will sustain your life."

"It looks great," Skylar said. "Thank you." She hadn't intended to sleep through dinner preparations.

Dinner was eerily quiet and Skylar assumed it was because no one wanted to address the white elephant in the room. She was relieved, because had the topic of Braznovich's whereabouts come up, she feared that she would have either exploded in anger or collapsed in tears; neither of which she wanted to do in front of Ernie and Greg.

After dinner, Skylar threw away their paper plates, rinsed the silverware, put away the left overs and then told Ernie that she would wait for him on the front porch. Sitting on the porch swing, Skylar's spirits sank. She had hoped to see Braznovich before she left and now she ached with disappointment. He wasn't coming and deep down she knew why. Her mind had reluctantly filled in the blanks, and her heart was broken by his betrayal.

Greg poked his head out. "Can you come in for a second?"

"Why?" Skylar slid off the swing and followed Greg inside.

"I want to show you something." He sat on the couch and motioned for Skylar to join him; and then he pulled up an email on his laptop.

"Campus will be as evacuated. As many off campus as possible tonight. Evidence uplinks to follow." The email came from a protected account and one, when Greg tried to trace it, looped around the globe in a massive mess of IP addresses.

Skylar smiled. This was great news. Sally had reached the mystery person and as a result, countless lives would be saved. "If only Braznovich were here to share in the good news," Skylar mumbled sarcastically.

"Go easy on him," Greg said, patting her knee. "There's probably a very good explanation."

Skylar rolled her eyes.

Ernie flicked his cigarette butt off the deck and then closed the sliding door. "Before we head out, let's go through the plan once more so we're all on the same page," he said.

"I'll use the temporary cell phone to call Greg the minute I reach Tess's apartment building so he can get me in and get Tess and me out. Then, we'll exit the main entrance prior to 8:15pm and meet Ernie at the rear of the campus, on the west side, outside the fence."

"If something goes wrong or you find yourself trapped, text me," Greg said. "I'll find a way to get you out."

"Until we hear otherwise, we have to assume Braz is going to follow the plan, attempting to get his nephew, Jonathan, out and then meet us in the rear after 8:15pm," Ernie said. "If that changes, I'll contact both of you."

Skylar exhaled sharply. "Whatever."

Ernie and Greg exchanged glances but no one dared to speak.

Pulling into the mini-mart lot, Ernie turned off the ignition and slanted his body to face Skylar. "Are you scared?"

"Scared doesn't begin to describe it," she exhaled.

"Good."

"Good?" She gawked at him. "Why is that good?"

"Because being scared pumps your adrenaline, helping you move faster, push harder and become stronger." He cracked his window and lit up a cigarette. "Remember how you felt when your car exploded? Well, you might have a similar feeling tonight. It's going to be loud, the kind of loud that will make your ears ring and your head split. The important thing is to keep moving. Move through the fear. Don't get frozen by it."

Skylar remembered the ear ringing sensation and the pounding headache that followed the explosion; and she definitely remembered the immobilizing fear. It's the kind of fear that grips from the inside out and makes your body shake uncontrollably.

"I know you have a gun, but take this." Ernie handed her a Taser. "In case you meet opposition you don't want to kill."

Chills darted up the back of her neck. What would she do if someone blocked her from reaching Tess? She had focused only on getting Tess and getting off the campus, but hadn't considered the possibility that she might actually encounter opposition. Skylar's eyes widened. "I don't want to kill anyone," she uttered.

"Now you don't have to," Ernie said, with the cigarette hanging from his lips. "This little baby will stop 'em long enough for you to get around 'em." He gave Skylar a quick lesson on how to use it and then showed her how to fasten it onto the belt loop of her jeans. "Whatever you do, don't Taser yourself." Her eyes widened and he chuckled. "Don't worry about it. You'll be fine."

Rod pulled his truck into the lot and parked on the opposite side. "There's your ride," Ernie said. "I guess one way or another I'll see you on the other side."

"That's not funny," Skylar scowled.

"You're right," he grimaced. "I'll see you on the other side of the fence. That's what I meant."

She opened the passenger door and started to slide out when Ernie grabbed her left hand and gave it a squeeze. "You look right nice in my shirt," he grinned. "That's my lucky shirt so you have nothing to worry about." She looked down at herself, forgetting that she had borrowed one of his flannel shirts to help her blend in with the construction guys. Thankfully the shirt was long enough to hide the Taser that was dangling from the front of her jeans and the 357 magnum that was stuffed in the back of her waistband.

"Thanks," she grinned, "for everything." She climbed down and shut the door behind her. *Ready or not, here we go.* She took a deep, shaky breath. There wasn't one tiny part of her that felt ready. Skylar watched Ernie drive away, a part of her wanting to chase after him, wishing she were still in the safety of his truck.

With her heart thumping wildly in her chest, she approached Rod's truck and climbed inside. "I was surprised when you called. I didn't think you were still coming," he said.

"I told you, I'm not leaving my sister there to die," Skylar uttered. "Let's just get this done."

"My kind of girl," he smirked. "Skip the foreplay and get right to the action."

Skylar rolled her eyes and let a tiny smile form on her lips. His humor calmed her nerves ever so slightly and his flirtation made her feel good.

As they neared the P3 campus, Skylar pulled her hair into a low ponytail and placed the white hard hat on top of her head. Slipping her arms into the bright, orange, construction vest, she fastened it in front and looked down at the badge that was clipped to the left side. "What's this?"

"That will get you through the gate and onto the campus."

"Someone's going to check this badge?" Panic filled her. She envisioned walking in with a group. She wasn't counting on a face-to-face inspection.

"Relax," Rod scolded. "All you have to do is place the badge under the scanner and you'll be logged in. They'll see you on the security camera but there's usually not a guard there in person."

"Usually?" Skylar repeated. "What if there's a guard there in person today?" She took a deep breath. Her hands were beginning to tremble and she had the sudden urge to either vomit or cry.

"There won't be. Relax. I'll go through with you."

They rode for another minute in complete silence, as horrifying thoughts bounced around Skylar's mind. What if she got caught? What if a security guard recognized her and called the police? Worse yet, what if he handed her over to Sagan?

Rod pulled a pair of mirrored sunglasses from the top of his visor and handed them to Skylar. "Wear these," he said.

"Thanks." She slid the glasses on her face and surveyed herself in the visor mirror. With the hard hat and the glasses, her identity was well concealed.

"Get rid of your lip gloss," Rod instructed, taking a sideways glance at her. "Most construction workers don't arrive all gussied up for work. There's probably a napkin or something in the glove compartment you can use to wipe it off."

Skylar opened the glove compartment and inhaled sharply when she saw two hand grenades. Rod must have heard her because he immediately offered an explanation. "They're just in case," he defended.

"Just in case," Skylar repeated. "In case of what?"

"Don't' worry about it," Rod muttered. "Just wipe off your lip gloss."

Skylar carefully slid a white napkin from beneath the grenades and closed the glove compartment. Despite the fact that the pins were in, the presence of grenades made her nervous. What if they got into a car accident? Would an impact be able to dislodge the pin and cause an explosion to go off in her lap? Skylar squirmed uncomfortably. *What does just in case mean? If he has bombs in every building, why does he need grenades?* She wasn't sure she wanted to know the answer and decided not to ask. This was one of those moments when ignorance was closer to bliss than knowledge. Wiping her lips clean, she turned to face Rod. "How's that? Better?"

"You could actually pass for one of the guys now."

"That's something a woman never wants to hear a man say," Skylar quipped and Rod laughed.

"Actually, with that shirt you sort of look like a lumber jack," he teased.

Skylar had borrowed the shirt in hopes of blending in with the other construction workers, but now she wondered if it would make her stand out instead of blend in. "Should I take it off?"

283

A sly grin spread across Rod's face. "That's a dangerous question."

Skylar blushed. "That's not what I meant."

"Damn," Rod teased. "I thought I was about to get lucky."

Skylar rolled her eyes even though Rod couldn't see them through her mirrored sunglasses. If anything, his flirtations had momentarily distracted her from thoughts of the grenades or what was about to happen at the campus, and for that, she was grateful.

Pulling into the construction lot located just behind the P3 complex, Rod parked and killed the ignition. He took the grenades from the glove compartment and placed one in each of his jacket pockets. "You got your gun, right?" He asked Skylar.

She nodded and pointed to the back of her jeans.

"Loaded?" He asked.

"Yep. I'm just hoping I don't need to use it."

"I wouldn't bet on that," he uttered, stepping out of his truck and closing the door behind him. Skylar slipped her hands into the gray work gloves that were lying next to her on the seat and then climbed out of the truck. The gloves were rubbery on the palm side and she clapped her hands together a couple of times to get used to the feeling.

"Now, walk confidently, like you belong here," he said and started walking toward the construction entrance.

"How do I do that?" Skylar scampered to catch up with him and keep up.

"Longer strides and don't fidget," Rod said without slowing the pace. Skylar lengthened her stride and kept up, but by the time they reached the gate she was out of breath. "Look like you know what you're doing," he whispered out of the side of his mouth. "And don't stare directly at the camera."

Thankfully, there was no guard standing at the gate. Rod placed his badge beneath the scanner and stepped through, letting it close behind him. Skylar followed his example and breathed a sigh of relief as she stepped through and the gate closed behind her.

Once they were out of range of the gate camera, Rod stopped walking and turned to face her. "Remember, this fence goes live at 8:00pm on the money."

"Goes live?"

"It's an electric fence and the gate is attached to it, which means that when the fence goes live the gate goes live. That means after 8:00pm the only exit you can use is through the main entrance."

"When you say 'goes live'... um... how live are we talking?" Skylar swallowed hard, trying not to show fear. "A little shock? A knock you on your butt kind of shock?"

Rod stared at her. "A roast you alive kind of shock. I'm serious, Skylar, after 8:00pm don't touch the fence." He patted the top of her hard hat. "Let's do this."

Skylar nodded affirmatively, but her stomach clenched into tight, nervous knots. "You'll be there when I get Tess out, right? You won't let anyone shoot her, right?" Her voice quivered. There was so much to remember and the timing had to be perfect, that she was now beginning to second guess whether she was strong enough to pull this off.

He took her by both shoulders and squeezed gently. "You have to trust me. You came to me for a reason, even if you didn't realize it at the time. It was a Divine appointment, you and me. I won't let you down. Just remember to watch the time and get you and your sister out of the main entrance before 8:29pm. I'll handle everything else."

Rod pointed her toward Tess's building and then disappeared toward the back of the campus. Skylar wanted to take off running toward Tess's building, but she didn't want to draw undue attention to herself. After all, why would a construction worker need to run across the campus? She needed to appear natural, normal, as if there were no cause for alarm. *Just a regular day on the job.*

Her heart thumped wildly as she reached Tess's apartment building and pulled open the heavy metal exterior door. Stepping inside, Skylar reached into her front jean pocket, retrieved the temporary cell phone from her pocket and dialed Greg.

"I see you," he answered on the first ring. "Don't take the stairs in front of you. Walk past them to the end of the hall. Go through the last door on your left and up those stairs to the fourth floor."

Skylar wondered why she couldn't take the staircase in front of her, but she didn't want to waste time arguing. She knew Greg had a better vantage point of the entire building and she trusted his judgment. The hall was long and stark white, just like in the main building. Fluorescent lighting ran along the ceiling and it was obvious to Skylar that Maxwell spent as little money as possible constructing the building. It was evident that he didn't care about aesthetics or comfort. His renters were given the bare minimum and charged a fortune for it. It sickened her. She strode quickly past the apartment doors which lined the hall, hoping no one would hear or see her and ask why a construction worker was in a building that was clearly not under construction. She began to dream up reasons just in case she was confronted.

"I'm at the door," she whispered into the phone.

"Go on. You're clear," Greg answered back.

Skylar pulled the door open, stepped into the stairwell and held the door as it closed so that it wouldn't slam loudly behind her. She then started up the steps. "Where is Tess right now?" She asked Greg.

"In her apartment, lying in bed," Greg said. "Caroline is sitting outside the door and Hannah is inside with Tess."

Crap! Skylar was hoping to catch Tess alone. She was actually hoping that Caroline and Hannah had been evacuated, but the more she thought about it, the more she realized that Sagan probably wouldn't allow Tess's guards to leave her for any reason. "P3 security can't see me on their cameras, right?"

"Right. I've blocked their feed. You're invisible, but you've got to hurry."

"Why do I have to hurry if I'm invisible?" Skylar didn't like the underlying angst in Greg's voice. "Is there something wrong?"

"No, but hurrying would be good," Greg barked.

He wasn't telling her something and it was obvious that whatever it was, he wasn't going to tell her. Skylar crept up the stairs as quickly and quietly as she could. As she reached for the handle on the fourth floor, the door burst open, bumping her in the chest. Skylar jumped backwards, letting out a tiny shriek and then gasped when she looked up and saw she was standing face-to-face with Braznovich's nephew, Jonathan.

"Sorry," Jonathan blurted. "I didn't know you were there."

Skylar nodded. "No problem." She said curtly.

"What are you doing way over here anyway? The building project is at the back of the campus..." his voice tapered off as he stared at Skylar, studying her face. Skylar's mouth went dry and panic gripped her.

"There's a problem with a fuse, a faulty fuse, and it's tripping everything, so we're checking each building..." Skylar muttered, trying to appear as if she knew what she was talking about.

"So you're checking the breaker boxes on every roof?" Jonathan asked.

"Yep, I'm headed to the roof," Skylar said, unsure of whether Jonathan was baiting and trapping her or if there really were breaker boxes on the roofs.

Jonathan narrowed his eyes. "What makes you think the problem is with this box and not another building."

"We've checked all the other buildings. It has to be this one," Skylar said with forced confidence. "Now, if you don't mind, I gotta get up there and see what's going on before my boss comes yelling at me for that holding up the job."

"Sure," Jonathan said and watched as Skylar turned and headed up the stairs.

"Nice adlib!" Greg blurted through the phone.

"Hey!" Jonathan hollered up the stairs. "Do you have a key to open the rooftop door?"

Skylar whirled around and looked down from the landing above. Her mouth went dry and she sucked in air as if through a straw. Should she Taser him? How loud was Tasering? Would it draw more unwanted attention? "I just told you, I've been checking boxes on every roof. There's no problem. With all the security cameras around here, your security officer buzzes me through the minute I reach the door." Was he buying her story?

Jonathan's eyes seemed to stare right through her. "Why were you about to enter the fourth floor door?"

"I had to use the bathroom," Skylar answered impulsively. "I forgot all about it when you hit me with the door."

"Workers are supposed to use the portable latrines set up at the construction site," Jonathan rebutted.

"Right," Skylar said, "but they're kind of nasty." She turned her head and pretended to speak into her cell phone. "I know, sir, but I've been delayed by someone who keeps asking me questions.

I'm going up now." She lowered the phone and looked toward Jonathan. "See, now my boss is pissed! Thanks a lot!"

Skylar stormed up the next two flights of steps and then paused. "Is he following me?" She whispered into the phone. She was shaking inside and out.

"Relax, he's on his way down the stairs. He must have bought it," Greg said. "But in case he didn't, you need to hurry."

"What time is it now?" Skylar asked.

"7:33pm. You have exactly twenty minutes until the first bomb goes off."

Skylar hurried back down the steps and through the fourth floor doorway. "This time tell me if someone is coming," she whispered to Greg.

"I'm sorry, I didn't see that guy until it was too late," Greg defended.

Skylar crept down the stark white hallway, made a left where it divided and immediately saw Caroline sitting crossed leg on the floor in front of Skylar's door. Butterflies danced wildly in her stomach. This was it. This was the moment they had been planning and she couldn't mess it up.

"Remember," Greg's voice filled her ear, "the alarm and sprinkler system will go off at precisely 7:43pm, that's ten minutes before the first bomb. Anyone left on campus should flood the halls and the campus grounds and that will give you some cover to get Tess out."

"Got it," Skylar whispered. "I'm hanging up now."

"I'll be watching," Greg said softly.

Skylar disconnected the call and slid the phone back into her jean pocket. As she approached Caroline, she removed her work gloves and sunglasses and then pulled the hard hat from her head. Caroline glanced up and immediately rose to her feet. She looked as if she had seen a ghost and Skylar surmised from her expression that Caroline knew exactly who she was. "I'm here to see my sister," Skylar said pointedly.

"I'm afraid I can't let you in," Caroline answered, her eyes wide with fear.

Skylar pulled the 357 magnum from her waistband and pointed it at Caroline. Big tears formed instantly in Caroline's eyes and guilt rushed over Skylar. She didn't want to make threats, but what choice did she have?

"They can see you," Caroline whispered and let her eyes dart up toward the cameras and back down to Skylar. "They can see us. If I let you in, they'll know."

"We've blocked their surveillance. They can't see you. Now are you going to let me in?" Skylar held the gun steady as Caroline turned and with trembling fingers, unlocked Tess's door.

Hannah, who had been sitting at the kitchen table, leapt to her feet with surprise. "What's going on?"

Skylar pushed Caroline through the door and then closed and locked it behind her. She instructed Caroline to join Hannah at the table and ordered them both to sit down.

"They can see you," Hannah blurted, crossing her arms over her chest. "Security will be coming through that door any second."

"She said they blocked the surveillance cameras," Caroline told her.

"That's impossible," Hannah scoffed.

Skylar checked her watch. It was now 7:37pm. "We don't have a lot of time so you need to listen carefully," she said. "I've come to get Tess, but also to rescue as many of you as I can."

"Who says we need rescuing?" Hannah scowled.

Skylar narrowed her eyes and glared at Hannah. She could see the resemblance between Hannah and Sally. "I know you like prophesies, so here's one for you. At exactly 7:43pm the fire alarm and sprinkler system in every building on campus is going to go off. P3 security won't be able to shut it down and the buildings are going to flood. You don't know this yet, but the flooding will actually be a blessing because it will help combat the fire from the bombs that are going to go off every six minutes starting at 7:53pm until the campus is destroyed."

Caroline's eyes grew wider and she put her hands over her mouth. Hannah sat staunch, her arms crossed in disbelief. "You're lying," Hannah spewed.

Skylar leaned down into Hannah's face. "I realize you're not used to prophetic words actually coming true, but this one will and if we don't hurry, a whole bunch of your friends are going to die."

"What do you want us do to?" Caroline asked, tears filling her eyes.

"She wants us to get Tess out," Hannah quipped. "All she cares about is her sister."

"Was the campus evacuated earlier this evening?" Skylar asked Hannah, but she refused to answer.

"Sort of," said Caroline. "There was a mandatory off-campus lecture this evening for all entry-level students and interns. It's about five minutes from here."

"Who's leading the lecture?"

"Saul Latham," Caroline answered. "Why?"

"No reason." Skylar took a deep breath. Whoever had arranged the off-campus lecture had only succeeded in protecting the entry-level students, meaning that they either couldn't force the leaders or higher-level personnel to attend or they didn't want to protect them. "Listen, your team leaders are specifically targeted to be killed. We have people trying to warn them, but they might be more prone to believe it, if they hear it from you. One of you could call them...."

Caroline cut her off. "We're not allowed to have cell phones."

Skylar felt righteous anger rising in her gut. "You could go building to building and warn them."

"I'll go!" Caroline jumped to her feet while Hannah sat motionless, staring at the top of the table. "C'mon, Hannah, what reason would she have to lie to us?"

"She'd lie so we would go running off while she sneaks her sister out. Do you know what will happen to us if she takes Tess?" Hannah stared up at Caroline and Skylar thought she saw fear creeping into her eyes.

"If you don't get off campus before 8:29pm you're as good as dead anyway," Skylar rebutted.

"Please," Caroline begged Hannah. "You know there's something wrong with this place. We've talked about it before." Caroline grabbed Hannah's hand. "This is our chance to get out. Please, Hannah?"

Hannah's bottom lip quivered slightly. "Hannah, your mother is working with us. She's the reason the mandatory lecture was scheduled. She's the reason every person at that lecture isn't going to be blown up tonight. You were supposed to be at the lecture too, but I have a feeling Maxwell wouldn't allow Tess's guards to go."

"You don't even know my mom," Hannah blurted.

"Sally Watts," Skylar said. "She's tall and thin and has long dark hair and brown eyes and she's a very brave woman." Skylar saw emotion fill Hannah's face. "Your mom loves you and she doesn't want to lose you the way she lost your sister."

Hannah abruptly stood up and walked toward Tess. There was a glimmer of hope behind her eyes. "She's been sedated," Hannah said of Tess, "so we'll have to help you get her down the stairs."

"Why was she sedated?"

"Maxwell's orders," Hannah shrugged.

"Does he order her sedated often?" Skylar posed.

"No. Never," Caroline explained. "He came here tonight and said he wanted her sedated because she was under a demonic attack."

Her blood was boiling, but Skylar swallowed the emotion. *I'll show him a demonic attack!* "Just help me get her to the stairs and then you two go warn the other team leaders and get off campus."

Skylar pulled the sheet off of Tess and her eyes instantly fixated on the bandages wrapped around Tess's arms, just above her elbows. *That son of a bitch cut her!* She seethed in her mind. *He cut my sister!* Rage consumed Skylar and she fought to maintain her composure and focus on what needed to be done. She needed to get Tess out; that was all that mattered now. Tess mumbled incoherently as Skylar, Hannah and Caroline lifted her from the bed and carried her down the hallway and to the front stairwell. Skylar scooped up the hard hat, glasses and gloves that she had left in the hallway and handed the hat to Caroline. "One of you should wear this, for protection." She shoved the gloves into the front of her jeans and slid the glasses into her flannel shirt pocket; she then glanced at her watch, 7:42pm. "You have one minute until the alarms and sprinklers go off. Get to the rear left building first. The bomb in that building will go off at exactly 7:53pm. Watch the time closely. The next building to blow is the rear right, six minutes later, then it goes to the left side of campus again, then the right and so on. The main building will blow at 8:29pm. You have to be off the campus before then." Skylar spoke rapidly and hoped Hannah and Caroline were able to follow. "Go. Tell everyone you see to get off campus. Hurry!"

Hannah and Caroline took off down the stairs and Skylar adjusted her grip beneath Tess's underarms. Tess was facing forward with the back of her head resting against Skylar's chest. "Tess, can you walk? Can you hear me?" Skylar inched her way backwards down the first flight with Tess's legs dragging lethargically down each step. "This would be so much faster if you could walk," Skylar grunted.

Pausing on the landing to readjust her hold, Skylar lowered Tess to the ground and stretched her back; then she bent over and reached for Tess's arms. This time Tess pulled away. "Stop it!" She slurred. "This is God's plan. Joel's Army is rising up to cleanse the Earth for our returning King."

"Shut up, Tess!" Skylar yelled. "This isn't God's plan." *This is Rod's plan!*

"No," Tess slurred. "We are fighting God's adversary."

"If we don't hurry, we're not going to be fighting anyone, because we'll be dead. Now, can you walk?" Skylar tried to speak calmly, but she knew they were running out of time.

"I'm not leaving," Tess slurred and slumped over onto the landing. "We are to build a wall of righteousness and remain."

"Maxwell didn't build a wall of righteousness. He built a prison of lies."

The alarm blast startled Skylar and the sprinkler system doused them with water. "We're running out of time," Skylar barked, but Tess didn't move. Skylar grabbed Tess's wrists, twisted her so that her back was facing the stairs and pulled her down the next flight of steps, her bottom and feet bouncing up and down on every stair. With the alarm sounding, Skylar expected the staircase to flood with people, but then she remembered that most of the students and interns had already been evacuated. Very few people entered the stairwell and they were in such a state of confusion and panic that they didn't seem to notice Tess and Skylar.

Just as they reached the next landing, Skylar's hands slipped off of Tess's wrists and Tess's head hit the landing. *Crap!* "I'm sorry, Tess!" Skylar bent down, but Tess just stared, seemingly unaware of what was happening. The water was making Skylar's grip slippery. Suddenly she remembered the work gloves. Skylar slid them from her waistband, quickly pulled them on, grabbed Tess's wrists again and headed down the next flight. While they were on the last set of stairs, the first bomb exploded and Skylar glanced at her watch. It was precisely 7:53pm. *I hope no one was in that building.*

Skylar dragged Tess through the front doors, as screams filled the night air. People were running, some toward the building where the bomb had just exploded and others running from it. Skylar felt a mixture of sadness and anger, as she witnessed the terror stricken faces of so many young people; but she squelched her emotions, knowing that she had to focus on getting herself and Tess out alive. When she heard a shot fired, Skylar's body instinctively tensed and she dove to cover Tess. She couldn't help wondering if one of the team leaders had been executed. It sent a shiver through her and she silently prayed. *God, help us.*

Adjusting her grip once more, Skylar began dragging Tess across the campus, toward the main building, careful to stay as far to the right as possible to avoid being seen. She expected the police to be flooding the main entrance at any moment, and God only knew what would happen if they found her. People were running in all directions, some calling out the names of their roommates or friends; and others wailing for help. They were almost to the main building when the second bomb exploded. Tess shrieked in her incoherent state and began to kick her feet against the ground. "No! No!" She cried. Skylar released her arms and squatted in front of her.

Placing her hands on Tess's face she stared into her eyes. "Can you walk?"

Tess didn't respond.

"Tess, if you don't get up now, we're both going to die!" Skylar's jaw tensed and Tess leaned forward, allowing Skylar to help her to her feet.

Tess wrapped her arm around Skylar's shoulder and Skylar wrapped her arm around Tess's waist, trying to support her weight. Tess was weak and frail from weeks of fasting and the effects of the sedative. Her legs were like Jell-O, offering no support, but Skylar's adrenaline enabled her to carry all of their weight. Hearing sirens rapidly approaching, Skylar led Tess toward a clump of bushes to the right of the main building, near the electric fence. She checked her watch, 8:04pm. That meant that the electric fence had already gone live and the third bomb would explode within the next minute.

Skylar lowered Tess to the ground and squatted next to her, trying to catch her breath and think. Swat teams now poured through the main entrance, heading toward the bomb cites. Two more shots rang out and Tess cried. "What's happening?"

There wasn't time to explain and Skylar was certain that Tess wouldn't remember the explanation anyway. She pulled out her cell phone and dialed Greg. "We're stuck by the front of the fence," Skylar blurted when he answered. "The cops are all over the place. I don't know where to go. We're trapped." Skylar's voice trembled. She remembered Ernie's words not to allow fear to immobilize her; to move through the fear. *How do I move through it when there's nowhere for us to go?*

The third explosion sounded and Skylar's muscles tensed again. She didn't know how much more she could take.

"The cops have the front entrance completely blocked. You'll never get out that way. You've got to get to the back of the campus," Greg told her.

"But the fence is live. There's no way out in the back," Skylar argued.

"I'm working on over-riding the fence system…"

"Can you do that?" Skylar screamed

"I think so."

"I need more than that," she blurted. "I need a guarantee, otherwise we're dead."

"I need more time," Greg yelled.

"Time is something I don't have," Skylar seethed.

"Just get to the back. I'll text you when it's safe to go over the fence."

Skylar disconnected the call and shoved the phone back into her pocket. Even if she could get Tess to the back of the campus without being seen, and even if Greg could get the fence shut down, how in the world was she going to get Tess up and over the fence by herself? Wrapping her arm around Tess's waist, she hoisted her to her feet. "I want to go to sleep," Tess whined. "I'm tired."

"C'mon, Tess, stay with me, we're almost out," Skylar groaned, staggering to keep Tess upright and make their way toward the back, being careful to stay behind the buildings and out of sight.

"Please, I need to rest," Tess slurred, slumping over and pulling Skylar to her knees.

"If we rest, we die!" No sooner had the words left her lips than she heard his voice from behind her.

"Thou shalt not steal," Maxwell gritted. Hearing his voice, Tess raised her head, let go of Skylar and crawled toward him, wrapping herself around his left leg and burying her face into his thigh.

"Tess!" Skylar yelled, stumbling to her feet.

"It appears that you are trying to steal what is mine," Maxwell said, never taking his eyes from Skylar, but reaching his left hand down to stroke Tess's hair with his fingers.

"You delusional son-of-a-bitch," Skylar spewed. "It's YOU who has stolen what belongs to God. It's YOU who has used God's name to deceive and manipulate and use people in order to make yourself feel powerful, and I don't think God's too happy about it."

Maxwell grinned sadistically and continued to pet Tess's head. "What I do, I do for the Father."

"Bullshit!" Skylar blurted. "What you do, you do for yourself and you don't care who you hurt or kill in the process."

"God removes the obstacles according to His plan," Maxwell stated calmly. "I am a mere tool, an instrument of His glory."

Skylar spit toward him. "You're a tool all right, but nothing you do brings glory to God."

Maxwell made a clicking sound with his tongue. "You were always rebellious and sinful. You will pay for what you've done here today."

"If it frees even one person from your sick control, it will have been worth it," she seethed and in one fast motion, pulled the 357 magnum from the back of her jeans and aimed it at Maxwell. "Let my sister go," Skylar demanded.

Maxwell lifted his left hand from Tess's head. "I'm not holding her. See." His grin grew wider and the evil in his eyes deeper and darker.

"Tess?" Skylar called to her. "Tess, come with me. Please."

"I don't think she wants to go with you," Maxwell clucked. "Your sinful ways sadden her."

"MY sinful ways. Well, if that isn't the pot calling the kettle..."

Before she could finish her sentence, Maxwell pulled a .38 from his jacket pocket and pointed it at Skylar.

"You might get a shot off, but so will I," Skylar uttered and tightened her grip on the gun. The truth was she didn't know what would happen if he shot first. Her dad's voice replayed in her mind from the day he presented her with her first gun. "He who hesitates dies," he had said. *He who hesitates dies. Maybe I should just shoot him now and be done with this.* Thinking it and doing it were two different things. She hated Maxwell, but could she kill him in cold blood? She didn't know if she had it in her.

The fourth explosion sounded and Skylar heard another shot fired in the distance. Did another team leader die?

Maxwell laughed and then took his gun and placed the barrel against the top of Tess's head. "Lower your weapon or this is the last time you'll see your sister," he growled.

Skylar's mouth went instantly dry and panic prevailed. She studied his eyes, with tears pricking at her own. There was no doubt in her mind that he was evil enough to kill Tess. *He never cared about her, not really. He only cared about himself. She's been disposable to him all along.* Skylar took a deep breath. *He's going to kill her unless I put down my gun. But if I do, he'll kill me. But if he kills me, will he let Tess live?* There were no guarantees. The only thing she knew for certain was that Maxwell was going to kill her and eventually kill Tess, too. Suddenly, her mind was a mesh of memories; strange memories of long ago, when she and Tess were kids. Dancing in their family room. Going on fishing trips with their grandpa. Singing in the car with their mom. Throwing footballs with their dad. Playing princess in the pool. Laughing so hard it felt like their sides would split wide open. Tears streamed down Skylar's face as she bent down and set the 357 magnum on the ground. "I love you Tess," she whispered. "I love you with all of my heart."

Maxwell grinned. "That is your problem. The heart is evil and cannot be trusted. If you love with the heart, you are corrupt. True love is loving with the spirit. That is God's love."

"You don't know anything about God's love," Skylar screamed, and suddenly she felt a righteous rage fill her. "You killed Ema and Mrs. Wright and Lexi!" She hollered as loud as she could.

"I believe it was your gun that killed them, wasn't it?" Maxwell chided. "You've made quite a mess of your life, but that's to be expected when you are led by a sinful heart."

"You murdered Pastor Goodwin and everyone else who stood against you and all of those innocent people in that African village. You murdered them all."

He made a clicking sound with his tongue. "Now, now, Skylar, let's not go making accusations. God is the one who removes obstacles, not me." Skylar's whole body shook as Maxwell lifted the .38 from Tess's head and took aim at Skylar. "Get down on your knees!" Maxwell commanded. She dropped to her knees in sobs as Maxwell took one step toward her.

"You're going to execute me, but there will be more like me, who will rise up against you. You won't be able to blackmail and kill everyone. You won't get away with this," Skylar tearfully seethed.

"What can I say, Skylar," he clucked. "The wages of sin is..."

Before he could finish his sentence, Tess bit into his upper thigh, causing him to jerk forward and holler in pain. He fired off a shot into the ground next to Skylar just as she dove forward, grabbed the 357 magnum and, without hesitation, fired two shots into Maxwell's chest. He flipped backwards, losing his grip on the .38 while Tess scrambled away from him. Skylar scrambled to her feet and keeping her gun aimed squarely at Maxwell, crept toward him. There were two gaping holes in his chest, but no blood coming from the wounds. Inching closer, Skylar noticed that he was wearing a Kevlar vest beneath his shirt. She gripped her gun tighter and let her eyes work their way from his chest to his head, gasping when she saw that a bullet had gone directly through his forehead. She covered her mouth and fought the urge to gag.

Skylar whirled around, scanning the area for the shooter. She knew that she had only hit him in the chest, so who put the bullet in his head? Was it Rod? Was it Ernie? Could it have been Braznovich?

Was it one of Rod's snipers? Whoever it was, they had saved her life.

The fifth explosion blast through Tess's apartment building, the closest building to them, and Tess covered her head and screamed. Skylar pulled Tess to her feet. "We've got to get out of her now!"

Tess stood up, saw Maxwell and vomited. "You killed him," she wailed. "You killed him."

Skylar knew how it appeared and she also knew it wasn't the right time to try to explain what had happened. She took Tess by the hand and pulled her toward the back of the campus. More shots rang out, but Skylar couldn't tell if the police were shooting at Rod's men, or Rod's men were shooting at the team leaders. Either way, it felt surreal, like a nightmare where everything moves in slow motion.

When they finally reached the back of the campus, Skylar released Tess's arm allowing her to slump into a fetal position, sobbing. Skylar took out her phone and text Greg. "We're at the back. Is the fence down?"

"Working on it" Greg text back. "Do you have Tess?"

"Yes, but we're trapped. Swat teams everywhere. Fence is the ONLY escape," she text.

"Hold tight. Getting closer," Greg text.

"HURRY!" Skylar text back and then crouched down next to Tess and held her while she cried.

Moments later the main building exploded and lit up the night sky. Skylar instinctively covered Tess's head with her hand, despite the fact that they weren't near the blast. Within seconds another bomb exploded, followed by another and another, all near the main building. *The finale.*

"What's happening?" Tess cried.

"The wages of sin is death…" Skylar muttered, her voice tapering off.

The finale of explosions drew the police toward the front of the campus, but Skylar knew they wouldn't stay there forever. She pulled out her phone. No message from Greg. She text: "We're running out of time."

"Psst! PSST!" Skylar heard from behind them.

She stood to her feet, pulled the 357 magnum from her waistband and whirled around. "Who's there?" She demanded.

"It's Rod," Rod said in a loud whisper. "Come toward the fence."

Skylar crept toward the fence until she could see him. He was standing on the outside of the fence, dressed all in black with a black ski mask covering his face.

"Don't touch the fence," he said emphatically.

"We're trapped," Skylar stammered. "How do we get out?"

Two more men appeared from behind Rod, both dressed in all black and both wearing ski masks. "We'll get you out. Sit tight."

Two helicopters with search lights flew over the campus, circling the entire area, shedding light on everything and everyone. "Police choppers!" Rod yelled to his men. "Let's hurry this up!" Then he turned to Skylar and tossed a black ski mask over the fence. "Put that on," he ordered.

"What about Tess?" Skylar asked, slipping the mask over her head and maneuvering it in place.

"The police aren't after Tess," Rod answered flatly.

Suddenly, Rod pulled out the grenades he had shoved in his pockets earlier. "Stand back!" He yelled. "Way back!"

Skylar grabbed Tess's arms, pulled her to a standing position and staggered with her away from the fence. *C'mon Tess, move faster!* She was getting frustrated, but knew deep down it wasn't Tess's fault. She was drugged and malnourished. When they were far enough away, Rod pulled the pin on one of the grenades and hurled it at the electric fence. The explosion was so loud Skylar instinctively dropped to her knees and grabbed her ears, while Tess screamed and slumped to the ground.

The choppers circled overhead. "You've got to get through the fence NOW!" Rod yelled.

Skylar tried to lift Tess again, but Tess fell back to the ground.

She could see several policemen off in the distance and knew it was only a matter of time before they would see the hole in the fence and start heading towards them. "Please Tess!" Skylar hollered. "Help me!"

All of a sudden Tess was swept from the ground in one fluid motion. Skylar recognized the muscular arms wrapped around her sister and looked up to see Braznovich. His hair was tussled more than usual, his black t-shirt was ripped and blood ran down his left bicep, but oh, was he a sight for sore eyes. Skylar stared at him, a rush of surprise overtaking her. "GO!" He yelled, pointing at the gaping hole in the fence and motioning Skylar to run through first.

Once they were all on the other side of the fence, they rushed into the trees; Rod's men disappearing in different directions. "I'll put Tess in Ernie's truck. You get in the Hummer," Braznovich instructed.

"I want to stay with Tess," Skylar objected.

"We'll meet up," Braznovich ordered. Skylar knew this wasn't the time to argue. They all needed to get to safety and she knew Ernie would take good care of Tess. She ran to the Hummer and climbed in, pulling the ski mask from her head.

CHAPTER 33

Braznovich left the headlights off until they were half a mile away from the P3 campus; then he flipped them on and made his way to the highway, headed toward the Kansas state line.

"I saw Sagan's body," he commented. "Did you kill him?"

"I shot him, twice, but he was wearing a vest," Skylar said.

He tossed her his phone. "Pull up the last picture."

She did and should have been surprised by what she saw, but, at this point, nothing surprised her. The photograph showed a picture of Maxwell, with his shirt torn wide open and the black, bullet proof vest openly displayed. Written in white lettering across the front of it was "Property of KC Police."

Skylar handed Braznovich his phone. "We already knew that he had the police in his back pocket," she sighed. So it wasn't surprising that he owned a police vest. "But how would he know to wear the vest tonight?"

"That's a good question," Braznovich said. "Somebody must have tipped him off."

"Who?" Skylar couldn't imagine any of Rod's team working for Sagan.

Braznovich took her left hand in his and gave it a squeeze. "Are you sure you didn't kill him?"

"Positive. I only fired two shots, both in his chest."

Braznovich raised an eyebrow and Skylar had the feeling that he didn't believe her, but she didn't care what he thought. Tess was safe, Sagan was dead, P3 was destroyed and Skylar was more concerned with whether or not there were other casualties. She hadn't seen bodies on the campus, but she had heard shots fired and could only assume that Rod's group had taken out the other team leaders.

"How many people died in this?" Skylar asked.

"I don't know," Braznovich said, and a heavy silence hung between them. So much had happened that there was ironically nothing left to say. It was time to process it all, yet Skylar felt mentally exhausted and utterly drained. As they put more miles between themselves and P3, the tension lessened and she slowly began to relax.

"I saw Jonathan," she said softly, breaking the silence.

"Me too."

She studied his face, growing concerned when she saw what she thought was sadness behind his eyes. "Did you talk to him?"

He released her hand and ran his hand quickly through his hair. "I did. I asked him to come with me, but he refused. He threatened to kill me if I tried to force him out." Braznovich shook his head. "He told me he'd kill himself before he'd go back home. I'm not going to tell THAT to my sister."

"So, what did you do?"

"What could I do?" He exhaled and Skylar closed her eyes. *You didn't leave him there!* "I did what every loving uncle would do. I Tasered him, tied him up and had Ernie transport him out of there."

Skylar's face lit up. "You didn't!"

"I did." The corner of his mouth curled up into a smile. "I figured it was time that I stop playing it safe and did what I knew was right."

Good for you!

"And you know what," Braznovich continued, "it felt pretty damn good."

305

Skylar laughed out loud. "I bet it did. So, where is Jonathan now?"

"At an undisclosed medical clinic. Ernie's taking Tess there too."

"What? Why?" Skylar was upset that this decision had been made without her consent. She had assumed Tess and Jonathan would be brought to Braznovich's grandfather's house with them. "I want to be with Tess."

"Right now it's more important for them to get healthy," he said. "They can't be trusted with our location. They will try to contact other P3 people and the police, so until we have evidence to prove your innocence and Sagan's crimes, we have to lay low; even from them."

She knew that he was right, but she didn't like it. More than anything, she wanted to see Tess and to assure her that everything was going to be okay. "When can I see her?"

"We'll talk to the doctors tomorrow and go from there."

"From one prison to another," Skylar mumbled, staring blankly out the passenger window.

CHAPTER 34

Walking through the front door, Skylar could instantly see the shock on Greg's face, as he rapidly punched keys on his laptop. "You won't believe it," he blurted and directed the news feed to the television above the fireplace.

"P3, which stands for Purposeful Powerful Prayer and sits in the heart of Kansas City, Missouri, lost their leader tonight in what can only be described as a brutal attack on the campus. Fifty-two year old, Maxwell Sagan, whom some considered to be a man of God and others labeled a cult leader, was murdered while trying to defend one of his up-and-coming leaders, Tess Wilson. The suspect behind the attack is said to be Tess's sister, Skylar Wilson, who, earlier this week was also accused of killing several other victims with ties to the P3 movement."

Skylar felt her knees buckle beneath her.

"The total number of casualties on the P3 campus is still unknown," the reporter continued. "You can see behind me that the compound is a ball of flames and fire fighters are diligently working to bring the fire under control. One eye witness had this to say." The camera angle widened and there, standing next to the reporter, was Hannah. The reporter placed the microphone in front of her. "What did you see here tonight?" The reporter asked.

"Skylar Wilson entered our building, put a gun in our faces and forced us to help her get her sister, Tess, out of the building. She told us that the whole campus was going to be blown up."

"Did you threaten them at gunpoint?" Braznovich asked.

"No, well, sort of; but I wasn't going to shoot them," Skylar winced.

"So it was clear that Skylar Wilson was behind this attack?" The reporter asked Hannah.

"Yes, she definitely knew what was going to happen and exactly what time the bombs were going to go off," Hannah stated matter-of-factly.

Braznovich threw his car keys across the room, watching as they smashed against the wall. He spewed several obscenities and then stormed out onto the back patio. Skylar stood motionless.

"What's his frickin' problem?" Greg blurted. "The police were already after you. This doesn't change anything. You just went from life in prison to the death penalty, if you get caught."

Skylar's eyes widened.

"Sorry," Greg murmured. "All I'm saying is that we needed proof to clear your name before and we still need proof to clear it now, so I don't know why he's so upset."

Greg made a good point. Nothing had changed regarding Skylar being a wanted criminal in the eyes of the Kansas City police and the world for that matter. So why was Braznovich so upset? Greg went back to clicking away at his keyboard while Skylar slipped onto the patio. Braznovich was sitting on the top step, staring into the woods. "Why are you so angry?" She asked, but he didn't respond. He shook his head from side to side and Skylar had the distinct feeling that he didn't know how to explain what he was feeling. She sat down next to him, resting her elbows on top of her knees. "It isn't that I'm in more trouble now, it's that we didn't get Hannah out, isn't it?" She sighed. "You wanted to be the knight in shining armor who rescued Sally's daughter."

He shifted his feet and shot Skylar a cockeyed look. "No, and yes." Running his hand through his tussled hair, Braznovich exhaled. "Every man wants to be someone's knight in shining armor, but I don't want to be Sally's." He shook his head, wearily. "I promised to get Hannah out and had I been able to keep that promise, Hannah would not be publically confirming your involvement in the attack tonight."

"It'll be okay..." Skylar's voice faded.

"From the moment I got Jonathan off the campus, I went back to search for you and Tess, but I couldn't find you. I was going crazy with worry and then when I found Sagan's body, I freaked out. I was so focused on finding you that Hannah never crossed my mind." His jaw tightened. "Had I kept my focus where it should have been, your name would be one step closer to being cleared, not further smeared."

Skylar nudged his shoulder with hers. "I know it looks bad, but it could be worse; at least we're all alive." He glanced sideways at her. "I mean, you may not have gotten Hannah into protective custody with Tess and Jonathan, but we managed to get her off the campus alive."

He grinned and turned to face her. "Always the optimist."

"It's not optimism," Skylar smiled. "It's faith. I believe in you and I believe that what we're doing here is for the greater good. And I believe God is helping us."

Braznovich tucked a piece of her hair behind her ear and then inched his way closer so that their lips were almost touching...

"Break it up, lovebirds!" Ernie rasped from the sliding door. "We got news."

Their kiss would have to wait. Braznovich leapt to his feet, grabbing Skylar's hand and pulling her up.

"Did you just get back?" Braznovich asked Ernie as they stepped inside.

"Two minutes ago. Tess and Jonathan are doing fine. We'll talk more about that later," he said. "Take a look see." He pointed to the television.

They all stared at the television as Clayton Richmond made a statement to the press. "On behalf

of Senator Patterson, I have been asked to issue this
release. Please hold all questions, as the Senator will
be happy to address them in person tomorrow
morning." Photographer's cameras flashed and
clicked away while the cameramen positioned
Richmond in the center of their screens. "Senator
Patterson has received substantial evidence exposing
Mort Radburn of the National Ecclesiastical
Transformation, Maxwell Sagan and numerous others
within the P3 organization, as co-conspirators in the
murder of Congresswoman Micah Belmont. Despite
the blatant attack against his campaign, Senator
Patterson is continuing his candidacy for the office of
President."

Braznovich's cell phone buzzed and he
motioned for Greg to mute the television while he
answered. They all stared in silence.

"Yes, sir, she is here," Braznovich said into
the phone. "He's asked me to place the call on
speaker," he said to Skylar, Ernie and Greg, and then
he held the phone out so they could all hear.

"Ms. Wilson, this is Senator Patterson. I
apologize for my inability to keep our meeting earlier
this week. I believe you will understand why at the
close of this conversation. After receiving your video
uplink, we conducted our own investigation and to
say that our findings were disturbing would be
putting it lightly. We initially felt our evidence
against Maxwell Sagan and the P3 organization was
inconclusive, but this afternoon, upon receiving the
rest of the information, we now have substantial and
concrete evidence of the illegal tactics Sagan used to
threaten, blackmail and even dispose of men and
women in high profile political and religious
positions."

"Sir?" Skylar questioned. "We didn't email
you anything this afternoon."

"Well, someone did, and you might say it has
literally changed the world, for me personally, for my
staff, for the people of Kansas City, Missouri and for

all those manipulated by this cult both nationally and internationally. We won't release this information to the press yet, but I wanted you to know that we now have conclusive evidence that Vice Presidential candidate, Micah Belmont, was murdered. We have blood test results confirming the use of Rohypnol and video coverage of Sagan and several other leaders placing the drug into the Sacrament of our Lord. The amount of compiled evidence is astounding. You have helped bring down a dangerous man, one who will be remembered as the religious Al Capone of this century."

Skylar didn't know what to say.

"Sir?" Braznovich interjected. "There is still the issue of corrupted law enforcement and the fact that Ms. Wilson's gun was stolen by Sagan's followers and used in several murders, framing Ms. Wilson for crimes she did not commit."

"Ah, yes, that's being worked on as we speak. You sit tight, Ms. Wilson, we'll not only have your name cleared, but you will be recognized as a brave woman, willing to fight for what is right and tenacious enough to win."

Skylar felt her cheeks flush. "Thank you, sir."

"No, Skylar. Thank you. We are indebted to you and your team for the information you have provided."

"One more thing, sir," Braznovich added. "Regarding what happened this evening, we were in no way responsible for the planning nor the implantation of this attack...."

Patterson cut Braznovich off mid-sentence. "Our official stance is that we know nothing about the attack this evening."

By the time Braznovich disconnected the call, Skylar was bursting with excitement. Her name was going to be cleared. The evidence against Sagan was going to be made public and everyone would know what a monster he was. The leaders who helped him murder and manipulate would be punished and the world's largest cult, known as P3, would be silenced. More than all of that, Tess was free. It would take time and healing, but Skylar was confident that once Tess was removed from the grips of this cult, she would be restored and have a normal life again. It was almost perfect. The only thing that could have made it better was if Sagan had been alive to face his punishment, although Skylar was certain he wasn't going to escape God's Divine judgment.

Skylar turned quickly to Ernie. "Did you kill Sagan?"

"Nope," Ernie said. "Braz said that he was shot in the head. I'd have shot him in the arms and legs and made him suffer before he died."

She took the cell phone from her pocket and text Rod. "Did you kill Sagan?"

A few seconds later a text came back. "Call me!"

Skylar stepped onto the patio and dialed Rod's number. "Five men!" He spewed. "I have five men down and ironically they were my snipers!"

"What?!" She gasped.

"Dead. My men are dead!"

"How?" She couldn't believe it.

"You tell me!" He snapped. "They were picked off one by one, like somebody knew exactly where to find them." Rod's rage seeped through the phone.

"But I heard shots..." Skylar was confused.

"Yeah, the shots that killed MY men!"

"Rod, I'm so sorry..."

"Save it, Skylar, just tell me who did it."

"I...I... don't know," she stammered.

"Did you leak our plan to the police?"

"No!" Skylar paced wildly across the patio. "You know I wouldn't do that."

"Then who did?" He screamed into the phone.

"I don't know."

"You tell your people that these were good, God-fearing men with wives and children. You tell your people I'm coming after them. An eye for an eye!" Rod hollered and then disconnected the call.

"Well?" Ernie said as she walked back inside. "Did he do it?"

Skylar shook her head, dazed.

"What's the matter?" Braznovich asked.

"He didn't kill Maxwell, but all of his snipers were taken out. Anybody know anything about that?"

All three men shrugged, as if it were news to them.

"How many snipers?" Braznovich asked.

"Five. All on the rooftops," Skylar explained.

"Greg, can you pull up any kind of surveillance feed that would show the rooftops?" Ernie asked.

"Maybe. If not a surveillance camera, maybe a satellite feed if I can find a live one," Greg mumbled.

"While you're at it, can you find a surveillance feed that shows Sagan being killed? Skylar asked.

"I already searched," Greg shrugged. "You were behind Tess's apartment building, between the building and the fence, right?" He asked and Skylar nodded. "Here's the surveillance camera that shows that area, but look." He played back the feed from the time frame when Sagan was killed. The feed was blank; no picture.

"What happened to it?" Braznovich asked.

"I have no idea. It just went black." Greg threw his hands in the air.

"Who would have the ability to mess with their security cameras?" Skylar posed.

"Anyone on the P3 security team, or someone like Greg who is hacking in," Ernie answered and walked toward the sliding door to light up a cigarette. "Whoever it was, they made sure we wouldn't know who killed Maxwell Sagan."

CHAPTER 35

It didn't take long for the elation to morph
into exhaustion and they all agreed to call it a night.
Despite how tired she was, Skylar tossed and turned,
her muscles wanting to melt into the bed, but her
mind churning; mulling over all that had happened.
Braznovich was snoring peacefully beside her and she
wished she could join him in slumber. Finally giving
up on sleep, she slid out from under his arm and
crept downstairs, where she found Greg sitting at the
kitchen table with a cup of hot tea and his laptop.
She fixed herself a cup of tea and sat down next to
him.

"It's been bugging me," he said.

"What?"

"Several things. First, where was Braznovich
all day today? Did you ever confront him?"

Crap! "No...I...um, I meant to, but I got
distracted," Skylar winced.

"You got distracted or he purposefully
distracted you?" Greg glared at her.

She didn't like what he was insinuating.
"What are you getting at?"

"Nothing. I don't know. Something just
smells fishy. It just seems odd that he vanished for a
whole afternoon and didn't tell anyone where he
went." Skylar crossed her arms and frowned. It did
smell fishy, but she didn't want to admit that to Greg.
"Second," he continued, "Braznovich didn't seem very
surprised when Patterson phoned him." Greg shook
his head. "I mean, if a Presidential candidate of the
United States of America calls my private cell phone
out of the blue, the shock is going to show on my
face; and I'm probably going to wonder how he got my

number, or how he knows my name for heaven's sake!"

Now that she thought about it, Braznovich did seem strangely calm when Patterson called, as if he were expecting to hear from him. "There's got to be a reasonable explanation," Skylar said.

"You had red flags about him earlier this week," Greg pointed out. "To the point that you sneaked out and stole one of his motorcycles to get away. What if your intuition was right?"

"It wasn't," Skylar argued. "That was a misunderstanding."

"Was it?" Greg's tone was sarcastic and Skylar didn't appreciate what he was trying to do.

"What's your point?" She demanded.

"The point is that all the pieces aren't adding up. You don't know Braznovich very well and I think he's hiding something."

Skylar grunted frustration and let her head plop down against the table. She felt like she was on an emotional rollercoaster. One minute up, the next down. One moment trusting him, the next doubting him. Was Greg right? It did seem odd that Patterson had Braznovich's cell number, and if he wasn't with Sally all afternoon, than where was he? Then again, was it any of her business? Did she have the right to demand to know his whereabouts?

"Then there's this." He scooted his laptop so they both had a clear view and pressed play on a surveillance camera feed which showed the P3 parking lot from earlier in the day. "The time frame on this is shortly after Sally delivered her message in the secret room and before we received the email that an evacuation would transpire."

Skylar watched intently as a person wearing a long, black, hooded trench coat and rounded dark glasses walked across the lot, carrying what looked like a file box and placing it into the trunk of a solid, black Cadillac. They did this four times, each time carrying at least one file box. "Who is it?" Skylar asked.

"I don't know, but I have a feeling that this is the person who planted the camera in the secret room. The one who had people like Lexi working for them, slowly building a case against P3," Greg explained.

"Braznovich would call that speculation," Skylar teased. "Anyway, it looks like someone is packing up their office files."

"Or boxes of files filled with evidence against Sagan," Greg stated. "And it looks to me like they're in a hurry to do it. The timing is a little too coincidental if you ask me."

"Can you get a read on the license plate?"

He zoomed the video. "Already tried, but I can only see the front plate and it doesn't have numbers or letters on it. It looks like some sort of emblem, but I can't zoom in close enough to see what it is."

"What about the driver?" Skylar asked.

"I can't see his or her face either. All I can see are black leather gloves gripping the steering wheel. It could be anybody."

Greg zoomed in closer on the face of the person beneath the dark glasses and trench coat, but zooming lost clarity and the picture was too blurred to see anything. "Is it a man or a woman?" Skylar squinted.

"Can't tell that either. The shoes look female. The glasses could go either way. It's all guesswork."

Skylar stared intently at the screen. This person looked oddly familiar. "I've seen that walk before. It looks feminine."

"Nowadays that doesn't mean much," Greg chided.

She smirked at Greg and then turned her attention back to the screen. She couldn't escape the feeling that she had seen this person before; and then all of a sudden it hit her. "Can you bring up the surveillance feed of the person who left the note on my car just before the bomb?"

It took a few moments for Greg to find it, but when he did they were both astounded by the similarity. "This is the same person," Greg blurted. "Same coat, same shoes, same glasses..." his voice trailed off.

"Same hair," Skylar said, squinting at the screen.

"Hair? The head's covered with a hood. We can't see the hair."

"Look," Skylar pointed to the very edge of the hood, just below the person's right ear lobe. "There's a piece of hair sticking out right there."

Greg zoomed closer on both pictures and confirmed that whoever it was had blonde hair and wasn't very good about making sure it remained tucked under their hood.

"Blonde, huh? Well, that doesn't help much," Greg rubbed his eyes. "Then again, it could be a wig beneath the hood," he posed.

"Maybe," Skylar uttered. There was always a chance that this person was nobody of consequence and her loading a car with file boxes was completely coincidental. Then again, if it was the same person who had placed the note on Skylar's car, warning her of the bomb, then this could be the person who had placed and monitored the camera inside Sagan's secret room. It was possible that this was the insider working against P3, the one Ema referred to as spies among them, and the one who sent Lexi to deliver the video uplink to Mrs. Wright. It was possible that this person was the one who was truly responsible for shutting down P3. If so, it was logical for them to remove the evidence from buildings they knew were about to be blown up. It was certainly worth trying to find this person and ask them some questions.

Skylar finished her tea and upon placing her empty cup in the sink, noticed Mrs. Wright's recipe box sitting on the countertop. She carried it to the table, sat down and began flipping through the recipe cards.

"What are you looking for?" Greg asked.

"I'm not sure," Skylar sighed. "I just feel like there's something we're missing in here."

After fifteen minutes of pulling out random cards and finding nothing relevant, Skylar excused herself back to bed. There was a lot to think about and though she was certain she would have trouble falling asleep, her tired body beckoned her to try.

Skylar lay in bed, staring at the ceiling, when all of a sudden a thought popped into her mind. It was a memory more than a random thought. She remembered being in Ema's hospital room, when Ema was using her last breath to communicate. She had said 'M' and Skylar thought she was referring to money or magic, but now, it seemed as if she meant something else entirely. Had Ema been trying to direct them to the mystery person who was building a case against Sagan all along?

"Omigosh," Skylar put her hand to her mouth as the memory flooded her mind.

Braznovich groggily rolled over. "What is it?"

"In Ema's hospital room, I think she tried to tell me who the mystery person is, but I misunderstood. Then she said 'P...Pr...' and I thought she meant prophet or prayer, but now I think she was trying to say the word 'President' and after that she said 'N.E.T.' ...." Skylar abruptly sat up, her eyes widening and her pulse quickening. "I think I know who our mystery person is..." her voice trailed off as disbelief swept over her. *It couldn't be.*

CHAPTER 36

Since neither of them could fall back asleep, Skylar shared her theory with Braznovich. She told him about the person in the trench coat, loading files into the black Cadillac with the odd license plate; and how she believed it to be the same person who had left her the anonymous notes. Braznovich didn't appear overly shocked. "It could be," he said. "It's at least worth going and talking to her."

Unsettled by his non-enthusiastic response, Skylar crossed her arms. "That's it? I've probably figured out who the insider is and you're lethargic about it?"

Braznovich chuckled. "In my defense, it is the middle of the night and I'm tired. Besides, we've known all along that there was an insider working against P3. It stands to reason that the person relocating the evidence would be the one who gathered it in the first place."

Skylar studied his face. He was so matter-of-fact, so calm, so not surprised and it bugged her. "Where were you today?" She blurted before she could stop herself.

NOW he looked surprised. "I wondered when you would ask, though I didn't think it would be in the middle of the night."

"Well?" She bulged her eyes and threw her hands up.

"I took Sally out for coffee and then made sure she made it safely back to her hotel," he explained.

"And then?" Skylar knew she sounded more accusatory than she intended, but in her defense, she was running on no sleep and she thought he should be more forthright with the information.

He reached over and tucked her hair behind her ear but Skylar pushed his hands away. "Don't try to distract me. You did that earlier today, but it won't work again."

"When did I try to distract you?"

"I don't know, just answer the question." Skylar scowled at him and Braznovich chuckled.

"Is that your pouty face?" Skylar dropped her chin and frowned. "C'mon, where do you think I was?"

"Well, all you've told me is that you had coffee with Sally and took her back to her hotel. You were gone for hours, so what am I supposed to think?"

Braznovich exhaled and then shifted in the bed, propping pillows behind him and leaning back against the headboard. "Come here," he said, reaching for Skylar and pulling her backwards against his chest. He wrapped his arms around her, weaving his fingers into hers, and resting their woven hands on top of her stomach. "I'm sorry. I wasn't very clear when I said that. We had coffee, I made sure Sally wasn't followed to her hotel and then I left and I met with Clayton Richmond."

"What?!" Skylar was shocked. "You met with Patterson's campaign manager?"

"Yes. See, your idea to contact them wasn't a bad one, even though it initially backfired. After we learned of Belmont's death, I contacted Richmond."

"Why?"

"I wanted to give him the autopsy report on Ema Wright and alert him to the possibility of drugs being used to murder Belmont."

"Wow," Skylar sighed. "What did he say?"

"He didn't return my call until yesterday afternoon and then he told me that he had already been contacted by someone at P3; someone asking him to pick up evidence that would take P3 down." Braznovich took a deep breath. "He told me that they were aware of the Armageddon attack and that, not in so many words, they would be watching."

"Who would be watching? The government?" Skylar gasped.

"I got the feeling that he was letting me know that this thing was bigger than just us, and that they were going to take care of it."

They sat for a moment in complete silence, thoughts bouncing around in Skylar's head. "Did he tell you who contacted him from P3?"

"No. I'm assuming the contact was made anonymously or that the information was classified."

"So, why did you have to meet? Why not just discuss things over the phone?" It was a good question. Skylar thought it was probably difficult for someone like Richmond, while in the middle of running a Presidential campaign, to just drop everything and meet with Braznovich.

Braznovich stroked her hair. "Richmond set up the temporary medical facility where Tess and Jonathan are being watched."

"What?!" Skylar sat up, climbed to the side of the bed and spun around to face him. "Why?"

"We agreed that until a full investigation was conducted, local law enforcement and hospital personnel couldn't be trusted. It was the only way to ensure that once we pulled them out, they would remain safe. I toured the facility this afternoon with Richmond."

"Where is it?"

Braznovich peered at her from beneath narrowed brows. "That's classified as well."

"You mean you get to know the location but I don't?"

"You're on a need-to-know-basis and right now, it's safer if you don't know." He answered flatly.

Skylar didn't like it, but it made sense. Tess's safety and health were all that mattered in the grand scheme of things.

"Remember, Tess was one of the up and coming leaders and she will undoubtedly be able to provide Richmond's people with insight into the inner workings of P3. The information she and Jonathan have can help dismantle some of Sagan's other houses of prayer and minimize the chances of another cult like this one spreading as far and wide. We have to remember that not every house of prayer is a cult."

Skylar nodded. She knew that he was right and that only the houses of prayer which followed Sagan's model fell into the cult category. Still, she couldn't help but feel repulsed by all of them, and that had nothing to do with her feelings for God, and everything to do with her experience with Sagan.

"Will Richmond show Tess and Jonathan the evidence against Sagan?" She asked.

"I think so, but not until they're ready to handle it."

"What about all of the other people from P3? They're going to be lost..." her voice grew silent.

"That was part of my meeting with Richmond this afternoon. They're lining up top-notch psychiatrists, psychologists, theologians, family counselors and those who specialize in cult and occult behavior to help these kids re-unite with their families and re-enter society. It will take time for them to find their way back to some form of normalcy. Richmond got Patterson to sign off on a rehabilitation facility and agree to help fund the program."

"What do you mean help fund it? He won't fund all of it?"

Braznovich gave her a wink. "It's all funded."

"You paid for a facility to help rehab these people, didn't you?" Skylar couldn't believe it.

"I helped. Besides, I think my grandparents would have wanted some of their money to be used to help others, particularly in this circumstance."

"I think you're right about that," Skylar said quietly. "I think your grandpa would be very proud of you."

He leaned forward took Skylar's face in his hands and kissed her squarely on the lips. "Now, Richmond's first priority is to clean out the corruption from the top down, and he's starting with the Kansas City police and getting your name cleared. Evidently the evidence given to him from this mystery person at P3 has a list of politicians, religious leaders, organizations, doctors, lawyers and mercenaries working with P3; and from what Richmond said, the list is lengthy." He kissed her again. "Once they are all indicted you can go back to a normal life."

"Are you sick of me already? Ready for me to move back home?" She batted her lashes with playful drama.

"Ms. Wilson," he smiled, "who said anything about you moving back home?" Butterflies fluttered in her stomach as he leaned closer and pulled her into a deep, passionate kiss.

CHAPTER 37

Skylar had just stepped out of the shower and slipped into her jeans and one of his black t-shirts, which hung almost to her knees, when Braznovich burst through the bathroom door, taking her by the wrist and dragging her from the room, down the stairs and toward the fireplace. His voice was frantic and his eyes were laced with fear. She had never seen him like this.

"Grab what you can and get downstairs," he ordered Greg, who was hurriedly unplugging wires and stacking laptops into a pile on top of the coffee table.

Ernie appeared through the sliding door, carrying several large guns. He tossed a rifle to Braznovich who caught it with one hand and with the other hand, he pulled the lever on the back of a fireplace brick, opening the door to the staircase that led down to the library. "Go," he said to Skylar. "Hurry!"

"What's going on?" She asked, sliding her temporary cell phone into the back of her jeans. Her voice was breathy with fear.

"Richmond called and warned us that this location has been compromised," Braznovich uttered.

"Compromised by whom?"

"I'll explain once we're all safe. Now go!" He pushed Skylar through the fireplace door. "Where's your gun?"

"In the nightstand drawer." Her voice trembled.

"I'll get it," Ernie hollered and made a dash toward the steps.

Greg grabbed the stack of laptops, blueprint designs, all of his notes and the stack of Braznovich's grandfather's P3 notes and hurried past Skylar down the steps and into the library.

"We got company!" Ernie barked from upstairs.

"How many?" Braznovich yelled.

Ernie peered through the upstairs window which sat at the top of the steps. "Two black SUV's approaching; I'm guessing three or four men in each." He dashed down the stairs, tossed the 357 magnum to Braznovich, who then handed it to Skylar; and then Ernie and Braznovich rushed down the stairs, closing the secret fireplace door behind them.

"Is this soundproof?" Greg whispered and Braznovich shook his head to indicate no. They needed to be quiet. Very, very quiet.

"Did you lock up the barn?" Braznovich mouthed to Ernie, who answered in a whisper.

"Yep, she's secured, but that don't mean they won't find a way in."

"They won't find the bunker, so we'll need to make our way there," Braznovich said.

Leading them into the office where Greg had originally set up his equipment when he arrived, Braznovich opened the doors to the giant armoire and Skylar's eyes widened when she saw what looked like a steel bank safe with a keypad in the middle of the door. Without a word, Braznovich punched the code into the keypad and the door clicked open. He ushered Skylar inside. It was dark and the air smelled stale. "C'mon Greg, let's go!" Braznovich ordered in a hushed tone.

"Wait a tick," Greg whispered. "Don't you want to see who these guys are?" He clicked wildly across his computer keyboard.

"This ain't P3 man," Ernie huffed, "there aren't security cameras all over."

Greg glanced up with a gleam in his eye. "Well, not all over, but I did plant a few."

"What?!" Braznovich took sudden interest, stepping out of the armoire and glaring at Greg's computer. "You planted cameras in my house?"

"Sorry, man, but when Skylar thought you were a P3 sympathizer and left, I figured I better do something to protect myself," Greg explained.

"Good thinking!" Ernie gave Greg a slap on the back. "So, what do we got going on up there? How many are there?"

Greg let his fingers work magic on the keys until a picture of the front porch and top of the driveway filled his screen. There were six men in total, probably arriving three in each SUV. They were dressed in full-scale SWAT gear, complete with Tasers, grenades, tear gas canisters, Sig P229 pistols, and Benelli M1 shotguns.

"Damn!" Ernie spewed. "They came locked and loaded."

"Who are they? Sagan's men?" Braznovich squinted at the screen.

"Dunno," Ernie answered. "But whoever they are, they mean business."

Greg's face grew ashen. "If they detonate one of those grenades, is the structure of the fireplace and the armoire tunnel going to hold?"

Braznovich and Ernie exchanged glances. From their expressions, Skylar surmised that they were both searching for the answer in the other's eyes and coming up empty.

"We gotta take 'em out first," Ernie said.

"We can't take out six guys in SWAT gear by ourselves," Braznovich uttered. "They have Kevlar vests and grenades. We have nothing."

Skylar inched her way out of the armoire. "Let me call Rod. I'll tell him the men who took out his guys at P3 are here now. He'll come with men, I know it!"

"No," Braznovich barked. "We're not giving Rod this address. This house isn't even listed under my name." His eyes flashed with what Skylar thought was anger. "I don't even know how these guys found us. For all we know these could BE Rod's guys."

"They're government agents," Greg mumbled, shock ringing in his voice.

Ernie leaned in closer to the screen. "I'll be damned. They're FBI."

Braznovich gawked at the computer. "Where do you see that?"

"It's not their standard issue digs, but look at the upper left lapel, see the small emblem?" Ernie pointed at the computer. "That's the United States Federal Bureau of Investigation's emblem right there."

"Did Richmond send them?" Skylar asked. "Maybe they're here to protect us?"

Ernie shook his head. "These guys ain't on a security detail."

A thought crossed her mind and Skylar hated verbalizing it, but she had to. "Is Richmond a P3 sympathizer? Did he send these men to take us out?" She asked. Her mouth grew instantly dry as an even worse thought crept in. If Richmond was on P3's side, then that would mean Tess and Jonathan were still in danger and all of the evidence against Sagan had been handed over to the enemy.

"No," Braznovich blurted in such a way that made Skylar feel that he was not only trying to convince her, but himself as well. "Richmond is clean. I met with him yesterday and he's clean."

"Since Patterson called you, is there any chance they've traced you by your cell phone?" Greg asked. "It's easy to do."

"I have a GPS locking system on my phone that re-routes any attempted traces to random locations overseas. It's a common PI gadget."

Skylar wasn't convinced about Richmond. While Ernie, Braznovich and Greg bantered about the best possible course of action, she sank to a sitting position on the edge of the armoire and secretly sent Rod a text, telling him that the men who killed his five shooters were here, posed as FBI agents, dressed in SWAT attire and heavily armed. "They're trying to take us out too. Please help." She typed in Braznovich's address and waited.

Seconds later, the cell phone silently vibrated in her hand and she glanced down to read the text. It read, "On our way, stay low."

"There are six men," she text, wanting to ensure Rod didn't show up alone and get himself killed.

"Got it," Rod text back.

Ernie looked up from the computer. "I need a smoke," he rasped. "I can't think without a smoke."

"Not down here!" Braznovich barked.

"Why haven't they tried to enter the house yet?" Greg asked, sweat forming on his brow. "They're just standing by their cars."

They all stared at the screen. "They're waiting for orders," Ernie said.

"Or waiting for someone else to arrive," Braznovich posed.

"Is it possible they've gained information that you own this place, but they don't think you're actually here?" Greg asked Braznovich. It seemed like a viable possibility to Skylar.

"Our cars are out front," Braznovich said.

"They know we're here. They're either waiting for orders or waiting for us to make the first move," Ernie said confidently.

"So, what do we do?" Greg asked, the tension in the room becoming more and more palatable.

"Where in the house did you place cameras?" Braznovich asked, without answering Greg's question.

"Upstairs hallway, family room, front door, the back sliding door and one in the barn."

"Back sliding door?" Ernie winced.

Greg nodded. "Yeah, I see you take a leak off the patio every night."

Braznovich shot Ernie a disgusted glare.

"What can I say, when you gotta go, you gotta go," Ernie shrugged.

A few minutes later, they had developed a plan. In lieu of the fact that they were clearly outnumbered in manpower and weaponry, Braznovich felt it was best to lay low, hoping that they wouldn't detonate a bomb inside the house, which could reveal the underground rooms. "If they enter the house, see that we're not home, they wouldn't have reason to utilize explosives," he speculated.

Ernie agreed that if they met no opposition, they would be less likely to use brute force. "However," Ernie pointed out, "we don't know whose orders they're waiting for and what they'll be ordered to do."

Braznovich instructed Skylar and Greg to get back into the armoire and follow the tunnel down a set of stone steps to a steel door with a combination lock. "Punch in the code, 1463721, and then close the door behind you."

"Aren't you and Ernie coming?" Skylar asked.

"We'll stay here for now and monitor what they're doing via the cameras. If we need to, we'll join you in the bunker," Braznovich explained.

"Bunker?" Greg asked, but no one answered him.

"Once you reach the steel door, it will open into the back of the bunker. There's a lever on the floor that will unlock the last door to the room I showed you the other day," he said to Skylar. "When you find the lever, pull up and to the right until you hear a click."

Skylar nodded, repeating the code and instructions in her mind. "Why can't we all go and monitor the cameras from there?" She asked.

"I want to have the advantage of being able to pick a few of these guys off before they get inside," Braznovich uttered. "Now, you two go."

Skylar's hands trembled. She didn't want to leave without Braznovich and Ernie. How would she know they were okay? Braznovich handed her the stack of his grandfather's P3 notes. "Put these back in the safe when you get to the bunker," he said. "The combination code is the same, 1463721." He gave her a light kiss on her forehead and closed the steel door behind them.

The tunnel was pitch black and Skylar's heart was pounding violently in her chest.

"Grab my shirt," Greg said and Skylar tucked Braznovich's grandfather's notes under one arm and took a hold of the back of Greg's shirt with the other. They walked slowly, baby-stepping through the darkness. Neither of them spoke until Greg announced that he had found the steps and they inched their way carefully downward. It seemed to take forever for them to finally reach the next door. Fumbling in the dark, Greg slid open the panel, revealing an illumed keypad and then he punched in the code. The door clicked open and they entered, pushing it closed behind them. It looked as if they were standing in a steel bank vault, tiny lights along the wall illumed the area just enough for Greg to locate the lever, lift up and angle to the right. They heard a loud click and Greg pushed against the door. It was heavy and mounted on hinges that made it want to propel back into a locked position. It took both Greg and Skylar pushing against it to open it enough for them to slide sideways through the opening, and then it swung closed, leaving them in darkness again. Skylar tried to visualize the bunker, but couldn't get her bearings because they had entered through a door that she and Braznovich had not used.

"We gotta find a light," Greg uttered and Skylar could hear him shuffling around.

"I know there's a switch somewhere, but I don't know where," she said. "I entered through another door and there were shelves to my left and shelves straight ahead and bunk beds to my right."

"I think we actually entered through the shelves," Greg mumbled, "because there are shelves directly behind us."

Skylar turned and ran her right hand along the shelves behind, her fingers brushing against what felt like a small safe. Presuming this to be the safe that once held Braznovich's grandfather's notes, meant that the bunk beds were to the left and the other door was directly across the room from her. Still holding the folders under her left arm, Skylar stretched her right arm out in front of her and made her way slowly across the room. Finally finding the switch, she flipped on the light and heard Greg exhale loudly.

"Thank God! I hate the dark," Greg sighed, which made Skylar smile. It was nice to know she wasn't the only one feeling afraid.

Skylar took a seat on the bottom bunk bed and set the folders of notes next to her. There was no telling how long they'd be forced to stay in the bunker, so she figured she'd keep her mind busy reading instead of worrying about what was happening outside. She lifted the photograph of Braznovich's grandmother's funeral from the pile and started to set it aside when Skylar stopped abruptly. Something in the picture caught her attention, something she hadn't noticed before. In the background, amid the masses of people dressed in black, was the face of a woman she knew. It was Mary Sagan. Why would Maxwell's wife attend the funeral of a woman Maxwell had had killed? This confirmed what Skylar believed Ema had been trying to tell her with her last breath. She was struggling to say a word that started with the letter M, and Skylar had the strangest feeling that Ema had been trying to say the name Mary. Did it mean that Ema was trying to warn them that Mary was evil? Or was Ema trying to tell them that Maxwell's wife was the insider, helping kids escape and silently building a case against her husband? The pieces fit. Mary would undoubtedly have had access to her husband's office and the secret room, and she had blonde hair. If she was the one who gave Richmond the evidence against Sagan and Richmond was bad, then Mary was in danger too.

Skylar's mind was racing almost as fast as her pulse. There was only one way to find out if Mary was good or bad, and that was to meet with her in person.

Skylar shared her theory and thoughts with Greg, who scowled at her. "I thought this was going to be over when Maxwell was dead." She knew his frustration. She, too, had hoped this whole thing would be over once Maxwell was stopped; but it now seemed that his tentacles stretched farther and wider than even she had imagined. "I didn't sign up for this," Greg spewed. "I agreed to help get Tess out, not to be hunted for the rest of my life."

"I know," Skylar said quietly.

Greg slipped an ear bud into his right ear and pulled a small transmitter/receiver box from his jean pocket. Sitting down on the bed next to Skylar, he handed her the other ear bud and twisted the channel knob of the box until they heard Braznovich and Ernie talking. Skylar's mouth fell open, but before she could say anything, Greg explained how he had planted a bug on Braznovich just before climbing into the armoire.

"Why?" She questioned.

"I don't trust him." He raised his eyebrows. "I want to know if I'm being set up."

Skylar didn't know what to say. Greg seemed paranoid, and yet if there was any situation in which paranoia was acceptable, this was it.

"We got more company," they heard Ernie say.

"How many vehicles?" Braznovich asked.

"None. We got shooters in the woods!" Ernie blurted. "Hot diggity dog, I think they're on our side!"

332

"What?!" They could hear the surprise in Braznovich's tone.

"Whoever they are, they're firing at the bad guys, which means they're on our side," Ernie repeated and Skylar could envision the grin on his face and the gleam in his eye.

Greg squinted at Skylar. "You contacted Rod didn't you?"

"Guilty," she shrugged.

"Braznovich is gonna be pissed."

"Better pissed than dead," Skylar answered flatly.

Greg and Skylar listened to what sounded like Ernie and Braznovich racing up the steps and into the family room. The moment they went through the fireplace door, Skylar and Greg could hear gun fire.

"Let's go out the slider and swing around the sides," Ernie said. "That way they'll be trapped."

"Good plan, you take the left," Braznovich instructed Ernie. "I'll go right."

They listened to the sliding door open and close. *Why are they going outside?* Skylar had hoped that Rod and his men would take down the bad guys and Ernie and Braznovich would be able to stay in the safety of the indoors. Once they went outside the gun fire became louder, pounding through the ear buds. They heard both semi-automatic fire and single shots, and Skylar couldn't stand not being able to see what was happening. She was imagining the worst. Leaping to her feet, she ripped the ear bud from her ear, drew the 357 magnum from the back of her jeans and headed for the door.

"Where are you going?" Greg gasped, his brows narrowed low over his eyes.

"This door leads to the barn. I'm going to go up where I can at least see what's going on."

Greg shot her an are-you-crazy glare and then rolled his eyes and conceded to following her; though he made it well known that he thought it was a bad idea. "I don't even have a gun," he moaned.

Pointing to the shelf of guns, Skylar told him to pick one and then they headed out, wading through the water in the tunnel, climbing up the ladder and finally exiting into the horse stall inside the barn. Once inside, Skylar was careful to find the button in between the wooden slats on the floor that closed the panel so, in case the barn was compromised, no one would find the bunker below.

The gun fire was loud, louder than Skylar had expected and as she stuck her head out of the side door she could hear bullets ricocheting off trees. "You can't go out there," Greg said. "It's suicide."

"I just want to step out and try to see Braznovich. I'm not going to go anywhere."

"Well, I'm not going with you," Greg shook his head, erratically and held up the .22 he had taken from the bunker. "It's insane! I'm staying here where I can hide and shoot anyone who comes in."

"That's fine. I'll be right back." She held the 357 magnum in front of her and stepped outside the door, flanking her back against the barn and sliding slowly to thc right, toward the front of the barn so she could see. The house was blocking her view of the driveway, so she made a dash across the front of the barn and into the trees, staying low. She had forgotten that she was bare footed until her feet met with the rough terrain of the woods. Had Braznovich given her a chance she would have slipped on her tennis shoes, but he had ripped her out of the bathroom so quickly, shoes had never even crossed her mind.

From a crouched position in the woods, she could see that there were three bodies in the driveway, all dressed in SWAT attire. She scanned the area, but didn't see anyone else. It was as if they were all hiding in the trees that lined the long, gravel road. Staying low and behind the trees, Skylar inched her way passed the house and further down the right side of the driveway. She froze, instinctively ducking lower as several single shots were fired. She was unable to ascertain from which direction they had come. Her heart beat wildly in her chest and clammy sweat flushed her skin. By the time she heard the crackling sound of footsteps behind her, it was too late. The steely barrel of a gun dug into the back of her head and before he uttered a word, she dropped her 357 and raised her hands. "You'll break the stale mate for me," he seethed. "Now stand up slowly and walk forward."

Skylar did as she was told. "If you kill me they're just going to kill you," she said trying to reason with him, but her words were met with a forceful shove.

"Shut up and keep walking," he screamed, digging the barrel into her back.

"Maxwell Sagan is dead. You don't have to follow his orders anymore."

"I don't work for Sagan," he sneered. "Sagan is nothing. I work for the Master."

What did that mean? If Sagan wasn't the true leader, if he wasn't the top dog, then who was? Skylar trudged to the edge of the woods and stepped slowly out from the tree line. She knew, now that she was in plain view, Braznovich, Ernie, Rod and his men would be rapidly thinking of a way to save her. Still, every muscle in her body clenched with fear.

Pushing her to the center of the gravel driveway, he ordered her to stop and place her hands on top of her head. Then he kicked the backs of her legs, forcing her to fall forward onto her knees, execution style. He held the gun against the back of her head and hollered into the trees. "This is over! Surrender immediately or watch her die!"

Tears ran down Skylar's cheeks and dripped from her chin. The two remaining SWAT members came out from wherever they had been hiding, forming a triangular guard stance around Skylar, and scanning the trees. The woods were eerily quiet but the sound of Skylar's heart thundered loudly in her ears. Her eyes darted from tree to tree, searching for any sign of salvation. All of a sudden she heard a man's voice.

"Big Bear! Whoop!" The man yelled, his voice echoing through the trees.

It had sounded like Rod's voice and Skylar glanced around, but she still couldn't see anyone.

The SWAT man to her left fired several shots into the woods and Skylar jumped, unsure whether he was aiming at someone in particular or firing randomly. She looked to her left just as a single shot hit him in the back of the neck, thrusting his body forward, face down and splattering blood all over the gravel. Skylar shrieked and clamped her eyes shut.

"Rattlesnake! Whoop!" The voice rang out again and Skylar peeled open her eyes and looked up. It was Rod's voice, she was sure of it, but she still couldn't see him. Almost instantly shots echoed and the SWAT man to her right crumpled forward into a bloody heap as a barrage of bullets took out his legs from beneath him. Skylar's body trembled uncontrollably as she brought her hands up to her face and covered her mouth.

"I'll kill her!" The man holding Skylar at gunpoint screamed. "I swear I'll kill her!" He grabbed Skylar by the neck and pulled her to her feet, using her as a shield as he inched his way back toward the SUV. His grip on her neck tightened. "Open the door!" He ordered. Skylar reached her arm backwards, running her trembling fingers across the car, but she couldn't find the handle. "Open it now or you're dead!" He screeched, and dug the barrel of the gun into the middle of her back.

"I can't reach it," she cried. "You have to let me turn a little to reach it."

He spewed obscenities and then angled her body just enough to allow her to she reach and lift the driver's door handle. The moment he released her neck and reached for the door, Skylar dove forward onto the gravel. The man whirled around to shoot her, but before he could, he was hit by a barrage of bullets that came from the trees and flew over the top of Skylar's head. Skylar screamed, wrapped her arms around her head and curled into a little ball, violently trembling. The man was thrust backwards against the SUV and then fell forward, his body draped over the top of Skylar and his blood spurting down the back of her neck and into her hair.

Her body convulsed uncontrollably and she fought the urge to vomit. The black t-shirt she had borrowed from Braznovich was saturated with blood and her elbows were bleeding from diving across the gravel. She wanted to move, but fear had her paralyzed. Her ears were ringing and the only other sound she heard was that of her lungs gasping for air beneath the man's dead weight.

She never heard the footsteps of Braznovich or Ernie approaching, but when the man's body was lifted from her and she knew she was safe, she slipped slowly into unconsciousness.

"What the hell was 'big bear, whoop?'" Braznovich demanded, as Rod and his men appeared from the trees, dressed head to toe in camouflage.

"It's our code to aim high, like you're shooting a big bear. Rattlesnake, whoop, means to aim low, like you're shooting a rattler," Rod explained.

"You could have killed her!" Braznovich seethed.

"They were going to kill her anyway. We had nothing to lose," Rod spat, pushing his chest out and bumping it against Braznovich. "Besides, I didn't see you fellas coming up with a better plan."

Ernie wedged himself between Rod and Braznovich. "He's right, Braz, she's alive and they're dead. Leave it alone."

"She doesn't think!" Braznovich uttered, lifting Skylar from the gravel. "She doesn't listen!" He ranted as he and Ernie carried Skylar inside.

Skylar could hear them talking, but she couldn't force her eyes open. She wanted to respond, but she felt trapped somewhere between a foggy dream and reality and her head was pounding with a horrendous headache. She must have hit her head when she dove forward onto the gravel.

"I told her not to go out there," Greg insisted, coming in through the sliding door. "But she wouldn't listen to me."

"She doesn't listen to anyone," Braznovich growled.

"She follows her instincts," Ernie said and all of a sudden Skylar could smell cigarette smoke. She was waking up. She could almost open her eyes. "And her instincts aren't too shabby either." Erie offered as he exhaled a ring of smoke. "Look how she knew to dive away from her captor so we could gun him down. She's one sharp cookie."

"Thank you," Skylar whispered, finally cracking open an eyelid.

"Well, lookey who we got here," Ernie smiled. "Welcome back to the land of the living."

Skylar looked around and saw that she was lying on the family room couch with a towel beneath her and a bag of ice on her forehead. Upon seeing her awaken, Braznovich sat down on the edge of the armed chair, and gently stroked her cheek. She removed the bag of ice and slowly pushed her way up into a sitting position.

"Hi," she mouthed to Braznovich, who scowled at her. Despite his anger, she saw a gleam of affection and relief in his eyes.

"You're in big trouble," he muttered.

"Don't be too hard on her," Rod said, entering through the front door. "If she hadn't contacted me, we might all be dead."

"We?" Ernie rasped.

"Sure as shit," Rod uttered. "Turns out a SWAT team showed up at my place while we were here helping you."

"Was anyone hurt?" Skylar asked.

"Nobody was there. My neighbor saw 'em come and go. I'm sure they'll be back, but we'll be ready for 'em."

"You and your men can stay here tonight," Braznovich offered. "Though, I don't know if it's any safer than your place." He shook his head and exhaled a deep breath. "I don't know how they found us."

"I was thinking the same thing," Rod said. "Me and my men all wore ski masks to Armageddon. There ain't no way they could have ID us, even if we were caught on video. It just doesn't make sense."

"No, it doesn't," Braznovich agreed.

Rod pulled the 357 magnum from his waistband and handed it to Braznovich. "One of my guys found her gun in the woods."

"It's your gun," Skylar said.

"It's yours now," Rod winked and then directed his attention back to Braznovich and Ernie. "You fellas mind if we take them vehicles? Or were you planning on keeping 'em?"

"We'll make you a deal," Ernie answered. "You haul the bodies out of here and the SUV's are all yours."

"Deal," Rod's face lit up. "Do you have some trash bags we could use?"

"Under the sink in the kitchen," Braznovich uttered. His tone was intense and Skylar knew his thoughts were distracted by the fact that he didn't understand how the SWAT team had found his grandfather's house.

Ernie fetched Rod the trash bags and then they said their goodbyes. Rod strode briskly toward the front door and then stopped and turned to face Skylar. "You ever need anything, you just holler."

"Thank you," she said quietly. "For everything."

After Rod and his men had gone, Skylar took a long, hot shower, scrubbing her hair and the back of her neck numerous times until she was certain that all of the blood was gone. She had more questions now than answers. Was Richmond behind this attack? If so, why would he have called to warn them? If he wasn't behind it, who was and was Richmond in danger too? What would happen when these men didn't report back to whoever had sent them? Would another SWAT team show up? And the question she knew was tormenting Braznovich, how did they find this house?

As she slipped on a clean pair of jeans and the light blue sweater Braznovich had given her, she couldn't escape the feeling that the answer to all of her questions lie with one person. Mary Sagan.

CHAPTER 38

"Are you sure you want to do this alone?" Braznovich asked.

"Yes," Skylar answered, pulling the last recipe card from Mrs. Wright's box and slipping it into her purse. She couldn't believe she had skimmed over it before, as now it seemed so obvious. It was exactly what Ema had tried to tell her before she died.

Ernie offered to tag along as well, but they all agreed that he and Greg should stay at the house in case anymore unwanted visitors showed up. Greg had placed cameras at the front of the long driveway and throughout the woods, surrounding the house, so he could monitor anyone approaching by vehicle or on foot. Ernie had moved the stash of weapons from the bunker to the house, strategically placing them throughout and claiming that anyone who tried to surprise them would be sorry. "If there is another attack, let's try and keep at least one of the guys alive," Braznovich urged. "It'd like to find out how they found this place."

"Good idea," Ernie said. "I'll call Rod and tell him too."

Braznovich raised an eyebrow. "Yeah, tell him to control his 'Big Bear, Rattlesnake, Whoop!" Braznovich mimicked Rod's voice and Ernie laughed out loud.

"Hey, that 'Whoop' saved my life," Skylar scolded, as she came down the steps.

Arriving at the P3 campus, Braznovich offered one last time, "Let me go in with you."

She understood his reservations. After all, they didn't know if Mary Sagan was good or bad; but this was something she needed to do alone. She had a feeling that Mary knew who was the mastermind behind everything and she thought that she might be more prone to talk woman-to-woman, than P.I. to potential killer. Climbing out of the Hummer passenger door, Skylar adjusted the 357 magnum in the back of her jeans and made sure her sweater covered it.

"I'll be right outside if you need me," he said. "Good luck."

She walked briskly toward the front door of the Real-estate office which, when facing what was left of the campus, sat to the far right side, unattached to the other buildings but sharing the same parking lot. A small bell dinged as she opened the door and entered the office, attracting the attention of a young, blonde receptionist who sat behind the front desk. She looked up and though she cordially smiled, Skylar witnessed a flash of uneasiness in her face. "May I help you?"

Skylar hesitated, staring at the woman behind the desk. She had the surreal rush of familiarity but she couldn't put her finger on where she had seen her. "I'd like to speak with Mary Sagan, please," Skylar said, hoping her voice wasn't as shaky as she felt.

"I'm sorry," the receptionist began, "but under the circumstances Mary isn't seeing anyone right now. If you'd like to make an appointment..."

Mary poked her head from her office doorway and met eyes with Skylar. "I'll see her," she said flatly.

The receptionist nodded, motioning Skylar to follow Mary into her office. "Can I get you some coffee?" She asked.

At the mention of the word 'coffee' the memory flooded Skylar's brain and with widening eyes, she gawked at the receptionist. "It was you who warned me in the coffee shop," Skylar uttered, breathlessly. "You wrote on the bottom of the cup."

The young woman's eyes bulged and she shot Mary a panicked glare.

"I'll see you now," Mary said, forcefully interrupting before her receptionist could speak.

A bolt of energized adrenaline burst through Skylar's veins as she realized that this probably meant Mary was on the good side. It probably meant Mary had sent her receptionist into the coffee shop to warn Skylar. It probably meant that she was the one who had gathered evidence against her husband and helped people escape the movement. She knew Braznovich would say it was only speculation, but deep down Skylar knew that she was right.

Closing the door behind them, Mary ushered Skylar toward one of the plush, mauve chairs located in front of a large, red wood desk. Skylar let her eyes peruse the office while Mary walked around the desk and took her seat behind it. The office was decorated in different shades of pink, mauve and burgundy. There were fresh flowers on the red wood book shelves and floral patterned curtains that made the room feel bright and cheery. Skylar couldn't help but note the difference in the aura of Mary's office and the rest of the stark, white P3 campus. "What can I do for you?" Mary asked, folding her hands on top of her desk.

Skylar cleared her throat. *So, we're going to play it this way, huh? You're going to pretend not to know why I'm here.* Skylar took a deep breath and locked eyes with Mary. "I think you've already done enough."

Mary's steely blue eyes returned Skylar's stare with equal fervor. "I beg your pardon?"

Skylar leaned forward. "I know it was you," she whispered. "You planted the camera in the secret room behind Maxwell's office; you recorded the evidence against him and sent the evidence to

Patterson's people, which is helping to clear my name."

Mary blinked rapidly. "I don't know what you're talking about."

"You were one of the only people with unlimited access to Maxwell's office and to the secret room. You tried to help Ema escape and you gave Lexi the video to take to Mrs. Wright in the park. Ema was trying to say your name when she died."

Mary swallowed hard, her jaw tightening and her eyes watering slightly.

"You left the notes on my car to warn me of the bomb and to direct me to Braznovich because you knew..."

"I said, I don't know what you are talking about," Mary interrupted.

Skylar didn't stop. "I know you were the one who scheduled the mandatory meeting to help evacuate the campus. We checked the building record where last night's meeting was held, and the hall was rented in your name and it was rented after you received Sally's message asking for help in evacuating the campus." Skylar leaned in even closer to the desk. "What I don't understand is why you sent Saul to lead the meeting instead of Maxwell..." her voice trailed off. "Unless you were the one that ki..."

"Is that it?" Mary interrupted, slamming her hands down on top of the desk and leaping to her feet.

Skylar rose slowly. "I understand why you have to deny everything, but I wanted you to know that I know it was you and I'm grateful for everything you did."

"You don't know anything," Mary barked. "You have no idea what I've done or what I've suffered."

She made a good point. Skylar didn't know what she had been through and she couldn't imagine what it was like to be widowed, even if a person may

344

have been the one who killed their spouse. Still, it had to be emotionally disturbing at best. Skylar wanted to know the truth but she didn't want to push too hard. She realized that she was probably coming across as cold and unsympathetic, and that wasn't her intent. "I have proof," Skylar said hesitantly.

"What proof?" Mary whispered, sinking back down into her chair. Skylar sat back down and retrieved the recipe cards from her purse.

"Mrs. Wright wrote her recipes on the top line, but she wrote her contacts on the second line." Skylar pointed to the card that read: Alexia Graham 3:00pm Kernodle Park. Then she handed Mary the card with her name on the second line. "All of the spies, as Ema called them, were listed on cards in Mrs. Wright's recipe box with the dates and times that Mrs. Wright met with them."

"That doesn't prove anything," Mary spat.

"That alone, no, it doesn't," Skylar agreed. "But coupled with the handwriting from the note you left on my car and on my apartment door, which matched the handwriting on the envelope that was mailed to Mrs. Wright; and the fact that Ema tried to say your name before she died..." Skylar paused as Mary's face grew ashen, and she stared, glassy-eyed into space. "I am sorry for your loss," Skylar uttered softly, lowering her eyes to the floor and thinking that maybe this wasn't such a good idea.

She stood up and slowly made her way toward the door when Mary uttered, "I'm not sorry." Skylar whirled around to face her, noticing that her eyes had gone from glazed with emotion to aflame with anger, and her lower lip was quivering. "Maxwell may have died yesterday, but I lost my husband a long time ago." She pulled a tissue from her top drawer. "Maxwell started living this lie a long time ago. He distorted truth so much that he finally lost sight of it altogether. He lost touch with reality and he couldn't find his way back, not even to me." Mary slumped

345

down into her chair. "He wouldn't even come back for me."

Skylar didn't know what to say. She stood silently listening.

"I have watched so many people come here in search of the Lord and never find Him because of Maxwell's lies. Countless kids died from illnesses related to malnourishment and dehydration or because Maxwell had pushed them too far with the Rohypnol and the mortification." Rage flashed in Mary's eyes. "I can't tell you how many helpless parents came to me, begging me to allow them to see their child, pleading with me to relay messages to their sons and daughters." Tears streamed down Mary's face. "It broke my heart. I tried to tell Maxwell that it was wrong, but he wouldn't listen. He was becoming powerful in the eyes of political and religious leaders; and I couldn't compete with that power." Mary wiped her nose with the tissue. I wasn't the only one who tried to warn him, but he degraded anyone who stood against him. He destroyed their churches, their reputations and even took their lives. I couldn't stop him." Mary slumped lower in her chair and it looked as if the whole world was pushing down upon her shoulders.

Skylar didn't know what to say. Her heart was pounding loudly in her ears, as Mary confessed to everything Skylar had already suspected. This was the confirmation Skylar needed for her own soul, but she felt guilty that it had to come at such a high price.

"I should have stopped him years ago when he first dreamt up his Divinity Design. I should have stopped him before he went public with it and with all of the lies; because once he went public we were trapped. His ego would never allow him to admit that the document was false. He would never admit that the whole house of prayer foundation was built on lies. The fall would have been too great, that's why he kept changing the wording and falsifying the prophecy even more and more." Mary pounded her fist on the desk. "It was lie upon lie upon lie!"

"I know," Skylar whispered.

"When he and his prophets from Kansas City were accused of false prophecy, Maxwell created scandals around the other prophets and cast them away so everyone would view him as the true man of God." Mary exhaled a short guffaw. "If that isn't ironic. The person people perceived to be the true man of God was someone who had nothing to do with God. All of his God encounters were man-made lies." Mary rubbed her eyes and tucked her bleached blonde hair behind her ears. "He even altered the Scriptures and had thousands of copies printed and handed them out to the students here, so that what he taught would match what they thought the Bible said."

Skylar almost couldn't believe what she was hearing. How could anyone desecrate the Bible and call themselves a man of God? It sickened her.

"I planned for years to leave him, but he wouldn't have let me go. I knew too much, so I began to gather evidence. For the past several years I've recorded conversations from the secret room where he conducted all of his meetings with politicians and high ranking officials, and from the mortification room where he tortured anyone who had doubts. I copied documents and gathered all the proof I could."

Skylar shuddered. She couldn't imagine the footage from the mortification room.

"I didn't know any other way to prove that what he was doing was wrong," Mary cried. "I originally planned on showing him the evidence and begging him to stop; but then I realized that he would think I was threatening him and he might..." her voice faded.

Mary didn't need to finish her sentence, Skylar knew what she feared. Wife or no wife, Maxwell would have had her killed and burned the years of evidence Mary had compiled against him.

"So you called Patterson's office," Skylar interjected, "and you gave the evidence to them."

"Yes," Mary answered. "After Micah Belmont was murdered, I knew I couldn't wait any longer. I couldn't go to the local police because they all worked for Maxwell." Mary met eyes with Skylar. "I was running out of time and options; so I spoke to Clayton Richmond and he arranged for his men to pick up the evidence."

"You did the right thing," Skylar said softly.

Mary didn't respond, she just stared off into space.

"Are you going to be okay?" Skylar asked, aware that the question seemed ridiculous. Of course Mary wasn't okay, but Skylar didn't know what else to say. "You saved my life and my sister's life and who knows how many others through the years..."

Mary cut her off, her gaze far away. "When I saw Maxwell pull a gun on you, I ...I..."

Skylar crept closer. "You were there, behind Tess's building?"

Mary nodded. "He pulled the gun and I couldn't believe it... I..."

"You...what?"

"There were snipers, SWAT teams and they were taking out your people."

They took out Rod's men. Skylar inched her way closer. *Is that what Richmond meant when he told Braznovich that they knew about Armageddon Friday and would be watching? Was Richmond the one that sent the SWAT team to take out Rod's men? Was their mission to protect Sagan? If so, that meant Richmond was probably the one who sent the SWAT teams to Braznovich's grandfather's house and Rod's house as well. That would mean Richmond was the mastermind.*

"Maxwell pulled the gun and I ..." Mary sucked in a labored breath and then fixed her gaze on Skylar. Rising slowly from her chair, she ran her fingers down the front of her navy blue skirt, smoothing it. "I did the only thing I could."

What did that mean? Was she admitting to killing Maxwell or not? Skylar studied her face but Mary gave nothing away. "Did you kill him?" Skylar's voice quivered. "Did you purposefully block the security surveillance because you knew you were going to kill him?"

"No," Mary's face flushed red. "Maxwell was the one who blocked the security surveillance. When I saw him do it, I knew that he had done it because he was going to kill you. I followed him, thinking I could stop him, but I... everything happened so fast."

"You killed him..." Skylar's voice grew quiet and silence filled the room, the truth hanging thick between them.

"I think we're finished here," Mary said, extending her arm and motioning Skylar toward the door.

Skylar turned to reach for the doorknob when she heard glass shattering from behind. She whirled around just as Mary fell forward into her arms, knocking Skylar to the floor beneath her. Someone had shot through the office window and Mary had taken a bullet in the back. Blood filled her mouth as she gasped for air, gripping Skylar's face between her palms. "Mort...Saul...have...F...B...I...connections," she uttered, each word labored as Mary fought to communicate.

"Stay with me," Skylar blurted. "Keep talking to me." Skylar tried to gently reposition Mary so she could reach the door and bang on it to get the receptionist's attention; but she didn't want to make any drastic movements or loud noises for fear that whoever had shot Mary would appear in the window and shoot her as well.

Mary's fingers slid down Skylar's face and dropped to the floor. She mumbled incoherently as her face fell forward against Skylar's chest.

"In…side…er…" she gasped for air and the blood made a gurgling sound in her throat.

"Who? Who is the insider?" Skylar shook Mary. "Please, keep talking to me. Is Richmond the insider?"

"Com…pu…ter…" Mary's words staggered. "Trai…tor…" her voice faded.

Skylar banged on the door with her fist. "Stay with me, Mary," she pleaded. "Keep talking." She banged against the door again and then felt Mary's body go limp as the last breath left her. "No," Skylar gasped. "No, no, no!"

Mary's receptionist must have heard either the knocking or Skylar's sorrowful moans because she tried to push the door open, ramming it against Skylar's shoulder. Peering inside the office, she inhaled upon seeing Mary's bloody body and broke into sobs.

"Get Braznovich!" Skylar blurted. "He's right outside. Hurry!"

By the time Braznovich came in, maneuvered the door open and freed Skylar from beneath Mary's body, they could hear sirens off in the distance. "We need to leave now!" Braznovich barked.

Rushing toward the front door, Skylar stopped abruptly when she saw Mary's receptionist, huddled in the corner behind the front desk, trembling and weeping. "We can't leave her here," Skylar told Braznovich. "If they came for Mary, they might come for her too."

She could see the wheels in Braznovich's brain spinning. "Fine, bring her."

Reaching her hand toward the receptionist, Skylar tried to coax her to come, but she was in a state of non-responsive shock. Finally, Braznovich pushed Skylar out of the way, lifted the receptionist up and slung her over his shoulder.

As they raced toward the Hummer, Skylar asked Braznovich. "Who called the police?"

"Maybe she did," he said, shoving the receptionist into the middle of the front seat, while Skylar and Braznovich climbed into the sides next to her and Braznovich sped out of the lot. The last place they needed to be caught was on the P3 campus. Until they could identify the mastermind behind the whole operation and publically clear Skylar's name, it wasn't safe to be seen anywhere, much less at P3.

On the way back to Braznovich's grandfather's house, the receptionist calmed down enough to tell them that her name was Rebecca Milner, that she was from Columbia, Missouri and that she originally became involved with P3 because her mother had left her and her father to follow Maxwell. After her dad drank himself into oblivion and died in an alcohol related car accident, her mom had no choice but to let Rebecca, who was merely a teenager then, come and live with her. "I faked being a P3 member for a long time, just so my mom would love me," she told them. "I used to pretend to see visions and make up prophesies just to fit in."

Skylar winced. That sounded terrible and yet a part of her understood the feeling. Through the years she had often felt that if she had faked supporting P3, Tess might have loved her too.

"Then I met Mary and she let me work in her office, and she became like a mother to me," Rebecca began to cry again and Skylar squeezed her hand.

"Where is your mother now?" Braznovich asked.

Rebecca shrugged. "She just left one day and I never heard from her again..." her voice broke with emotion.

"Just out of curiosity," Skylar said, "did you call 9-1-1 when Mary was killed?"

Rebecca shook her head.

"Well, it couldn't have been someone who heard a shot, because I didn't even hear one," Skylar explained. "All I heard was the sound of the window shattering."

"There wasn't a shot. I was outside the whole time and would have heard it. Whoever killed her used a silencer," Braznovich said matter-of-fact.

"Then how could someone know to call 9-1-1?" Rebecca asked but neither of them answered. It was a good question and Skylar couldn't help but think about the obvious answer. Whoever killed Mary knew Skylar was there and wanted her to be caught by the police.

Walking inside, Braznovich introduced Rebecca and filled Ernie and Greg in on what had transpired while Skylar showered again, this time washing away Mary's blood. As the water poured down on her skin, the emotion flowed from within and Skylar wept.

CHAPTER 38

After her shower, Skylar slid the 357 magnum into the back of her jeans and returned to the family room, taking a seat on the floor between the edge of the couch, where Rebecca was sitting, and the fireplace. Her hair was still damp, but she had put on some lip gloss and mascara and felt, at the very least, presentable. She noticed that Rebecca's face was red and blotchy from crying and Skylar wished there was something she could say to make it better, but she knew mere words couldn't soothe Rebecca's soul. Mary had been a mother-figure in her life and only time was going to heal that ache.

Glancing around the room, Skylar didn't see Ernie and Braznovich. She was just about to ask Greg where they had gone when she caught a glimpse of them outside on the patio, engaging in what looked like a heated discussion. She wished they would come back inside, not just because she was curious to know what they were discussing, but more because she was worried that another team of assassins might be sneaking up at any moment. It wouldn't be difficult for a trained member of the FBI to pick off two grown men standing out in the open.

"What are they talking about?" Skylar asked Greg, who shrugged his shoulders and narrowed his eyes.

"How should I know? It's obviously something they don't want us to hear." His tone was a mixture of frustration and sarcasm. "Anyway, did Mary say anything before she died?"

"Yes, she said 'Mort Radburn and Saul have FBI connections.'" Skylar replayed the memory in her mind. She wasn't sure exactly what Mary had been trying to tell her. She knew from the secret video that Mort Radburn, Sagan and Saul Lathum were working together, at least from a political angle. They now knew that Sagan obviously had members of the FBI on his payroll, but who and how many was still unknown.

"That's it?" Greg asked and Skylar nodded.

"That and something about a computer, a traitor and an insider, but I couldn't really hear what else she was saying."

"That doesn't make sense," Greg huffed.

Braznovich's face shown deep concern as he walked inside and Skylar grew worried. Was he afraid of another attack? Or was it something else? Skylar studied his eyes as he paced back and forth the length of the family room, occasionally glancing over to watch Ernie exhale smoke out of the sliding door.

"Do you think the SWAT guys are going to come back?" Skylar asked, confronting the white elephant in the room.

No one answered for several seconds and then Ernie spoke, "If they do come back, we'll be ready."

That didn't exactly make Skylar feel better. If they came back, she was certain it would be with a vengeance; more weapons and manpower than before. They could always hide in the bunker, that is, if they could get to the bunker before they were under a full-scale attack. The thought brought a knot to Skylar's stomach.

Braznovich's phone buzzed and Ernie immediately shot him a glare that Skylar couldn't interpret. It appeared to be anger, but it was laced in angst and piercing with venom. Skylar had never seen Ernie's eyes this way. She could tell something was terribly wrong. Not wanting to interrupt, she sat quietly and watched as Braznovich answered the call, stopped mid-stride across the room and turned to face Ernie. His jaw tightened and his face turned a deep shade of red. "I understand," he gritted into the phone. "Thank you." In one fluid motion, he disconnected the call and drew the .45 from his waistband, taking aim at Greg.

Ernie's cigarette dropped from his mouth and he followed suit, drawing his gun and pointing it at Greg. "What do we got?" Ernie said to Braznovich.

"Our traitor," Braznovich seethed.

"What?!" Skylar leapt to her feet and Rebecca slid off of the couch and backed toward Skylar.

"That was Richmond. They nabbed the P3 insider in Patterson's organization, a man named Lockton. He confessed to everything," Braznovich explained.

Greg sat motionless, his eyes narrowing. "What does that have to do with me?"

"Lockton listed the names of his contacts in the N.E.T, the FBI and P3; and guess whose name is on that list?" Sarcasm seeped through Braznovich's voice.

"I'm being set up," Greg muttered, but something told Skylar he was lying. Something in his face and in his body language was suddenly different. Mary's words flashed through Skylar's mind. *Insider. Computer. Traitor.* Had Mary been trying to warn her about Greg?

Ernie took two steps forward, keeping his aim on the back of Greg's head. "Braz doesn't work on speculation, so whatever he has, it's concrete. You better start talking."

Greg didn't say a word.

"Richmond has been running traces on all incoming and outgoing correspondence from everyone on Patterson's payroll, searching for a connection. Well, today they found their insider and ran traces on all of Lockton's communications, and guess who he's been in constant contact with the past several days?" Braznovich explained.

"I was following up on some leads, trying to locate the insider myself," Greg stammered.

Braznovich took a step closer. "Bullshit," he blurted. "You're not the only hacker in the world, and you're not even the best hacker. Every communication you sent and received has been found, despite your attempts to hide the trail." Greg opened his mouth as if to say something but Braznovich kept talking. "You told them Skylar would be at Mary's office today and YOU called 9-1-1 less than thirty seconds after Mary was shot so that Skylar would be caught by the police and take the fall for the attack on P3, as well as all of the other local murders."

"What?!" Skylar gasped. "How would he know exactly when Mary was shot?"

"Cell records prove the 9-1-1 call came from this location, less than thirty seconds after Greg received an internet text from Lockton instructing him to make the call," Braznovich seethed.

"That's a lie! I'm being set up," Greg gritted.

"It was YOU who gave Lockton this address and set us and Rod up to be ambushed by their SWAT teams. Then, when Skylar wandered from the barn into the woods, you told them where to find her!" Braznovich's voice now echoed off the ceiling. "Tell me, Greg, when did you decide to betray us? Was it the minute Skylar called to ask for your help, or did you take some time to think about it?"

"You don't know what you're talking about," Greg huffed.

"Are you sure?" Skylar asked Braznovich, her voice broken with disbelief.

"Richmond is uploading the data to my email as we speak," Braznovich answered. "Pull up my email on my laptop and read it for yourself."

Skylar's hands were trembling as she carried Braznovich's laptop from the coffee table to the kitchen table, clicked on his email and found the latest note from Clayton Richmond. Opening the file, Skylar skimmed the data, tears filling her eyes and emotion catching in her throat.

"It's true," Skylar uttered, scanning through the file. "Every phone call and text message and email is here."

"How much did they offer you?" Braznovich asked. "Or was this about revenge? Were you so heartbroken over Tess that you wanted everyone to pay?" Braznovich hollered with such a rage that it startled Skylar and sent Rebecca to her knees in a tearful heap in front of the fireplace.

"I loved Tess!" Greg yelled, leaping to his feet and inadvertently knocking his laptop to the floor. "I gave her everything! Everything! And Sagan stole her away and YOU let it happen!" He pointed at Skylar and screamed. "YOU sat back and did nothing to convince her to stay with me!"

"Sit down," Ernie warned Greg.

Greg's face was bright red and the veins in his neck were protruding as he shouted until his voice was raspy and hoarse. "I hate you! I hate that bitch I married! I wanted you both to burn in hell!" Greg sank down onto the couch spewing obscenities and then, in a smooth, calculated motion he pulled a .22 from between the cushions and took aim at Skylar. Before he could pull the trigger, Braznovich fired, hitting Greg in the right shoulder and forcing him to drop the gun. Ernie kicked the gun across the room toward the fireplace and then cuffed Greg's hands behind his back.

"That'll keep you from trying anymore stunts like that," Ernie huffed.

Skylar was speechless from shock. She couldn't believe Greg had just pulled a gun on her. She couldn't believe any of this was happening. "You were going to shoot me?" She asked, sinking down into one of the kitchen chairs, and trying desperately to fit all of the pieces together. "You were going to shoot me with the gun you took from the bunker," she said more to herself than to him.

"You told me to take my pick," Greg sneered. "I wanted to shoot you the minute I picked it off the shelf..."

"Then why didn't you?" Skylar yelled.

"Because we'd have known he did it, for one," Ernie said.

"And if he killed you, he couldn't frame you," Braznovich added.

Skylar stared at him as if she were dazed. "You told Lockton about Armageddon Friday and where Rod's men would be stationed. That's how they picked off his men." The pieces were beginning to fall together. "You told them where to find me, and Tess, too, didn't you?" Skylar's eyes widened. "That's how Maxwell knew to wear a bullet proof vest. He knew the attack was coming and he knew precisely what time I would be getting Tess out." It was all making sense now. All this time Maxwell seemed to be a step ahead of them and it was because Greg had been feeding him information. Skylar's hands began to tremble as her rage grew.

"Yeah, I told Lockton where to find Rod's men but I didn't tell Maxwell anything. I wanted you to kill that son of a bitch and then I wanted you to take the fall for the attack on P3 and for everything," Greg coldly answered, wincing slightly from the pain in his arm.

"That's why you wouldn't turn off the electric fence," Skylar uttered. "You wanted me trapped inside; but why?"

"So Tess would blame you for everything and leave you forever just like she left me!" Greg spewed.

"That's why you told me to take the back staircase to Tess's floor and didn't tell me that Jonathan was coming through the door. You wanted Jonathan to catch me and turn me over to the police," Skylar said, as the puzzle was almost complete in her mind. "You were on Sagan's side the whole time," she uttered in disbelief.

"You're stupid!" Greg screeched, followed by a high pitched laugh. "I was never on Sagan's side. I planned on killing him the whole time. I just didn't know how to do it until you showed me the Patterson/Belmont video from the secret room. When I saw how far up his contacts went, I devised a brilliant plan. I figured out a way to work both sides in my favor."

"I don't understand," Skylar mumbled.

"We were useful to him," Ernie interjected. "One by one we were finding the P3 spies from Ema's journal and one by one he was giving their identities to Maxwell's people."

"Making him look like a hero," Braznovich added, his lip tightening.

Skylar's stomach knotted as the realization of what that meant struck her. "You were the reason Lexi was killed, and you blabbed about my planned meeting with Patterson, which ultimately got Micah Belmont killed."

"Yeah, so?" Greg's eyes were hard and cold.

Skylar felt enraged. All of this time she had blamed herself and it was him. "I trusted you!" She gritted. "I brought you in because I thought you were one of the only people in the world I could trust to help take down this cult." She shook her head side-to-side, as if her brain just couldn't wrap itself around what was happening. "Why would you even pretend to side with Maxwell when he caused you so much pain?" Tears filled Skylar's eyes. "Why?' She wanted to understand.

"You don't get it. You and Tess and everyone at P3 went on with your lives. You were happy and you left me with empty memories. I wanted the memories to be gone. I wanted them to be gone, forever! When you called, I knew this was my chance to make everything right again."

"So this was about revenge?" Skylar asked.

"Revenge on Maxwell and on you, sure, but then I'd have Tess back, all to myself; just me and

Tess the way it used to be. No more P3 and no more family to get in the way. Just me and my Tess." Skylar saw a flash of genuine insanity behind his eyes. How had she not seen it before? How had he slipped so far from reality and no one noticed?

"He knew our chances of beating P3 were slim to none, so whether we got caught or killed..." Braznovich began but Greg cut him off.

"It was a win-win-win," he smirked with an evil gleam. "Maxwell gets dead, you get blamed and I get to start my life over with Tess, as her hero."

"I would imagine you were promised a substantial amount of dough to provide information," Ernie added.

"I was set for life. Still am." Greg grinned cockily and something inside of Skylar snapped. She couldn't handle the injustice of everything that had happened, nor the responsibility in knowing that she was the one who brought Greg in. Anger morphed quickly into rage and Skylar pulled the 357 magnum from the back of her jeans and took aim.

"What is she doing?" Greg wailed to Ernie and Braznovich. "You're not gonna let her shoot me, are you?"

"You had Rod's men killed, and Lexi and Mary!" She gritted. "You set me up to take the fall, so give me one good reason I shouldn't drop you right here."

"Do something!" Greg whined to Ernie and Braznovich.

"You have five seconds to give me one reason!" Skylar yelled, tightening her grip on the gun and taking another step closer.
"Five...four...three...two..."

Before Skylar could finish her countdown, Rebecca grabbed the .22 that Ernie had kicked toward the fireplace, screamed in a piercing tone, and fired a shot into Greg's foot.

No one had to tell her to drop the gun because immediately following the shot, she let it slide from

her fingers and fell to her knees in an emotional heap.
Rage had obviously overtaken her. Skylar stared in
awe, as Ernie removed the gun from within Rebecca's
reach, and shoved it into his waistband.

"She shot me!" Greg wailed. "She shot my
goddamned foot!"

"You're lucky she didn't aim at your balls,"
Ernie rasped with a chuckle and all of a sudden
Skylar couldn't stop the grin from spreading across
her face. She couldn't believe it. Sweet, quiet, tearful
Rebecca shot Greg!

"She's crazy!" Greg cried. "You're all crazy!"

"NOW we should probably think about getting
him some medical attention," Ernie calmly noted.
"With two gunshot wounds the likelihood of bleeding
to death just went up."

"Call a doctor!" Greg spewed.

"After you answer a few more questions, like
how did you know to contact Lockton?" Braznovich
asked.

"I'm not telling you shit!" Greg spewed,
writhing in pain.

Skylar stepped closer, taking aim at Greg. "I
still have my gun and you still have one good foot."

Greg's eyes widened and he shook his head
frantically from side to side. "Don't let her shoot me!
She's crazy!"

"You know what they say about women. Hell
hath no fury..." Ernie's voice faded as he placed a
cigarette between his lips and lit up. "Looks to me
like all you gotta do to keep that good foot is answer
some more questions," Ernie rasped.

"Okay. Okay. After I saw the video with
Patterson and Belmont in it, I knew Sagan had to
have a back-up plan if either candidate decided to
default on their agreement, so I tapped into Sagan's
personal email file and found out that Lockton was
his insider in Patterson's organization." Greg winced
in pain. "So I called Lockton and told him about the
secret video and that I had sent it to Belmont."

"That explains why Belmont was killed almost immediately after receiving the video uplink. She was probably planning to go public with it," Braznovich said.

"Which was my plan," Skylar added. "If Belmont or Patterson would have gone public with it, P3 would have been under instant scrutiny and people might have been freed without all of the violence."

"Well, now we know why the plan backfired," Ernie huffed.

"And how much did Lockton pay you?" Skylar whispered.

"Are you going to let me bleed to death or take me to a hospital?" Greg belted, ignoring her question.

"Bleed to death," Ernie, Braznovich and Skylar answered in unison.

Ernie chuckled. "You know what they say about great minds."

"Fifty thousand dollars in an off-shore account and all I had to do was help them find the spies inside P3 and keep them one step ahead of you," Greg wailed in what sounded like breathless agony. "I didn't have anything to do with the N.E.T. or the FBI. I swear. My only contact was Lockton."

Braznovich's cell phone buzzed and he glanced down, obviously reading a text message. "Turn on CNN," he said to Ernie.

They all watched as Ernie turned on the big screen television and the CNN reporter spoke: "What started as an attack against a cult organization in Kanas City, Missouri has turned into a full-scale breach of national security; involving the FBI, N.E.T. and members of Senator Patterson's campaign. Originally thought to be the work of twenty-nine year old, Skylar Wilson, sister of up-and-coming P3 leader, Tess Wilson; we have since learned that Wilson has been cleared of all charges pertaining to the murder of several Kansas City residents and Police Officers and was NOT a part of the attack on the P3 compound. Apparently, Wilson's .22 had been stolen and used, by P3 personnel, to frame her in the aforementioned murders and the eye-witness who stated that she saw Skylar Wilson at the scene of the P3 attack has retracted her statement. Authorities have received substantial evidence that Maxwell Sagan, founder of the P3 movement, had been working in conjunction with N.E.T. founder, Mort Radburn; Senior P3 leader, Saul Latham; Patterson's Financial Advisor, Graham Lockton; and the Director of the Federal Bureau of Investigations, Henry Gleitner, to propagate what is being called the P3 Agenda. Sagan was murdered earlier this week, but the other gentleman on this list have been taken into custody and indicted on charges of murder, conspiracy to commit murder, misuse of funds, illegal use of narcotics, and frankly the list goes on and on." The reporter shook his head. "This has had national and international ramifications both politically and religiously, as people worldwide are fleeing houses of prayer said to be built upon Sagan's model. The Republican Party has suffered a stifling blow...a blow analysts are saying will dramatically affect this year's election. We take you now live to Washington to hear what President Towman has to say..."

The feed was re-routed to the White House, showing President Towman, wearing a dark suit and a blue tie, stepping behind a podium in a room filled with journalists. He cleared his throat before he began. "There has been much speculation over the events that have transpired this week and I am here to set the record straight. The cult group known as P3 has been officially shut down and I have just been informed that its leaders, namely Maxwell Sagan and Saul Latham have either been killed or taken into custody, as have several high-ranking government officials within the Republican Party, the N.E.T. and the FBI. My Administration has in no way condoned the P3 Agenda nor the actions that have been taken against the public in the pursuit of this agenda. A deeper investigation is underway, including evidence suggesting that these men were behind the scandals resulting in the resignation of two Democratic House members earlier this year, behind the killing of Supreme Court Judge, Stanley Mikakis, and most recently, the sudden death of Congresswoman, Micah Belmont."

"Omigosh," Skylar gasped.

"You can say that again," Ernie rasped.

"I consider these actions to be an attack on the government of the United States of America and they will be treated as such. We are a nation built upon the foundational truth that 'in God we trust'. We are not built upon the principal that in God we blame, in God we judge, in God we threaten, in God we blackmail or in God we kill our fellow man. These crimes are inexcusable and dishonor the core freedoms upon which we stand."

Ernie muted the television when Braznovich's cell phone buzzed and he excused himself to answer the call. Returning moments later, he told everyone that Richmond was sending officers to pick up Greg and had assigned two officers to protect them until they could be certain that they were no longer in jeopardy.

"So Richmond really is a good guy?" Skylar asked.

"Yep," Braznovich said. "His concern is our safety and exposing other government agents who are pushing the P3 Agenda. He's also scrambling to handle the backlash this whole thing is going to have on the Republican Party, Patterson's campaign in particular."

"Geeze, I'd hate to be in his shoes," Ernie said. "Looks like the Democrats are gonna run away with this election."

"Richmond also assured me that he and Patterson were the only ones, aside from me and Ernie, who knew the location of the rehabilitation facility holding Tess and Jonathan," Braznovich explained.

"What about the employee's working there?" Skylar asked.

"Richmond said they were thoroughly checked out."

"I hope they weren't checked by Henry Gleitner of the FBI," Ernie snapped, and a pit formed in Skylar's stomach.

"That's not funny," she frowned.

"Richmond gave me his word that Tess and Jonathan are safe and I believe him." He glanced at Skylar, his eyes softening. "But, we can go by there first thing tomorrow if you want."

This made Skylar feel a little better.

Two officers transported Greg from the house, while two other officers, dressed in military camouflage, stood guard outside; one in the front of the house and one in the back. While Ernie and Braznovich stepped outside to talk with the officers, Skylar pulled Rebecca from the floor to the couch and sat down next to her. "You're going to be okay now," she said. "We're all going to be okay. It's over." Rebecca buried her face in Skylar's shoulder and cried. It was going to be a long road toward healing, for everyone; but it was finally over. Tess was safe. P3 was shut down. And her name had been cleared on national television. By the time Ernie and Braznovich came back inside, Rebecca was dosing against her shoulder and Skylar wasn't far behind. She could feel her eyelids drooping. Braznovich offered everyone an1843 bourbon on the rocks, but Ernie was the only one who took him up on it. Under normal circumstances, Skylar would have enjoyed sipping a nightcap, but tonight she was just too tired. With drink in hand, Braznovich sank into the comfort of the arm chair and let out a sigh. He shot her a small smile and Skylar noted how he looked as exhausted as she felt. Ernie opened the sliding door and lit up a cigarette. "It's ironic," he rasped, sending a smoke ring up and out through the slider.

"What is?" Braznovich asked.

"Well, if Lockton, who everyone thought was one of the good guys hadn't really been a bad guy, we'd have never found out that Greg was a bad guy who was posing as a good guy." They all stared quietly as Ernie spoke. "And you know how we found out?" Ernie raised his eyebrows into the top of his forehead.

"By a trail of emails and texts...." Braznovich's tone indicated the answer was obvious.

"By their fruits!" Ernie grinned at Skylar and she burst out laughing, noting instantly how good it felt to laugh. "Just like that verse said, we had to look at the man's fruits."

"Deep man, really deep," Braznovich teased.

They sat in silence for a moment, each one mulling over their own thoughts, until Braznovich finally broke the silence. "You know what gets me? There have been cult groups that have ended badly, like Jonestown, for example, but..."

"Geez," Ernie interrupted with a shudder, "I haven't been able to drink Kool-Aid since that incident."

"But those cults were different because they only affected the people inside. Through this one, Sagan gained a substantial amount of control within our government." Braznovich shook his head.

"That's scary stuff right there," Ernie rasped.

"It's a shame radical extremists like Sagan and Jim Jones, who claim to bring people closer to God actually push people away from Him," Braznovich stated with certain introspection.

"If I were God that would really piss me off," Ernie said.

"If you were God, we'd all have bigger problems," Braznovich joked and Skylar laughed, inadvertently shaking her shoulder and waking Rebecca.

"I bet it makes God sad when people hurt others in His name," Skylar said.

"Yeah, but I don't think He was sad when Rebecca shot that son-of-a-bitch in the foot," Ernie chuckled. "In fact, I think I heard angels applauding."

They all laughed and Rebecca's mouth curled into a smile. "I don't know why I did that," she said quietly. "I've never even shot a gun before."

"That was pretty good aiming for a first time," Ernie said, exhaled smoke out of his nose.

"He can't have me arrested for attempted murder or anything can he?" Rebecca asked with surprise, as if the idea just popped into her head.

Ernie, Braznovich and Skylar stared from one to the other. "I didn't see anything," Skylar said.

"Hell, I saw the fool shoot himself in the foot," Ernie uttered and Rebecca's grin grew bigger.

Skylar leaned her head against the back of the couch and exhaled deeply. Despite acknowledging that there was still an uneasiness plaguing her, Skylar felt a certain warmth. Her sister was finally free and because the P3 campus was destroyed, thousands of students and interns would have no choice but to return to their homes and families. Skylar believed families and friendships would be restored in time, just as she believed her relationship with Tess would be restored. She just wished it hadn't come at such a high price. So many good people lost their lives to shut it down and that reality weighed heavily on her heart.

"God will remove all the obstacles," Rebecca said quietly. "Mary used to say that that was the only thing Maxwell was right about...that God would remove the obstacles."

"And if He won't, all we gotta do is give you a gun," Ernie joked and Skylar saw Rebecca's face flush as she giggled.

CHAPTER 39

Rebecca was too frightened to sleep alone, so she slept in Ernie's bed while Ernie slept on the floor next to the bed. Crawling into bed next to Braznovich, Skylar laid her head against his chest. "Aren't you glad my name is cleared and I can go back home and you can get away from me?" She teased.

He wrapped his arm around her and stroked her shoulder with his thumb. "I was just thinking about that," he paused, and she jolted up to look into his eyes.

"You were just thinking about getting away from me?" Skylar frowned and Braznovich smirked with delight.

"You didn't let me finish."

"Well, if that's how you're starting, I'm not sure I want to hear how you're going to finish." She plunked her head back onto his chest and he chuckled.

"I was thinking we could get away for a while. Maybe take the bikes and go somewhere where no one can find us..." his voice tapered off. "A get-away." He lifted his hands and made quote marks around the words 'get-away.'

Skylar blushed. "Oh, a get-away sounds good." She ran her fingers over his chest. "Where would we go?"

"I have a spot in mind. Very secluded." He planted a light kiss on the top of her head.

"We can see Tess and Jonathan first, right?" Skylar asked, knowing that she couldn't leave town in peace without seeing for herself that Tess was safe.

"Right."

"And what about Rebecca? I don't think she should be left alone." Skylar thought Rebecca was a sweet girl, but deep down she was worried about her mental and emotional stability. Rebecca had been inside P3 for a long time, not to mention that she had just seen Mary killed, she had shot Greg in the foot, had no idea where her own mother was and probably had no friends for support.

"Ernie will stay with Rebecca," he answered matter-of-factly, as if he had already thought through the details. "In fact, I think he's looking forward to it." Braznovich winked. "I think she pretty much won his heart when she shot Greg." Skylar laughed out loud. It was still hard to believe she did it.

"Speaking of which," Braznovich stopped and cleared his throat, "you weren't really going to shoot him were you?"

Skylar smiled. "That's for me to know and you to find out," she answered playfully, but the truth was she didn't know the answer. She might have actually shot him. That fact was unsettling, but it was true nonetheless.

"Can I go home and pack some of my own clothes before we go on our get-away," she asked, purposefully changing the subject.

"Oh, Ms. Wilson, I don't think you'll be needing any clothes," he reached his hand over and lifted her chin so their lips were dangerously close. "Besides, I'm not letting you out of my sight," he whispered, his lips gently brushing against hers.

"Why not?" She whispered back and he paused momentarily, the longing of a kiss hanging tensely between them.

"Because you can't stay out of trouble," he smirked.

"That's not true," she rebutted.

"In fact, sometimes I think you ARE trouble," he grinned.

"That's not true," she said.

"I don't think you know what's true," he
teased.

"Then tell me."

"I don't think you can handle the truth." He
raised his brows, his eyes sparkling.

"You know what they say, the truth will set
you free." Skylar smiled, pulling back slightly so she
could look into his eyes.

"The truth is...I... love... you," he said slowly
and softly, and an eruption of butterflies fluttered
wildly in her stomach. She had the feeling that these
words weren't something Braznovich spoke often. He
had gone out on a limb and she felt as if she might
explode with joy.

"I love you back," she whispered and he
pulled her into a deep and passionate kiss.

Reaching over and turning off the lamp which
sat on the night stand, Braznovich laid down and
Skylar snuggled against his chest. They weren't in
bed for long before she felt his body relax beneath her
and his breathing deepen. Skylar wasn't as
fortunate. Her body sought slumber but her mind
was once again tormented with the re-playing of all
that had taken place that evening.

"Braznovich?" She whispered.

"Yes, Skylar?" He answered back in a hushed
tone.

"Were you asleep?"

"Does it matter?" He teased.

"Do you think Maxwell created the scandals
that caused those two democratic House members to
resign?" She couldn't escape the nagging suspicion
that Maxwell had been hand selecting a government
that would adhere to his false prophesies and push
through the P3 Agenda.

"I think you think too much and you need to
go to sleep." He squeezed her shoulder.

He was probably right, she did think too
much; then again, something was bothering her, and

she knew she wouldn't be able to sleep until she identified it. If Maxwell was indeed hand selecting a government to follow his false prophesies, why did only two democratic House members resign and why was only one judge killed? Wouldn't there have needed to be more scandals and more resignations? As terrible as it sounded, surely he would have needed to blackmail or kill more people before he'd be able to take control. Or did he already have that much control? Was he already controlling the majority in both the House and the Senate? Her heart beat a little faster as her mind mulled over the possibilities. "What party holds political power right now?" She blurted.

"President Towman is a Democrat, now go to sleep," Braznovich wearily answered.

"I know that. I meant, what majority are the House of Representatives and the Senate? Are they leaning Democratic or Republican?"

Braznovich groggily inched his way up into a sitting position. "Right now, the House and Senate are held by the Republican party, why?"

"So in this next election, if the House and Senate could keep a Republican majority and Patterson wins the election..."

"The Republican party would have the power to pass just about anything they wanted," Braznovich finished her sentence.

Skylar's eyes widened as she recalled the words of Saul Latham resounding in the prayer room. *"We must overcome all barriers of corruption in our government, in our education system and in our culture!"* Shane's mouth went dry as his words continued ringing in her ears. *"We must put an end to the hypocrisy in the church and in America and in the world. It is better for a man to be dead than to be a homosexual. It is better for a woman to die than to abort her baby."*

Skylar sat up in bed. "The judge that was killed..."

371

"Stanley Mikakis," he interjected.

"Was he a Democrat?"

"You could say that. He was well-known for his strong stance in favor of Roe vs. Wade." Braznovich leaned over and turned on the bedside lamp. "What is going through that brain of yours?"

"Sagan's agenda. The P3 Agenda."

"Who knows what that lunatic's agenda really was?" Braznovich shrugged. "But he's dead now, so you don't have to worry about it." He intertwined his fingers with hers and stroked the top of her thumb with his. "You need to breathe. It's over and tomorrow we will be on our way to a romantic spot where no one will find us." He lifted her hand to his lips and kissed it.

Skylar wasn't so sure that it was over. Yes, Maxwell Sagan was dead but the power of his lies and the agenda he put into motion were still very much alive.

Suddenly their bedroom door burst open and Ernie paraded in. "We got trouble!"

Braznovich bounded off the bed in one giant leap, grabbing his .45 from the night stand. "What's up?"

"Our two guards are missing," Ernie rasped.

"How do you know?" Skylar asked.

"I was watching the surveillance cameras Greg set up on his laptop. They were there just a few minutes ago and now they're gone."

"Maybe they wandered into the trees to take a leak," Braznovich posed, sliding on his jeans and then checking the clip in his gun.

"Together? Leaving us unattended?" Ernie shook his head. "And if that's the case, they're taking a long leak," he quipped.

Rebecca stepped into the doorway, fear sweeping over her face. "I heard a noise downstairs," she whimpered.

Ernie pulled Rebecca into the room and told her and Skylar to stay put, then he and Braznovich crept out of the door, down the hallway and toward the steps. Skylar's heart was racing, pumping with adrenaline driven fear, as she held Rebecca's hand in her left hand and the 357 magnum in her right. Hearing the front door open and close, Skylar pulled Rebecca closer to the bedroom door so she could listen to what was happening downstairs.

"Mr. Braznovich," an officer spoke, "I was called in because one of our men went missing and I believe it is in your best interest if we move your party to a safer location."

A lump of dis-trust rose in Skylar's throat. *No!* She had a bad feeling about this.

"Okay, give us a few minutes to gather our things," Braznovich answered.

"Certainly, but with all due respect, the sooner we leave, the be..." Skylar heard the man's voice crack loudly mid-sentence, followed by a thump.

"What the hell are you doing?" Braznovich blurted.

"What?" Ernie threw his hands up. "You told me you wanted someone to interrogate, so here he is." "You just Tasered a Federal Agent!"

"I know, but I don't trust him," Ernie said.

"Based on what?"

"The fact that he isn't one of the two men originally assigned to protect us," Ernie rasped. "And the fact that we know the FBI is tainted."

"He just told us he was called in because one of the other officers was missing," Braznovich argued.

"That's a bunch of BS. How did he get here? I was watching the surveillance camera and I never saw a vehicle. Now, help me search his pockets."

Skylar and Rebecca rushed to the top of the steps and peered down over the railing, seeing the officer face down on the floor.

"Is he dead?" Rebecca gasped, throwing her hand over her mouth.

"Nope, just stunned," Ernie said, grabbing him by the arm and flipping him onto his back.

"Need help?" Skylar asked.

"No, just get dressed and go pack whatever you can. There's a duffle bag in my closet," Braznovich instructed.

Skylar and Rebecca rushed into the bedroom and filled the duffle bag with clothing and toiletries, then joined the men downstairs. "What do we do now?" She asked.

"Pack up the laptops," Braznovich ordered. "Yours, mine and all of Greg's equipment."

Skylar and Rebecca began unplugging computer wires and shoving the laptops into several briefcases. Noticing Rebecca's hands were trembling, she wished she had words of wisdom to calm her; but there were none. She wasn't even sure what was happening and who they could trust, so how could she possibly reassure Rebecca. They left Greg's laptop out so they could continue to monitor the outside cameras.

Braznovich's cell phone buzzed and he pulled it from his pocket and read a text message aloud. "It's from Richmond," he said. "It says 'Location compromised. Get out now!'"

"He's a little slow with his updates," Ernie quipped.

Was he purposefully slow? Skylar couldn't help but still question Richmond's loyalty. She and Rebecca piled the briefcases and duffle bag into a corner by the front door, while Ernie tied up the Federal Agent he had Tasered and Braznovich sent a text back to Richmond.

Skylar sat down on the edge of the steps and stared at Greg's laptop. "I don't see anyone else outside," she said.

"That doesn't mean they aren't there," Braznovich quipped.

Ernie glanced over her shoulder. "I don't see anybody either. I think we can make it to the Hummer."

Braznovich glanced down at his phone, obviously reading another text. He paused momentarily and an idea lit his eyes. "I have a better idea. I think I know how we can end this once and for all."

Moments later, Skylar was gripping Rebecca's hand and leading her through the fireplace, down the steps, into the armoire and through the tunnel that emptied into the bunker. Neither of them spoke. Once inside the bunker, Skylar waited for a text from Braznovich, giving them the all clear. When the text came, she led Rebecca out of the bunker, through the watery tunnel, up the ladder and into the horse stall inside the barn. They entered quietly, though Braznovich had assured her that the barn was safe. Pulling the set of keys that he had given her from her pocket, she unlocked the Lamborghini and she and Rebecca climbed in. Braznovich's instructions re-played in her mind. Start the car first and then open the barn door using the remote opener on the visor, pull out fast and speed like a demon down the road, remembering to close the garage door behind them. Skylar handed Rebecca the remote opener. "Open it right when I turn on the ignition and close it as soon as we're out."

Rebecca nodded.

Skylar took a deep breath. She couldn't believe she was about to drive a Lamborghini, much less one that had only been driven from the lot to the barn. Her stomach felt hollow, as she placed the key in the ignition and turned it. The engine roared. Rebecca hit the opener and Skylar floored the gas, peeling out of the garage and onto the gravel road. Rebecca pressed the opener again and looked over her shoulder to make sure the barn door was closing; and then she gripped the handle above the passenger door as Skylar whipped the car around the house and down the long driveway through the trees. As they passed the house, Skylar noticed that the Hummer was backed up to the front door and Ernie and

Braznovich were loading something large into it. She could tell it was something that was so heavy that it took the two of them to lift. She couldn't imagine what it was. A part of her felt compelled to stop and see if they needed help, but that wasn't a part of the plan and she knew Braznovich would get pissed if she strayed even slightly from the plan.

Reaching the end of the gravel road, Skylar peeled out and turned right, heading south. Once they were exactly ten miles from the house, she handed Rebecca the cell phone that Ernie had retrieved from the Federal Agent's pocket, and Rebecca dialed the numbers that Braznovich had jotted on the inside of Skylar's wrist. She then put the phone on speaker and pressed the call button. It was time to end this.

"Is it done?" Came the man's voice through the phone, after only one ring. "Are they dead?"

"Not exactly," Skylar answered, flatly.

"Who is this?" He demanded.

"Your worst nightmare," Skylar sneered.

"How did you get this number?"

"YOUR man gave me your personal number. He said it was okay that I called."

"My man? He feigned innocence but Skylar could hear the fear behind his voice.

"Yes, you know, the man you sent to kill us," Skylar paused dramatically, and then added, "he's dead now; and so is your career."

He cleared his throat. "I don't know what you are trying to imply Ms. Wilson, but you're way out of your league..."

"Save your breath, Senator Patterson," came the voice of Clayton Richmond through the phone. Patterson obviously didn't realize that he was on a three-way conference call, one being recorded and transmitted directly to President Towman and the Attorney General. "We have all the evidence we need. The man you sent to take out the Federal Agents I had assigned to guard Skylar and her team, sang like a canary. We know you signed off on the murder of Micah Belmont, promising to announce Lockton as your next running mate; and that's just the tip of the iceberg."

"Clayton, you don't know what you're talking about. These are void accusations. Think this through. If I go down, your career is over. You go down too!"

"Save it. The Attorney General is on his way as we speak."

Senator Patterson disconnected the call, leaving Richmond and Skylar on the line. "Good work," Richmond said. "I'd have never suspected he was working with Lockton and Sagan and, hell, God only knows how many other people. This whole thing is unbelievable."

"Yes, it is..." Skylar sighed, her voice fading from exhaustion. She knew Sagan's tentacles ran deep but she had no idea it was this deep.

"As soon as we hang up, ditch the phone you're using because it's government issued and Patterson has a lock on the signal," Richmond warned. "Until we have identified all of the players, I wouldn't trust anyone."

"Got it."

"Don't go back to Braznovich's home or anywhere familiar until you hear from me," he instructed. "Until we get this mess cleaned up, it's too dangerous." Skylar could hear the exasperation in Richmond's voice. "Hopefully it'll only be a couple of days. Braznovich told you where to go?"

"Yes. And Richmond?"

"Yep?"

"Braznovich said that Patterson knew where Tess and Jonathan were being kept?"

"I've taken care of it," he said. "Tess is tucked away in a place where no one will find her. She's going to come out of this alive and so are you. Just lay low for a while."

Upon hanging up, Rebecca turned off the phone, disconnected the SYM card and threw both pieces out of the window. "It's finally over," she said quietly.

"I hope so," Skylar replied.

Skylar took Highway 69 south and less than an hour and a half later, she took the Fort Scott exit, turned right onto East Wall Street, right onto Hendricks and then followed the signs toward the center building of the Fort Scott National Historic Site. Pulling up directly behind the building, she killed the lights but left the ignition running. Glancing over at Rebecca, Skylar saw the same trepidation in her eyes that she felt in the pit of her stomach. She wanted to reassure her that everything would go according to plan, but there were no words that would make two young women, sitting in a Lamborghini, in the dark, in an unfamiliar town, awaiting a confrontation with a stranger, feel any less vulnerable. The plan was simple. They were to wait for their contact to show up. If he proved his identity with the correct key phrase, they were to follow him. If someone showed up who did not know the key phrase, they were to high tail it out of there, using whatever force necessary. This was the reason she left the car running and had checked the clip in her gun twice already.

Glancing to her left, Skylar's heartbeat sped up as she saw a man in camouflage approaching. He was an African American man, standing around six feet tall, with no hair and a machine gun slung over his right shoulder. He approached the car, then stopping approximately six feet from the driver's door, he removed the gun from his shoulder and laid it on the pavement. He stepped back, placed his hands palms up in front of him and slowly turned, as if to show Skylar that he was unarmed. She appreciated the gesture, but without hearing the key phrase, she wasn't going to trust him. Skylar depressed the button that rolled down the window and held the 357 magnum steady in her grip. The moment the window went down, he addressed her.

"My name is Lieutenant Jeffries," he spoke clearly and directly.

"Key phrase?" Skylar asked, tightening her grip around the gun and slowly reaching over, dropping the gear into drive, so she could peel out before he would have a chance to retrieve the machine gun from the ground.

"God will remove the obstacles," he said and gave her a slight nod.

Skylar breathed a sigh of relief. This was their contact. "What do we do now?" She asked him.

He bent down, retrieved his weapon and slung it over his shoulder. "Keep your lights off and follow me." He then turned around and led them down a path the size of a sidewalk, stopping in front of a small, white house, which looked to be at least one hundred years old. Two men, both dressed in camouflage appeared from the darkness, pulled open what looked like a garage door and Lieutenant Jeffries motioned for Skylar to pull the Lamborghini inside.

Once inside she turned off the ignition and squeezed Rebecca's hand. "We're okay," she said, hoping it was true, but feeling her stomach flip flop with fear.

Skylar stepped out of the car, keeping the 357 tightly in her grip, while Rebecca climbed over and slid out of the driver's door next to her.

"Ma'am, if you and Ms. Milner will join us downstairs we'll brief you on the new developments," Lieutenant Jeffries said, extending his arm toward a door in the far right corner of the garage.

"How does he know my name?" Rebecca whispered, slipping her hand into Skylar's and squeezing it tightly.

They followed the Lieutenant through the door and down a long flight of concrete steps. "Fort Scott is one of the oldest military bases in the United

States, built way back in the 1800's. It used to be one of the largest ones too. Now, on the outside, it's a National Historic Site for tourism, but below it…" his voice faded as they reached the bottom of the staircase and he pushed open a large steel door, "…is a secret division of the US Military called DARC. Defense Against Radical Cults."

Skylar couldn't believe her eyes. It looked like an underground office building, slash hotel, slash mini-city. There was a lobby area with potted plants and blue, cushioned chairs. Just beyond the lobby were three hallways, one painted white, the other red and another, blue. "The white hallway represents our business. It houses the debriefing room and all of the equipment we use to protect our nation," Lieutenant Jeffries explained. "The red hallway is our town beneath the town. There's a coffee shop, a cafeteria, barber shop, recreational activities, you name it, if they got it up there, we got it down here." Lieutenant Jeffries smiled and for the first time Skylar noticed his brown eyes sparkled just like Braznovich. She felt her body begin to relax.

"What's the blue hallway?" Skylar asked, sliding the safety on and slipping the 357 into her waistband.

"That's where we live while we're stationed here. That's where you'll be staying as well."

He led them down the white hallway, passing several doors with glass panels in them. Skylar peeked in as they walked by and was impressed by how much the rooms resembled conference rooms found in four-star hotels. "You said you would brief us on new developments?" Skylar asked as they continued down the long hallway.

"Yes ma'am, we're almost there," he answered, briskly gliding toward a door on the left side of the hall and pulling it open. "Please, have a seat," he said, gesturing them toward a large conference table with eight chairs; three on each side and one on each end. "Coffee and water are over in the corner," he

pointed. "Help yourself. I'll return shortly." He was
gone as quickly as he had appeared and as soon as
the door closed behind him, Skylar made a dash for it
and pushed on it. When it opened, she breathed a
sigh of relief. They weren't locked in, which she
surmised to mean they weren't prisoners here.

It felt as if it took forever for Lieutenant
Jeffries to return. By the time he did, Skylar had
polished off two cups of coffee and Rebecca was
dosing with her head on top of the table. Skylar's
heart leapt for joy when the door swung open and she
saw Braznovich and Ernie following Lieutenant
Jeffries into the room. Jumping out of her chair, she
threw her arms around Braznovich's neck, burying
her face into his chest. He appeared equally as
relieved to see her, squeezing her tightly against him,
while Ernie made a beeline for the coffee.

"Sir, as soon as you're ready, we can begin,"
Lieutenant Jeffries said.

"We're ready," Braznovich nodded and
motioned for Skylar to return to her seat.

Skylar had so many questions but she
decided it was best to listen first and ask later.
Braznovich took a seat at the far end of the
conference table, with Skylar to his left and Ernie to
his right. Rebecca sat on the other side of Skylar.
Lieutenant Jeffries nodded toward the door and the
two men who had opened the garage door earlier,
stepped inside the room and sat on the opposite side
of the table, next to Ernie. Once everyone was seated,
Lieutenant Jeffries lowered himself into the chair at
the head of the table.

"We have arranged for you to stay in our
quarters until we can place you into a protection
program," he began and Skylar felt her breath catch
in her throat. "The protection program is run by the
FBI, and for obvious reasons, we cannot assume your
new identities will remain undisclosed until our
investigations are complete and the Bureau has been
thoroughly removed of all P3 conspirators. Until we

can assure your safety, you'll remain our guests here."

What? No one said anything about protection program. Skylar felt her chest constricting as she tried to inhale a deep breath. Braznovich must have seen her internal struggle because he reached under the table and squeezed her hand.

"What about Tess and Jonathan?" Skylar uttered, her voice cracking with emotion.

"They are being transported here as we speak," Lieutenant Jeffries explained and Braznovich was visibly shocked, as was Ernie.

Skylar saw Braznovich's jaw tighten and his eyes flash with a heated intensity. "Who ordered their transfer?"

"Colonel Bilingswad."

"Why?" Braznovich demanded, releasing Skylar's hand and agitatedly tapping his fingers on the table.

"Clayton Richmond believes the location of the rehabilitation facility may have been compromised, so he contacted the Colonel."

"Who's transporting Tess and Jonathan? And how do we know they are trustworthy?" Braznovich questioned.

Ernie got up from the table and refilled his coffee. "Let's back up. How did you boys know to contact us?"

"Clayton Richmond. He was one of us. He served as a member of the DARC for a long time; long before he decided to enter the political world. He would have only stationed trustworthy personnel around you and your loved ones. I guarantee you, Tess and Jonathan are safe." Lieutenant Jeffries adjusted in his chair and crossed his arms atop the table. "Richmond contacted us the minute Ms. Wilson called Senator Patterson and informed him about the video that was made at P3. P3 had been on our radar for years, but when we got Richmond's call, we knew that Maxwell Sagan was expounding his scope from a religious cult to a political takeover and we took action. I am not authorized to fill in all of the details, but when Richmond discovered that you were slated to be murdered at your home this evening, he arranged for us to intervene."

"So, under Richmond's orders, you sent two DARC men to guard us," Braznovich said.

"Affirmative," Lieutenant Jefferies replied.

"That explains why you wanted us to bring the bodies?" Ernie said.

"DARC is a secret military operation. We fly under the radar of both local and federal law enforcement. Should our identity be compromised, well, let's just say our identity cannot be compromised."

"So you didn't want the police to find the bodies," Ernie nodded. "And what are you going to do with the FBI guy, who took out your two men?"

"You brought him with you?" Skylar gasped, realizing now why it took Ernie and Braznovich so long to load the Hummer. She hadn't been privy to the knowledge that they were bagging bodies and bringing them along. No wonder he didn't want her and Rebecca to go with them. There would have been no way she would have been able to ride in the same car with two dead bodies next to her. The mere thought made Skylar shudder.

"Richmond told us to bring him," Braznovich replied.

"So, what will you do with him?" Ernie repeated.

"That's classified," Lieutenant Jeffries answered curtly and then rose from his seat. "I understand your apprehension and the fact that you have questions. A lot has happened. We will answer what we can and you will have to trust us with the rest. Protecting the nation and the people of our great nation is our job and we do it well." He extended his arm and the other two soldiers stood up. "Lieutenant Barkley and Lieutenant Sincowitz will show you to your quarters. We will make sure you are informed the moment Tess and Jonathan arrive and we will reconvene in this room tomorrow morning at o-nine-hundred hours with Colonel Bilingswad and Clayton Richmond."

"What about the others that have helped us?" Braznovich asked. "Sally Watts and the McCulleys..."

"And Rod," Skylar added.

"Do you have reason to believe that they could be in danger too?" Braznovich questioned.

"We've got our people watching them. If necessary we'll bring them in," Lieutenant Jeffries answered assuredly.

No one said a word as they exited the conference room and followed the soldiers back down the white hallway and into the blue one. Skylar was a whirlwind of emotion, elated about the prospect of being with Tess, but fearful and angry at the thought of being forced into some type of witness protection program; and still curious as to how high Sagan's P3 tentacles of deception reached.   They now knew Patterson was involved, but were the President and the Attorney General also involved?

As they walked down the blue hallway, Skylar slid her hand inside Braznovich's. Until the answers were brought to light, they would all have to remain in the DARC.

ABOUT THE AUTHOR

S.R.Claridge, nominated for the 2010 Molly Award, 2013 Pushcart Prize and awarded the 2011 Rocky Mountain Fiction Writers Pen Award, writes full-time and lives in Colorado. She loves autumn, moonlight and Grey Goose martinis with bleu cheese or jalapeno stuffed olives. She believes Friday nights are for indulging in Mexican food and margaritas and Sunday mornings warrant an extra-spicy Bloody Mary. Growing up in St. Louis, Missouri and earning her BA in Psychology from the University of Missouri, Columbia, S.R.Claridge is a mixture of mid-western family values and western wild nights. She loves Jesus, believes in the power of prayer, in the freedom of forgiveness and that life is a gift that should be enjoyed to the fullest. With a background in theatre, S.R.Claridge creates characters with dramatic flair and is known for her intense plot twists and engaging humor. S.R.Claridge would rather walk dangerously where there's a view than sit in idle safety and let life pass her by. Her spirited outlook comes shining through in her novels, as she takes readers to the edge of their seats with bone-chilling suspense.

AUTHOR ACCLAIM

"Terrifically twisted!"
-NYMagazine

"The Just Call Me Angel series is suspense at its
best."
- RipeReviews

"A unique series from a one-of-a-kind author."
- APEX Reviews

"Riveting!"
- TrueBlueEbookReview

"One thrilling moment after another!"
- CanadaReviews

"A best-seller candidate indeed."
- BookWatchMagazine

BOOKS BY S.R.CLARIDGE

Tetterbaum's Truth *(book 1 in the Just Call Me Angel series)*

Traitors Among Us *(book 2 in the Just Call Me Angel series)*

Russian Uprising *(book 3 in the Just Call Me Angel series)*

Death Trap *(book 4 in the Just Call Me Angel series)*

Loose Ends (*book 5 in the Just Call Me Angel series*)

Divine Intervention *(book 6 in the Just Call Me Angel series)*

Petals of Blood *(short story; Pushcart Prize Nomination 2013)*

House of Lies (*Political cult suspense*)

Spouse in My House *(poetic short story a la Dr. Seuss)*

No Easy Way *(debut novel; nominated for The Molly Award from the HODRW 2010)*

The Candy Shop *(Suspense Thriller)*

Made in United States
Orlando, FL
17 February 2024